THE CAULDRON

A STRUGGLE FOR SURVIVAL

JOE CLARK

Dedicated to Anita Sherkness Cronberry Clark
Friend, Lover, Wife
November 9, 1941 – April 17, 2024

Contents

Preface

John White Geary (December 30, 1819 –February 8, 1873) was born and raised near Pittsburgh. At age fourteen, he entered nearby Jefferson College to study engineering and law. His father's death forced him to drop out of school to pay off debts and support his family. He worked as a surveyor and a land speculator in Kentucky. He returned to college and graduated in 1841. Two years later, he married Margaret Logan. The couple had three sons before she died in 1853.

He was commissioned as a lieutenant colonel in the Second Pennsylvania Infantry during the Mexican War (1846 – 1848). His exploits at Belen Gate earned him a promotion to colonel. He returned home a war hero. President Polk appointed him postmaster of San Francisco in 1849. A year later, he was elected the city's alcalde – chief administrator and judge. That same year, California achieved statehood, and Geary was elected mayor of San Francisco. He returned to Pennsylvania in 1852 because of his wife's failing health.

President Pierce appointed him governor of Kansas territory in 1856. Although initially neutral, he had joined forces with the abolitionists by the end of that year. In a letter to President Pierce, he blamed the pro-slavery faction for problems in the territory. Incoming President Buchanan fired Geary in March 1857.

At the start of the Civil War, he raised two regiments – the 147th (regular army) and the 28th Pennsylvania Infantry (volunteers). He used his own money to outfit the 1500 soldiers and fifty-one officers from Philadelphia and other sections of the state who formed the volunteer regiment. In July 1861, he resumed his rank of colonel and assumed command of the 28th Regiment.

My mother's grandfather Thomas J. Donal and his older brother John were among the men who signed up for a three-year enlistment on a fateful day in July 1861.

According to the unit history:

"During the four years' service of the Twenty-eighth Regiment, its casualties were about equal to the number of its original muster and, although in its organized condition, it served in twelve different states of the union, and was engaged in as many skirmishes and battles as any regiment in the United States Army, it never lost a single wagon or ambulance or any other description of property, by allowing it to fall into the hands of the enemy. The officers were frequently changed in consequence of death, resignations and promotions, the regiment having had four colonels, four lieutenant colonels and nine majors. It also produced one major general and three brigadiers …

"The members of the regiment who remained at the end of the war were mustered out of service on the 18th July, 1865, and were heartily welcomed home, their privations, sufferings, laborers and gallant services having endeared them in the warmest affections of the highly gratified and truly grateful loyal people of the country. Their soiled, torn and tattered flags, carried triumphantly through so many bloody battlefields, attesting the unfailing courage of the men who bore them, have received a hallowed place in the archives of the Commonwealth, whilst the brave and noble soldiers who fought beneath and around them, have returned to the peaceful pursuits of life and enjoyment of the multiform blessings their struggles and triumphs have secured to their country and the world."

1

Philadelphia 1861

William Smith, Esq, walked south along Ridge Avenue, enjoying the mid-July weather. He came to the shoe shop a block after turning right onto 10th. Young Tom was on the sidewalk shining shoes and selling copies of the Inquirer. Smith enjoyed talking to him.

Tom's father had died from influenza ten years earlier. His family struggled but seemed to be coping. Tom and his older brother were making steady profits from their shoe business. His sisters were employed as servants in some of the best households in Philadelphia. His mother worked at the Mercantile Bank.

"Shoeshine, Mr. Smith?" Tom called.

Smith stopped more for the conversation than the shine. Tom was going to sell him a newspaper but, in the process, he would cover important events. The young man had taken the time to study the day's edition. He had the headlines down and he knew the stories behind them.

"Yes, sir," The gentleman replied as he took a seat and placed his feet on the iron pedestals.

Tom handed him a paper. "We're gettin' whupped," the boy said. "Mr. Lincoln is going to have to do sumthin'."

"Is that a fact?"

"Yep. Them rebels chased our boys all the way back to Washington."

"What is the president going to do about that? Lead the troops in the next battle?"

Tom stopped shining shoes long enough to shoot a glare at Smith. "No, sir. He's puttin' a new man in charge."

Smith chuckled. He was still furious that Lincoln had tried to put Robert E. Lee, a slaver, in charge of a battle to end slavery. "That should be interesting. Who do you think he'll choose?"

"General McClellan. No question. He whupped the Confederates last week."

"We'll see."

"You won't have to wait long. We're gonna take the fight to them pretty quick."

"What makes you say that?"

"We're being mustered in," the boy crowed. "This may be the last time I get to shine your shoes."

Smith studied his friend. A runt. A blonde, gray-eyed runt. He could not have weighed more than a hundred pounds soaking wet. But he was aching to get into this fight. "Well good luck. If I don't see you again, I hope you do well." He reached into his pocket and pulled out three pennies for the shine and the paper. "I don't know that I would be as eager as you for this fight."

Tom grinned. "That's okay for you, but if you're Irish you have to prove you're an American too."

The big man flashed a tight-lipped smile. He nodded and found two more pennies for the boy. "Good luck."

Smith folded the paper under his arm and continued his journey to the office. A block away, he caught sight of his reflection in a storefront window. Pausing to admire the elegant figure mirrored in the glass, he straightened his red bow tie. Not that it needed straightening. He smiled and gave a slight nod to the smooth, black face that smiled back at him.

But he couldn't get the conversation out of his head. Yes. He believed Lincoln, a farm boy and a fighter, would find a way. He knew how to win. He would beat the rebellion. But he wouldn't do anything about the plight of blacks in the South. Slavery would go on just as it had for the last two hundred years. That would only change if Smith and his friends made it change.

He scowled and shook his head. Dark times were coming. The group would have to seize control and force whites to end slavery. If that's what had to be done, that is what they would do.

Give the rebellion some time to play out. The chaos it was creating could provide the perfect opportunity for a takeover.

2

Washington, June 1861

John Clark, a strapping young man in a dress military uniform, stepped into the spacious office. The woman seated at the large desk in the center of the room looked up. A faint smile. Her blue eyes sparkled.

The visitor said, "Tell the Old Man I'm here,"

"He's expecting you." She rose and stepped gracefully to the door behind her. Her red hair was pulled back in a bun. Her dress was plain but stylish – black with a white "V" over her chest. She pushed the door open and leaned in. "Sir, Major Clark is here for your meeting."

"Send him in," a deep, raspy voice growled. Clark strode across the room, stepped into the office and shut the door.

General Winfield Scott, the hero of the Mexican War and the most admired military man in America, was now commanding Lincoln's army. The job was wearing him down. He was losing his battle for control of the war with the secessionist states. Scott had recommended former West Point superintendent Colonel Robert E. Lee to lead the Union Army. Lee had declined, resigned his commission, and joined the rebel army. General George McClellan, dubbed America's Napoleon by the press, was emerging as President Lincoln's favorite for the role.

There was a lot to be said for McClellan. He had graduated second in his class at West Point in 1846, despite being the youngest. He went on to serve with distinction in Mexico, earning a promotion to colonel. After leaving the military, he became a railroad executive. Several states had wooed him to lead their militia when Lincoln issued his initial call for troops in April 1861. McClellan picked Ohio. He then developed a detailed plan for defeating the Confederacy. It looked good on paper, but to Scott's practiced eye, it was too complicated.

The old warrior came up with his own plan. He wanted to use the eighty thousand men who made up the newly formed army and navy to take control of the Mississippi River while blockading ports on the Atlantic and Gulf coasts. Newspapers derisively dubbed it "The Anaconda Plan."

General Scott handed a packet of documents to Clark. "Major, these regiments are to report to General Banks at Harper's Ferry immediately. He needs the reinforcements for his defensive perimeter along the Potomac."

"Yes, sir." The major saluted sharply. He pivoted and marched off to carry out the orders that would send men into combat.

3

Off to War

One of the units activated by Scott's orders was the 28th Regiment of Pennsylvania Volunteers, the Goldstream Regiment, recruited by Colonel John White Geary, a veteran of the Mexican War. Before the war over the US border with Mexico broke out in 1846, Geary had graduated from college and worked as an engineer for the railroads. He was commissioned as a lieutenant colonel in the 2nd Pennsylvania Infantry and served with distinction. Following the war, President Polk appointed him postmaster for San Francisco. In 1850, he was elected mayor of the city, the youngest man to hold that position. A few years later, Polk made him governor of the Territory of Kansas. When newly elected President Fillmore replaced him, Geary returned to Pennsylvania and took up farming.

During his short stint as governor of Bleeding Kansas, the Mexican war veteran got a first-hand view of the increasingly violent conflict between the anti-slavery and the pro-slavery factions. He realized a broader, more deadly struggle was coming.

After the attack on Fort Sumter, he put together a militia unit. His soldiers, drawn from Philadelphia and nearby towns, were mostly young and poor. Geary personally paid to outfit the unit with uniforms, muskets, and other equipment. He was still organizing his men when orders came to report to Major General Nathaniel Banks at Harper's Ferry.

Early on Saturday, July 27, 1861, the colonel marched his regiment's fifteen companies to the Philadelphia Naval Shipyard, where they boarded vessels that carried them to Baltimore. From there, they marched to Harper's Ferry, seventy miles inland.

The trek ended at a level plain bordered on one side by the Potomac River and by majestic mountains on the other. Tents covered the ground as far as the eye could see. One exceptionally large tent stood at the edge of an open area. A solitary man, tall and broad, with a full head of black hair and a short white beard, stood in front of that tent. He projected an air of authority, leaving no doubt who was in charge.

Colonel George Henry Thomas waited patiently as the new arrivals, young men with eager faces and fresh uniforms, lined up on the field in front of him.

When the formation was ready, Colonel Geary stepped to the front center and saluted Thomas. "The Twenty-Eighth Pennsylvania Volunteers reporting for duty."

Thomas returned the salute. "Welcome, colonel." Thomas's slight southern drawl marked him as a Virginian who had remained loyal to the Union. He approached Geary and the two men shook hands. Thomas said, "I believe we served together in Mexico."

"We did, sir."

"Fine looking soldiers. Are they ready to fight?"

"They'll hold their own."

"They had better. We are surrounded by rebels."

Thomas stepped back and addressed the regiment. "On behalf of Major General Nathaniel Banks, I welcome you to the Department of the Potomac. Maryland is a Union state because loyalists hold a majority in the legislature. Out here in farm country, Confederate sympathizers outnumber our friends. That river behind you, the Potomac, is all that lies between us and the Confederacy. Virginia is a Confederate stronghold. Our mission is to prevent Virginians from crossing the river and taking control of Maryland. For now, your job will be to extend our right flank. Sooner or later, we will be sent across the river to conquer Virginia.

"You have no doubt heard that this war will be over in a matter of months. A year at most. But you have also heard what happened when we fought them at Bull Run. They are not pushovers. They fight like demons. Our job is to beat them into submission. Is that understood?"

The troops responded in unison, "Yes, sir."

"You left your families and homes to join this war against an unholy rebellion. Your patriotism, your courage, and your generosity are deeply appreciated. Welcome to the Department of the Potomac."

Turning to Geary, Thomas said, "Dismiss your men and join me so we can discuss your assignment."

The situation was precarious. Maryland, a slave state with mixed loyalties, remained in the Union, but in rural areas, most people favored the South. General Banks's encampment was an outpost in hostile territory.

Confederate soldiers fired on Union pickets from the Virginia side of the Potomac. Mounted citizens working as an ad hoc cavalry roamed the rugged woodland on the Maryland side. An armed militia conducting guerrilla warfare in support of the rebel cause.

Within days, the 28th was deployed in a thirty-mile defensive line along the Potomac from Noland's Ferry to the Antietam Aqueduct. Pickets were positioned every four hundred yards where the terrain permitted. The soldiers also took over operation of the telegraph, post office, the Baltimore and Ohio Railroad, and the Chesapeake and Ohio Canal. Communications and transportation had to be protected.

Tom Donal held the rank of sergeant in Company C. His brother John was a lieutenant.

The soldiers were assigned picket positions in groups of four. They learned about digging in, an important skill that had not been covered in basic training. They scraped out a long, deep trench where they could eat and sleep without worrying about enemy musketry. They constructed wooden parapets that would shield them from musket balls while they stood watch.

The work took less than a week. Sergeants walked up and down the line supervising privates. Junior officers supervised the sergeants. Lieutenant Donal stopped by to check on his brother twice. He nodded in Tom's direction but did not speak to him.

Once the parapets were up and ready, Tom and his fellow soldiers settled into the routines required to keep a lid on rebel activities. The pickets had to fend off raiding parties from Maryland and Virginia. Cavalry patrolled the woodlands and the hills surrounding the Union camp every day. The southern sympathizers remained active. Spies, many of them women, carried information back and forth across the river.

Cooking was another skill the fledgling soldiers had to master very quickly. Undercooked food was hard, if not impossible, to digest. Many of the men suffered from diarrhea before they learned how to prepare camp meals. At home, Tom's mother made the meals. Now he had to cook sow belly and flapjacks over an open fire.

He took up new habits as he settled into army life. Facial hair developed into a beard and mustache. He began drinking coffee for the first time in his life. And he took up smoking a pipe in the evening after dinner.

It was at this time he met two men whose companionship he would value throughout the war. One introduced himself as Sam Goldman. He was a tall, swarthy New Yorker with angular features, a thick mop of black hair and matching eyes. The other called himself Jim Kennedy. He was as tall as Goldman but broad-shouldered and barrel-chested. He was fair, like Tom, with sandy hair and blue eyes. He said he was from New York, but Tom could hear his old man when he talked. Tom's father had come to America from an area in Northern Ireland known as The Plantation. He may have been Irish, or he may have been a transplanted Scot. Tom had settled on Scotch-Irish.

Goldman and Kennedy were members of a unique, informal band of soldiers. They were the camp equivalent of the *Philadelphia Inquirer*. Traveling around at night, they traded gossip with others who preferred to sit and puff on a pipe. Over the course of an evening, they would pick up all the important news and scrub the stories to the bare-bones truth.

They knew everything worth knowing.

Both men had been recruited by Major General Banks before he was awarded his rank for being the top recruiter in the Northeast. Kennedy said, "He's a great politician, but he'd be doing us a favor if he took a bullet and died a hero."

"What does that mean?" Tom demanded.

"He can't command troops in the field."

"Who would you put in command?"

"Colonel Thomas. He graduated from West Point and he's fought Mexicans and Indians."

"He's a schmuck. His family owns slaves," Goldman countered. "He and Lee are good friends. They've been together since the Mexican War."

"His wife's a New Yorker," Kennedy said. "I've met the family."

"Schmuck," Goldman repeated.

"Lee quit and joined the Confederacy," Kennedy growled. "Thomas stayed."

4

Kat

A patrol led by Lieutenant Luke Dahlgren returned with some locals he had taken into custody on charges of insurrection. Eight men and a woman. The young, freckle-faced redhead sat behind the lieutenant because she didn't have a horse.

The prisoners were turned over to Colonel Geary for processing. The men had been on their way back to their farms after harassing Union pickets when they ran into Dahlgren's column. They were belligerent but surrendered to the superior Federal force without a fight. Geary paroled them after receiving their signed promise to stop their attacks on Union soldiers.

The woman was escorted into the tent that served as Geary's headquarters. He was sitting at a table with maps spread out in front of him. "Please be seated."

She chose a chair directly across from the colonel. "Thank you, sir."

"You gave your name as Katherine McAllister?"

"Yes, sir."

"I'm Colonel Geary."

"People call me Kat."

"Okay, Kat. You were caught trying to ambush our patrol. What do you have to say for yourself?"

"That's not true," she purred. "I was hunting. Men on horseback caught me by surprise and I tried to hide. I guess I wasn't quick enough."

Geary grinned. "You were hunting? Why weren't you home doing chores?"

"The chores are all done. I needed a rabbit for dinner."

"Doesn't your husband do the hunting?"

She shot a fierce look at her captor. He did not miss the fire in her green eyes. "I'm not married, sir." The woman drawled, barely suppressing her fury. She paused, then added, "My father and my brothers are off fighting the war, so I have to do everything myself."

Geary straightened and studied the woman. "Where?"

"They're with Fremont. Out West."

Geary walked over to Kat's escort and examined the musket she had been carrying when she was arrested. "Enfield. That's a nice weapon. It's what we gave our soldiers."

"Yes, sir."

"How did you get it?"

"I went with Pa and my brothers to enlist."

Surprise registered on Geary's face. "Never met a woman who wanted to enlist."

"I'm sure you have. You just didn't give her a chance. They laughed at me and said they needed men to do the fighting. I told them I could fight as well as any man and I could shoot better than most."

"What did they say to that?"

"A colonel, like you, came over to see what was going on. I explained that I was there to enlist." Kat sneered. "He got that silly grin men use to put us women down. I said I could outshoot any of the men that were signing up. He had a sergeant issue me that Enfield, a pouch of caps and a pouch of balls. And we went outside. He had one of the privates put his cap on a tree limb at fifty paces. I loaded up and shot that cap off the limb. The colonel said" - the woman deepened her voice to mimic the officer - "I admire your spirit but I still can't recruit you. You can keep the musket and the ammunition as an honorary member of my regiment."

"Think you could do that again?"

"I think I could do it with my eyes closed."

Geary handed the woman her musket and led her to an open area near the tree line. He ordered her escort to go over to the trees and put his hat on one of the branches. As the man stepped up to put his hat on a projecting branch, a startled hare darted from its hiding place and raced for a new one. The woman shouldered her musket, aimed and nailed the rabbit in mid-leap. She raised the musket triumphantly and whooped, "Dinner."

Kat retrieved her kill and returned to Geary. "Do I have to shoot that man's cap too?"

He chuckled. "No. You've convinced me."

"I can help you if you don't mind working with a woman."

"In what way?"

"I know every family within fifty miles of this place. I could let you know when something is brewing."

"Let's go back inside and talk about that."

"I can't, sir. I wasn't expecting to be gone long when I left this morning. I got chores that need tending to. I'll come back tomorrow."

5

Espionage

Confederate troops and their allies continued frequent, sometimes daily, attacks on Union positions. Kat began visiting Geary one or two afternoons each week. They would go over maps, and Kat would identify homes and families in the area. Geary brought in other officers to get detailed intelligence from the young woman. Lieutenant Dahlgren proposed taking her on patrol to help scout the roads. Geary agreed. Kat was issued a uniform and given use of a horse.

In mid-September, rebels attacked pickets above Harper's Ferry. The attackers retreated after a two-hour battle. They left behind eighteen killed, seventy-three wounded, and a twelve-pound cannon.

Ten days later, five hundred Confederates attacked the regiment's left flank from the Virginia side of the Potomac.

The raiders were defeated and driven off. Homes in the area were searched. Those that had sheltered the retreating rebels were destroyed.

A few days later, Lieutenant Donal led Company C in an attack on a fortified position set up to support forays across the river. He destroyed the rebel stronghold and took prisoners.

A similar incident took place on the right flank at the beginning of October.

Geary asked for a volunteer to work with Kat. The spy would pose as a hand, helping McAllister with work on her farm. He would spend time talking to men in the nearby towns and taverns. Sergeant Tom Donal got the job.

As Kat was leaving for home after a mid-October visit, Geary said, "I want one of my men to join you as a farmhand."

She turned and studied him. "I don't need a farmhand."

"I have a farm back in Pennsylvania. It's a big job."

"I'm handling it by myself. I don't need help and I don't want your soldiers hanging around my home."

"The information you're providing me is coming from women you associate with," Geary explained. "I want someone to get to know the men in the community."

"Do I have a choice?"

Geary nodded. "Of course. I hope you choose to go along with my plan."

"And if I don't?"

"I'm not sure how much use you are going to be to me."

Kat scowled and shook her head. She sighed, "Okay. Bring him in so I can meet him."

"Send him in," Geary ordered. An aide stationed at the entrance to the headquarters tent ushered Tom in.

The colonel made quick introductions, "Kat, this is Sergeant Tom Donal. Tom, Kat McAllister."

Tom had not been told what he was supposed to do, so he stood at attention, rigid and expressionless. Kat gave him an appraising look and turned back to Geary. He proposed living arrangements. She made her modifications, wheeled and walked out of the tent. She was gone before Tom realized what was happening. He heard the colonel clear his throat and started after her.

Tom was trailing a few steps behind Kat by the time they reached her spread. A house and a barn encircled by a log fence. He had seen farms like this on the outskirts of Philadelphia, but he had never thought about living on one. The low clapboard house sat atop a slight rise. The barn, a hundred paces away, looked big enough to house ten or twelve animals and the fodder they would need to get through the winter.

Tom went straight to the barn and found a place to sleep. He dropped his knapsack and walked up to the house. Chickens wandered about the yard. A pen held a few indolent pigs. The woman hollered as he approached the cabin, "I got chores. Sit on the porch. I'll call you when dinner's ready."

That didn't suit him at the moment. He needed to be moving. He set off following a cow path along the fence. The ground rose, topped a small hill and descended to a creek running across the property. He crossed the stream on a footbridge and started up the next hill. Eight cows lolled in the shade of trees near a corner of the property. Tom gave them wide berth but continued to follow the railing around the edge of the farm. It looked like it hadn't been tended to for a while and needed repairs. He passed furrows where crops had been planted. Corn stalks, he recognized. Everything else was a mystery.

Kat stepped out onto the porch just as Tom returned from his jaunt. She said, "I got to bring the cows home, then I'll make dinner."

"Mind if I go along?"

"Looks like y'all just finished takin' a walk."

Tom nodded. "But I got plenty a walkin' left in me."

The woman shrugged and set off to fetch her cows. They became attentive and restless well before she reached them. Making her way through the small herd, she slapped a switch against her skirt. The animals immediately ambled toward the barn. They deviated slightly from their well-trod path to get around Tom but otherwise ignored him.

He followed Kat as far as the door. He would have followed her inside, but she held up a hand and scowled. He waited on the porch and fretted. When she did let him in, the scene dismayed him. He stepped into a modest room furnished with a table and five chairs. At one end, two rockers sat next to the fireplace. At the other, a partial wall created a smaller room with an iron stove, cabinets and a table.

Three doorways without doors lined the back wall. The room nearest the kitchen had a curtain across the opening for privacy. That was her room.

At dinner, Tom mentioned the fence needed some fixin' and offered to take care of that if she was willing. Kat studied him. "Ever mend a fence?"

"No, ma'am," Tom admitted, "but all I've done lately is things I never done before. I reckon I can mend your fence."

She chewed while she mulled over the idea. "I'll get you started in the morning."

Two nights later, Kat broke the silence halfway through supper. "They would like you."

Tom stopped eating to study her. "Who would?"

"Pa and my brothers." She smiled at her guest. "You're a good worker. We'll go into town tomorrow. I need some supplies and you should start getting familiar with things."

A couple of nights after that, she said, "No need for you to sleep in the barn. You can use my brothers' room. They ain't comin' home anytime soon."

Kat continued reporting to Geary and consorting with Dahlgren.

Tom accompanied her on these outings. He met with the regimental exec, Major Tyndale, who was concerned about the young soldier's situation. Spying was a hanging offense.

The arrangement had several benefits for Tom. He didn't have to stand watch, and the food was better. Mixing with the local men felt a lot like selling the *Inquirer* back in Philly. He just had to be careful what he said. Each night, he made notes on a sheet of paper that went into an envelope for his reports to his superiors.

His partner was the problem. Kat had been the woman in a household dominated by adult males since her mother's death. She seemed comfortable with Tom in her house. Sometimes too comfortable. She seemed to want more intimacy. She would say, "Goodnight." Then she would stand, staring as if she expected him to do something. When he didn't respond, she shuffled to her room and closed the curtain.

Tom would have been tempted if Major Tyndale hadn't given him strict instructions. And if his mother had not drummed proper treatment of women into his head. Following his instincts would lead to trouble as sure as the sun was going to rise.

Once they returned early from a trip to headquarters. Dahlgren was away on an extended patrol. Tom was certain they would have stayed overnight if the lieutenant had been in camp. Kat seemed more clingy than usual. She kept brushing up against the young soldier. He acted like he didn't notice. She came to say goodnight wearing a shift with a bow at her neck. The sleeves covered her shoulders. Her breasts were conspicuous under the flimsy garment. Stiff nipples pushed against the sheer cloth.

"Tom," she said. "I'm feeling distraught. Could you hold me?"

He looked up. Scrunched his lips and shook his head.

"Tom, please."

The reluctant Irishman stood and walked over to the sad-eyed woman. He wrapped his arms around her shoulders. She sighed and rested her head on his chest as her arms clamped around his waist. The longer they cuddled, the more uncomfortable Tom felt. He tried to pull away. "This ain't right."

She looked up at him. "What's wrong?"

"I shouldn't be touching you."

"Why not?"

"I just shouldn't. That's all."

"Why?" she repeated. "I asked you to hold me. I need your embrace."

"We got a job to do." He put his hands on her shoulders and pushed gently but firmly. "We can't let nothin' get in the way of that."

"Sex ain't gonna get in the way," she countered with a wry smile. "My parents had a job to do and they managed to make three babies."

"That's another thing," he snapped. "What if you get that way?"

"I won't," she scoffed. "If I do, that's my problem."

He clamped his mouth shut and shook his head. She reached up and massaged his shoulders. "We both need this and you know it."

"What about Lieutenant Dahlgren?"

Kat shoved him away. She glared and hissed, "What about Lucas? We're not married. I'm not his property."

"But he is a lieutenant," Tom objected.

"Not in your regiment," she snorted.

"He can still make trouble."

"He can spread rumors. So what?" Kat began unbuttoning his shirt. "There are rumors about him and me, and there are rumors about you and me."

Tom's mouth dropped open.

She smirked. "You are probably the only man in that camp who doesn't believe you and me are sharing a bed." She kissed his chest. "You might as well get some pleasure out of it."

Tom's eyes shut. His right hand ran through his hair. Kat pulled his head in for a kiss. A long one that kept getting hotter. She pushed the shirt off his shoulders. He untied the bow at the top of her gown. She opened his breeches, and he slipped out of them. He pushed the gown off her shoulders. It fell to the floor. She took his hand and led him to her bed.

6

Homeless

With the harvest complete, life turned to preparing for winter. The men cut down trees, split logs and stacked firewood. Women preserved fruits and vegetables and laid up a supply for the coming months.

Men spent more time in the evening at the local tavern. Tom chatted and listened. Several men approached him, urging him to join a group. He wouldn't commit, but he left the door open.

Kat visited her neighbors to socialize and trade goods. Over tea and biscuits, she collected hints of what the men were up to.

Putting it all together, they had a detailed picture of an armed militia forming in the area. They reported what they had uncovered, including names and addresses of participants, to Geary and Tyndale. A raid was ordered when army brass became convinced there was enough solid information.

Dahlgren took two companies to make arrests and otherwise disrupt the plot. They found stockpiles of weapons and other military equipment hidden in barns and outhouses.

Stunned silence settled over the town in the aftermath of the raid. The life of the community seemed to come to a sudden halt, as if the sortie had been a physical assault on everyone in the area. Tom visited his favorite tavern to catch up on the gossip some days after the raid. The tension in the air was palpable. Men who had been friendly avoided him. He sat alone at a table nursing a pint and then left.

The next day, Tom watched people passing the McAllister spread. The activity was unusual. He saw too many on the roads, and they seemed too interested. Late in the afternoon, a little before dinner, one man stopped at the gate. Tom recognized him from the tavern. His name was Isaiah Smith. He wasn't a secesh, as the rebels were called back at the camp. But he never came out as pro-Union. Tom left his chores and went to meet the man.

Smith said, "Tom, somebody passed information to the Federals. That's got everybody upset." Tom nodded. The man went on. "Kat was born and raised here. She's one of us. People have come to like you. But a lot of them think you're working with the Federals."

Tom met Smith's gaze with a blank expression that hid a growing dread of what was coming next. Smith said, "There's a lot of ugly talk. Some insist there's got to be a lynching."

The two men locked eyes for a minute before the visitor stalked off.

Tom went immediately to the house. Kat met him at the door. She was outwardly calm, but her eyes betrayed the terror she felt. He confirmed what she was thinking. "That was a warning. We have to get out of here."

They stuffed what they could in knapsacks and bags, grabbed their muskets, and set off for the camp. The next day, Dahlgren took Kat and a patrol to check her farm. It had been burned to the ground. Nothing was left. There were no carcasses. The animals had been taken away before the fire was set.

Geary agreed to find a place for Kat. He cautioned Tom to leave the woman alone. "Whatever was going on between the two of you has to end immediately. You have a bright future. Don't ruin it by cavorting with loose women."

About 150 women were attached to the 28th. Many of them were married to officers or enlisted men. Officers' wives were treated well. The wives of enlisted men were tolerated. Some women came to the camp to care for wounded soldiers. A few were trained nurses. Most were volunteers who took care of important but less glamorous tasks – feeding, bathing, and cleaning up after the patients.

The rest of the women made themselves useful cooking, cleaning and sewing when they weren't entertaining the men. The women in this group were vagrants forced to fend for themselves, immigrants from Germany, Ireland and elsewhere, and runaway slaves. Each regiment was authorized to hire four cooks per company. Kat was hired as a company cook.

7

November 9, 1861

My Dearest Mother,

I just received your letters today. My mail was held for several weeks while I was away on an assignment. I worked as a farmhand while I gathered information on the local secessionists. Secrecy was very important for the success of the mission.

The locals around here are quite different from the people we encounter in Philadelphia. They are mostly farmers with strong opinions on life and politics. They are either for the Union or for the Confederacy. There is no middle ground.

Many of the people in this part of the state are ready to secede and join the rebellion. I uncovered a plot to form an armed militia that would declare western Maryland part of the Confederate States of America. My reports helped foil the plot.

  I learned a great deal about farming while I was collecting information on the rebels.

  I trust John has kept you apprised of developments here in the camp.

Your devoted son,

Tom

8

The First Battle of Bolivar Heights

Ten days after the militia incident, Banks ordered a raid on the Confederate grain supply a few miles outside Bolivar, Virginia. Colonel Geary took two enhanced companies and Company C with an artillery piece across the Potomac. The enhanced companies returned with grain they had liberated from the mill that evening. They said the others would be returning the next day.

The sound of artillery and gunfire erupted on the Virginia side of the Potomac in the morning. The day was no more than an hour old. Officers were finishing their breakfasts and discussing plans. The battle raged for hours, but no reinforcements were sent to rescue Geary and his men. Kat fretted until the fighting ended, and the colonel led his troops back across the Potomac. He was limping. Tom helped an injured soldier hobble along with the rest of the company. The wounded were taken to a nearby mess tent for treatment.

Kat raced to her tent and grabbed her medical supplies. By the time she reached the mess tent, Geary had the injured men resting on tables while he waited for the surgeon. His face had a pasty look that suggested his injury was serious. Kat walked up to him and said, "Take a load off your feet so I can look at that leg."

"Take care of the men."

"I'm starting at the top. Lie down and make yourself comfortable."

"You're not qualified. I'll wait for the surgeon."

She glared at him and snapped, "I've cared for men and horses and hogs and dogs all my life. I haven't lost a patient yet."

The colonel recoiled, shocked by the woman's temerity. But he let her push him back onto a table. She tore a rag from her petticoat and wiped away the blood. Bone was visible. "That's pretty nasty."

"Shrapnel."

She opened a bottle and poured fiery liquid into the wound. He grimaced. "Whisky. Where did you get that?"

"It's easy to come by. My friends use it to pry money from your men."

"So, you're settling in?"

Kat covered the gash with a poultice that smelled and felt like horse manure. She began bandaging his wound with another strip of cloth torn from her undergarment. "There's only two men in this place I'd fuck, and you won't have me."

Geary chuckled. "What about Lieutenant Dahlgren?"

"Make that three."

"Sergeant Donal is an innocent young man. I don't want him led astray."

The woman paused to stare incredulously at the colonel. "I heard a lot of shooting this morning. I imagine Tom was trading bullets with the enemy."

"Yes. He gave a good account of himself."

"You seem to be doing a fine job of leading him astray without any help from me." She tied off the bandage. "You have children, colonel?"

"Three. Two in the army."

"So, it didn't turn out all bad when a woman led you astray."

He guffawed in spite of himself. By then, Captain Mills was looking over Kat's shoulder and admiring the way she had dressed Geary's wound. "How bad?"

She turned to face him. "Cut to the bone. Have to make sure it doesn't become infected."

The medic sniffed the open bottle of whisky and dabbed some of the poultice on his tongue. He nodded. "You'll do. Follow me. I'll examine them and tell you what I want done."

When the work was finished and the wounded were being led from the tent, Mills grabbed Geary. "I need her on my staff."

The commander looked puzzled by the unexpected request. "She's a cook."

"She has medical training. She speaks English. She follows directions. She should be taking care of injured soldiers not dishing out slop."

Kat was transferred to the regimental hospital later that day.

That night, while the men were seated around a fire eating their dinner, a guard approached Tom. "Come with me, soldier."

He looked up. The voice was familiar, but it didn't fit with the uniform. Tom followed the messenger along a path toward the headquarters tent until they came to a trail that would have been missed by anyone who didn't know the area. It led into a thick stand of trees. When the pair reached an open spot well back from the main route, the guard's cap came off. Her hair cascaded down over her shoulders. She threw her arms around his neck and squeezed. He wrapped her in his arms and pulled her body against his. She whispered, "I knew you were over there. I was afraid I'd never see you again."

"I'm okay. Not a scratch."

"Some men were killed. You could've been one of them."

He squeezed her again, his cock pushing against her crotch. She breathed in his ear, "Do you want me?"

Tom nuzzled her neck. "Always." He pulled back. "But this'll get us into a lot of trouble."

"Men pay the women and the women give them what they want. Every night. No one gets in trouble."

He gave her an exasperated look. She pulled his head in for a kiss. When their lips separated, Kat whispered, "I need you."

His hands slid to her butt. He squeezed the soft flesh with both hands. Kat pressed against him with all her strength. He opened her knickers and reached inside for bare flesh. While his hands explored up under her shirt, she pushed his breeches aside and stroked his rock-hard shaft. "That's quite a bayonet you've got there, soldier." She giggled and toppled back, pulling him down as she fell.

When they had satisfied their savage hunger, they pulled their pants on and cuddled. "Tell me what happened."

Tom kissed her on the forehead and rolled onto his back. Clasping his hands behind his head, he gazed at the stars while he composed his answer. She rolled over and rested her head on his shoulder, her fingers toying with his thin, silky beard. "Our orders were to wipe out the rebel grain supply at a mill on the other side of Bolivar. Colonel Geary had Company C take an artillery piece up the heights to cover the operation. The rest of the regiment went to the mill, loaded up all the grain they could haul back and burned the rest. The rebels didn't give us any trouble. But it was dark by the time our troops had made it back across the river. The colonel decided we should stay put until morning." He turned to look at her. and she kissed him. "We were on open ground on our way back when they hit us. It was a company of mounted irregulars supported by a company of Confederate infantrymen." Tom grimaced. "We raced to the edge of town and set up a defensive perimeter." He took a breath and sighed. "They kept coming. There was a lot of shooting but we held them off. The Old Man ordered a couple of squads to work their way around the rebels and hit their flank. That ended the fight pretty quick. They took off running."

Tom pointed at the moon high in the night sky and said, "I've got to get back before I'm reported missing."

He got to his knees. Kat grabbed his head and kissed him. He straightened, pulling free from her tender clutch.

9

February 23, 1862

My Dearest Mother,

Thank you for the letter. As always, you provided a much needed boost to my spirits. The gossip I've heard in camp agrees with what you wrote. All the goings-on in Washington have not produced a whit of progress against the rebels. Only the weather, which has been wet and cold, has slowed the secessionist harassment of our troops.

General McClellan defeated the rebels last summer but he has not done anything since he came to Washington.

We were all cheered by the news that General Grant had captured two forts. I am told that means the Confederates have lost Kentucky and will soon lose Tennessee. It appears that we, Colonel Geary and the Twenty-Eighth Regiment, will be crossing over into Virginia tomorrow as ordered by President Lincoln.

Four companies of cavalry from Michigan are joining us on this mission. We will drive the rebels out of Virginia.

I am eating well. By luck, my tent mate, Aaron Wilson, is a veteran some years older than me. He has taught me to cook as well as many other things that I need for survival.

Your devoted son,

Tom

10

1862 – Into Virginia

President Abraham Lincoln found himself in a difficult position after the defeat at Bull Run in July 1861. Confederate General Joseph Johnston occupied Manassas, a day's march from the Federal capital. Lawmakers and people on the street in northern cities were demanding vigorous action. Some feared the war might have been lost already.

General George B McClellan, a thirty-seven-year-old West Point graduate and Mexican War veteran, emerged as the man of the hour. The *New York Times Herald* hailed him as the "Napoleon of the Present War."

Lincoln brought the young general to Washington and made him commander of the Military Division of the Potomac. McClellan immediately set about rebuilding the Union army. As the ranks swelled with volunteers, he organized. He drilled the troops to prepare them for battle, and he showed up frequently to review the drills. Morale soared.

McClellan clashed with Scott over strategy. When the old warhorse retired, Lincoln appointed McClellan as his new General in Chief. It was a rocky marriage from the beginning. The two men battled over goals and timing. While the general dreamed of a grand assault on Richmond that would bring the Confederacy to its knees, the president feared an assault on Washington that would bring the Union to its knees. Either Johnston, with his troops thirty miles south of the city, or Jackson, rampaging in the Shenandoah Valley less than a hundred miles to the west, could march on the nation's capital as the British had done fifty years earlier.

Tensions increased over the winter months. In mid-January, Lincoln called a meeting of the top generals to press for action. McClellan announced his plan to land his army at Urbana, Virginia, a port city fifty miles south of Richmond, but he gave no operational details. Ten days later, the president issued orders for all of the armies to commence operations by February 22, Washington's Birthday. A week later, he ordered the Department of the Potomac to take the offensive against the rebel stronghold at Manassas.

Winter weather had shut down operations for the regular army, but the secessionists kept up their guerrilla warfare. Attacks and skirmishes continued into the early months of 1862, forcing Union soldiers to man their picket positions in all kinds of weather. Cavalry patrols remained active and continued to round up locals who were consorting with the rebels on the Virginia side of the Potomac.

Goldman and Kennedy brought stories of civilian pressure on the president to do something. Ordinary Americans reading their newspapers at home feared the North was losing the war. Congress pressed for action. Many feared that if the Federal Army didn't get going soon, the rebels would win by default. Goldman said his war correspondent cousin told him Lincoln was getting fed up with McClellan's excuses and delays.

President Lincoln's demand for action by the end of February forced the encampment into a flurry of plans and preparations. Colonel Geary's orders were to establish Union control in the Loudon Valley, including the Manassas Gap Railroad, which ran from northeastern Virginia into the Shenandoah Valley. He was to block any attempt by Confederate General Stonewall Jackson to advance from the Shenandoah Valley and attack Washington.

Four companies from the First Michigan Cavalry were attached to the 28th Volunteer Infantry Regiment to beef it up for its new role.

Kat found Tom in the evening. "I heard that you're going after the rebels tomorrow."

"Four-thirty. We should start crossing the river by daybreak but it will take all day. And we have to kick the rebels off that mountain over there. We're going to take control of that railroad they used to bring reinforcements and win the battle at Bull Run last year."

She led him to an ambulance, where she laid out some blankets they could use as a bed. They lay talking for a while after making love. But Tom had to get back to his tent. He pulled away and dressed.

Kat said, "Tom." He stopped to study her. "I'll catch up. You won't get very far without supply wagons and we'll travel with them."

He smiled, nodded and disappeared into the night.

Geary began crossing the Potomac on February 24. The morning was raw. A biting wind chilled men to the bone. Rain fell intermittently. Geary had to get five thousand men and a thousand horses across the Potomac before dark. Six men drowned when a sudden squall capsized their boat. But the beachhead was established. That part of the operation was a success.

The 28th spent the next four days fighting its way up Loudon Mountain in cold, wet late winter weather. They pushed rebels from entrenched positions as they worked their way up the two-thousand-foot climb.

On March 1, Geary led his men to Lovettsville, a Union friendly German settlement. When he reached the town, he learned the enemy was getting ready to torch Waterford, ten miles away. He sent his cavalry ahead to avert the disaster. The foot soldiers followed after a short rest.

The advance paused for three days while supply wagons caught up and the troops replenished their food and ammunition. On March 5, they continued to Leesburg. The Confederates were in full retreat, burning supplies and bridges as they moved. Geary took Leesburg without opposition. He took over Fort Johnson and renamed it Fort Geary.

The colonel left a small garrison at Leesburg and continued his pursuit of the fleeing rebels. By the 15th, he had set up a perimeter along the eastern border of Loudon County. Over the next week, he expanded his perimeter west along the Manassas Gap Railroad as far as Front Royal.

Rumors of a naval battle reached Tom in mid-March. A Confederate ship with steel armor had sunk a couple of Union blockade ships at the mouth of the Elizabeth River. It was driven off by the Union's steel ship the next day.

Near the end of March, a civilian wearing a bowler hat and a black woolen overcoat strolled through the camp until he came to the fire where Tom and his friends were drinking coffee and smoking pipes. He studied the group of grubby soldiers and said, "Tom Donal? I'm Josh Goldman. My cousin Sam told me to be sure and say hello."

The greeting baffled the soldier, but he recovered quickly. "How is Sam?"

"Quite well. The local secessionists keep him busy. Keeps him from pining for home."

"And what brings you here?" Tom asked.

"I'm a war correspondent for the *Inquirer*. I've been assigned to report on Colonel Geary."

"It's pretty quiet here. All we're doing is guarding the railroad. Sit down and have some coffee," Tom suggested. "If you've got some news to share we'd be obliged to hear it. We haven't seen a newspaper in over a month."

Josh sat down and made himself comfortable while Tom poured him a cup of coffee. "What would you like to know?"

"Is McClellan ever going to leave Washington?"

"He's on his way to Fort Monroe right now."

"I thought he was going to Urbana."

"Plans change. The Confederates have an ironclad that's blocking our ships from sailing up the river."

"But he's still going to march on Richmond."

"That's what he says."

Another soldier asked, "What happened to all the rebels that were supposed to be camped down here getting ready to march on Washington?"

"General Johnston took them south to block McClellan."

Geary pulled back to the east and set up camp in The Plains, midway between Front Royal and Manassas. Rebel cavalry attacked on April 1. The battle with the rebel forces spread as far south as Warrenton and continued for several weeks, except for a short break when a snowstorm kept both sides in their respective camps.

At the end of the month, the regiment was detailed to repair roads, bridges, telegraph lines, and rails. Work on that stretch of wooded road snaking through broken country over ravines and hills was demanding. The troops had to live off the land, foraging for food and harvesting lumber needed for the repairs. Rebel militia and cavalry kept up constant pressure with lightning attacks.

A four-day rainstorm swelled the rivers, wiping out some of the bridges that had to be replaced.

But by the end of April, the telegraph lines were in working order and the railroad tracks were in good shape.

11

April 20, 1862

My Dearest Mother,

We are taking a day of rest in honor of Easter. The day started with a sunrise service celebrating the resurrection of the Lord. We sang hymns and listened to a sermon. Our chaplain assured us that God will deliver victory to the North for our cause is just and righteous. But I think God is testing us.

We received news of success out west. General Grant delivered a major blow against the Confederates at Shiloh. Here in the east, we have little to show for our efforts. General McClellan is fighting his way up the peninsula toward Richmond, but there is no news of him attacking the city. For our part, we are stuck with inconsequential tasks.

Rebel cavalry began attacking us a month ago. Some say it was the spring campaign. Two weeks ago, it snowed so hard for four days that all the fighting stopped. But it has picked up again. We are rebuilding bridges and corduroying roads so our wagons can get around. Last week, a rainstorm swelled the rivers and washed out the bridges we had just built. We'll build new ones next week.

You mentioned General Banks and his battles with Confederate General Jackson. The men here do not have much confidence in General Banks. He is a politician. General Jackson has made a career of the Army. He graduated from the Military Academy and has been leading troops in combat for the last twenty years. Besides, Jackson grew up in these mountains. Banks is from Massachusetts.

Our Colonel Geary has been promoted to General and put in charge of a brigade. Lieutenant Colonel DeKorponay has been promoted to Colonel and given command of our regiment.

Your devoted son,

Tom

12

Back with Banks

The Shenandoah Valley is the depression between the Blue Ridge Mountains on the east and the Allegheny Mountains on the west. It extends over a hundred miles from the Potomac River in the north to the James River in the south. Much of it was farmland that supplied the Confederacy with food during the war. The rest was woodland. Trees overrun with dense vegetation. Most of the roads were haphazard trails created by farmers and trappers. Some of the more important roads were corduroyed, with tree trunks and branches placed across the dirt surface so it would not turn to thick mud in wet weather. Jackson commissioned new maps drawn up in 1862. The North continued to rely on maps created a century earlier.

Banks and Jackson fought for control of The Valley throughout March and April. Banks won at Kernstown at the end of March and seized Winchester in mid-April. Tom and his friends, discussing the situation around a fire at night, concluded Jackson was keeping Union forces engaged so they could not support McClellan.

Josh Goldman confirmed rumors that General Johnston had moved the Confederate army from northern Virginia down the peninsula to block McClellan's attack on Richmond. But McClellan had won a major battle at Fort Magruder, forcing Johnston to retreat.

Geary and his troops were reattached to Banks's army at the beginning of May. He was assigned responsibility for a fifty-mile stretch of track on the Manassas Gap Railroad and nearby roads. The work was back-breaking. The troops had to live off the land again, foraging for food and harvesting lumber, while dealing with hit-and-run attacks by rebel militia and cavalry.

Near the end of May, Confederate forces overran the small garrison at Front Royal. Troops under Colonel John Kenley made a stand but were forced to retreat to Cedarville. The following day, Jackson attacked Banks at Winchester and drove him out of the city. He chased the Union general all the way to Point of Rocks on the north shore of the Potomac.

On May 28, Geary led his regiment out of Manassas to patrol gaps in the Blue Ridge Mountains in support of an expected counterattack against the Southerners. A week later, the regiment was ordered to go back to guarding the railroad from its camp near Manassas.

The new situation was an improvement. Tom still had to take his turn on the picket line, but there were no rebels in sight. Instead of cutting trees and building bridges, the troops drilled every day. Their rations included fresh vegetables and beef. And Kat managed frequent visits with Tom.

While they were marking time on railroad duty, rumors about a big battle north of Richmond reached Tom. The Confederates had attacked McClellan's forward units, which were trapped by sudden flooding on the Chickahominy River. McClellan repulsed the attack. According to reports, the Confederate commander had been killed, and General Robert E. Lee was taking his place. The change was considered a loss for the rebels because Johnston was reputed to be their best general.

Jackson's audacity and success in the Shenandoah Valley astounded Lincoln. He devised a plan to trap the Confederates between three small armies. Major General John Fremont was ordered to cross the Alleghenies and attack from the west. Brigadier General James Shields was ordered to recapture Front Royal and attack from the east. Banks was to recross the Potomac and attack from the north.

Banks balked. His troops were in no condition for another battle after being forced out of Winchester. Fremont struggled to cross the mountains on muddy roads in bad weather. Shields retook Front Royal but paused to wait for reinforcements.

Jackson marched up The Valley on a corduroyed highway. On June 8, he sent a division to confront Fremont at Cross Keys. The Union general deployed a fraction of his force, which was easily repulsed by the Southerners. That failure broke Fremont. He withdrew and returned to Missouri.

The following morning, Jackson attacked Shields at Port Republic. With Banks and Fremont out of the fight, the Union general was isolated and outnumbered. He had to retreat to avoid being crushed.

Kennedy, Sam Goldman and his cousin Josh came by one night. Kat showed up in uniform with a canteen full of whisky. They talked long into the night. Josh said, "McClellan made it to Richmond and was getting ready to pounce when everything went wrong all at once." He sipped his whisky and let the suspense build.

"What happened?" Tom demanded.

"Johnston didn't wait for McClellan to get his forces organized. He attacked. He hit a weak spot and pushed our boys back, but they recovered and made a stand." Josh looked around and grinned. "Then God unleashed a rainstorm that changed everything. The battleground turned into a swamp. The Chickahominy overran its banks and washed out the bridges McClellan needed for maneuvers. His big army was divided into two small armies. But just as Johnston was ready to finish McClellan, he was shot off his horse and the Confederates had to regroup."

"Killed or wounded?" Kat asked.

"Wounded. He's alive but out of the job. Davis put Lee in charge of The Army of Virginia." Josh sipped his whisky. "The first thing he did was change the name to The Army of Northern Virginia."

Kennedy asked, "Any idea what Jackson is up to?"

"None. He disappeared into the mountains."

Sam said, "He's on his way to Richmond."

"I don't know," Josh countered. "His presence in The Valley has kept everyone on edge. He gives Lincoln nightmares and that keeps troops from joining McClellan." He swirled the tin he was using for a cup and took another swig of whisky. "In fact, he took one army corps away from McClellan and stationed it in Maryland to protect Washington in case Jackson left The Valley."

"If he was supposed to be in The Valley to threaten Washington, he would make sure we knew he was in The Valley," Sam insisted. He pressed his lips into a tight line and nodded. "He's on his way to Richmond to make sure McClellan is beaten once and for all."

Geary moved about the Blue Ridge side of the Shenandoah throughout June. He marched to a new location every few days, but did not encounter any significant rebel forces.

Tom shared dinner with Kennedy and Goldman several times in between moves. The same questions came up in each discussion: "Where are the Confederates? What's Jackson up to?"

They were certain there was only one answer. Jackson had left The Valley. "He's going to reinforce Lee at Richmond," Goldman insisted.

On July 3, Josh reported that Lee had driven McClellan back to a defensive position along the James River sixteen miles from Richmond. Sam predicted Banks would be ordered to attack the Confederate capital within a week.

13

July 4, 1862

My Dearest Mother,

We are taking a day off to celebrate the birth of our nation.
The news is not good. McClellan has been chased from Richmond by Confederate General Robert E. Lee. Our troops are now camped too far down the James River to be a serious threat to the Confederate capital.

We have been searching for rebels in the Blue Ridge Mountains for weeks. There are none to be found. They likely left for Richmond before we got here.

General John Pope is putting together the Army of Virginia. His successes under General Fremont in the West are cause for hope.

Our mission will be to force Lee into a battle and defeat him. General Pope says this will be easy once he has introduced the methods used to defeat the Confederates in the West. Many find his attitude offensive. His strict orders regarding personal conduct have upset many, particularly older soldiers. Officers are reportedly vexed because he has limited what they can carry with them on the campaign.

I've heard that Fremont has resigned rather than report to a former underling.

We begin training with the rest of the army next week.

Your devoted son,

Tom

14

The Battle of Cedar Ridge

General John Pope formed the Army of Virginia to take on Lee's Army of Northern Virginia at the beginning of July. The Department of the Shenandoah under Banks, the Department of the Mountains under Fremont, and the German Militia under Franz Sigel were being united under a general with a history of success against the Confederates in the West. Geary's unit became the First Brigade in the Second Division under the command of General Christopher Augur.

Pope announced himself with a bold statement. "I come to you from the West, where we have always seen the backs of our enemies; from an Army whose business it has been to seek the adversary and beat him when he was found, whose policy has been attack and not defense."

His orders to his soldiers gave clear insights into his philosophy and approach.

The troops would have to live off the land where they were operating. They would have to forage for their food and other necessities.

Officers were ordered to give up their luxury tents and cut their baggage to the bare minimum.

Men in the civilian population would be required to sign an oath of loyalty. Any man who refused would be imprisoned or exiled.

The general deployed his army in a wide arc across northern Virginia. On his right, I Corps, under the command of General Franz Sigel, was stationed in Sperryville on the eastern slopes of the Blue Ridge. III Corps, under the command of General Irvin McDowell, was stationed at Falmouth, on the Rappahannock near Fredericksburg.

II Corps, under the command of General Banks, encamped at Little Washington near Leesburg in the Loudoun Valley, fifty miles northeast of Sigel. Banks drilled his troops every day for the remainder of July.

August 1 was a day of mourning for President Van Buren, who had died on July 24. Two days later, Pope reviewed the corps.

That night, Kennedy and Goldman joined Tom and a few others around the fire. They puffed on their pipes, sipped their coffee and wondered what was going to happen.

Tom said, "We've been marching in place for three weeks. When are we going to do something?"

Goldman replied, "Soon. Very soon it will plotz."

Kennedy grinned and shook his head. "Plotz?"

"Boom! Explode. Pressure's building toward a big one."

Tom said, "What makes you think that?"

"Pope has fifty thousand men here in Virginia and McClellan has a hundred thousand trapped on a peninsula near Richmond. That situation can't last very long."

"Meaning?" Kennedy demanded.

"Richmond is the target. McClellan has lost twice to the Confederates. Pope wants to go on the offensive. We're going to march down to Richmond and trap Lee in between two armies."

By this time, Josh Goldman had joined the group. "I doubt that."

"Why?" Tom asked. "It makes sense."

"Halleck is now General in Chief. He won't allow anything like that."

"He's a schlemiel," Sam growled and shook his head.

"We have them outnumbered two to one," Tom said. "Capture Richmond and this war is over."

Josh shook the suggestion off. "Halleck wouldn't move when McClellan ordered him to attack. He wouldn't allow a move when Grant wanted to follow up on a string of victories. He's not going to make a bold move now."

"That was when Grant was number two in Tennessee," Kennedy said. "He's aggressive. Now that he's in charge, he'll take the war to the rebels."

Josh considered the possibilities for a moment. "Grant isn't in charge in Tennessee. Halleck hasn't said who is going to take over that position, but it probably won't be Grant. The word in Washington is that Grant messed up so badly at Shiloh, he will never be trusted with a major command."

Banks broke camp on August 6 and began moving toward Culpeper Courthouse, sixty miles to the south. His objective was to capture the railroad junction at Gordonsville. The Second Division under Augur was in the lead.

On the eighth, Lieutenant Dahlgren intercepted them and reported that Confederate troops led by General Stonewall Jackson were marching in their direction. They had driven Dahlgren and his men from their position on Lookout Mountain. The 28th Regiment was ordered to retake the position and hold it at all costs.

Pope ordered Banks to set up a defensive position along Cedar Ridge and hold the rebels until Sigel arrived with reinforcements. Augur took the center with Crawford on his right. Geary and Prince were on his left. By nightfall, the troops were in position and the Union was back in control on Lookout Mountain.

August 9 started hot and got worse as the day went on. Jackson led a sluggish advance across the Rappahannock. By eleven, the Confederates were in range of Union artillery, and Banks opened up. The artillery duel continued into the late afternoon. Brutal heat took its toll. Heatstroke decimated gun crews.

On Lookout Mountain, there was nothing for an infantryman to do but wait. Tom found an abandoned spyglass and a perch where he could watch the action. An intelligence team also watched the developing battle and kept Banks informed. What they saw was confusion. Jackson's infantry was too disorganized to fight.

Banks was not going to allow a promising opportunity slip away. He sent Geary and Prince to attack Jackson's right flank. The charge met with ferocious musketry. Men in blue, racing to take on the rebels, began dropping well short of the mark, but their comrades kept charging. The right side of the Confederate line buckled. Men in gray bolted to the rear. As they did, thousands of fresh troops led by an officer on horseback raced forward to hold the line. The Confederate front recovered and stiffened. The Union assault stalled.

On the other flank, Crawford's men charged across a wheat field with such ferocity that the rebels turned and ran.

Disaster threatened the Confederate ranks until a lone horseman rode to the front, waving his saber in one hand and a battle flag in the other. The rebels rallied and followed the cavalier in a counterattack on the Union troops. Tom had no doubt the daring rider was General Stonewall Jackson.

Momentum shifted. Augur's men began to fall back. The fighting continued late into the night. In the end, all Tom could see were muzzle flashes from muskets.

As August 10 dawned, Pope had his army back together, and Jackson had pulled his men back across the Rappahannock. Both sides had suffered heavy casualties. Prince had been captured. Geary had been wounded and was in a field hospital recovering. Half the men in the brigades that saw action had been killed or wounded. Several hundred men had been taken prisoner by the rebels.

Halleck ordered Pope to disengage. He was not going to risk a futile attack on a well-defended Confederate position. That decision opened the door for Lee's move into Northern Virginia, Maryland and Pennsylvania.

15

Bull Run Again

The Army of Virginia settled into bivouac north of the Rappahannock. Without a plan or goals, its soldiers were left marking time. Life took on a languid pace while the men waited for orders that would send them into battle.

On a night visit, Kennedy said, "Jackson has pulled back to Gordonsville."

Goldman added, "Molasses McClellan is on his way back to Washington. That means Lee can move north. Last week's fight with Jackson was probably just the beginning."

"That would leave Richmond unprotected," Tom objected.

"The best defense is a good offense," Goldman observed.

"Besides, if Lee ever gets north of the Potomac, this war will be over," Kennedy said.

"We aren't losing," Tom retorted. "We've captured Kentucky and Tennessee. And we can still march down to Richmond."

"Our top general marched on Richmond and was sent packing without firing a shot," Kennedy said. "And we just got thrashed."

"Antiwar sentiment will force the president to recognize the South as an independent country," Goldman said.

Days later, news of an attack on Bristoe Station reached the camp. Jackson had managed to march around the Army of Virginia and strike at the rear. The 28th was sent to drive him off and repair the damage. The rebels engaged Union troops and torched the supply depot at Manassas Junction before pulling back across Bull Run Creek.

A division sent by Pope to pinpoint Jackson's position was attacked. The battle raged until nightfall. The following day, the rest of the Army of Virginia arrived to drive the Confederates off.

Pope's assault was a disaster. While he was launching a series of disjointed attacks that accomplished nothing, Lee reached the battlefield with reinforcements. On the third day of the battle, the rebels broke the Union offensive with a strong move against the left flank. The Federal line fell back but managed to hold off Lee's army until dark. Pope withdrew across the Rappahannock overnight and retreated to the defenses around Washington.

16

September 6, 1862

My Dearest Mother,

The battle last week was a disappointing loss. It was bloody. Almost a thousand good men lost their lives, and another thousand were wounded. I did not participate in that battle. The 28th had been assigned to repair damage inflicted on a railroad station by rebel soldiers.

We now have news that General Lee is leading his army down the Shenandoah Valley into Maryland. Our orders are to march north and link up with General McClellan near Harpers Ferry. Then we will be back in the same situation we were in this time last year. I expect that I will spend this winter encamped up there just as I did last winter.

I have not heard what the future holds for General Pope and the Army of Virginia. I can tell you that these last two battles have not helped his reputation with us soldiers.

Your devoted son,

Tom

17

Antietam

McClellan led the Army of the Potomac from its encampment at Harrison's Landing on the Peninsula back to Washington on August 4. Shortly after that, Lee began moving north for a bold strike into Maryland. A week later, he provided reinforcements that enabled Jackson to crush Pope at the second Battle of Bull Run. He continued north through the Shenandoah Valley toward Harpers Ferry. McClellan was sent to intercept the Confederate forces and drive them back into Virginia. The remnants of Pope's Army of Virginia were ordered to join up with the Army of the Potomac.

Lee had moved into Maryland, expecting to be welcomed by a crowd of frustrated secessionists. He found himself in hostile territory with an enemy army marching to confront him. He retreated over South Mountain just ahead of the

Army of the Potomac led by McClellan, the man he had defeated in seven days of fighting south of Richmond. After crossing the mountain, Lee paused to make a stand outside the town of Sharpsburg. His rearguard had done little to slow McClellan's advance.

Major General Ambrose Burnside, who would suffer a humiliating defeat at Fredericksburg before the year ended, was set up on his right flank. Major General Joseph Hooker, who would fail at Chancellorsville, encamped on his left. Brigadier General George Mead, who would claim victory at Gettysburg, was squarely to his front. But McClellan was in charge and the Union attack developed at his pace. Lee strengthened his defenses while he waited.

Jackson had just captured Harpers Ferry. He was on his way to reinforce Lee as he had done in the Seven Days Battles two months earlier.

Lieutenant Colonel Tyndale led Geary's brigade to the edge of a field with endless rows of cornstalks eight feet high, picked clean of ears and wilting under the scorching summer sun. The men had left Thurmont before sunrise, crossed Mount Catoctin, and pushed twenty-seven miles through heat and choking dust to reach this place of rest after the sun had set. In the last hours, they had marched to the thunderous sounds of an artillery duel. The roar of cannons continued as the soldiers rolled out their bedding to get some sleep before the battle that would come with the dawn.

Southern artillery began firing before the first dim light of day. Hooker's big guns answered. At 5:30, his lead division started from woods bordering the north side of the cornfield. Their objective was the high ground where a small church stood. Hooker called a halt before the division reached the cornfield. Bayonets glittering amid the rows of corn had caught his attention. He turned his artillery on the field, instantly flattening everything between his men and entrenched rebel pickets.

The first division charged across the rows of stubble only to be stopped by a hailstorm of artillery and musket fire. Another division advancing through the woods on the west side of the cornfield came face-to-face with the rebels and pushed them aside. They were slowed to a halt by reinforcements coming up from the Confederate rear.

XII Corps was called up to reinforce Hooker. Tyndale roused his weary troops from their breakfast to face charging rebels. They engaged the Southerners with bayonets and pushed them back to their entrenchments.

Tom was sprinting across the road that separated the two armies when he saw a man aim directly at him and fire. The ball whistled past his head. Tom kept charging. With no time to reload, the rebel swung his musket like a club. The young soldier drove his bayonet into the man's chest before the rifle's butt could get around. He pushed the lifeless body back and slid over the fence in one smooth move.

The 28th fought hand-to-hand all the way to the Dunker Church. They drove off the Confederate artillery and dug in while Southerners fired at them from the nearby woods. Reinforcements from the Union reserves were supposed to come forward and secure their gains. After two hours passed with no sign of the reinforcements, they were pulled back to a safer position.

The focus of the battle moved to the left toward the southern end of the rebel position. When the sounds of battle finally died out, except for scattered musketry and an occasional lonesome cannon blast. Major Danson led the regiment in a retreat to their camp on the other side of the cornfield. A mini ball had struck Tyndale in the head during the charge up to Dunker Church. He was not expected to live.

Tom noted the setting sun. This day was almost over.

Eight-foot high cornstalks had been cut down to the ground in the battle. Possession of the field had changed hands a dozen times as the Federals and the Confederates attacked and counterattacked. In the end, it belonged to neither side. The dead had claimed it for their final resting place. A man could walk across it without stepping on the ground. Danson led the regiment around the perimeter out of respect for fallen comrades.

Goldman found Tom preparing dinner. He sat in silence while the young Irishman cooked enough for both of them. "Where's Kennedy?" Tom asked as he sat to eat.

"Haven't seen him since yesterday."

"He was with II Corps, right?"

"They made a final assault on the center of the Confederate line. The rebs were dug in pretty good."

A gloomy silence settled over the meal until footsteps announced another visitor. Kennedy stepped out of the darkness. "Hi, boys. Glad to see you made it through the day."

"I was worried you didn't," Tom said.

"The road was so low they could stand and shoot at us from behind a mound of packed dirt. They were slaughtering us. We got around 'em and up a little rise. Then we were shootin' them like fish in a barrel."

Tom asked, "What happened?"

"Those that could, ran. We chased 'em."

"Then what?" Goldman asked.

"Longstreet was waiting for us. General Richardson was killed. Colonel Barlow went down. General Hancock, the adjutant, took over and ordered us to retreat. We needed reinforcements. At least another brigade."

"It was about the same with us," Goldman said. "Burnside was supposed to attack the right flank to keep pressure off Hooker. We sat around all morning waiting for orders. Then he was going to send us over the bridge. But the Confederates mowed us down before we got halfway. Finally somebody offered a brigade of New Yorkers extra whiskey. They charged the position and sent the rebs running. But another division of Johnnies counterattacked and pushed them back across the bridge."

A mischievous grin spread across Kennedy's face. Goldman caught his stare and demanded, "What?"

"Boom. You got your plotz."

Late into the night, shadowy figures moved among the dead, emptying their pockets of valuables they no longer needed. By morning muster, the distinctive odor of rotting corpses was everywhere. Soldiers from both sides were dispatched to search for wounded men among the dead bodies. Officers met at the edge of the turnpike that separated North and South. They talked and then sent someone to carry a message to headquarters. Eventually, a truce was negotiated. Wounded prisoners were exchanged, and the grisly business of identifying and burying the dead got underway.

The sun was high in the sky and the air was thick with the nauseating odor of decaying flesh. Flies were everywhere. Bugs swarmed over lifeless bodies. Burying the remains was hard, sweaty work that required an iron will and an iron stomach.

Late in the afternoon, Tom spotted the forlorn figure of a woman picking her way in his direction. When she got closer, he could see it was Kat, looking pale and exhausted. She wrapped her arms around his waist and buried her head in his chest. He put his arms around her shoulders. "Are you okay?"

"No." She sobbed. "How can people do that to each other?"

"I guess it's something that has to be done."

"Why? For God's sake why?"

"The dispute has to be settled one way or the other."

"Not like this."

"Looks like this is how it's going to be."

"Why can't we just get along? We did before."

"President Lincoln said we can't be half slave and half free. The seceches have decided they won't give up their slaves without a fight." Tom kissed her on the forehead. "And where I come from, we aren't going to give up our country without a fight."

Tom led her to a tree where they could sit and hold each other. "Looks like you could use some rest."

"They turned the Miller farmhouse into a hospital. It's not big enough. I spent the last two days tending to wounded and dying men. I held a stranger's hand while he died. I helped hold men down while their limbs were sawed off. I've got nothing left."

"I spent yesterday fighting men who looked like me except they were wearing gray. I killed more than a few." He closed his eyes, shook his head and heaved a sigh. "Today I helped bury them."

They sat in silence for a while and dozed. When they woke, the Confederate Army had faded from the battlefield. Tom figured they had gone back to Richmond to lick their wounds and get ready for the next campaign.

Four days later, President Lincoln issued a warning that the southern states had until January 1, 1863, to end their rebellion and return to the Union or lose their slaves.

18

September 28, 1862

My Dearest Mother,

I am well and eager to get on with this war. General Geary has returned to duty, although his arm is still in a sling. He has been given command of the Second Division of XII Corps.

V Corps pursued the Confederates when they withdrew from the battlefield at Sharpsburg. They caught up with Lee's rear guard as it was crossing the Potomac. Their initial attack put the rebels to flight. A counterattack the next day chased our troops back across the river. A regiment from Massachusetts in combat for the first time suffered severe losses.

That ended the pursuit of General Lee and his army. We are encamped on Loudoun Heights and I expect that is where we will spend the winter.

I am sure you have received the news about John. A mutual friend informed me that she had written a letter for him and sent it to you. But I would be remiss if I did not at least mention his situation. He has mostly recovered from the wound he received in the last battle. He still has his right arm, but it is practically useless. He has difficulty making it through the day as fever and chills bedevil him.

Colonel Tyndale, whom I am sure you met before we left Philadelphia, is making a miraculous recovery. The day after the battle, they were certain he was going to die. Now he is back at work and seems to be okay. He still wears a bandage on his head to cover the wound, but that is the only evidence he had been shot.

The President's proclamation was announced to us in camp. Free the slaves. I don't see that we have any other choice. We cannot treat some like property and still say that we believe all men are created equal. We cannot have slavery and say we believe in the unalienable rights of life, liberty and the pursuit of happiness. The Golden Rule tells us to treat others the way we want to be treated. None of us wants to be treated like a slave.

But why only the slaves in rebel held territories? What happens to the slaves in Maryland and Missouri?

What happens if the Confederate states end their rebellion before the end of the year? Will slavery go on as it has in the past?

Many of my fellow soldiers are unhappy with the proclamation. We were recruited last year to save our country. There was no mention of slaves or slavery when we were asked to commit to a three year enlistment. Now we are told we are fighting to free the slaves in the South.

Many say that the slaves are not their problem. They have not enslaved anyone. They have not bought slaves. They do not use slaves to do their work. Most have never met a slave. Slavery has been around for a long time. It is an established institution in the South. We can deal with it after we put down the rebellion.

Many insist that as soon as the slaves are freed, Blacks will move north and take their jobs.

It is a contentious issue.

Your devoted son,

Tom

19

December 21, 1862

My Dearest Mother,

I send all my love to you and our little family with deepest regrets that I will not be with you for Christmas. I join you in praying that 1863 will see an end to this conflict and bring peace to our beloved country.

When last I spoke with John, he had accepted a medical discharge and was going home to be with you where he can recover properly.

General Mansfield was killed in the battle at Antietam. General Albert Slocum is now in command of XII Corps. General Geary is officially commander of the Second Division. Colonel Ruger has taken command of his old brigade, including our regiment.

Our camp was moved to Bolivar Heights at the beginning of November when we were assigned as a garrison for Harpers Ferry.

We were ordered to leave Bolivar Heights on December 9 and join the rest of the Army in the assault on Fredericksburg. The battle was over by the time we arrived.

As I understand the situation, General Burnside's plan was to capture the city on November 18 and march on Richmond before the Confederates could get in position to block him. But the pontoon bridges he needed to cross the Rappahannock River did not show up until the first week of December. By that time, General Lee had gotten his army in a good defensive position. General Burnside crossed the river and captured Fredericksburg, but attempts to dislodge the rebels from their well fortified positions around the city resulted in a slaughter. The blame will likely fall on the commander, but he would not have had to attempt that assault if the pontoon bridges had been delivered on time.

This is the sort of thing that makes me wonder if our leaders in Washington are serious about winning this war.

We are now in garrison near Dumfries, Virginia. That puts us in a good position for another attempt to take Fredericksburg and march on Richmond when the weather improves.

Your devoted son,

Tom

20

February 21, 1863

My Dearest Mother,

We are pausing to celebrate President Washington's birthday. A small respite from the monotony of our daily routines. Last year, our orders were to get busy fighting the Confederates. This year, we are in winter camp, recovering from our wounds and preparing for God knows what.

It is not surprising that General Burnside was replaced by General "Fighting Joe" Hooker after the second debacle at Fredericksburg. Morale was so bad the Army of the Potomac could not have mounted another campaign. Conditions in the camp were ghastly. The food was moldy. Clothing and other necessities were in short supply. I was not paid for two months running. And this in the midst of a harsh winter.

I have heard rumors that the top brass and even President Lincoln were opposed to General Hooker, but gave him the command because they had no other choice.

We soldiers love him. We are being paid on time, and our back pay has been delivered. Fresh meat and vegetables have replaced the putrid stuff we were being fed. The weather is still miserable, but I am told General Hooker is working to fix that.

Your devoted son,

Tom

21

Hooker Takes Command

For three months, Major General Joseph Hooker, newly appointed commander of the Army of the Potomac, could do no wrong. He successfully rebuilt the Army of the Potomac after Burnside's missteps had left it in shambles.

He boosted morale. He made the well-being of his soldiers his top priority, and lapses in that area were quickly corrected. Newly issued unit patches promoted cohesion by giving the soldiers a sense of identity and pride in the accomplishments of their unit.

Officers and men returning to duty after recovering from wounds received at Fredericksburg played an essential role in bringing the Army of the Potomac back to life. Battle-proven leadership at the regiment level was key to enforcing discipline and raising performance standards.

Hooker developed the Bureau of Military Information (BMI) to replace outside organizations. Allen Pinkerton and his detective agency had been the source of McClellan's faulty assessment of Confederate strength.

The Peace Democrats, the Copperheads, gave an unintended boost to esprit de corps that winter. Men who had fought, shed blood and lost friends battling the rebels wouldn't stand for a negotiated peace.

Games and celebrations were encouraged to distract the men from thoughts of war. The biggest and the best in that winter of 1863 was the celebration of St. Patrick's Day hosted by Brigadier General Thomas Meagher, commander of the Irish Brigade. General Hooker and thousands of his men joined in the games, the feasting, and the dancing.

The day started with the men chasing a greased pig, which would belong to the man who caught it. At the top of a fifteen-foot high, greased pole was a ten-day furlough for the man who got there first. Then there were foot races and jumping contests.

The quartermaster had secured thirty-five hams, a side of beef, turkeys, chickens and small game to feed the crowd. He also had champagne, whiskey and rum.

In the afternoon, officers raced horses over a steeplechase course with four hurdles, five ditches and two artificial rivers.

Sam Goldman and his cousin Josh found Tom relaxing with Kennedy in the shade of an oak tree. Tom raised his cup. "Have a seat, gentlemen. We're drinking to a quick end to this bloody war."

Josh extended his cup. "To war's end."

The four men clicked their cups together, and the newcomers formed a circle under the branches of the oak tree. Tom said, "To our leader, General Hooker."

As the four men tapped cups, Sam added, "And good riddance to that putz Burnside."

"He had some bad breaks," Tom said.

"He was lucky that attack in January ended before it got started," Kennedy replied. He took a minute to study the shocked expressions. "A lot of us in II Corps were ready to throw down our weapons and quit rather than follow him across the river."

Josh said, "Lincoln was against it but he let Burnside convince him to give it a try."

"I've heard Lincoln doesn't like Hooker," Tom said.

"He's ambitious and he's not afraid to let it be known," Josh replied. "The word going around is he sabotaged Burnside."

"Ignoring Burnside's taking the job because he didn't want Hooker to have it," Sam threw in.

"Now that Fighting Joe has the job, let's hope he does it right," Kennedy said as he raised his cup.

Three more cups touched his, and Tom proclaimed, "To Hooker and success."

22

Chancellorsville

President Lincoln set three goals for his army at the beginning of 1863. Grant was to capture Vicksburg, the last remaining Confederate stronghold on the Mississippi. Rosecrans was to drive Confederate General Bragg out of Tennessee. Hooker was to crush Lee.

The commander of the Army of the Potomac devised an elegant strategy. He would have to avoid frontal assaults on Confederate troops in well-fortified positions while getting them to attack him in his well-fortified position.

Lee's army was deployed in an arc from Port Royal, Virginia, twenty miles south of Fredericksburg, to the US Ford of the Rappahannock five miles north of the city. Half of the Army of the Potomac was encamped at Falmouth directly across the river from Fredericksburg. Confederates positioned on Marye's Heights, where Longstreet had held off Burnside's assaults, could easily monitor activity in the Union camp. Hooker let them watch his preparations for a fresh assault on Fredericksburg. In the meantime, the other half of his army, spread out in camps north and east of Falmouth, got ready to march around the Southerners and attack them from the rear. Lee would be trapped in a classic pincer, forcing him to fight a superior army or retreat to Richmond.

The third element of Hooker's plan was an attack on the supply and communication lines that connected Lee to Richmond. Initially, the cavalry was to cross the river upstream of Lee's left flank. Heavy rains swelled the river and forced the commander to abort the cavalry attack. He revised his plan.

On April 27, General Henry Slocum took III Corps, V Corps, XI Corps and XII Corps west in a sweeping move across the Rappahannock at Kelly's Ford and the Rapidan at Germanna Ford before turning east to confront Lee. Two days later, General John Sedgwick started VI Corps and I Corps across the Rappahannock a few miles east of Fredericksburg. The next day, General Winfield Scott Hancock led two divisions of II Corps across the river at US Ford against the Army of Northern Virginia's left flank. The Confederates did not oppose his crossing. By the time he had set up camp on the south side of the river, the four corps led by Slocum were taking up positions around Chancellorsville.

That same day, April 30, Major General George Stoneman led the cavalry toward Richmond to cut Lee's supply and communication lines.

Operations picked up at eight the following morning. Two divisions of Meade's V Corps advanced along River Road with the objective of taking control of Banks Ford. They made good progress with only light resistance by the rebels.

General George Sykes, advanced with the Third Division east along the Orange Turnpike. He was soon confronted by a division under the command of Confederate General McLaws, a West Point classmate. A two-hour battle followed. Sykes and his men were pushed back until reinforcements arrived to help him mount a successful counterattack. The Yanks seized the high ground around a local church and began digging in.

Slocum led XII Corps along the Orange Plank Road, which swung south of the Turnpike, intending to take control of the fork where the Plank Road split off from the Turnpike. He collided with the Confederates a couple of miles east of Chancellorsville. The rebels gave ground, but a brigade using an unfinished railroad running parallel to the road circled around the corps and attacked its right flank. The assault hit the first brigade of Geary's Second Division. The 28th Regiment wheeled and charged the rebels.

Tom found himself in another deadly firefight. His regiment began to waver when Major Chapman was felled by the intense musket fire. Geary rushed to take command of his old unit. Under his leadership, the regiment drove off the attackers. XII Corps gained high ground around a local church a mile south of Sykes's position.

A few hours later, Hooker issued orders for his commanders to pull back to the wooded area around Chancellorsville, known as The Wilderness. The day ended with the Army of the Potomac setting up a defensive position in a vast thicket of stunted trees, bushes and vines - hostile territory for a large army.

That evening, the men received a chilling message. "The Major General Commanding trusts that a suspension in the attack today will embolden the enemy to attack him."

The following day, the Northerners waited in tense anticipation for that attack. Tom heard nothing. Saw nothing. The men of XII Corps were isolated from the unmistakable signs that the enemy was preparing to unleash overwhelming force in the attack that the "Major General Commanding" hoped for.

Not far away, the artillery division of III Corps watched for hours as Confederate troops marched around them toward their right flank. They shelled the rebels with little effect. The III Corps commander, General Dan Sickles, came out to confirm the observation and notified Hooker. The commanding general sent a message to General Howard on the right flank, informing him that the rebels were headed in his direction and might be planning to attack his position. Howard replied that he was preparing his defenses.

Hooker also ordered General John Reynolds to bring I Corps up from Fredericksburg to reinforce Howard.

At 5:30, Howard's men stacked their muskets and sat down to dinner. The first sign of trouble was animals stampeding through the encampment, desperately fleeing some unseen danger. Before any of the soldiers grasped the peril, screaming rebels crashed into the camp, sending the Union soldiers in a panicked rush for safe haven. Thirty thousand Confederate soldiers poured through the breach in the Union line, wreaking destruction as they went.

Federal resistance stiffened as the horde rolled across their position. The Wilderness prevented a route that night. It was as inhospitable to Jackson's men as it was to Hooker's. The Southern forces became confused, disorganized, chaotic as they forced their way through the tangled undergrowth. The attack ground to a halt as evening faded into night.

Every man in the Army of the Potomac, from Major General Hooker to the lowliest private, knew the pause would not last. The enemy was gathering itself for a fresh attack.

Hooker used the respite to reconfigure his defense. He set up a rectangle anchored on the river to secure his position and protect his escape route across the US Ford. The late arriving I Corps formed the western edge of the box. V Corps provided the southern edge, and Howard the eastern edge. II Corps and XII Corps formed an arrowhead shaped salient that protected the artillery position at Fairview Cemetery and the army's headquarters in the Chancellorsville mansion.

The Confederate attack resumed at 5:30 on the morning of May 3. The rebels drove III Corps, with its artillery, from the Hazel Grove and set up their big guns to support later operations. Within hours, the rebels attacked XII Corps. It was a costly assault that gained little ground. Successive artillery strikes on the Chancellorsville mansion severely damaged the building and knocked Hooker unconscious. A third push by the Confederates forced XII Corps and II Corps to give ground, collapsing the salient that protected the Union headquarters. Hooker ordered his second in command, General Couch, commander of II Corps, to lead a retreat to the main defensive perimeter.

VI Corps, under orders from Hooker, stormed the rebel entrenchments on the ridges east of Fredericksburg. The Southerners were forced to retreat at about the same time the defense of Chancellorsville collapsed. Sedgwick organized his men and marched west to join up with Hooker. A detachment from Lee's forces at Chancellorsville met him at Salem church. The battle lasted until dark. Sedgwick withdrew across the Rappahannock.

Hooker held out for another day, but he had no plan and no hope. After nightfall, he crossed the Rappahannock with his artillery, leaving Couch in charge on the south bank. Meade and V Corps followed him across. XII Corps was the last across. Tom and the rest of Geary's fighting Pennsylvanians, the 28th Regiment, brought up the rear.

That night, Kennedy and Goldman joined Tom and others around a fire, rehashing what had happened. They were bitter to the last man. Tom stoically puffed on his pipe while he listened and observed. When he had heard enough, he asked, "How did we lose that one? We controlled high ground. We were winning. What happened?"

Goldman grinned. "The Major General Commanding retreated to low ground to get Lee to attack." He shook his head sadly. "As if Lee needed an excuse."

Another soldier said, "We saw them moving across our front. It took them all morning to get past us. Sickles even came out and saw them. He sent Birney to attack them but it was too late."

Someone else said, "It was the krauts. They took off running as soon as the rebs showed up."

"Ve fight," another man objected. "Sure. Ve run. Too many of dem."

Kennedy said, "If Sickles knew, Hooker knew. Why didn't he send reinforcements to protect our right flank?"

Another voice said, "That's what we were supposed to do. We were south of Fredericksburg when we got the orders. We had to cross the pontoon bridges, march up the north bank, and cross the Rappahannock again. The battle was over by the time we got to Chancellorsville."

"A better question," Goldman said, "why didn't we attack Lee while half his army was maneuvering around to our right flank?"

"Who was going to do that?" Kennedy asked.

"V Corps," Goldman replied. "They did almost no fighting."

Tom said, "Our strategy was to defend against their attacks."

"So, Fighting Joe didn't fight because they didn't attack?" Goldman sneered. "We sat for a whole day cornered by an army half our size because they didn't attack?" He paused and swept the group with a challenging gaze. "Schmegegge. They attacked us Saturday night. Why didn't we make them pay?"

23

Down but not Out

The Army of the Potomac's retreat back across the Rappahannock was devastating. The psychological impact far outweighed the military result. Lee had defended his territory against a much larger army. Common wisdom at home and abroad held that the Union could not prevail. Lee was invincible. Richmond and the Confederacy would survive no matter what Grant did in the West.

The Army of the Potomac had suffered its third disaster in less than a year. Bull Run in August. Fredericksburg in December. And now Chancellorsville. Antietam, the one bright spot, barely qualified as a victory. The Copperheads, pacifists who wanted a negotiated peace with the Confederacy, were encouraged. Leaders in England and France were on the fence but leaning toward recognizing the Confederate States of America.

Hooker had proven to be a timid, ineffective general. The defeat had cost him dearly, and he was lucky the price was not higher.

He could lay the blame on others. Howard had failed miserably despite being warned that Jackson was about to attack him. Reynolds was too slow. Sedgwick was too passive in Fredericksburg. But the prevailing opinion put the blame on the commanding general.

Major General Couch, his second in command and commander of II Corps, resigned in protest over Hooker's refusal to attack Lee.

General in Chief Henry Halleck wanted to get rid of Hooker. Lincoln was not ready to take that step. The two generals soldiered on in spite of the animosity.

Hooker's immediate problem was rebuilding an army that had just lost seventeen thousand men in a fruitless three-day campaign. Lee would probably act quickly to follow up on his victory. He may have already begun preparing his next offensive. Immediate, concrete action was required. The Federal army had to be ready to go back into battle at any time.

The Army of the Potomac had suffered severe structural damage at Chancellorsville. High-ranking officers, including generals, had been killed or put out of action during the fighting. Some regiments, and even some brigades, had suffered so many casualties that they could no longer function as effective combat units. In some cases, regiments could be merged to create new regiments. In other cases, soldiers were reassigned to new units, and the old regiments were removed from the books. Unit history, pride and cohesion suffered in the process.

New recruits were arriving daily to replace the wounded, the dead and the missing in action. Many of these newcomers were draftees. The green soldiers were assigned to units based on need and best fit. It was guesswork. The choices were not entirely satisfactory, but there wasn't time to rebuild from the ground up.

Tom bumped into Josh Goldman one afternoon near the end of May. The reporter asked how he was doing. Tom said, "Not bad but I could be better."

"You weren't killed, and it doesn't look like you were wounded."

"No. I've been lucky. But I don't like spending my days on drills."

"How's the army doing?"

"Nobody's happy."

"So, you're ready to take on Lee again."

Tom spat. "The war's not over." He grimaced and shook his head. "Any news from out West?"

Josh considered for a moment. "Grant got around behind Vicksburg. It's just a matter of time."

"When did he do that?"

"April thirtieth. The same day you reached Chancellorsville."

24

June 15, 1863

My Dearest Mother,

I regret taking so long to answer your letters. The situation here is very trying. They have reassigned men to new units and gotten rid of some of the old units. The 28th took some heavy casualties at Chancellorsville, but enough of us survived to keep the regiment alive. It is being built back up with new recruits. Some of these men are willing, but many are draftees, or worse, bounty men taking the place of draftees. None of them are soldiers. That takes time.

You wrote about Colonel Grierson's raid. That was some story. He made the rebels look like fools while he rode around, tearing up their tracks and bridges. They got so busy trying to catch him they forgot all about Grant. Now he's in their backyard, hoping to capture Vicksburg.

Earlier this week, our cavalry led by General Pleasanton was in a fearsome daylong battle against JEB Stuart and the Confederate cavalry. According to camp rumors, it started with a dawn raid after we learned the rebels were massing near Brandy Station. The seceches foiled the initial surprise. Our boys didn't win, but they didn't lose. They held their own against one of the best cavalries in the world.

Today we received reports of fighting in the Shenandoah Valley near Winchester. That's a sure sign General Lee is moving north again.

Tomorrow we will be marching up there to take him on.

Your devoted son,

Tom

25

Meade Takes Command

"… The private soldier carried his shelter–tent or rubber blanket, and he and the comrade who was his 'partner' made of the two a comfortable protection from the weather. His haversack contained his rations, his canteen and a small tin coffeepot or pale clattered at his belt, and, in half an hour of halt, the veteran knew how to prepare a wholesome and abundant meal. The ration of meat, bread, coffee, and sugar was a large one and of excellent quality, and by foraging or traffic extras could be added to it on the way.

"The general officers could not manage in quite the same simple style. From the adjutant-general, the surgeon, quartermaster, the commissary, the ordinance and mustering officers regular statistical reports were required by army regulations, and enforced by stopping the pay of delinquent commands. At each headquarters, therefore, a good deal of business had to be transacted and much clerical work had to be done in the

intervals of fighting. The order to leave all baggage behind for four days implied only a short interruption of the usual routine, but when it was, by the circumstances, extended to nearly a month, it involved no small trouble and privation…"

Sherman's Battle for Atlanta, by General Jacob D. Cox

By the end of May 1863, "Fighting Joe" Hooker had convinced himself that he was the winner at Chancellorsville. He had taken more casualties, but the Army of Northern Virginia had been hurt more by its losses. The death of General Stonewall Jackson was a critical loss for the South. He could not be replaced.

The Army of the Potomac was already back to full strength. Hooker was beginning to believe that he could succeed where Burnside had failed. He could march through Fredericksburg and on to Richmond. When he learned the Confederates had attacked Winchester in mid-June, he made plans for another campaign deep into rebel territory.

General in Chief of the Army Halleck ordered Hooker, the commanding general of the Army of the Potomac, to head north and stop Lee before he could attack a major city. Washington, Baltimore and Philadelphia were all inviting targets. Hooker argued that Lee would be forced to abandon his move north of the Potomac and come after him if he was marching on Richmond. The already testy relationship between the two men took a turn for the worse. Daily arguments over tactics and strategy were heated.

Lincoln, monitoring reports from all over the country, had concluded that the South's preeminent general had already moved north of the Potomac to strike a decisive blow. He needed his best army to act immediately. In a message to General Hooker, the president said General Halleck was the

Commanding General of the Army, and the Commander of the Army of the Potomac was expected to obey his orders without question.

Hooker responded by offering his resignation. On June 28, the President, the Secretary of Defense and the General in Chief of the Army accepted his offer and appointed Major General George Meade as the new Commander of the Army of the Potomac.

Lee's army had been moving steadily north and east for weeks. On June 26, General Jubal Early clashed with Pennsylvania militia around the town of Gettysburg and laid the borough under tribute. He continued deeper into Pennsylvania, intending to capture the state capital, Harrisburg, and secure a route to Philadelphia.

The brigade marching to Philadelphia ran into a group of Pennsylvania militia, Union vets and colored troops fresh out of boot camp, blocking the approach to the Wrightsville bridge. The Confederates drove off the defenders, but not before they burned the bridge, thwarting an attack on Philadelphia.

Meade was camped at Frederick, Maryland, when he learned that he had been promoted from Commander of V Corps to Commander of the Army of the Potomac. He pushed his right wing forward to engage Early and ordered a division of cavalry dispatched to investigate the situation at Gettysburg.

The next day, Early pulled back to rejoin Lee and the Army of Northern Virginia at Cashtown in the foothills of South Mountain, a few miles west of Gettysburg. That is where the Confederates planned to meet and destroy the Army of the Potomac. Events moved the showdown to the hills south and east of a small Pennsylvania farming town.

26

Showdown at Gettysburg

General John Buford reached Gettysburg with a division of Union Cavalry while a division of Confederate infantry was in town for supplies and information. Both sides recognized the presence of the enemy, but there were no hostilities. These were reconnaissance missions. The rebels left town, heading northwest along Chambersburg Pike. Buford sent a message alerting Meade that Lee was in the area.

The town sat at the north end of a long valley between Seminary Ridge and Cemetery Ridge. A series of smaller ridges paralleled these two massive formations. Buford deployed his 2500-man force across Chambersburg Pike between McPherson's Ridge and Oak Ridge, a mile west of the village. He set a skirmish line in an arc a mile farther out. His mission was to hold the position until reinforcements arrived.

Early the next morning, Confederate troops advanced down Chambersburg Pike toward the little town of Gettysburg. Their formation was neat and precise, four men abreast on the country road, as if for a review. Yankee skirmishers, hiding in trees, began taking potshots at the rebel column. As the Southerners advanced, the Union attack increased in intensity, using the same hit-and-run tactics that citizen soldiers had used against the British a century earlier.

The Confederate column slowed and deployed into the woods to confront the snipers. One battle line north of the Pike. The other south. The delays bought Buford's grizzled veterans time to set up a defensive position on the ridges. They could hold off the rebels for a while, but they were badly outnumbered. And across the valley in front of them, rebel artillery was setting up on Herr's Ridge.

Buford sent a message to headquarters with his assessment of the Confederate forces massing against him. He needed infantry support post-haste to prevent the enemy from taking control of the high ground to his rear.

I Corps arrived on the scene at mid-morning. General John Reynolds raced ahead and found Buford at the north end of Seminary Ridge at the institute that gave the ridge its name. After assessing the situation, Reynolds asked Buford to hold on a little longer while he brought his lead brigades to the battlefront. The cavalry position was crumbling, but the dismounted horse soldiers held their ground until the Iron Brigade reached them on McPherson's Ridge.

Reynolds sent an urgent message to Meade with a fresh assessment of the developing situation. He ordered Howard to bring XI Corps up at quick time. Then he went back to charging about positioning troops and artillery to hold off the Confederate onslaught long enough for the Army of the Potomac to reach the high ground south of Gettysburg.

He was still deploying his men and setting up artillery positions when a musket ball hit him in the neck, killing him instantly. General Abner Doubleday took over.

The struggle was running out of steam by the time XI Corps reached the hills south of the town. Howard sent two divisions forward to support I Corps. He kept his remaining division in reserve on Cemetery Hill.

The narrow dirt road leading from Cashtown to Gettysburg slowed the Confederate brigades making their way to the battlefield. But the Southerners kept arriving in a steady stream. By midday, they outnumbered the embattled Union forces.

Confederates returning from their failed attempt to reach Philadelphia turned south on Harrisburg Road to join the fray developing around Gettysburg.

The Southerners had numerical superiority when fighting resumed in the early afternoon. They flanked the Union troops west of Seminary Ridge, forcing them into a fighting retreat. Ewell hit isolated brigades north of the town with crushing force, sending Yanks racing through narrow streets and alleys. The Federals regrouped behind XI Corps's reserve division on Cemetery Hill.

Major General Winfield Scott Hancock, II Corps Commander, arrived in time to breathe new spirit into the exhausted troops. He fashioned units that had lost 20 to 30 percent of their manpower into a stout, combat-ready defense.

Under orders from Lee to carry Cemetery Hill if practicable, Ewell evaluated the Union defensive works and declined to attack. XI Corps had earned back the respect it had lost on May 2 in The Wilderness outside Chancellorsville.

The Southern onslaught paused as the day ended. One final attempt to take Culp's Hill on the eastern side of the ridge was easily driven off by pickets stationed on the prominence.

Both armies converged on the battleground over the night of July 1 and into the morning of July 2. Meade spent the night surveying his position and his forces. He had his men deployed in a fishhook that started on Culp's Hill, swung around Cemetery Hill, down Cemetery Ridge, past the Peach Orchard and the Wheatfield, to Little Round Top. Lee had deployed his forces on Seminary Ridge less than a mile to the west. His line ran in a five-mile arc roughly parallel to the Union line.

General Gouverneur Warren, Meade's chief engineer, recognized the importance of Round Top and Little Round Top and took special care in setting up the defense on those cliffs. General George Greene, commander of Geary's Third Brigade and an engineer by training, had gotten XII Corps to build elaborate works for their position on Culp's Hill.

Meade had chosen to defend. If there was going to be a fight, and that is what both armies had come for, Lee would have to attack. An uneasy quiet settled over the Union perimeter as soldiers waited for the Southerners to make their move. Major General Daniel Sickles, commander of III Corps, was the exception. He moved his divisions from their assigned position to a hill half a mile away, overlooking a large wheat field.

By the time Meade reached his corps commander to demand an explanation, Confederate artillery had begun shelling the position in preparation for an infantry charge. After Meade pointed out that Sickles's new position was exposed and vulnerable to attacks from multiple sides, the corps commander offered to move his men back to the original position. Meade decided it was too late for that and set about bringing reinforcements from his right flank.

A couple of hours later, the battle erupted. Lee had massed one-third of his army against Meade's left flank. The rebels attacked with the ferocity of madmen. Assault after assault was repulsed, only to be followed by a new onslaught.

The Army of the Potomac did not flinch. Its men fought with the fury and desperation of cornered animals.

Little Round Top was a prize worth dying for. Thousands did, as unyielding Northern troops held out against relentless waves of Southerners.

III Corps was shredded in its fight for the wheatfield. Brigades sent in to continue the battle fared no better. The Irish brigade lost almost half its strength in a hand-to-hand melee amid the amber waves of grain. A hundred dead. Sixty wounded. Two hundred missing.

Confederate Divisions moved up Emmitsburg Road to swarm the center of the Federal defensive line on the western face of Cemetery Ridge.

The battle raged for hours from midafternoon into the evening. In the dying hours of the day, the tide of battle was turning in favor of the rebels. The embattled Union commander called up reserves to bolster his faltering defensive line. Williams and Geary were ordered from Culp's Hill to Little Round Top and the southern slopes of Cemetery Ridge.

Ewell sent three brigades in a night attack on the depleted Union right flank. Greene, fighting from behind the elaborate works he had constructed earlier in the day, successfully fought off the assault. Some of the attackers were able to seize and occupy portions of those works vacated when XII Corps divisions were shifted to the left flank.

When Geary returned to Culp's Hill early in the morning on July 3, he found that the Union had held the upper works at the crest of the hill, but the rebels had gained a foothold in the lower works. He planned an attack to drive the enemy off his hill.

The Army of the Potomac had survived a second day of intense fighting. The victory was costly, but not decisive.

Ewell renewed his offensive against Culp's Hill early on the morning of July 3. Geary's men, who had been preparing for an offensive to drive the Confederates out of their works, found themselves defending against a fierce attack. But the Second Division was dug in at the top of the hill. Devastating artillery and a hailstorm of musketry fired from their stronghold decimated the rebels pushing up the slope. The struggle went on for six hours despite the loss of life and limb.

An hour later, Southern artillery began an intense bombardment of Cemetery Ridge. The Union's big guns responded cautiously as if conserving the last of their ammunition. After two hours, the shelling stopped, and the infantry assault began. Confederate Major General George Pickett led fifteen thousand men in a charge that would forever bear his name. The legions of gray-clad infantrymen marching in formation and firing their muskets were awesome. It might have been terrifying to untested troops, but the Yanks on the ridge remembered their own charge at Fredericksburg and would not be denied their revenge. As the Confederates pressed toward the top of the hill, they came under heavy artillery and musket fire. The few that reached the Union line were repulsed with bayonets, rifle butts and even fists. The assault ground to a standstill and then fell back, leaving half its force behind, dead or dying.

An eerie silence followed the artillery fusillade and grand Confederate assault on the Union line along Cemetery Ridge. Meade acted to take advantage of the pause. He ordered the troops put on four-hour watches. Half the men would be at the ready while the other half would be resting.

Tom was sitting down to dinner when Kennedy showed up and said, "I saw your woman. She asked about you."

Tom looked up, shocked by his friend's unexpected greeting. "What? When?"

"An hour ago. I escorted a prisoner to the back. She saw me and walked over." Kennedy attempted to mimic Kat's voice. "Hello, James. I'm glad to see you are okay."

"I nodded. 'Thank you, ma'am.'"

In Kat's voice, "Have you seen Thomas? How is he?"

"I shook my head. 'No, ma'am. I'll check on him as soon as I get back to the front.'"

"A prisoner?" Tom asked.

"Yeah. A Reb was lying ten or fifteen feet in front of us moaning. He kept begging for water. Finally, I said I'll give you some water to shut him up."

"He was quiet for a while, then said, 'Y'all gonna git me some water or not?'"

"I said, 'You'll have to come get it. I can't go to you.'"

"He rolled over and looked at me. 'How'm ah gonna do that?'"

"I said, 'Crawl. Or lay there and die of thirst.'"

Tom said, "So he dragged himself over and you took care of him?"

Kennedy nodded. Tom continued, "And you ran into Kat?"

Kennedy nodded again. Tom said, "Did he tell you anything?"

"He thinks they've lost half their army. This is over. They couldn't attack again if they wanted to."

"But they're sitting there thinking about what they could do."

"They're hoping we'll attack them."

"Will we?"

Kennedy's face scrunched into a sneer. He shook his head. "Meade's thought about it, but we're in as bad a shape as they are."

"Too bad they replaced Hooker," Tom said. "We finally got Lee to attack us in a strong defensive position."

"It's a good thing they got rid of him. Hooker would've found a way to lose."

The two soldiers were still talking when Sam Goldman showed up. Looking at Kennedy, he said, "I see you made it back alive."

Kennedy nodded. "I was lucky."

"Luck of the Irish?"

"It was the Irish Brigade. We were all Irish. Only half of us came back in one piece," Kennedy retorted bitterly.

Tom said, "What about you, Sam?"

"I was on Little Round Top."

"So you drove the rebels back at bayonet point," Kennedy said.

Goldman shook his head. "That was another regiment. It was something to see." He thought for a minute. "How about you, Tom? What did you do all day?"

"Something went wrong," Tom said. "We did a lot of marching. When we got back here, the rebs had managed to take over some of our defensive works. It took us all morning, but we drove them out."

Kennedy and Goldman left together for their next stop.

That night was tense but uneventful. It was raining when Tom awoke in the morning. The corpses in front of his position had been lying exposed to the elements for almost two days. They were decomposing, swelling up and turning black. Flies covered the bodies in spite of the weather. The stench of rotting flesh was everywhere, overpowering every other smell.

The order of the day was watch and wait.

Around mid-morning, a detail came through with ammunition and food. A soldier in a fresh-looking uniform stood over Tom and said, "I see you survived."

He looked up and smiled. Kat was grinning down at him.

He said, "As did you."

"We had one scare."

"What happened?"

"Their cavalry was getting ready to attack. General Custer came to our rescue," She smirked. "He cuts a fine figure."

Tom shook his head. Kat said, "I can't stay, but I'll be back."

The Confederates began their withdrawal that afternoon. As they moved out, Tom and other troops were detailed to search for the wounded and bury the dead. Walking among the thousands of bodies and checking to see if any were still alive was a gruesome task.

Mass graves looked like the only way to get the job done. One work party dug a big hole. Another party dragged nearby bodies into the pit using a rope tied around the ankles. The hole would hold ten to twenty corpses. There was no way to determine who was being buried because every pocket had been picked clean. When the pit was full, a third crew shoveled dirt over the remains. It was vile work.

That night, some women came around. For a buck, you could get a shot of whiskey. For two, a quick fuck.

27

Pursuit

Tom's turn on the watch ended shortly after daybreak on Sunday, July 5. As he surveyed the scene from the top of Culps Hill, a tall brick building on the crest of an adjacent hill caught his attention. The area around it looked like a cemetery, but several artillery pieces sat on the open ground, waiting to be reclaimed.

Tom walked over to investigate. By the time he reached the site, a woman, visibly pregnant, was busy cleaning up the mess created by the battle. Gravestones had been knocked over. Some had been shattered. All of the windows had been broken out of the building, which served both as the caretaker's home and as a gateway to the cemetery. Flies swarmed over dozens of horse carcasses. The artillery pieces could not be moved until the dead draft animals had been replaced.

Dead bodies, some in blue, some in gray, bore witness to a fierce battle for control of this valuable perch.

The young soldier introduced himself and asked if he could be of service. The woman gave her name as Mrs. Elizabeth Thorn and politely declined his offer. "My husband Peter is the caretaker. He is serving with his regiment in Virginia. This work helps me get through his absence. It keeps me connected to him. But I thank you for your kind offer."

On his walk back, Tom saw hundreds, perhaps thousands, of carcasses lying in the valley to the west. Horses, cows, pigs. Farm animals vital to the lives of the locals. Innocent victims of the great battle. Thousands of human remains still lay where they had fallen, subject to nature's primordial cycle of life, death, and decay. They should get a Christian burial. With or without, they would be put into the ground because that was needed for a return to normality.

A Lieutenant Evans, who had been studying at Harvard Divinity School when the war broke out, organized a prayer service to thank God for the victory. He spoke about Joshua and David defeating the Philistines and led the soldiers in singing hymns. When he was done, the troops were ordered to pack their gear. The Army of the Potomac was going after Lee.

General Slocum marched II Corps and XII Corps as far as Littlestown, about ten miles to the southeast, before calling a halt. Exhausted soldiers were grateful for the break. Torrential downpours had turned the roads to quagmires that seized the wheels of artillery caissons and supply wagons and held them fast. Every mile of the march had been gained at a heavy cost.

War news spread through the camp during the delay. Vicksburg had surrendered to Grant, and Rosecrans had defeated Bragg, forcing him to take refuge in Chattanooga.

Tom received two letters while he was stuck at Littlestown. The one he opened first was from his mother:

My Dearest Son,

We have received news of fierce fighting at Gettysburg. John says that you must have been involved because your regiment was mentioned in the reports. Please let me know that you are okay as soon as possible. I pray for your safety every day.

Your loving mother.

He wrote back:

July 8, 1863

My Dearest Mother,

We were engaged with the enemy for three days almost without rest. The fighting was spirited and the death toll was staggering. By the grace of God, I was not injured. We are chasing that devil Lee to stop him from making it back to Virginia. But at the moment, rain is falling so hard we cannot move.

Your loving son, Tom

The second, he read and reread, but could not answer.

My dearest Tom,

I spend what little time I have for sleep dreaming of you. You are beside me, atop me and inside me. I long for your embrace constantly. It is my most earnest desire to tell you this in person. I am told there is but 10 miles between us. I could leave at daybreak and be with you by midday. But now is not a good time. I am needed here as you are there. The wounded and dying fill every available space, and still, many are forced to sleep on the ground with no protection. I cannot abandon them. Besides my heart is so full of sorrow I would not be a fit companion.

Do not forget me – our sweet lovemaking. I will come to you as soon as we have put an end to the present horror. I will bring caresses and kisses, and I will be yours without restraint. Until then, always remember that I love you.

Yours forever, Kat

The delay presented more problems. The troops had to stretch their rations, and the artillery brigades had to find food for the horses. Supplies were waiting for them in Jefferson, thirty miles to the southwest.

The march resumed on July 8. Men and horses, ignoring the rain, sloughed through mud, dragging caissons and supply wagons along until they reached the city, where they would find food and rest.

But there was little rest. The following day, they marched to Rohrersville, and the day after that, to Hagerstown. They joined the Union line on July 11. The men had trekked seventy-five miles on starvation rations in pouring rain through ankle-deep mud, in many cases without the benefit of boots.

When Meade reached Lee's defensive works in front of Williamsport, he found the roles reversed from Gettysburg. The Army of the Potomac stretched in a long line opposite the entrenched Army of Northern Virginia. Lee's army occupied a fortress with rifle pits for its sharpshooters and turrets for its artillery. A mile of open ground and a marsh separated the two armies. If the Federals were going to capture Lee before he crossed the river, they would have to charge across that killing field and over those parapets sitting on a ridge a hundred feet above them. One soldier told Tom he couldn't stop thinking about Fredericksburg.

A couple of miles west of the wall, the Potomac River, swollen to flood stage, blocked the Confederate army's march back to Virginia. Lee was using boats to ferry wagons over to Virginia and supplies back from the other shore.

His engineers were building a pontoon bridge to get his troops across the river into Virginia. The floodwaters were receding. It would soon be possible to make the crossing without a bridge.

Meade would have to attack at once if he was going to crush Lee while he was trapped in Maryland. However, some observers in the Union army were convinced Lee was getting ready to make a stand like he did at Antietam.

While preparations for an assault on the Confederate stronghold were underway, Meade received orders to dispatch some regiments to New York City to suppress an outbreak of violence. The rampage began as a protest against the draft, which had been ordered in March but was only now being enforced. The demonstration evolved into a race riot, with poor Irish workers taking out their frustration on poor Blacks.

Tom was embarrassed and appalled. Kennedy just shook his head and said, "This war is now about slaves and slavery in the South. Rich white men, some for slavery and some opposed, are sending poor white men off to fight and die to settle the issue. The poor whites doing the killing and dying have never owned a slave and never could. But they are being drafted and forced to fight because there aren't enough volunteers. All white men are eligible for the draft but most are not called. If a rich man is drafted, he pays a bounty to get some poor bastard to take his place. When a poor man is drafted, he has to quit his job and serve in the army. After this war is over, everything will be the same for the poor Irishman who was drafted except that he will have no job to support his family. He was forced to give that up so he could fight to end slavery. Explain the fairness in that."

The thirteenth was spent getting ready for an attack on the Confederates. When the Union officers studied the rebel fortress for a weakness, they found none. Meade and his staff became concerned that an assault would result in a disaster that would cancel the success at Gettysburg. The commanding general called a council of war. He settled on a reconnaissance in force. The Army of the Potomac would attack, but only to feel out the rebel defenses.

The charge advanced unopposed the next morning. Meade's men reached the stronghold and found it deserted. Lee had slipped his army across the Potomac and into Virginia during the night, using smoke and fog to conceal the escape. Confederate soldiers stood on the Virginia shore, mocking their foe.

Meade sent his cavalry in pursuit. Buford and Kilpatrick caught Lee's rearguard and captured two thousand prisoners. But these turned out to be misfits that Lee did not want with him on what promised to be a grueling march back to The Wilderness east of Chancellorsville.

Meade's engineers needed three days to build bridges the Army of the Potomac needed to get across the river and continue chasing the Army of Northern Virginia. During the forced layover, supplies arrived from Frederick. The men stocked up on food, ammunition, and other necessities.

A steady stream of criticism of the commanding general's performance dominated the northern press. Apparently, taking a cue from President Lincoln, the papers accused Meade of avoiding a confrontation with Lee. According to the headlines and opinion pieces, he pursued the Southern army just hard enough to ensure that it left northern soil but never pushed for the battle that would lead to the end of the Confederacy.

Halleck waffled. The president was disappointed. But when Meade asked to be relieved of his command, the commanding general of the army demurred, saying that General Meade's victory at Gettysburg was appreciated and that he had done nothing to justify removing him from command. Halleck encouraged Meade to use his own judgment, then let him know President Lincoln was disappointed in his decisions.

In private, George Meade wrote to his wife Margaret, "I have fulfilled my duties to the best of my ability." Later, he told her in another letter, "From the time I took command till today, now over ten days, I have not changed my clothes, have not had a regular night's rest, and many nights not a wink of sleep, and for several days did not even wash my face and hands, no regular food, and all the time in the great state of anxiety. Indeed, I think I have lived as much in this time as in the last thirty years."

28

July 17, 1863

My Dearest Mother,

We are waiting to cross the Potomac in pursuit of the seceshes. We're headed back into the Loudoun Valley where we spent much of last year.

The engineers have been working on the bridges we need to cross the river. We have used the time to get caught up after all the fighting and marching. Food has been plentiful for a change. I got new boots. One of my boots got stuck in the mud on the march down here. I threw the other one away. You can't walk with just one boot. They issued me a new pair two days ago and I'm breaking them in.

What you read in the newspapers is wrong. We were not waiting around to give Lee a head start. He sat in camp for a day daring us to attack. But he was dug in on Seminary Ridge and we were in no shape to attack. We were tired and hungry and pretty shot up. He pulled out overnight and our cavalry pursued him. The whole army set out to cut him off at the Potomac that afternoon. We were all in poor condition. The horses we had left after all the fighting and killing were hungry and tired. But we gave chase in pouring rain. The mud was so deep on the roads that we could barely move.

We laid over for two days at Littletown but not to avoid a showdown with them. We had to be careful that General Ewell did not go around us and attack Philadelphia or New York.

When we got down close to the river, we could see that the rebels had built themselves a very strong fort. It was at the top of a hill on the other side of a marsh. They had turrets for their artillery and in between the turrets they had pits for men to stand and shoot down at us while we charged up that hill. Any assault was guaranteed to be bloody. There was no guarantee that the Johnnies would be defeated and their fortress captured.

Last Tuesday morning, we marched on their position. It was abandoned. They had skedaddled back to Virginia during the night. We took their fortifications without firing a shot. But it wasn't us that wouldn't fight.

People may say that we waited for them to pull out because we were scared of them. When we saw the defenses they had built, we figured they were planning on staying and fighting until we forced them to leave.

The Confederates are hurting after that battle but so are we. A lot of good men were killed and many more were shot up so bad they can't be with us to fight the rebs now. The ones who are here need time to rest and get their strength back but we are going to keep chasing them and see if we can finish them off.

Your loving son,

Tom

29

To the Rappahannock

The Blue Ridge Mountains rose majestically like a wall separating the Shenandoah Valley from the Loudon Valley. Gaps between the peaks were used as corridors to connect the valleys. Lee had chosen to lead his army south through the Shenandoah Valley, where he was protected by mountains on both sides. He would have to use one of the gaps to get back to his home turf around Culpeper. He could also use one to head east and threaten Washington DC.

The Army of the Potomac lurched into the Loudon Valley, hoping to trap the Confederate army while blocking an eastward thrust by Lee.

The mountains also served as a shield that prevented the two generals from monitoring what the other was doing. But Lee had the advantage. The people living in this part of the country were strongly secessionist. Seceshes. They were eager to serve as Lee's spies.

Two days after crossing the Potomac, Meade paused in the vicinity of Snickers Gap, which was the main route east to the nation's capital. A corduroyed road through the mountains followed an old Indian trail that predated the arrival of European settlers. It led west to Winchester, which had served as Stonewall Jackson's headquarters during the Valley Campaign a year earlier. Meade set up his camp across that turnpike, intending to wait until he was sure of his foe's plan.

After two days of marching, the bivouac was welcome. It meant sitting down, eating supper, drinking coffee and smoking a pipe in peace. But a blazing summer sun followed days of heavy rains. Sweat soaked Tom's uniform. A dust cloud hanging thick in the air sopped all the moisture from his mouth. He needed to keep drinking to ease the dryness. But he had to nurse the water in his canteen.

Kat lured him to an empty ambulance. They cuddled. There wasn't much news to discuss. She had overheard talk about the pressure to find the rebels and finish them off. Meade was not going to be bullied into rash actions. He would not move until he was certain.

The army remained stalled the next day. Skirmishers were posted. They were rotated every four hours.

Kat was in her infantry uniform, eating dinner with Tom, when Kennedy and Sam Goldman showed up. Kennedy said, "You know they could hit us at any time."

Tom pressed his lips together and scowled. He considered before shaking his head and saying, "I don't think so."

Goldman said, "They are operating at the north end of the valley."

"How do you know that?" Tom asked.

"They almost captured a brigade of West Virginia Volunteers." Goldman gave a smug smile. "A slave overheard some of the rebel officers talking about it and managed to get word to General Kelly. He was able to pull back across the Potomac before the rebels could get in position."

Kennedy said, "I heard they're moving south."

Goldman chuckled. "I guess we'll be stuck here until Meade figures out what they're up to."

"What if they're doing both," Tom wondered.

"They're on the run," Kennedy said. "They have to pull back to safety so they can regroup and replenish their supplies after that last battle."

"They could send a couple of divisions north to attack a big city like Philadelphia," Tom countered. "No militia would be able to stop them. We'd end up chasing after them."

Kennedy shook his head. "Supplies. We're running out of food. They can't be doing any better. They have to move south to connect with their supply lines."

On Wednesday, July 22, orders were issued for the Army of the Potomac to resume its march. Rumors spread through the camp that the cavalry had spotted rebel troops moving south, and the sightings had been confirmed by mountaintop observers. The rebs were heading back where they came from.

The army responded like a bear coming out of hibernation. But by noon, III Corps was on its way to Manassas Gap. I Corps followed in close support. II Corps was moving down to Ashby's Gap. XII Corps was held in reserve at Snickers Gap. XI Corps moved east to Warrenton to seize the railroad and secure supply and communication links with Washington.

The late start meant the troops would spend the rest of the day and evening marching. Action would have to wait until the following morning.

Buford and the cavalry were sent ahead to Manassas Gap and Chester Gap, five miles farther south. They met no resistance at Manassas Gap but found Confederate troops pouring through Chester Gap on their way to Culpeper. The outnumbered Union cavalry could only observe the rebels from a distance.

At daybreak, Major General William H. French, commanding III Corps, began deploying troops to push through Manassas Gap and hold it for the rest of the army. French had been a division commander at Antietam, Fredericksburg and Chancellorsville. He took over command of III Corps at Gettysburg after Sickles was wounded. He had a reputation for bravery, boldness and decisiveness. But this day, the major general was cautious to a fault. He had already stationed over half his corps along his flank and rear to protect against a surprise attack. He held off launching his assault until I Corps was in position.

The trail through the gap was a boulder-strewn dirt road hemmed in by steep, rocky walls. Those walls limited the effectiveness of French's division. A small but determined rebel force dug in along ridges overlooking the trail through the gap was enough to block the Union advance. French failed to force the passage despite a day of heavy fighting.

The rebels were still dug in and holding on, but they knew the outcome would be different if the battle went on for another day. That night, they withdrew from Manassas Gap and joined up with the rest of the Army of Northern Virginia on the long trek south.

Federal troops continued arriving at the east end of the gap throughout the night. At dawn on July 24, the assault against the rebel positions was renewed. Too late. The Southerners had abandoned their foothold. French's men pushed on to Front Royal. They found a token rear guard in the town. It bolted as soon as the Union troops approached. Lee had gotten his army across Maryland and out of the Shenandoah Valley to safety.

The Army of the Potomac withdrew to Warrenton, where it could be resupplied before continuing its pursuit of the Army of Northern Virginia. By then, the quarry was setting up camp in Orange County.

Mead's pursuit of Lee ended at the Rappahannock River three weeks after the Battle of Gettysburg. His army had been on the march for almost two months. It had won a major showdown with the Army of Northern Virginia, at the cost twenty-three thousand officers and men killed, wounded or missing. The ones who had survived were tired and hungry. They needed time to rest and recuperate after the long chase back into Virginia.

30

On to the Rapidan

The Army of the Potomac had lost over a quarter of its men in two months of campaigning. Those who remained were used up. Meade had to rebuild.

Nine generals had been killed or wounded at Gettysburg. John Reynolds, commander of I Corps, had been a top candidate for commander of the Army of the Potomac. Another would assume command of I Corps, but Reynolds was one of those men who could not be replaced.

II Corps needed a new commander. Hancock was on indefinite leave because of wounds he had received at Gettysburg. Major General Warren took his place, but there was little hope that he could fill Hancock's shoes.

As a division commander in Sickles's ill-fated III Corps, General Andrew Humphreys had held off determined Confederate charges on Cemetery Ridge during day two of the fighting. He was taking over as General Meade's chief of staff.

New recruits were streaming in. Wounded soldiers were returning to duty. Enlistments were expiring. Some veterans reenlisted and went on leave. Others returned home to their families.

Depleted regiments were merged into new, full-strength regiments. The numbers made sense, but in real life, a regiment is more than a bunch of men thrown together in a pinch. Soldiers must fight as a unit and support each other in the worst circumstances. A regiment needs spirit to give it life. History and tradition develop over time.

Commanders had to turn the newly minted regiments into a force ready for combat. The men would have to sweat and struggle to achieve that goal.

Meade's encampment spread north and east from the Rappahannock River. XII Corps was stationed near Kelly's Ford. V Corps was on its left across from Chancellorsville, and I Corps was on its right near Rappahannock Station. VI Corps anchored the right flank at Sulphur Springs. XI Corps guarded the vital Orange and Alexandria Railroad. II Corps, the reserve unit, was stationed behind XII Corps, where it could rush to support any of the other units.

Life settled into a comfortable rhythm. Daily drills and picket duty. The men spent two days on the picket line every other week. Tom looked forward to those stints. There was some shooting, but it had little effect. For the young soldier, being alone in the wilderness was unlike anything he had experienced growing up in Philadelphia. Much of the time, he kept a solitary vigil at the river's edge with lush woodland at his back. Birds kept him company. The constant chirping began to make sense to him. Furtive animals would venture from hiding to investigate him. He took an interest in the stars at night and began to learn about some of the constellations.

The training regimen gave Tom more time with Kat, but he never mentioned her in letters to his mother.

On the morning of August 1, Meade sent his cavalry across the Rappahannock to find the Army of Northern Virginia and test its defenses. The foray gave the general something to report to Washington in response to the constant pressure to attack Lee.

Buford set out at dawn. He crossed the river at Kelley's Ford, then rode north and west to Brandy Station. The decimated Confederate cavalry offered little resistance. A single brigade engaged in a fighting retreat for about five miles until it reached the railroad station. An infantry division encamped nearby rushed to the aid of the beleaguered rebel horse soldiers.

The Federal cavalry was forced to race back to Rappahannock Station, where I Corps was waiting on the south shore of the river. It was a bad ending for Buford, but Meade was pleased with the results. The general now had a good idea where his enemy was hiding.

Josh Goldman showed up at the beginning of September. "Something big is about to happen out West."

"Grant?" Kennedy asked.

"Rosecrans," Josh answered. "He's going after Bragg."

"That won't be easy. Bragg's dug in behind strong fortifications," Sam observed.

"Since the beginning of July," Josh admitted. "But don't underestimate Old Rosy."

A week later, the Army of the Cumberland had encircled the Confederate position in Chattanooga, threatening to cut off its supplies. Bragg abandoned the city and retreated to the mountains. Northern papers proclaimed, "Rosecrans Delivers Crushing Blow to the South."

A New York paper followed up with a scoop about Confederate troops from Lee's Army of Northern Virginia being transferred to Tennessee to support Bragg.

Halleck immediately demanded an attack on Lee. Meade sent his cavalry across the Rappahannock at dawn on September 13. Gregg, on the right flank, crossed at Sulphur Springs. Kilpatrick, on the left, used Kelly's Ford. Buford crossed near Rappahannock Station.

Initial resistance by the rebels was light but determined. Union divisions pushed stubborn Confederate regiments back. When they reached Brandy Station, JEB Stuart made a stand with his entire force. After an hour of pitched battle, he pulled back to Culpeper Station. The standoff lasted a couple of more hours before Kilpatrick organized a coordinated three-front assault. Stuart withdrew to Pony Mountain to avoid being captured.

The Union cavalry followed and dismounted at the base of the mountain. They charged up the slopes and forced the Confederates to withdraw across the Rapidan River. The next day was spent in a futile search for places along the river where Meade's army could cross. Lee had fortified entrenchments guarding all of the fords.

The next day, Tuesday, September 15, the Army of the Potomac crossed the Rappahannock and marched to the Rapidan but did not attempt to cross. Meade sent a message to Halleck saying that any attempted crossing would be too costly. He recommended that his headquarters be shifted to Fredericksburg, where he could attack Lee's flank or even march on Richmond.

Halleck responded that the best way to defeat Lee, and perhaps the only way, was a general assault and a pitched battle.

The Army of the Potomac set up camp in the southeast corner of Culpeper County in a valley known as the Iron Triangle. The Rappahannock River ran northeast along its right flank. On the left, the Rapidan flowed east toward the ocean. The Orange and Alexandria Railroad, the army's lifeline, cut through the valley on its route between Washington, DC and Lynchburg, at the northern end of the Shenandoah Valley.

The Confederate Army of Northern Virginia was encamped a few miles away, southwest of the Rapidan River.

31

Chattanooga

While the Army of the Potomac recuperated in Virginia, the Army of the Cumberland began an assault on Braxton Bragg's Army of Tennessee - action General Rosecrans had put off for over a month. He was responding to an order from General in Chief Halleck to get moving and report progress daily.

Bragg was headquartered in Chattanooga along the Tennessee River. The city was a major railroad hub that connected half the Confederacy's arsenals. It was vital for the movement of raw materials, weapons and ammunition.

Rosecrans divided his army into three elements to force the Confederates to abandon their stronghold without a bloody assault. Crittenden was to attack the city from the west with XXI Corps, while Thomas led XIV Corps over Lookout Mountain, attacking from the south, and McCook led XX Corps around to the southeast, cutting Bragg's link to Atlanta.

McCook crossed the Tennessee River on August 29. The next day, Thomas crossed. Crittenden followed on August 31. These movements caused the Confederate high command to mobilize reinforcements for the Army of Tennessee. Lee dispatched Longstreet with his corps on September 4. Bragg abandoned the city on September 8 in spite of these reinforcements because the Union movements had cut his supply lines.

Rosecrans took control of Chattanooga on September 9. Lincoln expected him to keep aggressive pressure on Bragg because he wanted the rebel army driven out of Tennessee. But the deployment that successfully ousted the Confederates from a strongly fortified city had left the Union army divided and disconnected. The Army of the Cumberland needed to regroup before launching another offensive. However, in a move opposed by his senior officers, Rosecrans sent Crittenden with XXI Corps in pursuit of the Army of Tennessee. After a week of skirmishing, Bragg turned on his pursuers, intending to defeat XXI Corps as a first step in turning the tables on Rosecrans and taking back Chattanooga.

The Confederate attacks on September 18 caught the Federals off guard, but Rosecrans was able to recover and limit the damage. The battle continued the next day over thickly wooded rolling hills. Although a day of maneuver and counter-maneuver left their positions little changed, Rosecrans found himself in a more difficult tactical situation. He had only five fresh brigades and his ammunition was running low. And Confederate reinforcements were on the way from Virginia and Mississippi to beef up the Southern forces.

Rosecrans concluded that he could not attack the Confederates because of their superior numbers, and retreat would be unacceptable to Washington. He mapped out his defensive strategy.

The rebel offensive got off to a late start on September 20, giving Thomas time to throw up a strong breastwork. XIV Corps repulsed the initial assault, but Thomas requested reinforcements. Rosecrans ordered a division to shift from the center of his line to the left flank in support of Thomas. That created a gap in the middle of the Union line.

The Southerners launched a fresh attack just as the gap opened up. The rebel army stormed forward, and Federal troops ran to the rear in panic. The retreat turned into a mad dash for the safety of Chattanooga. Rosecrans and his staff were forced to abandon the field and fall back to the city. Before he raced back to set up his new defensive position, the general turned command of the troops in the field over to Thomas.

Disjointed elements of the Union army found a good defensive position on Horseshoe Ridge and made a stand. The ragtag army, now under the command of General Thomas, held out until dark. As the night wore on, weary soldiers made their way back to Chattanooga to join what was left of the Army of the Cumberland.

The three regiments on Horseshoe Ridge kept fighting until the Confederates surrounded them and forced their surrender.

Bragg had won the battle, but he had failed to crush the Army of the Cumberland. He seized the high ground surrounding Chattanooga and cut off the railroad needed to resupply soldiers and civilians in the city.

Rosecrans was exhausted and demoralized. His army was trapped in a strong defensive position with no means of feeding itself. There was not even enough grass to keep the horses and mules alive. Without them, the artillery caissons and supply wagons would be useless.

Lincoln sent reassuring messages to his general, but he worried. The worry became alarm when Rosecrans pushed the idea of retreating from the city. Two days after the defeat at Chickamauga, the president ordered XI Corps and XII Corps detached from the Army of the Potomac and transferred to the Army of the Cumberland. On September 24, the newly formed corps, with Hooker in command, traveled by train from Culpeper County to Nashville.

When he reached Tennessee, Hooker left Geary with a division at Murfreesboro to guard the railroad while the rest of the corps continued south to Bridgeport, Alabama, where it encamped on October 27.

On September 27, Lincoln ordered Grant to send reinforcements to Chattanooga. A week later, he placed Grant in command of the Military District of Mississippi, with rescue of the Army of the Cumberland and the recapture of Chattanooga as his highest priorities.

32

September 24, 1863

My Dearest Mother,

General Rosecrans has made important contributions to our cause, but there's been a reversal since you penned your last letter. He suffered a stunning defeat at Chickamauga Creek four days ago. I am being sent west along with others to reinforce him.

When we learned that General Lee had sent a large contingent from his army to support General Bragg, we planned to attack Lee. Rumors that we were about to go across the river and finally settle things with the Army of Northern Virginia circulated through the camp.

Before we could mount our attack, we received word that Rosecrans had suffered a severe defeat. Then orders came down from Washington, transferring XI Corps and XII Corps from the Army of the Potomac to the Army of the Cumberland. In other words, we are being taken from Meade and given to Rosecrans.

We will be leaving in the morning for Bridgeport, which is in Alabama not too far from Chattanooga.

Your loving son,

Tom

33

———

October 11, 1863

My Dearest Mother,

We are in Tennessee on garrison duty. We had to disembark at Murfreesboro to fend off a Confederate cavalry raid aimed at cutting our supply and communication links. We were able to thwart the attack, but not before they did some damage. We have made repairs and are now guarding the railroad between Murfreesboro and Bridgeport.

We cannot join up with Rosecrans in Chattanooga because there isn't enough food in the city. Civilians are suffering as well as soldiers. The horses and mules are starving. General Rosecrans seems to have given up hope of attacking the rebels and breaking the siege. I have heard rumors that he is planning to abandon the city.

Your devoted son,

Tom

34

Bristoe Station

In early October, Meade was alerted to unusual activity on the Confederate side of the Rapidan. Large units, divisions, were on the move. Lee had employed all his skill to conceal the activity, but Union spies watching from two mountaintop vantage points picked up on it. The Union commander climbed to the top of Pony Mountain to see for himself.

Meade reported the movements to Halleck and observed that they signaled one of two things. Either Lee was contracting his position so he could send more troops to support Bragg, or he was about to attack the Union army's right flank. Meade continued sifting through intelligence reports, trying to divine his foe's plan. When that failed, he decided on a daring gambit. He sent his left flank forward to pursue and challenge the Confederates while he prepared for an attack on his right flank.

Wagon trains began pulling out of the Iron Triangle and moving to the north side of the Rappahannock on the night of October 9. The infantry broke camp at daybreak. Kilpatrick crossed the Rappahannock at Sulphur Springs to protect the right flank. Buford on the left flank crossed at Germanna Ford. Sedgwick, leading VI Corps, V Corps and II Corps, marched north to find and destroy Lee.

By midmorning on October 10, the information reaching Meade convinced him that the bulk of the Army of Northern Virginia was marching around Madison Courthouse to attack him in the rear. He ordered his infantry to return to Culpeper Courthouse. II Corps was to take up a position to the left of III Corps on the right flank. I Corps was to march northeast and cross the Rappahannock at Kelly's Ford.

The rebels had too big a head start. Their cavalry, supported by a large infantry force, attacked Kilpatrick and French, forcing them to pull back towards Culpeper.

As the afternoon wore on and the Confederate attack developed into a massive onslaught, the Union commander decided to abandon the Iron Triangle and move back to the north shore of the Rappahannock. VI Corps formed his new left flank. V Corps, II Corps and III Corps crossed the river and formed the center and right of his new line.

The following day, the Army of the Potomac developed its line along the north shore of the Rappahannock. While the infantry prepared for a Confederate attack, the cavalry under Buford and Kilpatrick battled across the Iron Triangle from the Rapidan to the Rappahannock with rebel cavalry in hot pursuit.

Meade continued studying reports as they flooded in. He could not convince himself that he understood Lee's strategy. Worse, he did not know where the Army of Northern Virginia was hiding. The Southern cavalry was doing a masterful job of shielding the infantry. The Union commander dispatched Sedgewick and VI Corps with V Corps and II Corps in support to find the enemy. By nightfall, his army was once again split - half north of the Rappahannock, half south.

The next morning, Union pickets at Jeffersonton on the right flank were hit by Confederate cavalry. A messenger carrying an alert for Meade was wounded and captured. The Southerners renewed their attack in the afternoon. Two regiments from Gregg's division initially repulsed the rebels, but Ewell reached the scene with infantry and artillery in time to turn the tide. The rebels chased the retreating Yankees and captured the bridge at Sulfur Springs.

The Confederates had tipped their hand. During the skirmishing, Union cavalrymen had observed the southern infantry marching around the right flank. Gregg sent a message to alert Meade. It didn't reach the general until evening. Meade immediately ordered Sedgwick to pull III Corps and cavalry supporting it back to the north side of the Rappahannock, a movement that took most of the night.

In the morning, II Corps was ordered to continue east to Auburn to shore up the right flank. The men reached their new position around six that evening. In the early hours of October 14, Warren received orders directing him to continue east to Centreville, where Meade planned to make his stand. He rousted his men in the pre-dawn gloom. General Caldwell's division crossed Cedar Run first and deployed at the top of Coffee Hill to serve as a lookout while the rest of the corps crossed the creek and continued toward Centreville. Heavy fog limited visibility.

Sam Goldman was eating breakfast when rebel artillery shells began raining down on the prominence. He dropped the meal and scrambled down the side of Coffee Hill to get away from the rebel guns. Caldwell turned his artillery on the Confederates and sent a brigade of New Yorkers to capture the tree-lined knoll where the enemy was hiding.

Sam was soon charging at the double quick through a storm of musketry. He was still racing up a hill toward the trees when a company of gray-clad horsemen brandishing their sabers poured out of the woods at a gallop. When the two forces collided, it was saber against bayonet. The foot soldiers subdued the horse soldiers, but not before the main rebel force had retreated to safety, with their guns in tow.

A new threat materialized almost immediately. Columns of Confederate infantry were closing in from the north. Warren left Caldwell and his men to deal with them while he got the rest of II Corps on the road toward Centreville.

Caldwell's division held off the rebels throughout the morning, pulling back to join the rest of II Corps around noon. Stalwart New Yorkers brought up the rear, fighting as they retreated. They moved forward a few yards, stopped, turned and fired. Then advanced a few more yards. The artillery caissons were pulled forward while crews loaded their guns, then halted while they fired.

When the Yanks reached Cedar Run, soldiers splashed across the stream while horses pulling artillery dashed over the bridge.

II Corps moved rapidly along the Orange and Alexandria railroad as Caldwell and his division raced to catch up.

The corps was making good progress toward Bristoe Station and Broad Run, the last obstacle between them and Centreville. Rebels were also marching toward Bristoe Station. When General Webb, commanding Warren's lead division, was alerted to Confederate movements, he left the railroad and continued along an unimproved wagon trail. As he approached an intersection a quarter of a mile south of the railroad station, he could see Confederates on a parallel road north of it, chasing V Corps, which was crossing Broad Run.

Webb sent one regiment of skirmishers forward to confirm the identification of the other troops. He deployed the rest of his division along the railroad embankment. A Vermont battery with four pieces was ordered to unlimber and support the infantry. After a regiment of New Yorkers was shifted to create a firing lane for the artillery, the cannons opened up on the right flank of the Confederate column.

The rebels reacted quickly, turning from their pursuit of V Corps to face the enemy setting up behind the railroad bed. While they executed a complex right wheel maneuver, the rear guard of the fleeing V Corps halted and formed up to join the fight. Webb ordered his division to slide to its right to join up with V Corps. II Corps troops continued to arrive and take up positions along the embankment. Artillery batteries set up and unlimbered as they reached the scene. They rained death on the Confederates to their front, but the rebels persevered, charging the hated Federals no matter the cost.

When Warren reached the battleground, he countermanded Webb. V Corps was too far away. The men along the railroad embankment were ordered to hold their fire until the command was given.

Dread of what was about to take place seized Kennedy. He forced himself to keep busy getting his squad ready for the charge. When he caught sight of Warren seated on his horse, he paused to wonder what the general was thinking. Probably the same things as the corporal, except he had ten thousand men to think about.

When the Southerners had formed their line of battle, they started forward. Four thousand men moving as one across five hundred yards of rolling hills in the face of heavy artillery and occasional musketry. A hundred yards from the embankment where the Yanks waited, they reached an open plain with no obstacle to slow their charge. They broke into a sprint.

They were less than fifty paces from the embankment when the defenders got the order to fire. Thousands of muskets poured mini balls into the gray line and, for the first time, it faltered. Many dropped in their tracks. Some wavered and fell back. Others surged forward and reached the earthwork that protected the Yanks. They were quickly dispatched by the defenders.

The charge had collapsed so abruptly, rebel soldiers found themselves trapped in a kill zone. Many turned and ran. Not all made it to safety. Others dropped to their knees and raised their arms in surrender. Some retreated in dignity, firing their muskets as they withdrew to the safety of their lines.

Warren went about the business of getting ready for the next wave. He repositioned his artillery and consolidated his line. Caldwell had arrived. His corps was back together. Union casualties had been light, but the Confederates were beginning to mass on his left flank.

Skirmishing and artillery exchanges continued throughout the afternoon and into the night. Officers and men of II Corps endured tense hours knowing that the Army of Northern Virginia was within striking distance.

Warren ordered a withdrawal to Centreville under the cover of darkness. Three divisions of armed men stole away from their position in front of the enemy. No talking. Weapons and other equipment kept quiet. Ford the frigid waters of Broad Run without making any noise that would betray the escape.

The retreat was horrific. Wounded Confederates lying in the field where they had fallen begged for help. Water. Food.

Blankets. Anything to ease their misery. But this was no time for pity. Exhausted Union soldiers slogged on in spite of everything. The sick and wounded were put on wagons for the trip. Others were bullied into continuing the march. About 150 never made it to Centerville.

Lee's plan to destroy the Army of the Potomac had foundered on Warren's stand at Bristoe Station. But the situation remained dangerous. If Meade's right flank could be turned, he would be forced to retreat to the defenses around the capital.

The Union commander was under pressure to take the offensive against the Confederate army. Lincoln and Halleck believed the tactical situation was favorable. And they were sure the Army of the Potomac had advantages in overall strength. Lee was too far north to keep his army supplied. But Meade could not plan an operation against the wily southerner, because his whereabouts were unknown.

The Union cavalry searched for Lee. The Confederate cavalry probed Meade's defenses.

Meade learned that the Confederates had begun to withdraw on October 16. Torrential rains and swollen rivers prevented him from pursuing Lee for two days. The Union army began moving on October 18, with Kilpatrick's cavalry division in the lead, while Gregg and Buford protected the rear and flanks.

The following morning, Custer and the Michigan brigade were in the lead. They encountered Confederate pickets east of Broad Run and drove them across the stream. Custer ordered an assault against the Southerners. But they were dug in and held their ground. Kilpatrick ordered his cavaliers to cross the stream on either side of the entrenchment. Hitting the enemy on both flanks forced them to withdraw.

The Union cavalry continued southwest to Buckland, where they crossed a stone bridge, and Kilpatrick called for a halt to assess the situation. Davies took the lead when the march resumed. Custer's orders were to follow the First Brigade, but he delayed to give his men time to eat and recuperate from the morning battle. The Michigan brigade only paused for an hour before mounting and setting out to close the gap. Custer left a regiment behind guarding the bridge.

He had not gotten far when the sounds of a fight back at the bridge brought him racing to the rescue of his rear guard. A division of Confederate cavalry had come up behind him in an apparent effort to trap Kilpatrick's division between two divisions of rebels. Custer deployed his troopers in a defensive line and turned his artillery on the attacking Southerners. He held the bridge until he ran out of ammunition, then he led his brigade back across Broad Run and rejoined the main army at Gainesville.

The division of rebel cavalry in front of Kilpatrick gave ground as Davies pressed forward. A few miles down the road, it disappeared behind a line of low hills. Moments later, the Confederates came charging out from behind the hills with sabers drawn. Stunned Federals stopped in panic. Davies, realizing that he was trapped with only one way out, gave the order, "Every man for himself." He rode north toward Thoroughfare Gap, then swung southeast to join the main army. Southern horsemen, out for blood, chased the Northerners for several miles.

The Army of Northern Virginia tore up track from Bristoe Station to Culpeper Station and burned bridges as it retreated across the Rappahannock River.

Meade made repairs as he worked his way south. Pursuit by the Army of the Potomac ended at the river's edge.

35

October 25, 1863

My Dearest Mother,

We are waiting for developments that will allow us to move on to Chattanooga. I don't think we will have to wait much longer.

General Grant arrived in Bridgeport a few days ago. I was one of the men selected to escort him to Chattanooga. The route we followed winds through the mountains. It is steep and dangerous in places, even under normal conditions. Recent rains have made it almost impassable. General Grant is hobbled by an injury he received when his horse fell on him. He needs crutches to get around. He did well enough on horseback but when it was necessary to dismount and walk, we had to carry him in a litter.

He was courteous and friendly with us enlisted men. He looks frail. He is about a head taller than me but I would guess he weighs no more than me. Still no one questions what he says.

Conditions in the city are worse than I had imagined. Soldiers have been living on half rations for some time. They will not last much longer without additional supplies. The little that we can get to them over the trail I mentioned above barely sustains life for the populace. The animals are dying by the thousands.

Plans are in the works for breaking the Confederate stranglehold. They have made pontoons and a boat to ferry supplies up the river. They need a direct overland route to the supply depot. I believe that will be our mission.

You get much more news about the war than I get here in the camp. But do not believe everything you read.

The newspapers have reported that Meade defeated Lee again a week ago. That is confirmed by stories circulating in camp. The Confederates attempted to encircle him, but the Army of the Potomac slipped out of the trap, and General Warren inflicted heavy damage on their infantry.

The editorial you sent me argues that it would be foolish for General Meade to try to capture Fredericksburg. General Burnside and General Hooker tried and failed. We should not waste any more good men on a third attempt. But the third time is a charm, as they say.

General Burnside's operation was doomed when Washington failed to deliver the pontoons he needed for a bridge.

General Meade showed what he could do at Gettysburg. I am among those who believe that we could have defeated Lee last spring if General Meade had been in command. Capturing Fredericksburg and entrenching along the heights to the west still makes sense. That is a good place to launch an attack against Richmond. Therefore, it is a threat that General Lee cannot ignore.

    I do not trust the Washington politicians who are running this war.

Your devoted son,

Tom

36

Wauhatchie

Tom sat alone by a small fire, puffing on his pipe. He had thrown a blanket over his shoulders to ward off the chill night air. Clouds hid the moon. Kat was shunning company because of her monthlies. Kennedy and Goldman were back in Virginia. The young soldier had nothing to keep him company but thoughts and reflections on two years of a war that seemed to have no end.

A soldier walked over to him and extended a hand. "Mac."

"Tom. What can I do for you?"

"You look like you could use some company."

"Want some coffee?"

Mac unhitched a cup from his belt and handed it to Tom. "I hear your operation got called off."

Tom filled the cup and handed it back. "First time I ever heard of anything being called off because of the weather,"

Mac lit his pipe and puffed. "You'll go tomorrow. They're gonna take Brown's Ferry tonight. The road to Kelly's Ferry has to be secured."

"Good night for it. Too dark for the rebs to see what's on the river."

As predicted, Hooker led his patchwork corps to secure the road between Kelly's Ferry and Brown's Ferry early the next morning. He detached Geary's division to guard Wauhatchie Station and the wagon train with supplies and support personnel. Hooker reached Brown's ferry that afternoon and connected with the assault force that had captured the landing.

Two Confederate divisions hit Geary at midnight. The attack was expected, but not at that time of night. Geary quickly formed his men into a V to confront attacks coming from two sides at once. His outnumbered division held its ground for hours. When their ammunition ran low and it looked like they would be overrun, XI Corps charged to the rescue. The sound of horses bringing fresh combatants ended the battle. The Confederates withdrew before they could be trapped by the reinforcements.

37

Rappahannock Station

After his failed offensive in September, Lee established his headquarters at the Culpeper County Courthouse, a stop on the Orange and Alexandria Railroad in the center of the valley bordered by the Rappahannock and Rapidan rivers. He expected the Army of the Potomac to try to retake the valley.

Meade settled his army parallel to the Rappahannock from Warrenton in the northwest to Catlett Station near Fredericksburg. Engineers repairing the railroad had it ready for use as far as Warrenton by the first of November. Cold, wet weather and a lull in the skirmishing led the average soldier in the Army of the Potomac to hope that fighting was over for the year.

But the press kept up a steady drumbeat demanding an attack on Lee, who had to be weak after suffering major defeats.

On November 4, Kilpatrick's cavalry division was sent out to respond to a reported foray by Confederate cavalry. They ran up against skirmishers and chased them back to Fredericksburg. They spent the rest of the day exchanging musketry with rebels sheltering in the town.

On November 5, Meade visited his corps commanders. Across the river, JEB Stuart and Robert E Lee held a review of the Confederate cavalry near Brandy Station.

That night, Kennedy, Sam Goldman and a small group of friends sitting around a campfire were joined by Josh Goldman. The main topic was what's next. Many in the group were looking forward to shutting down for the winter. Sam Goldman said, "The press is pushing for another offensive before winter sets in. Opinion pieces say that if we attack Lee one more time, he will collapse."

Josh said, "The press is printing what the White House is preaching. The president is disappointed that his army hasn't done more damage to Lee."

"What does he want us to do?" Kennedy asked.

"Something," a voice called out. "Anything."

"They're right across the river," somebody else said. "We should go over there and have it out with them."

"There are three things we can do," Sam answered. "We can go north around their left flank just like they attacked us last month. But that takes time, and we'd need a wagon train to carry our food and ammunition."

"If Lee can do it, why can't we?"

"Maybe we could, if Lee was our commander," Sam said. "But we're stuck with Meade." He paused to gauge the reaction. He went on, "We could also go around the right flank. Take Fredericksburg and head south toward Richmond."

Josh grimaced and shook his head. "Lincoln has already said no to that idea and he's not going to change his mind."

"So, we have to go straight at them," Sam said.

"March across Kelly's Ford and keep pushing until we have them pinned against the Rapidan," Kennedy suggested.

"Except that they can cross the river farther north and attack our flank while we're trying to get across," Sam objected.

"What's the solution?"

Sam grinned. "General Meade will have to answer that question."

November 6 was cold and rainy. Reveille sounded at 4:30 on the morning of November 7. Near freezing temperatures with brisk breezes promised an autumn day that would be perfect for a fight.

Two hours later, the Army of the Potomac was on the move. Meade had split his army again. Sedgwick led VI Corps and V Corps toward Rappahannock Station with orders to take the Confederate fortress on the north shore by nightfall.

French led III Corps and II Corps south to Kelly's Ford with orders to force a crossing and establish a beachhead.

The cavalry took up positions on the flanks. Buford to the right of Sedgwick, and Kilpatrick to the left of French. I Corps was held in reserve.

Sharpshooters advancing ahead of French's wing reached Mount Holly church about a mile from the river crossing around 1:00 p.m. The sun was high in the sky, and temperatures had risen to a pleasant sixtyish.

The artillery gained a lodgment on the hills overlooking Kelly's Ford while the infantry prepared to attack. Surprise was essential. Twenty thousand men moved stealthily as they prepared to pounce on the unsuspecting enemy. When they were ready, the command was given: "Charge."

Union cannons began bombarding rebels on the south shore. Confederates responded quickly to the shelling and the sight of blue-clad soldiers advancing with their bayonets gleaming in the sun. The battle went on for two hours. Determined Southerners, fighting from trenches designed to fend off skirmish lines, not brigades, were forced to retreat to buildings in nearby Kellysville. Union artillery took aim at those structures, blasting holes in the brick walls and the roofs until the defenders threw down their weapons and surrendered.

As the sun set, French was able to report that he had accomplished his mission. III Corps had forced the crossing and established a defensive line a mile inland. A pontoon bridge was in place, and II Corps was ready to cross the ford. Confederates were massing in front of his new position.

Sedgwick's report had not yet reached headquarters. He had spent hours deploying V Corps and VI Corps behind a ridge that was supposed to hide them from the Confederates. But rebel pickets atop the bluff had watched the maneuvers and alerted the rest of the army.

Around three, just as the defenders in Kellysville were surrendering, Sedgwick gave the order to advance. The Union line charged to the top of the ridge, pushing back outnumbered pickets. When they gained the summit, the Yankees were greeted by the sight of a fort on the north bank of the river. Two redoubts on small, steep hills rising about seventy-five feet above the plain. Trenches with firing pits and traverses that spread out from the sides of the redoubts connected the two structures to the river and each other. The fortifications were about a half-mile from where the Federals stood. The ground in between was open with no obvious protection from rebel fire.

The Union line continued pushing toward its goal, and the gray-clad defenders continued to fall back.

Late in the afternoon, with temperatures dropping and shadows lengthening, Sedgwick and Wright, his stand-in VI Corps commander, rode forward to assess the situation. Union skirmishers had encircled the Confederate bridgehead. Only a few hundred yards stood between them and the enemy. Sharpshooters from both armies kept up a steady exchange. The artilleries blasted away in a futile attempt to eliminate enemy cannons.

It looked like a stalemate to the generals. Sedgwick concluded he would not be able to take the rebel works.

General David Russell, standing in for Wright as division commander, also ventured forward to make an assessment. He went all the way to the front line for a close look at the rebel bastion. It reminded him of the Confederate defenses on Marye Heights outside of Fredericksburg. He had dislodged the rebels from that fortification six months earlier during the Chancellorsville campaign. He saw no reason why he and his men could not do the same thing here. He sent his plan to Wright, requesting approval for an assault. The round-trip exchange took some time, but the attack was okayed.

Russell quickly organized his men into three waves and sent them forward. The first wave was decimated by enemy fire. A few of the attackers reached the stronghold and harassed the defenders. The second wave was more successful. Federal soldiers charged into the enemy trenches, where they fought hand-to-hand with the rebels. The third wave brought overwhelming force. The struggle went on for an hour, but in the end, the Southerners who survived were forced to surrender.

Sedgwick didn't know the outcome when he sent a late afternoon report to Meade. The army commander learned preliminary details around eight o'clock that night. The final report arrived two hours later. Meade reported the day's successes to his bosses in Washington. Staff members at Meade's headquarters celebrated enthusiastically. But the Major General Commanding found new things to worry about.

Confederates were still entrenched on the south bank of the river at Rappahannock Station. Only III Corps had made it across the river that afternoon. It could be crushed if Lee brought his whole army down on it in the morning. He began issuing orders to make sure that didn't happen. II Corps would cross at dawn and join III Corps. V Corps would march down to Kelly's Ford in time to follow II Corps across the river. I Corps would follow V Corps. French would send a division north to support Sedgwick's crossing.

The Army of the Potomac was on the move by four on November 8. Regiments sent out on reconnaissance by French advanced over a mile without encountering the enemy. While II Corps was taking up a position to the left of III Corps, Warren climbed a small hill and observed Confederates gathering near Brandy Station. Meade formed his troops in a line and began a stately sweep across Culpeper County. Southerners attacked the advancing Federals several times but retreated before a battle could develop. Reports reaching Meade throughout the day led him to believe that Lee had once again slipped out of his trap. He went into bivouac.

The victory at Rappahannock Station bolstered Meade's standing. He was once again a hero. But he couldn't overlook the obvious. The Army of the Potomac and the Army of Northern Virginia were back where they had started last summer, before Lee began his offensive into Pennsylvania.

That night, the mood around the campfires was jovial. This had to be the last of the fighting for the year. And Lee had been beaten again. "Lee's magic seems to have departed about the same time as good old Stonewall Jackson."

Josh Goldman joined some soldiers with Sam and Kennedy. He poured a cup of coffee and studied the group. "The Old Man missed another opportunity," he said. "I rode down to the river crossings in the southwest this morning. Hundreds of wagons were making their way across the Rapidan. The army couldn't get across until all those wagons were safe on the other side. Lee was trapped with his back to the river most of the day. Meade had him, but he stopped pushing."

38

Addressing Gettysburg

Sometime after the victory at Gettysburg, work began on a national cemetery to give the Union soldiers who died in the battle a proper burial. In October of that year, with the work half completed, the oversight committee decided to hold a commemoration ceremony in November before the weather got too bad. Edward Everett was chosen to be the main speaker. The president was invited to attend and make a few remarks.

Lincoln left Washington by train on November 18. His retinue included cabinet secretaries Seward, Usher, and Blair, along with a few foreign dignitaries. To those who accompanied him, he looked debilitated. His complexion was a sickly gray. He complained of weakness and headaches. The symptoms were put down to fatigue brought on by the burdens of the war effort.

Frustration with the lack of progress had spurred the Commander in Chief to superhuman efforts in his search for a winning strategy.

Four months earlier, Meade repulsed Lee at Gettysburg while Grant captured Vicksburg and Rosecrans drove Bragg out of Tullahoma. Since then, the Army of the Potomac's commander had been tentative. Lee had repeatedly slipped from Meade's grasp as he staggered back to Virginia. The pattern repeated in the months that followed. The Union army won battles but failed to destroy the enemy.

The upshot was that Longstreet was now in Tennessee. He had been a key to Bragg's victory over Rosecrans at Chickamauga. And just a week ago, he had launched a strike that drove Burnside into the defensive works around Knoxville. Grant had refused to go to Burnside's aid, insisting he couldn't go on the offensive until Sherman reached Chattanooga.

The Confederate army had won time and again despite its disadvantages. The Federal army had failed to capture Richmond, and now it was unable to corral the Southerners and force them into a decisive battle. Overall, Lincoln's army had proven to be expensive but ineffective.

The president stoically endured the commemoration ceremony. After a two-hour oration by Everett, he rose to deliver his comments. A big, powerfully built man, Lincoln strode boldly to the podium and paused to survey those in attendance. The audience appraised him and judged him to be the rock on which the country's future could be built. After a moment of silence, he intoned:

"Four score and seven years ago our fathers brought forth on this continent a new nation, conceived in Liberty, and dedicated to the proposition that all men are created equal.

Now we are engaged in a great civil war, testing whether that nation, or any nation so conceived and so dedicated, can long endure. We are met on a great battlefield of that war. We have come to dedicate a portion of that field as a final resting place for those who here gave their lives that that nation might live. It is altogether fitting and proper that we should do this.

But, in a larger sense, we cannot dedicate - we cannot consecrate - we cannot hallow - this ground. The brave men, living and dead, who struggled here, have consecrated it far above our poor power to add or detract. The world will little note, nor long remember what we say here, but it can never forget what they did here. It is for us the living, rather, to be dedicated here to the unfinished work which they who fought here have thus far so nobly advanced. It is rather for us the living to be here dedicated to the great task remaining before us - that from these honored dead we take increased devotion to that cause for which they gave the last full measure of devotion - that we here highly resolve that these dead shall not have died in vain - that this nation, under God, shall have a new birth of freedom - and that government of the people, by the people, for the people, shall not perish from the earth."

On the train ride back to Washington, Lincoln's condition worsened. Doctors determined that he had a mild case of smallpox.

39

November 21, 1863

My Dearest Mother,

I trust this letter finds you well. I am okay. The mood here is upbeat and the days pass quickly.

We secured the route from Kelly's Ferry to Chattanooga with only minor resistance from the rebels. They attacked us one night. The fight went on for a couple of hours but we drove them off. Sadly, General Geary's son was killed in the battle.

Chattanooga has been busy as a beehive since we opened the cracker line for supplies. I have been working on the road between Kelly's Ferry and Brown's Ferry. It is now a plank road that will hold up through the winter.

General Sherman has arrived with reinforcements. We now have 70,000 men. Plans have been made to oust the Confederates from their roost on Missionary Ridge. I don't know the plan, but I'll find it out soon enough.

Your devoted son,

Tom

40

Missionary Ridge

Four days after the president's appearance at the Gettysburg battlefield, a series of events produced a dramatic shift in the war's outlook.

General Grant received reports of troops leaving the Confederate stronghold on Missionary Ridge and heading north. Realizing they were going to support Longstreet's efforts to capture Knoxville, he ordered Thomas to cross the river and capture Knob Hill, threatening the center of Bragg's position.

The move forced the Confederate general to recall his troops.

The following morning, Grant sent Sherman north around Bragg's right flank. At the same time, he sent Hooker across the Tennessee River to demonstrate against Bragg's left flank.

Hooker ordered Geary to drive the rebels from their stronghold on Lookout Mountain.

Tom led a company of sharpshooters through a defile along the river at the mountain's base. The men advanced rapidly for an hour before encountering rebel pickets. The Southerners retreated without putting up much of a fight until they reached The Ledge. The main Confederate force was dug in on this three-hundred-foot wide plateau halfway up the mountain. Shooting started immediately. It escalated as the rest of Geary's division arrived and took up positions. A dense fog limited the effectiveness of muskets and artillery, but the exchanges continued into the evening.

When Geary's men awoke in the morning, they discovered that the Johnnies had slipped away during the night. New orders from General Thomas sent the Yankees north toward Missionary Ridge. Progress was slow because the rebels had burned bridges as they retreated to their stronghold atop the bluff. While pioneers, the men who carried tools instead of rifles so they could clear the way and build or tear down, set about rebuilding the bridges. While that work progressed, troops used makeshift footbridges to advance. By midafternoon, Tom led the division through Rossville Gap and up Missionary Ridge. As Geary's men ascended, they could hear a fierce battle to their left on the mountain's eastern slope.

When they reached the top, they saw that the rebels had lost the fight to hold their line along the edge of the cliff and were racing north in disarray. The Southerners reorganized in the northwest corner of the mountain and made a stand. That night, they abandoned their works and retreated toward Dalton, Georgia.

Hooker pursued the Confederates as far as Ringgold Gap, where he encountered a strongly entrenched rear guard. After attacks on both flanks failed to dislodge the Southerners, Grant called off the effort and ordered him to return to Chattanooga.

Two nights later, Mac and others filled Tom in on what had happened. On the first morning, Sherman captured Billy Goat Hill, a mile short of Missionary Ridge. In front of him was a deep ravine and, on the other side of that, Tunnel Hill, where the rebels were preparing strong fortifications. The next morning, Sherman launched his assault on the rebel position. After two frontal attacks failed, Grant ordered Thomas to capture rifle pits at the base of the mountain's east face. That was easy enough. But when his men occupied the rifle pits, they were sitting ducks for sharpshooters entrenched along the summit.

Ignoring orders, rank and file soldiers took it upon themselves to mount an attack along the eastern face of the mountain. They stormed up the slopes, battalion by battalion, each in a "V" formation with the flag bearers leading the way. It was horrific. The flags changed hands as the bearers fell, but the dogged charge would not be deterred. The men in blue stormed the rebel pits and sent the enemy running for cover.

The next morning, Grant sent Sherman north with thirty thousand troops to drive off Longstreet and lift the siege on Knoxville. The Confederate general pulled back without a fight and began moving east to rejoin Lee.

41

Disaster at Mine Run

A mid-November meeting with Halleck in Washington convinced Meade that he would have to attack Lee in his stronghold south of the Rapidan. His superiors had been unwilling to even consider an alternate approach.

The first good news was that the lower fords on the Rapidan were unprotected. Meade would be able to lead his men across the river and around Lee's right flank. Speed would be necessary. He couldn't give his opponent time to concentrate his forces against the attack. But that was how he had beaten Lee two weeks earlier.

On November 20, the Union commander was informed that the O&A Railroad had been repaired as far as Brandy Station. He could stockpile supplies for the planned operation. Heavy rains drenched the area for two days, making roads unusable, but the 22nd was sunny and mild. Meade met with his corps commanders to explain the battle plan and discuss their roles.

The operation was to start at daybreak on the 24th.

Warren would take II Corps across Germanna Ford to Robertson's Tavern on the Confederate right flank. French would lead III Corps over Jacobs Ford. Sedgwick was to cross at Jacobs Ford after III Corps. Sykes would cross at Culpeper Mine Ford and march to New Hope Church on the Confederate left flank. Newton would follow Sykes.

Troops were to carry ten days' provisions with them. Only artillery caissons and ambulances would accompany the troops across the river.

Rain pushed the offensive back two days. But it got off to a promising start on the morning of the 26th. II Corps had crossed Germanna Ford by ten o'clock. V Corps was across the river by eleven. III Corps was late. Meade was forced to halt the river crossings while he waited for French to catch up.

The III Corps commander had allowed his men to sleep late because he had not received his orders in time. Once he got them to the river, he took extreme precautions before crossing. As a result, III Corps did not make it across the Rapidan until late afternoon. VI Corps was stuck north of the river.

Speed and surprise were now out of the question. Three of the five corps had crossed the river. It would take another day to get the other two across. Pickets that had been pushed aside as the Army of the Potomac began crossing the Rapidan would have alerted Lee.

Lincoln had declared November 26 Thanksgiving Day. Meade had nothing to be thankful for. His army was once again divided, and the situation was about as bad as it could get. His army was encamped in the secondary growth woodland that had doomed Hooker's campaign and was about to do the same to his. And his dinner, like his men's, consisted of hardtack and sow belly.

The Army of the Potomac was on the move by seven o'clock the next morning. Warren had II Corps at Locust Grove near Robertson's Tavern by ten. Meade ordered him to wait for III Corps. The Confederates showed up first. They began engaging with Warren's pickets around eleven.

At the same time, Gregg's cavalry division was taking on the rebel cavalry at New Hope Church, two miles away.

Meade received a message from French at eleven-thirty. III Corps was at the Orange Plank Road, waiting for Warren. The army commander replied, "He is waiting for you. Move forward as rapidly as possible to Robertson's Tavern where your corps is wanted."

Two hours later, a note from French informed Meade that a large enemy force was attacking his right flank, and he was making dispositions as necessary. Meade ordered French to move his left forward to connect with Warren while fighting the enemy to his front.

Meade was in a near panic. Lee had mobilized his army and was attacking the Army of the Potomac before it was ready to meet him. But neither commander was ready for battle. They both ordered their troops to hold their position while they maneuvered to get organized for the fight.

General Henry Prince, commanding the lead division of III Corps, held almost half of Meade's army hostage as he cautiously crept across the Rapidan. French allowed the situation to go on too long. While the fastidious Prince moved his men into position for battle, his Confederate counterpart swung into action. After an hour of maneuvering, the rebel force hit the defense-minded Federals with the ferocity of a tigress. Union troops broke and ran. They raced across an open field and sought shelter on tree-covered high ground. They regrouped and prepared for the Southerners' next attack.

The rebels came. Fighting continued all afternoon and into the evening. But the Southerners could not dislodge the numerically superior Northerners in spite of their reckless ferocity. When nightfall brought an end to the struggle, both sides retreated to entrenched positions.

While III Corps struggled with the unexpected rebel offensive, V Corps on the army's left flank, supported by I Corps, battled with Lee's forces along the Orange Plank Road. An isolated II Corps held the center against aggressive probes. An all-out attack by Lee could wipe it out. Warren leaned toward caution until Sedgwick arrived with VI Corps on his right flank in the late afternoon. Then he had his skirmishers drive the rebels back to their main defensive line. He was confident he would be able to take the Southerners' position in the morning.

Meade ordered an all-out attack on the Confederates at first light on the morning of November 28. I Corps on the left. II Corps in the center and VI Corps on the right. He found the Confederate trenches empty. Lee had pulled back overnight. Meade ordered his army to move forward and locate the Southerners' new defensive line.

Progress was slow. The morning was cold and rainy. A biting wind chilled men to the bone. Wary soldiers pressed forward through dense woodland over muddy country roads. When they reached Mine Run, a small tributary to the Rapidan, they found the new rebel works atop a hundred foot rise three hundred yards west of the marshy stream.

While Meade pondered his next move, Warren came to him with a proposal. He had reconnoitered the Confederate line and determined that he could take II Corps around the enemy's right flank and attack it in the rear. Meade approved the plan but delayed the move until morning.

That night, temperatures dropped below freezing. Sleep was almost impossible. Early morning activity provided welcome relief. II Corps pulled back from the line and marched around I Corps to the edge of the two armies. The sun was setting when Warren reached his launch point. The enemy's supply wagons stood before him, unprotected except for some poorly constructed works and a few pickets. In the morning, his soldiers would deliver a blow that would cripple, if not destroy, the Army of Northern Virginia. But they would have to endure another cold, sleepless night before they could mount that attack. And they could not light fires that would give away their position.

Kennedy became aware of someone shaking him and yelling in a gravelly voice, "Corporal!"

He looked up. Recognizing the face staring down at him, he said, "Morning, Sarge. What time is it?"

"Three. We jump off at eight. Get your men ready."

The Irishman pushed himself out of his warm, comfortable nest and stretched. He walked around rousing privates and shouting orders. The men were to carry blankets with them to make burial easier. The final instruction was dire. "If you don't make it over the rebel works, you'll be shot."

Kennedy ventured to the edge of the woods to see what they were up against. The breastworks he'd seen the night before had been replaced. The Johnnies had spent the night building a bastion and covering the ground in front with abatis, trees and other debris that would slow the Union assault to a standstill. A division, if not the whole damned rebel army, stood ready to cut the charging Yanks to pieces. The planned attack would be suicidal and most likely fail.

As the morning wore on, more and more men wandered forward to take a look at their target. Word spread, and the mood darkened. Men sewed names inside their uniforms so they would not be consigned to an anonymous grave. They said their last goodbyes to their friends and made peace with the Lord. The chaplain was busy that morning.

Eight o'clock came and went. Men waited anxiously for the order that would send them to their death. But Warren had already called off the attack. After riding forward to inspect the enemy works, he had concluded that the assault was doomed. He kept his men at the ready while he notified his commander and waited for confirmation of his decision.

Kennedy caught a glimpse of Meade as he rode up to confront Warren. The Old Man was furious, and he made no attempt to hide his feelings. But after a loud conference, the army commander agreed they could not go forward with the assault. He rushed orders to the other corps commanders who were preparing to make their attack in conjunction with Warren's.

That night, Meade held a council of war. The conclusion was that another opportunity had been lost. The best course of action was to get out before Lee went on the offensive. By December 2, the Army of the Potomac was back in the Iron Triangle with the Rappahannock on its north and east and the Rapidan on its south and west. The men settled into their winter quarters to wait for a continuation of the struggle in the spring.

42

December 15, 1863

My Dearest Mother,

Good news. I will be coming home for Christmas. I might not make it until January but I will be home.

We are in winter camp. No more fighting for a few months.

A veteranizing campaign is underway. The goal is to hold onto veteran troops until the end of the war. We are being asked to sign-up for three more years or until the war is over. In return, we will get a bonus and a thirty day furlough. I will be promoted to Sergeant. I would have agreed anyway but the benefits appeal to me.

General Geary got us together and gave a rousing speech. He said America was like our mother, who sheltered us and fed us all our lives but was now struggling and needed help. This country will fall apart if brave men don't step up and save it. The past year has been difficult. We are all tired, but if we stop now, our struggles, our sacrifices, our suffering will go to waste. If we keep fighting, we will emerge victorious. He said he thought the rebels could hold out for a while longer but no more than a year. We just need to keep going until we have beaten them. He assured us that is what he was going to do. He asked that we continue to follow him as we have done in the past.

That doesn't sound like much when you read it in a letter. But when General Geary said it, every man who heard it was moved.

I will be on my way home as soon as I can make the arrangements.

There is one thing that I want to ask of you. I would like you to welcome a friend I have asked to accompany me. Her name is Katherine McAllister. I invited her to join us so she would not have to spend Christmas alone. Kat has been with our regiment almost from the beginning. The seceshes burned her farm to the ground after she warned us about a plot they were hatching. She took care of John after he was wounded. I'm sure he can tell you all about her.

There will not be time to get your response. I will have to trust that you will agree because you are my mother and I'm your son.

I will see you soon.

Your loving son,

Tom

43

Furlough

Hooker's army went into winter quarters at Bridgeport, thirty miles downriver from Chattanooga, at the beginning of December. Tom was looking forward to some relief from the past few years. He had reenlisted with his promotion to sergeant in the regular army guaranteed. He had a furlough coming, and he planned to go back to Philadelphia for a visit with money in his pocket.

Kat had no official position and no promised rewards. Winter quarters meant a break from the sounds of battle and the constant demands of the wounded and dying. She and Tom had more freedom than they'd had at any time in her memory.

Going with Tom to visit his family was both appealing and terrifying. Kat was eager to be alone with her man but dreaded meeting the rest of the family. She was ready to get away from the camp. Southern Maryland would've been her preference, but she might not be welcome there. Some of those who had wanted to hang her would not have forgotten her betrayal. Philadelphia wasn't a bad second choice. She had never been to a big city, and she was curious about Tom's life before the army. But that would mean spending time with people who would want her to marry him.

Marriage hung over them like an overzealous parent. An unwanted presence that could not be dismissed.

Tom knew he was too young. He didn't have a real occupation, so he couldn't support a family. He did not want to go back to the shoe shop. He had learned a great deal about railroads over the last couple of years. They interested him. He thought he might like to go to California and look for gold. He was not ready to settle down.

Kat wanted a family like the one she grew up with. She couldn't have that with the destruction and bloodshed continuing for the foreseeable future. She would not bring children into a world filled with such horrors. Even if the war were settled tomorrow, the country would not be restored easily or soon. If marriage was proposed, she would say no without hesitation.

"I will go with you," Kat said, "but if the visit becomes contentious, I will be on the next train back here."

Tom chuckled. "Agreed."

"What is your brother going to say?"

"My brother?"

"John."

"Why? What can he say?"

"He suspects we're intimate. What's to stop him from bringing that up in front of your mother?"

"He wouldn't do that."

"I patched him up after he was wounded. The way he looked at me, he wanted to ask. I didn't give him a chance."

"He might ask me but he'd never say anything to our mother or sisters."

"How does your mother feel about Presbyterians?"

"As long as you're not Catholic, you're okay." Tom pursed his lips and considered his next words carefully. "I think we should tell them that we are engaged and planning to get married when the war is over."

"I'm not committing to any such thing," Kat snapped.

"I know," Tom soothed. "But changing plans will be a whole lot easier than fighting about it."

Kat crinkled her nose. Shook her head. Then shrugged.

They joined some wounded men in an ambulance for their ride to Murfreesboro Station, where they began their journey to Philadelphia. John met them at the station when they reached the city. He had arranged a carriage to take them to the Donal residence, a few miles outside Philadelphia proper.

Tom's other brother, Robert, the oldest of the three boys, had avoided active duty because he was married and could argue that he was supporting his mother. His two sisters, Angie and Bess, worked as domestic servants in nearby households. Angie, the oldest of the brood, was two years older than Robert. Bess was between Robert and John. Neither was married.

The matriarch of the family, Bridget, ruled with an iron will. At sixty, her dark hair showed streaks of gray, but her face was unlined. Her manner was pleasant, but her eyes betrayed an intense ferocity. Her dress and bearing were formal, prim. She moved with an easy grace but with no waste in her movements. She had held things together for a decade after her husband died. When her sons joined the army, they sent her money to help with the finances.

Robert's house painting business had done well enough to support him and his family. John joined the business when he had recovered enough to work productively. Together, the brothers had built a thriving enterprise. John's income eased the burden his mother had been carrying.

When the sisters learned that Kat had cared for their brother after he was wounded at Antietam, she became a family favorite. John, a budding politician, burnished her reputation as a nurse and an asset to the regiment while avoiding mention of an unseemly relationship between her and Tom.

The visit passed pleasantly enough. The couple did some sightseeing - the Liberty Bell, Constitution Hall, Franklin's grave, and things like that. They went downtown to watch the Colored Troops parade along Main Street and attended a comic opera, "The Enchantress," at the Arch Street Theater.

Tom and Kat took advantage of an extension on his furlough to tour New York City and Baltimore before returning to the camp.

As soon as they were alone, Kat demanded, "What's the matter?"

"John's getting married," Tom grumped.

"You should be happy for him. He's getting his life together and he's found someone he loves."

"He's going to move into the house and take over."

The tone in Tom's voice made Kat pause. "He and his wife will need a place to live. And he is a big help to your mother."

"There will be nothing here for me if I manage to come through this war alive."

"I thought you didn't want to go back."

"I don't want to go back to the shoe shop. Philadelphia is my home."

That conversation hung over them like a threatening storm for the rest of the trip. They rented a room on the second floor of a townhouse in Manhattan while they spent a week sightseeing in the big city. Kat insisted on visiting Sam before they left town.

"How are we going to do that?"

"We'll hire a carriage. Isn't that what you city folks do?"

"If we knew where he lived."

"I do. He gave me directions."

"Why?"

"I asked. A girl has to know these things."

They arrived at a stylish two-story home on a modest property in a suburb west of the city. A uniformed maid greeted them, took their names and disappeared inside. Moments later, Sam came to the door, followed by his mother and father. He invited his friends in and introduced everybody. His father was Baruch and his mother Caroline.

The interior seemed much more spacious than the outside suggested. A stairway led to a second floor. To the right, a large, well-furnished room with a picture window looking out onto the street. The visitors were led down a dim hallway to a sitting room. Plush chairs and a settee against the long wall were arranged in a circle around an oval table in the center of the room. Heavy winter drapes covered the windows. A fire in a fireplace at one end of the room kept it warm.

While guests were seated, a man in uniform was given instructions and sent off in the family carriage.

An hour later, the conversation was interrupted when he returned, accompanied by a lady. Kat immediately realized she must be Sam's sweetheart but was surprised by her appearance. A full-figured woman as tall as Sam. Her round, milky-white face was framed by black hair pulled back into a bun. A single strand of pearls set off the understated red dress that clung to her body's curves. This was Sylvia.

Her head bent forward in a slight bow, but her downcast eyes surveyed the room and locked on the newcomers. A moment later, her face lit up as she realized who they were. She squealed, "Kat." And charged across the room to hug the redheaded rebel who wore men's clothes, smoked a pipe, drank coffee and whiskey from a tin and talked war with the men. "You came," she chirped giddily. "You came. Samuel said you would. I didn't believe it. But here you are. We need more women like you. Thousands more," she gushed, "to make men listen to what we have to say."

When Sylvia paused to take a breath, she noticed the young man staring open-mouthed and pulled him into her embrace. "You must be Tom. It is so good to meet you. Samuel has told me so much about you."

The momentary awkwardness was rescued by a maid who brought in a fresh pot of tea and served everyone. The conversation returned to normal. Tom said he and Kat were planning one last day of touring New York. Sam insisted that he and Sylvia would accompany them. Baruch invited his guests to stay for dinner and spend the night at his house.

When the dinner conversation had run its course, Baruch stood and raised a glass of kosher wine made from choice grapes and aged to perfection. "I propose a toast to the young people who are about to take over the world. I salute my son, and Sylvia his intended, and his friends Thomas and Katherine." He paused, his face beaming with joy, and nodded. "You are engaged in a great struggle. You did not begin this war but you are committed to bringing it to a proper finish. At the same time others are raising a false hope, a false god, peace with the slavers. There can be no peace with such men. Slavery was banned in the modern civilized world thirty years ago and yet it has continued in this country that proclaims equality and liberty for all. Peaceful solutions have been offered and rejected. When the election of Abraham Lincoln held out a promise that slavery would be ended in this country, they went to war. There is nothing to do but fight that war and settle the issue once and for all. That falls upon you, my children. Our hopes and our future are in your hands. May Yahweh grant you victory."

In the morning, a carriage showed up at the Goldman residence to take the four young people into the city for a day of touring, shopping and dining. The day ended with a show at the Winter Garden Theater, followed by dinner at the LaFarge House next door. When there was a break in the conversation, Tom turned to Kat and asked, "Where does Kennedy live?"

She scrunched her nose and shook her head. Sam said, "Jim doesn't have an established residence. He enlisted a few months after he arrived in this country. I'm sure he plans to go back to Ireland and join the revolution when the war is over."

Kat said, "His father is in the British Army. He lived most of his life in England or in one of the British provinces when his father was overseas. He enrolled in the university when he turned seventeen but he dropped out. He said he'd rather be a poor man in America than a man of wealth and privilege in England."

Sam added, "He once told me that in England an Irishman is expected to eat crow and proclaim it to be the finest cuisine he has ever tasted."

Tom and Kat took a train to Baltimore, where they spent another week. From Baltimore, they took a train to

Indianapolis and then south to Murfreesboro. A local farmer gave them a ride to Bridgeport. They hiked the rest of the way to the winter quarters.

By the time they reached home, as they thought of it, changes were already underway. XII Corps and XI Corps had been merged into a single Corps in the Army of the Cumberland. They would be designated XX Corps. Tom would still be in General Geary's division, and Kat would be part of his unofficial staff.

Tom made the acquaintance of Patrick Burns, a war correspondent for the *Philadelphia Inquirer*. When the two men introduced themselves, Burns said, "My mom is a Donal. Where are you from?"

"Philadelphia."

"I can see that. Where is your family from?"

"Northern Ireland. County Antrim. My father came to America in 1827."

"Mom's family is from Ayrshire."

"We're Scots," Tom said. "My family moved to Ireland when the crown offered free land to get British subjects to settle there. How did you get stuck out here?"

"General Sherman and I go way back. After his father died, our neighbors, the Ewings, took him in. I got to know him pretty well before he left for West Point."

Burns had little to offer despite his connections. He said, "They tell me less than they tell you. I get my information by listening to what men like you have to say."

Some news made it into the camp. In early March, Major General Banks undertook a campaign along the Red River in Louisiana. One of Tom's buddies opined, "If Banks is running that operation, the rebs will win for sure."

A month later, Banks sent his army into a Confederate trap and had to retreat without getting close to his objective, Shreveport.

A few days later, on April 12, a cavalry force under Confederate Major General Nathaniel Bedford Forrest recaptured Fort Pillow, a stronghold on the Mississippi River. The badly outnumbered Union garrison surrendered, but the Confederates killed three hundred of them, mostly colored troops. Witness accounts and forensic evidence supported a charge that prisoners of war had been massacred. But Forrest, backed by Confederate leadership, claimed the Union troops had refused to surrender. The episode hardened Union soldiers' attitude toward Southerners.

At the end of April, General Geary led an expedition down the Tennessee River to Guntersville, where the rebels appeared to be massing for an attack on Bridgeport. He defeated them and moved farther downriver to Triana, where the rebels were assembling a fleet of scows for their attack. He had the forty-seven boats broken up and burned.

Sherman's army pulled up stakes and started east on May 5. They paused at the Georgia border.

Burns found Tom sitting by a small fire, eating his dinner. "How's it feel to be on the march again?"

Tom pursed his lips and rocked his head. "Feels good to be doing something. But I'm not looking forward to what we're going to be doing."

Burns nodded. "This is a fight to the finish. Lincoln needs to put an end to the war if he hopes to get reelected in November. He picked Grant to take on Lee and destroy the Army of Northern Virginia. Looks like Grant ordered Sherman to destroy the Army of Tennessee. That should put an end to the rebellion."

44

Kennedy Takes a Wife

1864 came with high expectations. The Army of the Potomac had defeated Lee at Gettysburg, and had ended the year on the offensive. Meade had forced Lee into a fight, even though the commander had withdrawn from the field rather than send his troops into a pointless bloodbath.

The new year also brought the most convulsive reorganization in the history of the Union army. Veterans were going home as their enlistment expired. A reenlistment campaign offering a furlough and a bonus enjoyed some success. About as many men agreed to reenlist and continue the fight as decided to pack up and go home.

Recruits were arriving, but not in the numbers needed to replace the losses. Meade responded by consolidating divisions and brigades. Men whose old units were too small to fight effectively found themselves merged into new units with no history and no identity.

I Corps and III Corps were decommissioned and dismantled. Hancock returned to take command of II Corps. Warren was given command of V Corps. Sedgwick retained command of VI Corps.

The restructuring and the addition of green soldiers meant retraining officers, men, and units. Everyone spent hours on daily drills.

The routines were softened by the development of a social life. Wives and sweethearts came to visit the men in their winter quarters. Christmas was celebrated. Anything to put the men in a mood to enlist for another tour of duty.

The Army of the Potomac's winter camp stretched for miles in all directions from Brandy Station. The troops were housed in rows of huts, each eight feet by ten feet with wooden walls and a tent for a roof, organized by corps, division, brigade, regiment and company. Confederate infantrymen had started building the huts when they believed they would be spending their winter in the Iron Triangle. Union soldiers finished the project, and the symbolism was not lost on them.

It hadn't taken long. The men threw their energy into building the barracks whenever they were not occupied with training or other tasks.

Kennedy was left out in the cold. It was not intentional. He had been away on furlough, and no one thought to save a place for him. He made no effort to correct the situation. The cold spell would be over in a month or two, and they would be going after Lee again. He was confident he could endure the hardship until the spring campaign began.

When someone told him life in the barracks was warmer, he replied, "Not as cold." He grimaced and pointed out, "I put up with those boys all day long. I don't want to be locked up with them all night too."

The Irishman had been one of the first to reenlist. He had no family and no lover to ease his days. He took his furlough over Christmas and went straight to Washington, then on to Baltimore. His days were spent in a drunken orgy. He was kicked out of more than one whorehouse, and he spent a few nights in jail rent-free.

A week or so after Kennedy returned to camp, he was sitting in the dark by a small fire, fighting off the cold with a cup of coffee, when two soldiers escorting a woman approached. "She says she's your wife, corporal," one announced.

The other said, "But you're not married."

Kennedy scowled at the trio before rumbling, "I didn't consider it a real marriage. I was drunk at the time."

"Do you want us to get rid of her?"

Kennedy smiled sardonically. He shook his head. "I'll handle it."

The privates saluted and returned to their posts. "Ah, ye're a right sly one," the woman observed.

"And you're as enterprising as you are fetching."

The woman smiled and nodded appreciatively. The NCO said, "Refresh my memory. What's your name?"

"Roishin O'Grady."

His lips curled in a cynical smile. "Ah. Irish. Where are you from?"

"Limerick, I am, same as yerself, Seamus."

"Been lookin' into me?"

"A wee bit."

"Whatta you want?"

"A bite to ate, aye? And a spot to rest me bones."

"I've got coffee and hardtack."

"An' rashers an' beans, is it?"

"A little."

"I do be hearin' tell they've rations for the wives visitin' their fellas. Aye?"

"Which explains your fabrication."

"Aye."

Kennedy shook his head. The woman added, "And a spot to sleep. Aye?"

"I've thrown together a small one."

"Arrah, that'll be grand, so it will. I'm just a wee lass, I am."

"But I'm no monk."

"Ahhh, nor am I."

The corporal fixed his visitor with a poker-faced stare as he considered the situation. He'd have some explaining to do. He'd have to convince the captain that the marriage had slipped his mind. Might even have to sell it to the colonel. His recollection of their last encounter was foggy, but he didn't see that he had anything to lose. "Sit down. I'll get you something to eat." He passed his cup. "You'll have to share my coffee."

The woman made herself comfortable on the ground. She sat as close to the fire as she dared, although it might as well not have been there for all the heat it provided. When Kennedy began cooking the bacon and beans, Roishin ventured, "Ah, look, there's wan more wee thing."

He looked up and waited, expecting some preposterous demand. She said, "I'm needin' a hundred dollars, I am."

It took a minute, but he answered, "So you know about my bonus." He raised himself to his full height. "That's a lot of money for what you're offering."

"Ah, ye get what ye pay for."

"Never heard of anybody paying that much."

"They're payin' a one-off for a lass who's no mind for bein' shared, aye? I'm offerin' ye somethin' grander: exclusive an' unlimited, 'til ye strike camp altogether."

"It's still more than I'll be paid."

"Ah, sure, it's not for meself. It's for them good souls who lent a hand when they barely had two pennies to rub together."

Kennedy nodded toward the tent. "Would that be more or less than what I've got?"

"Yer a man now, so ye are. Yer pride's intact. And a bloody hero, yerself."

"No more than anyone else."

The woman patted the ground next to her. "Would ye be after takin' a load off right here?"

A petulant Kennedy sat on the opposite side of the fire, staring into her blue eyes. He said, "I've gone for days without food. We barely ate or slept for three days at Gettysburg. Then we marched a hundred miles in a week. Barefoot. I haven't been warm in weeks. If that's being a hero, your friends can have it."

"Sure and haven't ya been livin' in New York. Ye know the way the Irish live there. It's just as rough on thim as it is on yerself. But ye know yer fightin' to save our country. What do they have, tell me?"

Kennedy served the pork and beans on his plate and handed it to the woman, along with a fork. "Maybe they should go back to Ireland."

She sneered, "Is that what ye're thinkin'?"

"If they want work that gives them pride and manhood, they can join us. We could use the help."

She sulked, "Ah, ye're a fierce hard man, Seamus Kennedy."

"I'm doing what has to be done and I'm not asking for favors. I've got no use for those who want a handout but won't lend a hand."

Roishin pouted. He said, "If you want to share my bed, you're welcome to stay the night."

That's where the conversation died. She couldn't hold out any longer. Kennedy watched her tear into her meal. A little later, she shed her clothes and crawled under his blanket next to him.

At reveille, the woman rose, slipped into her coat, and went out to rekindle the fire. She was making coffee when Kennedy emerged from the tent with food for their breakfast.

"I'll be doin' the cookin'," she offered,

He shook his head. "It's part of my routine. Go get dressed."

They ate in silence. Kennedy cleaned up and stowed his utensils. He was on his way to morning muster when he stopped and turned to Roishin, "I'll be busy all day. I don't know what the other women do, but I'm sure you can figure it out."

Life went on like that for a week. Sometimes they talked. Sometimes they didn't. Kennedy didn't want to talk about the war, but he was interested in the scuttlebutt the woman picked up during the day. He also wanted to know about Ireland. His parents had never said much about the old country. His companion was more than happy to share her memories.

One evening, during a lull in the conversation, Kennedy said, "Are we married or not?"

She looked into his eyes and held his gaze briefly before looking down at the food on her plate. He was struck by her composure. She had to know what was coming. "You can't stay if we aren't. Either we go to the chaplain and do it proper or we go our separate ways."

"I'm thinkin' you'd make a grand husband, and meself, a fine wife, sure. The choice is all yours."

The next day, the couple stood before the chaplain and swore to have and to hold until death. Sergeant O'Hare and his wife witnessed the vows. The legal paperwork that changed Roishin's name from O'Grady to Kennedy was completed. She was officially the corporal's wife, entitled to the benefits of that position.

The weather warmed to tolerable, and life settled into a comfortable rhythm.

Sam Goldman looked up his buddy Jim Kennedy after returning from furlough. He was surprised to find a woman he didn't know and had never heard of eating dinner with the Irishman. He was stunned when his friend introduced her as his wife. Sam stood frozen in shock for a full minute before he managed, "Congratulations."

Jim could tell by the look on Sam's face that he wanted to say more. He tried to smooth things over by explaining that he had met Roishin while on furlough, and the two had hit it off immediately. But when it came out that the meeting had taken place in a whorehouse, Sam's expression changed from mild disapproval to stony rejection.

Kennedy turned to Roishin and said, "Sam and I need to take a walk."

She smiled and nodded.

Goldman was horrified by the development but toned down his rhetoric. He earnestly appealed to his friend's good sense. The situation would be a disaster if it wasn't corrected. But the marriage could probably be annulled.

Kennedy said, "I don't imagine you planned on spending your days shooting other men and your nights living like an animal when you were growing up." A look of disgust on Sam's face answered the question. Jim continued, "All she wanted was a good man and a brood of chiselers. That wasn't possible in our country."

The men walked in silence for a while. Kennedy said, "When she arrived in Baltimore, she had no money. She could starve or sell herself in a brothel. That is how we met. She's of the opinion that I could make a good husband and I'm sure she'll make a good wife." He turned and smiled at his friend. "What else do you need?" Sam gave him a forlorn smile but said nothing. Jim continued, "When life deals you a bad hand, you play it as best you can and hope the next one's better."

Goldman was forced to admit to himself that his initial judgment was overly harsh. Roishin was not garbage that no self-respecting man would touch. She could be a strong, daring woman ready to take on the world, like Kat. He also began to wonder about Sylvia. She chafed at rules imposed by society. Did she love him, or did she look at him as a man who could be a satisfactory provider and father of the children she wanted?

45

Grant Takes Charge

The war lumbered on. Inhospitable weather and unusable roads forced armies into hibernation, but planning and preparations took no holiday.

The Bureau of Military Information, the BMI, one of General Joseph Hooker's most important contributions to the war effort, had grown and matured. Its tentacles spread across the Confederacy. Spy networks and casual informants fed it a steady diet of facts and rumors. Contractors like former army sergeant Judson Knight ventured behind enemy lines and reported their findings to Meade and, later, to Grant. Knight also worked with Richmond socialite Elizabeth Van Lew, who gathered information from her friends while posing as a loyal Confederate.

In 1863, General Ulysses S Grant forced the surrender of Vicksburg, seizing control of the Mississippi River for the Federal Government. Then he secured control over Tennessee by driving Bragg off Missionary Ridge and forcing Longstreet to abandon his siege of Knoxville.

In October of that year, he was given command of the Military Division of the Mississippi with responsibility for three departments, each with its own army and area of responsibility. These departments had been operating independently since the beginning of the war. They took their orders from President Lincoln and the Commanding General of the Army. Grant's mission was to turn them into a single army reporting directly to him.

Burnside had taken command of the Department of the Ohio after the Fredericksburg disaster at the urging of President Lincoln. IX Corps, which he had commanded in South Carolina, was transferred to his new command. He developed XXIII Corps from troops recruited in Tennessee and Kentucky. At the end of 1863, Burnside and IX Corps were transferred to Annapolis, Maryland, to serve as a reserve unit. His replacement, General John Foster, was left with XXIII Corps and responsibility for protecting transportation routes and communication lines. Failing health forced him to resign after two months.

General John Schofield took over XXIII Corps, also known as the Army of the Ohio. He convinced Grant to ignore Longstreet, wintering in eastern Tennessee.

Sherman had returned to Vicksburg and command of the Army of the Tennessee with orders to clear rebels from territory east of the Mississippi River.

Thomas, now in command of the Army of the Cumberland, was ordered to drive Bragg's replacement, General Joseph E Johnston, out of Dalton, Georgia, and hold the city. He failed to achieve those objectives, but his initiative had two important results. The Confederates were unable to send troops from Dalton against Sherman. And Thomas gathered a key piece of intelligence that played an important role in forcing Johnston off Mountain Ridge a few months later.

When Josh Goldman visited his friends at the Army of the Potomac encampment, he said that reliable sources were predicting Grant would capture Atlanta, driving a stake into the heart of the Confederacy.

On February 6, II Corps was put on high alert. Men of the Third Division were rousted from their beds before dawn and ordered to cross the Rapidan at Morton's Ford, where the water was only waist deep. Kennedy led his squad of skirmishers through the frigid stream to a shallow ditch on the opposite shore, where they waited in the rain while an artillery battle raged and Confederate sharpshooters sent a steady stream of mini balls at them.

They pulled back across the river after dark, and Kennedy discovered the true benefit of having a wife. Roishin handed him a cup filled with whisky as soon as he reached the tent, and cooked his supper while he changed into dry clothes. She passed on what she had learned about his foray across the river as he devoured the meal. According to chatter making the rounds, the assault on Lee's lines was designed to prevent rebels from going to the aid of Richmond, while Butler led the Army of the James in an offensive against the rebel capital. However, his attack never materialized.

The Third Division had lost 260 men in a pointless exercise. Even worse, wives and girlfriends had spent an anxious day witnessing their men in action. That was enough to convince them that it was time for their loved ones to leave the army and come home. Veteran reenlistments dried up.

A few days later, news reached the Army of the Potomac that a hundred Union officers had escaped from Libby Prison. Half of them made it to safety. Less than a week later, news of the capture of Meridian, Mississippi, reached them. Sherman was occupying that vital industrial center. He burned it to the ground. Later, reports had Sherman tearing up railroad tracks and destroying bridges as he made his way back to Vicksburg. But his cavalry column, tasked with putting an end to the reign of terror by the Confederate cavalry under Forrest, was routed when the two forces clashed.

On February 22, a grand ball was held to celebrate George Washington's Birthday.

A week later, word spread through the camp that Ulysses S Grant had been promoted to lieutenant general and given command of the entire Union army.

The new commander was secretive in his planning. He shared what was necessary with those who needed to know. But some things were hard to hide. When Grant took the train to Washington to accept his promotion, Sherman accompanied him as far as Cincinnati.

Within days, Sherman replaced Grant as military commander of the Division of the Mississippi. He moved his base of operation from Vicksburg to Nashville. His protégé, General James McPherson, was promoted to commander of the Army of the Tennessee.

Butler was reinforced. That could only be interpreted as preparation for a new attack on Richmond.

Burnside was ordered to take IX Corps to Culpeper and join forces with the Army of the Potomac. The world watched and guessed at the reasoning behind that move.

Troops poured into Meade's camp throughout March and April. Roishin gathered from Kennedy's grumbling that they came in three classes. There were raw recruits - volunteers and draftees. Some were willing soldiers, but none were ready for the coming battles. Along with them came bounty men - recruits who had accepted money to stand in for a draftee. In Kennedy's opinion, they were more trouble than they were worth. They had no stomach for a soldier's life, but they had learned the hard way that those who tried to skip out on their commitment would be shot. That was the Union Army policy for dealing with deserters. NCOs like Kennedy preferred to use brutal punishments to persuade these men to do their jobs.

The third group were soldiers who had spent the war on garrison duty at posts far from the actual fighting. These men were trained. And they were willing, even though they had been pulled from plush assignments. But they were soft, and there wasn't enough time to condition them for the marching and fighting that lay ahead.

Kennedy vented his frustration one night. "We're getting ready to move, but we're not ready to fight. We're a mob pretending to be an army."

In April, Sherman moved his headquarters to Chattanooga. The Macon and Western railroad, struggling to supply Thomas's Army of the Cumberland, was swamped by the added demands of Sherman's Grand Army. The general was forced to take drastic measures to increase the volume of supplies that could be shipped on the single-track line. He put out an order restricting use of the railroad to military goods and passengers. He seized engines and cars from other lines for use on his line.

Josh Goldman joined his friends around a campfire a few days after Passover. Anticipation was thick in the air. Preparations had gone on for too long. The conditions had been right for a campaign for weeks. But nothing was happening.

The newspaperman filled his cup and took a seat. He left his audience in suspense while he sipped his coffee. "I hear the fun is about to begin. Grant has been working hard to set up a coordinated attack on the Confederates. You are going after Lee. At the same time, Sherman will be attacking Johnston while Butler threatens Richmond and Banks attacks Mobile."

His pronouncement was met with stunned silence. Men who had been eager to break camp and get back to the fighting were shocked by the vision of what lay ahead. The first response was, "What if Lee don't cooperate?"

Kennedy laughed. "He won't. But we're goin' after him anyway."

"The debate that I've heard," Josh said, "is whether to attack his right flank or his left flank."

Sam said, "Attacking his left flank is out of the question. Keeping an army supplied in those mountains is too big a challenge."

"So we're going back to Mine Run?" Kennedy asked.

Sam nodded. "Unless Grant is a fool."

46

The Wilderness – Again

On May 3, Grant reviewed the entire Army of the Potomac. Men and beasts spent the day showing themselves ready to march against Lee and his legions. Over dinner, Kennedy asked Roishin, "Did you see that?"

She smirked and nodded. He continued, "Do you think Lee won't notice we're comin'?"

"Ah, I don't be thinkin' it matters a wee bit. He knows what everyone else is knowin'. Grant's hare to bate him. An' bein' the man he is, he's lookin' forward to the grand ol' fight."

The NCO went out to check on every man in his command. He inspected their knapsacks and ordered them to pack light but carry as much ammunition and food as they could manage.

The Army of the Potomac stirred and began moving well before dawn to foil spies watching from nearby Clark Mountain.

Roishin made coffee and breakfast while Kennedy was dressing. After they had eaten, he held her and said, "We may never see each other again. I am glad for the time that we have had. And I hope that you will be waiting for me, if I make it back."

She reached up and pulled his head down to kiss him. "You'll be makin' it back, Seamus Kennedy. An' I'll be hare waitin'."

With that farewell, the corporal walked out to join his men for a march into The Wilderness. They crossed the Rapidan unchallenged. The few pickets guarding the fords scattered without firing a shot. V Corps, commanded by Warren, crossed at Germanna Ford and proceeded to the Orange Turnpike to take up a position on the army's left flank.

Sedgwick and VI Corps followed Warren across the river.

Hancock led II Corps across at Ely's Ford. It was late morning when he reached the burned-out remains of the Chancellorsville mansion.

Sporadic musket fire gave notice that Union scouts had encountered rebel pickets. The ground was littered with eerie reminders of Hooker's expedition a year earlier. For veterans like Kennedy, the old battleground kindled feelings of rage, disgust, horror, and even melancholy. Small clues brought back memories of friends lost in that battle.

The dead had been buried where they fell. Time and weather had worn away many of the shallow graves, exposing skeletal remains. Sergeant O'Hare put his men to work, burying the bones of those fallen warriors in more suitable graves. That evening, the soldiers sat around a fire, smoking their pipes. Veterans began to reminisce about Jackson's attack and its aftermath. The strongest memory was of fires and of wounded men trapped and burned alive. An old-timer said, "It's about to happen again. Them rebs are waitin' for us in those woods, and that's where we're gonna fight. When we do, the fire will claim its levy in human flesh."

That dire prediction was enough to end the discussion. Soldiers drifted off to get some sleep in spite of muskets firing fitfully in the distance.

II Corps began its march before daylight. Twenty-seven thousand strong. They took the Catharpin Road around the rear of the army to form the left wing. After six hours of marching on a warm sunny day, they paused for a short break at Todd's Tavern near the intersection with Brock Road. Carrying a loaded backpack and a musket was backbreaking work.

The pause was interrupted by a courier with orders for Hancock to go back and reinforce V Corps. The rebels had struck in force.

By the time II Corps reached the battle, Warren had repulsed the initial attack with the help of Getty's division from VI Corps.

The Confederates soon launched a fresh attack on Getty. Meade ordered Getty to counterattack. He was not going to lose another opportunity for a crucial victory.

Hancock ordered his troops into the fray. Sergeant O'Hare and the other NCOs drove their men toward the raging battle. Progress through tangled underbrush over uneven ground was agonizingly slow.

Confederates lying in wait for that offensive met Union brigades with a devastating broadside. Thousands of rebels hidden by the dense, jungle-like undergrowth fired as rapidly as they could, creating a hail of musket balls. The Yankees were stopped in their tracks, but they held and returned the barrage. A dense cloud of smoke enveloped the close-range firefight. Combatants, unable to see their adversaries, aimed at muzzle flashes.

II Corps reached the front line in time to blunt Confederate General Hill's attack, but the Yanks didn't live up to their reputation. Some fought, but many units folded in the face of a deadly rebel fusillade. When the Southerners pushed forward with overwhelming force, a stubborn Irish Brigade resisted the advance with bulldog determination.

Kennedy moved tirelessly along the line, shouting orders and yelling encouragement. He found himself stepping over and around the bodies of the dead and wounded. At some point, he came across his friend Sergeant O'Hare slumped against a tree with brains and blood oozing from a hole in his head. The sight brought him to an abrupt halt. Sympathy for the man's wife threatened to overwhelm him. But the Irishman had no time for such sentiments. He was now the senior NCO responsible for holding everything together.

Union soldiers, in full retreat, scrambled over hastily constructed breastworks at Brock Road and joined entrenched defenders. Hill's attack reached these defenses and faltered, then ground to a halt. The Southerners pulled back, their bloodlust suddenly drained. II Corps regrouped. Hancock prepared his troops for a long night and more fighting.

After the musket fire died down, an eerie silence settled over the battleground. Evening darkened to night, and men worn down by a long day of marching and fighting settled into an uneasy rest. Kennedy made the rounds, bracing them for another day of the same.

When he spotted a soldier, an outsider he recognized, he called, "Wilkerson. What are you doing here?"

"I wanted to see the battle."

"Well?"

"It wasn't what I expected."

"Maybe you'll have better luck tomorrow."

"I'm going back to my unit."

"You'll be staying with us, soldier."

"I'm Artillery. I'm going back to my unit."

"You've got a musket and cartridges. You look like Infantry to me." Kennedy flashed a broad grin. "The pickets won't let you pass even if I was willing to let you go. Your mates are sitting on their butts, taking up space and eating our food. We need fighters up here. You're staying."

A grizzled veteran, a private named Sam Smith, butted in, "Let'im go. The fight's over. We'll be headin' back to Brandy Station in the morning."

Kennedy shot a glare in his direction. "Not this time. Grant's in charge."

"We'll see," the old-timer growled.

Somebody else chimed in, "Yeah. What makes you think he's any different?"

"He beat them at Shiloh. He made them surrender Vicksburg and he chased them off Missionary Ridge. He ain't gonna quit just because he got punched in the mouth."

"He's never gone up against Lee."

"And Lee's never faced him." Kennedy wheeled and continued his tour of the troops.

Grant ordered an all-out attack to begin at five in the morning. It was just getting underway when the sound of musket fire coming from the right flank heralded a Confederate attack on Sedgwick.

II Corps had been reinforced with divisions from V Corps and VI Corps. Hancock sent thirty thousand men against Hill and drove him back over a mile. But his left flank collapsed in the face of a rebel counterattack. II Corps was forced back to the breastworks at Brock Road. Rebels stormed those defenses and breached them. Cannon fire from artillery pieces Hancock had brought forward ripped into the rebel horde. Union soldiers took on the Southerners. Beat them back and sent them running.

Darkness brought an end to the clash of arms but not to the terrors of the battle. The day's fighting had sparked fires that burned into the night, killing wounded fighters who could not make it to safety. Kennedy again made the rounds, getting his men ready for the battle that he was sure would begin at dawn.

Private Smith cackled, "We'll be heading back to Brandy Station in the morning."

Kennedy shook his head. "We're not goin' anywhere. We're here to fight Lee and that's what we're gonna do."

Another man said, "We been puttin' together a tally. Looks like Grant's lost twenty-five thousand."

Kennedy smirked. "How many did Lee lose?"

The man shrugged and shook his head.

Kennedy said, "We gave him as good as we got."

"Word is they captured two generals and their brigades," the old-timer countered.

Another private threw in, "I hear Longstreet's dead."

"I heard he was shot," Kennedy allowed. "I don't know if he's dead or alive."

"By his own men," the private chuckled. "Maybe they'll shoot Lee if we give them a few more days."

Kennedy laughed. "I wouldn't bank on it."

May 7 dawned wet and dreary. The orders for the day were to strengthen the defensive front. It was a break from the battle, but not a welcome one. Sometime in the afternoon, word began to spread that the wagons were being moved to Fredericksburg.

As the day wore on, rumors of a move spread through the ranks. Warren had been ordered to maneuver V Corps around II Corps and proceed south on Brock Road to the Spotsylvania Courthouse. Sedgwick and VI Corps were to follow. Sheridan was to clear the path for the infantry. Burnside was to take IX Corps on a roundabout route through Fredericksburg to Spotsylvania. Hancock and II Corps were to remain in place to camouflage the movements.

As soon as it was dark, V Corps began its march with Grant and Meade at the front. Shouts and cheers from II Corps greeted the generals when they turned south toward Richmond. Union soldiers were eager to continue their fight with the Confederates. But the road was blocked by two divisions of Union cavalry. They had returned and set up bivouac across Brock Road after driving Confederate pickets from bridges along Warren's route.

Meade ordered the horse soldiers to get out of the road so his infantry could pass. He sent a message to Sheridan informing him of the orders.

47

Laurel Hill and Spotsylvania Courthouse

Luck was with the Confederates on the morning of May 8. They took control of Laurel Hill and began digging in before Warren reached the crossroads. His attempt to drive the rebels from their works was unsuccessful. An assault by Sedgwick and VI Corps that afternoon also failed.

Grant continued maneuvering to get around Lee's right flank. VI Corps set up to the left of V Corps. When Burnside arrived, he positioned IX Corps to the left of VI Corps. Lee mirrored these developments, reinforcing his right flank as troops reached the standoff.

The battle lines extended south and east six miles from Laurel Hill, past the Spotsylvania Court House and the Zion Church to the banks of the Po River near Critchfield.

Judson Knight led a patrol around Laurel Hill in the opposite direction to reconnoiter the Confederate left flank. He found an unprotected route into Lee's rear and reported the situation to Grant.

On the afternoon of May 9, Hancock received orders to move against the Confederates. He marched due south from Todd's Tavern, aiming to bypass the Southerners' defenses and attack their rear. II Corps reached the Po River upstream from the Confederate position the next morning. They constructed a pontoon bridge, and twenty-five thousand soldiers, with their artillery and wagons, crossed the stream. But the river curved back on itself. The Federals would have to make a second crossing the following day.

When Hancock reached the second crossing of the Po, he found rebels massed and entrenched on a rise overlooking the river. He reported to headquarters that a successful crossing would not be possible. By midmorning, that report, along with other scouting reports, led Grant to believe Lee had weakened his line to counter the threatened assault by II Corps. Adapting to the new situation, he ordered an all-out attack against the center of the Confederate line. II Corps would spearhead the assault with VI Corps on the left and V Corps on the right.

Hancock set out as ordered, leaving Barlow's division to menace Lee's left flank. The Confederates attacked the isolated division while Hancock was maneuvering into position for Grant's assault on Laurel Hill. The II Corps commander had to go back to support his stranded division, which was fighting a valiant retreat against a much larger rebel force.

After making it back to the safety of the Union defenses, Kennedy organized his men. With more rain on the way, pitching tents and cooking food became the top priorities, but they had to be ready for another attack. The sergeant assigned a rotating guard. Four hours on and eight hours off. Then he took care of his own needs.

After resting for a few hours, he looked up some buddies to catch up on the news. General John Sedgwick had been felled by a sniper bullet the day before. One sergeant muttered darkly, "If they did the same to Burnside, they'd be doin' us a big favor."

A dour voice quipped, "That won't happen. Old Muttonchops is staying out of this fight."

"Lee couldn't have attacked you this morning if Burnside was doing his job, Jim," another pointed out.

Kennedy grimaced. He'd heard bad things about General Ambrose Burnside, but he knew the man was in favor with Grant because he had held off Longstreet at Knoxville. Kennedy studied the rebel position on the hill in the distance. He shook his head. The Johnnies had fought them to a draw in The Wilderness and then beat them to Laurel Hill, and captured that vital piece of real estate. He pointed at the precipice and asked, "How come we're not of up there?"

A young sergeant who looked like he had just started shaving explained, "It was tough, Jim. We had to cross a creek on a narrow bridge. That slowed us down and gave the seceshes a chance to get ready for us. They were waiting behind a barricade they had thrown up. We chased them off and cleared the logs. A little farther down the road we ran into another barricade. We cleared it. That went on all night."

Kennedy said, "So you got here after daybreak ready to sit down to breakfast."

The sergeant continued, "We could see they were already on top of the hill digging trenches. Warren decided to attack. He sent us up and they sent us back with our tails between our legs. Warren wasn't ready to quit. He sent us back up, but the Johnnies held their ground. We couldn't push them out of their trenches."

An older sergeant said, "We were too tired. We'd been of marching and fighting all night. Taking that hill was a job for fresh legs." He paused and studied the tent that was serving as a makeshift roof. Between that canopy and some clever drainage, the spot where the men sat was dry. The sergeant puckered his lips and rocked his head. When he had fully considered his words, he said, "Warren sent a report to Meade explaining the situation. The Old Man told him to let us rest. VI Corps was on the way. Warren was to cooperate with Sedgwick in the next assault. Warren exploded. He didn't care who was in charge as long as somebody was. He had no intention of cooperating with anybody."

The younger NCO continued, "The Old Man insisted those were his orders. When Sedgwick began his assault that afternoon, all he got from Warren was token support. And that, Jim, is why we're not up there."

Kennedy snorted, "Cooperate?" He shook his head in disgust. "I'll wager they don't teach that at West Point."

Sam Goldman had joined the group. He said, "Meade had a busy day. He got into it with Sheridan. They were so loud everybody heard every word. It sure sounded like insubordination."

"But Grant shrugged it off and sent the cavalry on a mission to tear up tracks," the old sergeant said.

The Union assault on the Confederate center had been ineffective without Hancock's leadership, but there was a bright spot. VI Corps had succeeded against the west face of the Mule Shoe, a bubble protruding from the other-wise dead straight, east-west line of defense developed by the Southerners. The salient bristled with artillery and rifle pits, making it formidable and dangerous. It had thwarted Grant's attack on the center of Lee's line.

Like all salients, it was vulnerable to attacks against its sides. A colonel from VI Corps led his brigade through the trees to a launch point within two hundred yards of the rebel position. Union troops swept aside the abatis protecting the bubble and stormed the parapets, attacking the defenders with bayonets. The shocked rebels abandoned their pits and their guns but quickly reorganized and counterattacked. The colonel was forced to pull his brigade back to Union lines.

The next day was miserable. Overcast with occasional rain. All hands were assigned to digging trenches and building up fortifications. Skirmishes broke out up and down the line throughout the day. Late in the afternoon, it became clear that something was afoot. According to rumors, II Corps was going to assault the Mule Shoe.

At ten o'clock, Hancock formed up the troops. Barlow led the midnight march over narrow, muddy trails through dense woods in pouring rain. When they reached IX Corps headquarters, the predicament was clear. No one knew how to get to the launch point.

They marched back through the dense, overgrown wood-land until someone stumbled on the right trail. At two in the morning of the twelfth, the division reached the launch point and paused. Soldiers were told to rest until it was time for the attack. Bone-weary men found a patch of soggy ground and tried to sleep despite the rain.

At 4:30, Barlow's division charged the salient in the Confederates' defensive line. Pioneers ripped abatis out of the way to speed the infantry charge. Overwhelmed defenders gave way with only token resistance. But once inside the redoubt, the attackers quickly degenerated into a chaotic mob. Regiments pushed up against each other and units jumbled together. In spite of the disarray, they were able to capture men and artillery pieces.

A counterattack drove them back, wiping out most of the gains. Union resistance stiffened as soldiers retreated to the edge of the Mule Shoe. When the Yanks reached the hastily constructed wooden fence that outlined the stronghold, they made their stand. The Confederate charge slammed into an unyielding Union line.

Suddenly the war, the battle between two armies, disintegrated into a thousand struggles between men separated by a crude wooden barrier. The two sides were so close that the combatants fired their muskets without aiming. Load, point and pull the trigger. The mini-ball would hit something. Antagonists leaned over the fence and shot their foes point blank. The two sides were close enough that bayonets often worked as well as bullets. Heroic men stood atop the barrier, fired a musket, and handed it to a buddy on the left while reaching for a fresh musket from a buddy on the right until they themselves were shot down.

If a man didn't have time to reload, he used his musket as a club. Kennedy barely moved from the spot where he had planted his boots to take on the rebel onslaught. He shattered three muskets before the day was over. Each time, he was able to grab another weapon lying nearby and continue fighting.

The battle went on into the night. Sometime after midnight, the Confederates withdrew to a freshly constructed defensive line. The Union troops set up to defend their position along the Mule Shoe perimeter. The ground on both sides of the fence was piled deep with the dead and dying.

Many of the wounded were trapped under their lifeless comrades. No help would be coming that night.

The sun was high overhead when Lieutenant Agee had Kennedy dragged from his tent. The NCO pulled himself to attention despite screaming pain in his left leg. His head throbbed with the worst hangover he had ever had. "Why aren't you up there with the rest of your unit, corporal?" Agee demanded.

Kennedy winced and shook his head. "I don't know, sir."

"I've got a report that you deserted."

"Can you tell me what's going on, sir?"

"Dereliction of duty. You abandoned your post last night."

Kennedy shook his head again, trying to get his bearings. He recalled being in a slugfest with the rebs, but he couldn't remember how it ended. The lieutenant stared at a bloody streak along Kennedy's left thigh. "What happened to your leg?"

Kennedy looked down. His muddy, disheveled uniform had a bloody tear right where his thigh shrieked in protest and threatened to buckle. "I don't know, sir."

The officer slowly circled his quarry. He paused near Kennedy's right shoulder. "What happened to your head?"

"I don't know, sir." But more details of the fight were coming back. He might have been hit on the head.

Agee pushed blood-matted hair aside and inspected the damage. A diagonal gash across a good-sized lump was visible. "I guess that explains it. Lucky you've got a thick skull, that would 'a killed anybody else. Find a medic and see what he can do for you."

The officer wheeled and started in search of his next victim. Kennedy found a branch he could use as a crutch to keep the weight off his injured leg and limped to headquarters in search of a medic. He wished with all his heart that Kat was there to take care of him. He trusted her above all others.

The medics were little help. The sergeant's cuts and bruises would heal on their own. A mini ball had left a nasty gash on his left leg. They bandaged the wound and sent him back to his tent with orders to stay off his feet for a few days.

When he reached the tent, Kennedy discovered a letter.

Seamus, darling, I've made it to Fredericksburg. They're saying there's no use going further. Ye'd be having no time for the likes of me with the constant fighting. I'm working as a char-woman, to justify me being here. There is that much blood and misery, it's impossible to do all that needs doing. I visit with the wounded and write letters, just to take a breath from the constant drudgery. Yesterday, one of the lads asked me name. When I told him, he says his sergeant was a Kennedy. I had to walk away before I burst into tears. I came back today and told him my husband is Corporal Kennedy. He says, 'That's the one, but he's Sergeant Kennedy now'. I know ye were alive just a few days ago, and I believe with all me heart ye'll be alive to hold me the next time we meet. Love, Roishin.

Kennedy tore a sheet of paper from a diary he kept in his rucksack. He stared at it for a while before writing.

Roishin, I am indeed alive and your intelligence is correct. There have been lulls but the fighting has not stopped for over a week. When we are not fighting, we are marching. There is no place for tenderness in this hellhole. Sergeant O'Hare was killed in the fighting in The Wilderness a week ago and I have taken over his responsibilities. Nothing has been said about a promotion. Your letter was a wonderful tonic. I will keep it pinned over my heart for protection in what promises to be a long, bloody battle. Love, Seamus.

The days that followed were torture. Idleness did not suit the Irishman but there was little to do. He forced himself to get out and walk around. He scrounged up enough whiskey to fill a canteen. He started reading the novel *Rob Roy* by the Scottish writer Sir Walter Scott. It was a gift Roishin had stuffed in his knapsack when he wasn't looking. He picked up bits of news. II Corps was taking up a position between VI Corps and V Corps. Then, V Corps was ordered to attack Lee's right flank but couldn't pull it off. Unrelenting rain and muddy conditions made maneuvers like that almost impossible.

On his third day, he helped move some of the wounded to the back so they could be transported to a field hospital. He got to witness the arrival of several thousand green troops. Replacements for those lost in the recent fighting. Heavy artillery men pulled from garrison duty around Washington and thrust into a shooting war as infantrymen. Their spotless uniforms with carefully polished brass drew unwanted attention from scruffy, bloodied veterans waiting to have their wounds treated.

One of the vets said, "That's sixteen thousand fresh troops to fill our ranks."

Another responded sourly, "It won't take Grant more than a day to get them killed."

Two days later, Meade ordered another assault on the Mule Shoe, or as it had come to be known among the troops, the Bloody Angle. II Corps spearheaded the assault. VI Corps was on the left and V Corps on the right. The rebels had used the two day respite to beef up the works they had hastily constructed on the night of May 12. The Union assault never got close. Halfway up the hill, Hancock's men were subjected to a firestorm of musketry and artillery.

Union soldiers raced back down the slope, chased by screaming, bloodthirsty rebels.

That was the last straw for Kennedy. He took himself off sick leave and reported for duty. He got back to his unit just in time to learn that II Corps was marching south for a sweep around the Confederates' right flank to cut them off from Richmond.

Lee struck first. He attacked Meade's right flank, where the inexperienced heavy artillery troops were stationed. They were green, but they fought. They held off the rebels long enough for reinforcements to reach them. The Southerners withdrew with nothing meaningful to show for their effort.

Goldman stopped by to see how Kennedy was doing. He brought news of a victory. Sheridan had crushed JEB Stuart. The Confederate cavalry hero had been killed in the melee. Kennedy nodded. "A week ago. I heard about it."

Goldman gave a slight nod. Kennedy said, "I heard we outnumbered the rebs three to one. Seems like Sheridan could've left a division to support us."

Goldman said, "The rest of the news is bad. Grant's not getting the support he planned on."

Kennedy said, "I heard something about fresh troops underway to reinforce Lee."

"Our men in the Shenandoah aren't fighting," Goldman groused. "Sickles turned tail and ran."

"That's what he does," Kennedy muttered.

"A token force of Confederates is blocking Butler and his army."

"Wasn't he supposed to be attacking Petersburg?"

Goldman smirked. "He was. But he can't. The Army of the James is as useless as tits on a bull."

"So, Richmond can spare troops to reinforce Lee."

"They're on their way," Goldman said.

Grant had a new plan to get around Lee and attack Richmond. V Corps and VI Corps maneuvered into new positions while the rest of the army worked on entrenchments. II Corps pulled back from the front to an open field where many of the men hoped to get a good night's sleep after weeks of fighting and marching. Instead, they learned they would be marching south that night.

Wagons with food and fodder pulled onto the field. Each man was issued rations for six days. Then, wagons with ammunition pulled up. Men filled their cartridge belts. Each man received sixty rounds.

After dinner, Kennedy joined a group trying to puzzle out the meaning of it all. Everyone agreed that there was no hope of pushing the rebels from their entrenchments, but none believed another flanking maneuver would be successful. One man pointed to a circle on the map and looked up. "Telegraph Road is the best route and they've got a brigade blocking it. They can use it. We can't."

"That's why we're marching tonight. We're going around them."

"No chance. They already know we've pulled back. It won't take them long to figure out we're on the move."

A horse soldier who had joined the group said, "They not only control the best route, they have entrenchments set up all the way to Richmond."

Kennedy asked, "What are we supposed to do?"

"Use the cavalry. We can take Petersburg, but we can't hold it. Send Sheridan down to attack the city while you race down to reinforce us. Between the cavalry and II Corps we could hold the city forever."

"Spoken like a true cavalier."

"Has anybody explained this to Grant?"

48

Resaca

Bragg had taken his demoralized troops to Dalton after the crushing defeat on Missionary Ridge. General Joseph Johnston replaced him as commander of the Army of Tennessee and began the rebuilding process. When it became clear that Sherman was getting ready to attack, he moved to a defensive position on Rocky Face Ridge.

By the beginning of May, the three components of Sherman's army were in position near Ringgold, Georgia - Thomas in the center, Schofield on the left, and McPherson on the right.

On May 7, XX Corps spearheaded the movement south along the rail line toward Dalton. Rebels mounted stiff resistance at Tunnel Hill. IV Corps and XIV Corps maneuvered around the fight and continued the march on Dalton, where the Confederate Army of Tennessee was reportedly encamped.

A cavalry brigade under the command of Colonel Oscar LaGrange cleared the way for the infantry and captured Varnell's Station. The next day, LaGrange continued to Dalton. Entrenched rebels overwhelmed the single brigade of horse soldiers, capturing the colonel and many of his troops.

On May 8, Sherman established a line opposing Johnston's position along Rocky Face Ridge. Schofield, at the north end, facing the Confederate right flank. Howard and Palmer extended the Union line around to the west and south. Hooker led XX Corps to a position at Mill Creek Gap on the Confederate left flank. His Second Division under Geary continued beyond the rebel line to Dug Gap.

One of Schofield's brigades scaled the mountain and reached the top near the north end. It pushed south along the crest, driving rebel pickets as it went. After advancing a mile, the Yanks encountered a strong Confederate force dug in atop a steep rise. Finding themselves in a dangerous position on a narrow ledge, they retreated.

Tom led an assault through Dug Gap at the south end of the mountain. The regiment trekked through underbrush, over broken ground, until they reached a ledge. On the other side of that narrow foothold was a sheer wall, blocking any further advance by the Union soldiers.

While Thomas and Schofield battered the mountain with artillery and sent skirmish lines to pressure the Southerners along Rocky Face Ridge, McPherson took the Army of the Tennessee around the rebels' left flank. He made a feint toward Rome before heading south to Snake Creek Gap, a narrow pass through the Chattanooga Mountains. It was unguarded, as Thomas had predicted.

On May 9, McPherson marched his army of twenty-three thousand through the five mile long gorge on trails made by local farmers, trekking with their livestock and wagons along the shelf between the stream and the mountains. On their left, Snake Creek, an insignificant stream emptying into the Oostanaula River, and on their right, sheer slopes rising to the sky.

He set up camp at the south entrance, planning to continue to the nearby town of Resaca in the morning. There, he would destroy existing rebel supplies and tear up track, preventing the Western and Atlantic Railroad from delivering fresh supplies.

However, Confederate reinforcements from Alabama and Mississippi had been streaming into Resaca while Union forces were marching through Snake Creek Gap.

At dawn on May 10, McPherson dispatched two divisions under Dodge to take Resaca and destroy the railroad tracks as planned. The detachment was confronted by Confederate cavalry almost as soon as it left camp. Outnumbered rebels retreated but kept the delaying action going throughout the morning and into the early afternoon.

The Union raiding party reached a crossroads west of the town at two o'clock. Dodge left one division as a rear guard and pressed on. He captured a bastion called Bald Hill near the town's defensive perimeter and sent the rest of the division under McSweeney to tear up tracks south of the train station.

McPherson caught up with Dodge a couple of hours later. The unexpected presence of the enemy in large numbers at a small outpost only a few miles from Johnston's stronghold concerned him. Unwilling to risk being pulled into a fight with a superior force, he ordered his troops to return to their bivouac at the south end of Snake Creek Gap and sent a report on the situation to Sherman.

The army commander responded by issuing orders for his infantry to march on Resaca. Over the next two days, Thomas, followed by Schofield, joined McPherson at the south end of Snake Creek Gap. Soldiers stocked up three days' supplies in their haversacks and began moving toward the town. The supply wagons remained in the gap.

Mac found Tom and a few other men gathered around a fire, discussing the situation. The newcomer groused, "We should be down there in the town living off rebel supplies right now."

One of the men said, "The Old Man was pretty pissed when he heard what happened."

Tom shook his head. "He must've gotten over it. According to the version I heard, all he said to McPherson was you missed the chance of a lifetime."

Mac said, "Doesn't matter. Johnston's come down off the mountain and set up in Resaca. His whole army's waiting for us behind a strong line of entrenchments."

The Confederate line was anchored on the Oostanaula River and swung in an arc along Camp Creek, a slow-moving, marshy stream, to the Conasauga River.

On May 14, Sherman set out to encircle the Confederate army. McPherson was sent against the left flank with orders to capture the town and tear up the railroad tracks. He recaptured Bald Hill, a strategic summit for placing artillery, and held the position against repeated rebel counterattacks. But the railroad tracks curved away from the river and were now behind enemy lines.

Thomas used local country roads to get around McPherson and line up on his left.

Schofield followed Thomas but continued farther north before heading cross-country toward the rebels' right flank. Marching over broken ground was arduous. Dragging artillery caissons without the benefit of roads was worse.

Howard set up next to Schofield, anchoring the left flank. Hooker was held in reserve.

When his forces were lined up along the west bank of Camp Creek, Sherman gave the order to move forward. The right side of the line made a successful crossing. Palmer captured the bridge over the creek and dug in on the east bank.

Schofield had mixed success. His leftmost division, led by Cox, crossed the stream and established a beachhead on the east bank. But his right wing was hit with enfilading crossfire and forced to retreat after taking heavy losses.

Howard crossed the creek and connected with Cox. But the whole army was too far to the right. Howard couldn't anchor his left flank on the Conasauga River. Confederate forces attacked the weakness. Sherman ordered Hooker forward to reinforce Howard.

Tom and his comrades charged through a waist deep marshy bog in a race to prevent disaster.

The rebels got there first and overran Howard's left flank.

Schofield's artillery opened up with double canister rounds to slow the onslaught. XX Corps slammed into the attacking Confederates, driving them back in fierce close combat.

Johnston had his troops attack Union positions all along the line in front of Resaca. Sherman's men held their ground.

On the morning of May 15, Sherman ordered Schofield to pull back from the center and slide behind Hooker to extend the Union line to the river. The two great armies waged a ferocious battle in front of the small Georgia village throughout the day.

Johnston slipped away that night. He marched his men south along the railroad tracks to Adair.

The next morning, Sherman took possession of Resaca. He ordered Thomas to pursue the Southerners and force them to keep moving. The rebel cavalry held off the Yankee pursuit with a heroic fighting retreat.

49

May 16, 1864

My Dearest Mother,

The mail finally caught up with us and I received your letters. After a week of fighting, we are back to chasing the rebels. They are on the run. That's what they do best. I am a little worse for wear but otherwise in good health. In answer to your question, I have not seen much of Kat since we got back from furlough. For the past week, I have been directly engaged with the seceshes, and the action has provided her with more than enough work. I did have occasion to visit with her last night, and she was in good health. She sends her love.

We had the rebels surrounded twice, and twice they slipped away before we could finish them off.

I have heard that Grant tangled with Lee at Chancellorsville and did no better than Hooker.

It appears this war is going to continue for a while longer. At least I can't see how it will be brought to a close.

Your devoted son,

Tom

50

Kingston

The Confederate Army of Tennessee fled south through Georgia along the Western and Atlantic Railroad tracks, which ran through Calhoun, Adair and Kingston before turning east toward Cassville. Bridges were available for crossing the Etowah River south of Kingston.

The Army of the Cumberland pursued along that same railroad with Howard in the lead.

Schofield was sent east to cross the Oostanaula at Newton. McPherson was ordered to travel west to Rome before crossing the river.

When Howard reached Calhoun around noon on May 17, he encountered stiff resistance from the Confederate rearguard. As the rebels retreated, they threw up a series of hastily constructed barriers to challenge and slow the Union advance. They kept up their resistance all the way to the outer defenses around Adairsville, where they joined the main army behind stout entrenchments.

Howard sent a division against the rebel works. It was repulsed. He was preparing to try again when Thomas arrived and ordered him to stand down and dig in. They were within striking distance of the city.

By nightfall, Hooker had encamped in close support of Howard. Schofield was ten miles to the east, and McPherson was six miles to the west.

That night, word spread through the Army of the Cumberland that there would be a big battle in the morning. A showdown with the Johnnies. Men made preparations for what they expected to unfold in a few hours.

But the trenches were empty when the Federals advanced on the town. Johnston had withdrawn during the night. Two roads headed south from Adairsville. The main road, the one more suitable for a large army, led to Kingston. The other road led southeasterly to Cassville. It was clear that Johnson had split his army between those roads, but Sherman could only guess at his strategy.

Sherman's grand army was divided and vulnerable. The Old Man hoped to entice an offensive strike that could lead to a decisive battle. He was certain the Army of the Cumberland was a match for the Army of Tennessee. And he had no doubt his generals could handle any attack Johnston could throw at them.

Thomas marched toward Kingston on the broader, more direct road. Hooker took a route leading to Cassville, six miles east of Kingston. Schofield continued his westward march on a diagonal road toward Cassville. McPherson followed diagonal roads from Rome to Kingston.

Thomas entered Kingston on the morning of May 19. He ordered Howard to extend the left flank toward Cassville and connect with Hooker.

The deployment was interrupted when IV Corps encountered a large force of Confederate troops in battle formation. They were in an open area bounded by Two Mile Run Creek, a small stream running north of Cassville and south of Kingston before emptying into the Etowah River. The Yanks quickly deployed into a defensive line, expecting a charge by the rebels. But the Southerners pulled out of their offensive posture and retreated toward Cassville.

This intelligence brought Sherman at a gallop.

By the time the commander reached the battlefront, Thomas had taken charge, and IV Corps was posted in a line of battle, in preparation for an assault on Cassville. Trees blocked the view, concealing rebel strength and activity within the town, but on the hills behind it, the Southerners were entrenching and preparing for a fight.

Union forces converged on the town. Hooker encamped along Two Mile Run Creek near a seminary on the outskirts of Cassville. Schofield came up on his left. McPherson was ordered to bypass Kingston and come up on Thomas's right. Thomas pushed his line forward to the edge of the settlement. The Union army was in position for a showdown in the morning.

Skirmishing continued through the night. Sherman moved back from the front line to get away from musket balls whizzing all about his soldiers. But he stayed nearby and slept on the ground.

Federal troops were aroused before daybreak to make final preparations for the big battle. The assault began at dawn. It was too late. The Confederates had abandoned their works and started south.

Schofield sent General Gregg and his cavalry in pursuit. After a brief encounter near Cartersville, the Southerners escaped across the Etowah River, burning bridges so the Federals could not follow.

Sherman paused his march in Kingston to prepare for the next phase of the campaign. His army needed rest. The railroads and bridges had to be repaired. And the Southern general would be making his stand in Allatoona Pass, where he could hold off the Northern army indefinitely.

51

May 22, 1864

My Dearest Mother,

We are resting after weeks of fighting and marching. We chased the rebels about 30 miles to Kingston, which is a railroad town. They were setting up to give us battle at Adairsville and again at Cassville, but each time, they pulled out overnight and fled south. They have now crossed the Etowah River. It looks like we are in for more marching and fighting.

We laid over for three days in Kingston. The railroad had to be repaired so we could get fresh supplies. Then we had to stock up so we could go a week or more without additional supplies. I have heard the Confederates are entrenched in Allatoona Pass, and General Sherman plans to lead us around them. But we need control of that pass so our trains can bring us supplies.

Civilians had abandoned Kingston by the time we got here. They left a lot of stuff behind when they pulled out. I have been reading through the Southern newspapers. Half the time, they think their General Johnston is a coward for not fighting us. The other half, they think he is a genius leading us into a trap. We think we could march into a trap and still beat them. I guess we'll find out.

We are getting some news of the war in Virginia. The fighting in The Wilderness and at Spotsylvania was bloody, according to what I heard. The troops in the Shenandoah Valley seem to lack enthusiasm. I guess the main thing is that Lee can't help Johnston, and Johnston can't help him.

We had to cross the river naked last week because the water was above our waists. I was in up to my neck part of the time. We stripped down and carried our clothing and equipment on our heads so the stuff wouldn't get wet.

Your devoted son,

Tom

52

North Anna

"We were now to operate in a different country from any we had before seen in Virginia. The roads were wide and good, and the country well cultivated. No men were seen except those bearing arms, even the black man having been sent away. The country, however, was new to us, and we had neither guides or maps to tell us where the roads were, or where they lead to.... Our course was south, and we took all roads leading in that direction which would not separate the army too widely."

The Complete Personal Memoirs of Ulysses S. Grant

At ten o'clock on the night of the twentieth, Hancock started his men south. The mission was to threaten the Richmond Fredericksburg and Potomac Railroad, Lee's source of supplies and communications with the Confederate capital. General Alfred Tolbert and a small cavalry stitched together from state militia units led the way, clearing pickets and screening the infantry's movements.

Guinea Station was their first target. A rebel infantry regiment guarding the rickety wooden bridge that led to the station retreated across the river and set up a defensive position on the south bank as soon as the cavalry showed up. Tolbert left Union pickets in place on the north bank before continuing his march.

When Hancock got to the crossing, he decided against an assault on the train station. Continuing south, he reached Milford Station at noon the following day. He had it burned to the ground before setting up camp for the night.

A telltale dust cloud hung in the air off to the west. One of the soldiers grumbled, "That horse soldier was right. They'll be down there waiting for us."

Kennedy smirked. "Unless we're heading for Petersburg."

"Grant ain't that smart."

"Hooker wanted to get Lee away from Chancellorsville and The Wilderness. We put that behind us weeks ago. Burnside wanted to take Fredericksburg and drive on to Richmond. We're on our way to Richmond now."

"But we've been taking a beating."

Kennedy scoffed. "So has Lee. When he realized Grant was sending us south, he had to figure we were trying to get around behind him. He sent troops to block us. We'd be shooting it out with them right now, if they thought they could beat us."

"He wants us to keep charging his trenches and getting shot to pieces."

Kennedy shook his head. "Lee's aggressive. He'll attack if he sees an opportunity. Grant gave him one. Us against the Army of Northern Virginia. Lee should have attacked. Instead, he matched Grant by sending a division to block us."

II Corps stayed another day at Milford Station waiting for orders.

A letter reached Kennedy during the layover:

Me Dearest,

I trust this missive finds ye well. We've upped sticks from Fredericksburg and landed in Port Tobacco, a wee village it is, with docks on the Rappahannock River. I'm hearing the move shortens our supply lines, which means I'm a bit nearer to ye, glory be!

Sure, the work's the same auld grind, no different, and there's too much of it by half.

The war news is grim. Grant's still battling, but the Confederates are a stubborn lot, too. I've had a yarn or two with prisoners and deserters, and these lads are weary of the war, clothes tattered, bellies empty! Many were against it from the get-go. It's always the poor lads who suffer and die for the whims of them wealthy eejits.

I pray each night that this war ends quick. I long for the day we can be together, building a life that was denied us back in our homeland.

All me love,

Roishin.

He answered:

"My sweet Rose,

You are a blessing, a gift from heaven. From what you have told me, I think what we see here is very much like what we would see in our own country. Most of the men are gone. Caught up in the war I suppose. The women and children are poorly dressed. They blame us and hate us with a passion. I think these women would invite us to their bed so they could cut our throats while we slept.

Our latest march took us through Caroline County, a beautiful rural area. It seems to have escaped the ravages of war until we arrived. Our soldiers helped themselves to the bounty of local farmers. We feasted on mutton and ham, vegetables and fruits. This foraging was against regulations but no one tried to stop it. The women we encountered sneered and said, "Y'all think y'all are going to Richmond. Y'all's bones will be in the ground before y'all lay eyes on that city."

The taunts and other displays of hostility enraged our troops. They were ready to torch Bowling Green, the county capital. We prevented it, but only with great difficulty.

The march has given us a break from the constant roar of artillery and musketry. We haven't had to worry about sharpshooters. Even the rain has held off. Of course, with so many men moving in formation, dust is stirred up and hangs in the air. We breathe it and choke on it while the summer sun bakes us to a crisp. There is no escaping the misery.

Yours always, Seamus."

V Corps pulled back from Spotsylvania on the morning of the twenty-first and reached Guinea Station that night.

VI Corps and IX Corps stayed put an additional day to keep Lee in place, so Hancock and Warren could get a good head start.

Burnside left Spotsylvania about the same time Warren was arriving at Guinea Station. Wright followed him. They were supposed to march down Telegraph Road, the shortest route, but they encountered entrenched rebels and turned east toward Guinea Station. This change in the plans forced Warren to shift V Corps west to Harris's Store.

On May 23, with his army lined up in a wide arc, Grant issued orders for movements against the Confederates encamped south of the North Anna River. V Corps and VI Corps were to cross at Jericho Ford. IX Corps was to follow them. II Corps was to advance to Chesterfield Ford.

The supply wagons and ambulances remained at Milford Station.

The river was over a hundred feet wide, with steep banks on either side. At Jericho Mills Ford, it narrowed to fifty feet. It was only waist-deep there, but the banks were still formidable. The ridge on the south bank dominated that on the north, making it an ideal position to defend.

Warren reached the ford in the early afternoon and had a pontoon bridge laid in for a crossing. He ordered his First Division to wade across while the bridge was assembled. These movements went forward without opposition from the Confederates. By late afternoon, V Corps had gained the ridge above the river on the south bank, but before it could establish its defensive perimeter, rebels emerged from a ravine and charged across the open space. The Union Third Division gave way. Soldiers ran for their lives back toward the river and the bridge.

The Second Division under Griffin stood its ground, but the attack on its suddenly exposed right was taking a toll.

A brigade of fresh troops just arriving on the ridge rushed forward to shore up the crumbling right flank. An artillery colonel on the north bank quickly unlimbered his guns and poured double canister into the charging Confederates. The Southerners pulled back to their ravine. They withdrew from the field during the night.

When Hancock reached Chesterfield Ford, he discovered the bridge was protected by a small garrison of Southern soldiers lodged in a crude fort. He notified Grant, who ordered him to take control of the crossing but stay on the north side of the river.

The task fell to the Irish Brigade. Hancock had the redoubt shelled before the actual assault began. The Irish, led by Kennedy, quickly crossed the open ground but couldn't scale the walls. The sergeant had his men use their bayonets to make a dirt platform so they could mount the parapet and force their way inside. The Confederates were easily overwhelmed. Some escaped across the bridge. Many were captured.

Hancock pulled back from the river and set up his camp. The Army of the Potomac had formed a line along the north bank of the North Anna River. Kennedy could see the entire army from his vantage point.

The Confederates had offered little resistance so far, lending credence to the belief that Lee was retreating to the defenses around Richmond.

Burnside did not cross at Ox Ford on the twenty-third because it was late and his men had spent the day marching. The next morning, parapets could be seen along the ridge above the ford. The rebels were going to make a stand.

II Corps crossed the river on the morning of the twenty-fourth. They began advancing along the south bank but found the enemy entrenched behind strong defensive works two miles from the bridge. A thunderstorm followed by driving rain decided the issue. The downpour quickly turned the ground to mush. Hancock ordered his men to pull back and prepare for an attack. The trenches filled with water almost as soon as they were dug.

By nightfall, two entrenched armies faced each other across a no-man's land. By morning of the next day, it was clear that neither side could mount a successful offense. The combatants on both sides were stuck in the rain, waiting for something to happen.

The downpour didn't dampen the enthusiasm of snipers. Sharpshooters cut loose at anything that moved, forcing soldiers trapped in the standoff to hunker down behind walls of mud.

Late in the day, wagons began moving supplies back to the north side of the river. That night, the Army of the Potomac snuck from its trenches and began moving east in another attempt to outflank Lee.

Pulling back to the relative safety of the north bank was a relief. But that didn't last. II Corps sloshed through the rainstorm over roads covered with soupy mud. They paused for breakfast at Mount Carmel Church before continuing another fifteen miles to Chesterfield Station, where they restocked their ammunition and rations. Hancock's orders were to halt at Bethel church, but he pushed on a few more miles to McDowell's Mill, where VI Corps was setting up camp.

That night, some soldiers from VI Corps joined Kennedy and his friends as they sat around a fire discussing recent events.

Burnside had sent IX Corps across the river on another daft assault against rebels entrenched on a ridge overlooking steep banks. Fredericksburg had taught him nothing. One brigade led by a drunken general had attempted to charge up the hill. It was cut to ribbons. The general was captured, saving him the embarrassment of a court-martial.

The visitors complained that Warren had slept through the attack on his position at Jericho Mills. Kennedy asked, "What happened?"

"Griffin sent an aide to report Confederates massing in front of him. At first, Warren refused to meet the aide, then he told the man to get back to his post. He insisted the Confederates weren't going to attack. They were retreating."

Kennedy grimaced and shook his head. He wanted to defend Warren. The general had his reasons. Besides, Griffin had held his ground and driven the rebels back. But there was no point in getting involved in V Corps politics.

53

Allatoona Pass

In 1844, "... *when [I was a] lieutenant of the Third Artillery, I had been sent from Charleston, South Carolina, to Marietta, Georgia, to assist Inspector General Churchill to take testimony. ... And after completing the work at Marietta we transferred our party to Bellefonte, Alabama. I had ridden the distance on horseback, and had noted well the topography of the country, especially that about Kennesaw, Allatoona, and the Etowah River. On that occasion, I had stopped some days with a Colonel Tumlin, to see some remarkable Indian mounds on the Etowah River, usually called the 'Hightower.' I therefore knew that the Allatoona Pass was very strong, would be hard to force, and resolved not even to attempt it, but to turn the position by moving from Kingston to Marietta via Dallas; accordingly I made orders on the 20th to get ready for the march to begin on the 23rd. The Army of the Cumberland was ordered to march for Dallas, by Euharlee and Stilesboro; Davis's division, then in Rome, by Van Wert; the Army of the*

Ohio to keep on the left of Thomas, by a place called Burnt Hickory; and the Army of the Tennessee to march for a position a little to the south, so as to be on the right of the general army when grouped about Dallas.

"The movement contemplated leaving our railroad, to depend for twenty days on the contents of our wagons; and as the country was very obscure, mostly in the state of nature, densely wooded, and with few roads, our movements were necessarily slow. We crossed the Etowah by several bridges and fords, and took as many roads as possible, keeping up communication by cross-roads, or by couriers through the woods. I personally joined Gen. Thomas, who had the center, and was consequently the main column ... The several columns followed generally the Valley of the Euharlee, a tributary coming into the Etowah from the south, and gradually crossed over a ridge of mountains, parts of which had been worked over for gold, and were consequently full of paths and unused wagon roads or tracks. A cavalry picket of the enemy at Burnt Hickory was captured, and had on his person an order from Gen. Johnston dated at Allatoona which showed that he had detected my purpose of turning his position, and it accordingly became necessary to use great caution, lest some of the minor columns should fall into ambush, but luckily the enemy was not much more familiar with that part of the country than we were. On the other side of the Allatoona range, the Pumpkin Vine Creek, also a tributary of the Etowah, flowed north and west; Dallas, the point aimed at, was a small town on the other or east side of this creek and was the point of concentration of a great many roads that lead in every direction. Its possession would be a threat to Marietta and Atlanta, but I could not then venture to attempt either, until I had regained the use of the railroad, at least as far down as it's [detachment] from the Allatoona range of mountains. Therefore, the movement was chiefly designed to compel Johnston to give up Allatoona."

The Memoirs of General William T. Sherman

Sherman established his forward supply depot at Kingston while pausing to prepare for the next phase of his campaign. His crews repaired tracks and bridges as far as Kingston. He trimmed his entourage to essential combat personnel and support staff and loaded his wagons with supplies for a three-week maneuver. He was heading south and west to pick up the Dallas-Marietta Road and then east to capture Johnston's main supply depot at Marietta.

He established facilities for treating his wounded at Resaca.

The Union army moved out on May 23. McPherson and the Army of the Tennessee swung west to Dallas. Thomas led the Army of the Cumberland south toward New Hope Church while Schofield marched the Army of Ohio to the left of Thomas. Captured documents proved the Southerners were monitoring Sherman's progress from observation points on peaks along the defile. Skirmishing on May 24 near Dallas alerted the Union general to Confederate intentions.

Hooker had jumped to the front of the line and was leading the Army of the Cumberland. He surprised rebel troops, burning a bridge across Pumpkin Vine Creek, and drove them off. At a fork in the road, he split his troops. Geary and the Second Division to the left. The other two divisions to the right.

Geary ran up against some Confederate infantry regiments, which fought him every step of the way as they retreated to a ravine where rebel forces lay in wait.

In the early hours of May 26, Kat was summoned to the field hospital at Burnt Hickory. As she came out of the pouring rain into the tent, she noticed General Schofield being treated in an isolated corner. He had been on his way to meet with Sherman about strategy and get orders when his horse lost its footing and tumbled into a ditch.

A steady stream of men from a battle the night before were being helped or carried into the field hospital. Some would stay for a few days of recovery. Many would be sent back to the front line. The rest would be transported to Resaca.

Kat was tasked with identifying and evaluating the wounded as they arrived. Most had sewn a piece of paper with essential information to the inside of their coats. Many talked freely to her because she had been one of their own for the past three years. She pieced together a version of the battle from tales the soldiers told her.

General Geary had halted his pursuit of the rebels when he reached the edge of a ravine. Confederates were massed in force on the other side. It looked like a brigade. Geary began deploying his troops along the ridge facing the rebels. He extended his line, searching for the enemy's right flank. The sound of musketry and artillery brought Sherman to the scene. When the commander arrived, he ordered a charge to dislodge the rebels from their perch.

With his Second Division already deployed, Hooker put his First and Third divisions in a column of brigades. That took until five o'clock. Just as the lead brigade started down the steep bank, a thunderstorm let loose. The clay surface turned to mud, making for slippery footing. Vegetation broke up the formation as the men descended into the gorge. When they reached the bottom, they had to trudge through mud and dense undergrowth to cross an open stretch. Those who made it to the other side were gunned down as they charged up the ravine's steep, slippery wall to attack the enemy. The assault was readily repulsed by riflemen firing down from trenches at the top of the embankment.

The suicidal attack went on in drenching rain until after dark.

Kat didn't get an answer to her most urgent question until midmorning. The soldier she was talking to grinned in spite of his pain. "Sergeant Donal's okay," he said. "He's the one that dragged me out of that hellhole and back to our lines."

Kat now had a name for the slaughter: the Battle of the Hellhole. So far, it was not as bad as Antietam or Gettysburg, but it wasn't over. She loved these men, and she was glad she was not up north somewhere, waiting for one of them to come home.

Casualties continued to arrive throughout the next two days. Little more than a stone's throw separated the two armies. No great skill was needed to hit something that close. The musketry was deadly, and it never stopped. Some of the stories Kat heard led her to believe the army was in motion. Units were shifting from the right flank to the left.

On the morning of May 28, casualties began arriving at the hospital by the hundreds. One of the brigades in Howard's Corps had attacked the Confederate line. As Kat gathered the information for a report that would make its way up to Sherman himself, she pieced together an ugly story. The generals believed they had found Johnston's right flank and prepared to attack. But the launch point was moved twice because pickets discovered that the rebel line extended further than expected. It was late afternoon by the time Howard was convinced he had finally overlapped the Confederate line and ordered the attack. Logan's division was formed in a column three brigades deep. For some reason, only the lead brigade attacked the enemy.

The men marched a half mile through trees, bushes and underbrush before reaching a clearing in front of a heavily entrenched line. They charged. They were brave, fierce and determined, but the assault was stopped fifty yards short of the rebel position. Losses were heavy. Those who could run, walk, or crawl retreated. As they made their way back through the dense trees, they encountered a second brigade moving forward to be butchered.

It was already dark when Kat left the field hospital on her way to dinner and a night's sleep. She had not gotten far when a large, menacing man blocked her path. He barked, "Where's your salute, soldier?"

Startled out of her reverie, she realized she was wearing a uniform, and the man in front of her, with an eagle on his shoulder, was a colonel. She blushed, snapped to attention and saluted.

The officer returned her salute and grumbled, "Since when do we have women in this man's army?"

"Since never, sir." Kat smirked. "You won't let us enlist and you aren't going to draft us. But these are the only clothes I have. Sececches burned my house and all my possessions."

That was a small lie. She had taken to wearing a man's uniform because replacing her worn-out clothes had become practically impossible.

The officer nodded. "I presume you are the notorious Kat I've heard so much about."

"I go by Kat."

"Perhaps you can help me find Lieutenant Edwards. He's my brother."

"I'll be happy to take you to him," Kat said and turned back to the field hospital. The colonel stepped up beside her, and the two walked together. "Can you tell me what's going on, sir? Why are we suddenly taking so many casualties?"

He took his time answering. "They surprised us and we made mistakes. We expected General Johnston to hold

Allatoona Pass at all hazards. As long as he was entrenched there, he could block our supply line. Encounters over the last few days have convinced us that he abandoned the pass in favor of a surprise attack. We paid a high price for that intelligence."

"So we are in for more bloody battles?"

"No. We're going to slide around their right flank and capture the pass. General Johnston gambled and lost. He will be forced to retreat."

The next day, hundreds of casualties began arriving around noon. This time, only three hundred were Federals. The rest were Confederates. They had taken a beating in an attack against McPherson on the Union right flank.

Two days later, word reached Burnt Hickory that the cavalry had attacked Allatoona Pass and driven off a small Confederate force guarding the north end. Sherman would be able to extend his supply line all the way to Marietta.

The rain picked up again and continued for three weeks. Saturated earth turned to a soupy marsh. Clothes soaked through and stayed wet. Kat slept in the relative comfort of an ambulance.

A report that Johnston had abandoned New Hope Church and was pulling back to a new defensive position made the rounds at Burnt Hickory.

Sherman pushed his army south through the monsoon and mud to consolidate his control of Allatoona Pass and the railroad. His railroad crew followed the infantry, repairing the track as fast as the foot soldiers claimed it.

Orders to move out from Burnt Hickory were issued on June 9. Schofield escorted the wagons and support staff to his new headquarters at Allatoona Station. McPherson established his depot at Big Shanty at the south end of the pass, near Marietta. Thomas established his headquarters at Acworth.

The moves improved conditions, but relocating wagons with supplies, cattle and thousands of casualties was a daunting job under the best circumstances. The present circumstances were about as bad as they could get.

54

Cold Harbor

The Union army, in full retreat from its stand along the North Anna River, reorganized at Chesterfield Station throughout the day on May 27. Rations and ammo were issued in preparation for another march around Lee's right flank.

Goldman and Kennedy crossed paths as they rushed about getting ready for the next move. Sam said, "Looks like God granted us a miracle."

His friend nodded. "We'd have taken a beating if we'd had to fight Lee back there."

"And we pulled out without losing so much as a horse."

"We're going to need all the luck we can get, if we're going to win this fight."

On May 28, the Army of the Potomac split into two columns and marched toward the Pamunkey River. II Corps and VI Corps went southeast to Nelson's bridge, thirty miles away. V Corps and IX Corps trekked farther south and east to Dabney's Ferry near Hanovertown. The cavalry under Sheridan was already busy securing those crossings.

The march was gruesome. At the beginning of the day, mud on the rain-soaked roads, sometimes ankle-deep, sometimes knee-deep, made progress slow and painful. By late afternoon, the sun had dried the roads, but the scorching heat sapped men's strength. More than a few staggered off the road and fell into the grass to die of sunstroke.

Hancock's route led past grim evidence of a recent cavalry battle. The bodies of Union and Confederate horsemen were scattered over the battleground near the line of march. Repeating six-shot carbines lay next to the men in blue. The Confederate dead gripped Enfield muskets. The Southerners' clothing bore silent witness to their poverty.

Artillery caissons and supply wagons stretched out for miles behind the infantry. The heavily loaded wheeled vehicles crawled over mushy roads, driven forward by the exertions of men and beasts, straining to the limits of their endurance.

The army bivouacked east of the river that night. In the early light of morning, II Corps and V Corps began a reconnaissance in force. Hancock, advancing along the Richmond-Hanovertown Road, found the rebels entrenched on the south bank of Totopotomoy Creek and ordered his men to set up a defensive line along the north bank. Wright deployed VI Corps on Hancock's left.

Warren crossed the creek and advanced as far as Shady Grove Road. A rebel attack that afternoon collapsed his left flank and sent Crawford's division racing back to the creek. Warren regained control of his corps and turned it to face the enemy. His men repulsed the Confederates with a withering barrage of artillery and musketry.

The next day, Grant ordered a general movement against the Confederate position along Totopotomoy Creek. The Army of the Potomac probed the Southerners throughout the day. Only Barlow's division of II Corps made it past the rebels' first line of defense.

A cavalry clash on the Union left flank at Old Church went back and forth. Confederates arrived in force to push Union pickets back to Matadequin Creek. Two squadrons of Union horse soldiers were sent in to reinforce the pickets. The original line was restored. A second attack in the middle of the afternoon overwhelmed the Federals, who fought a dogged delaying action until more reinforcements arrived. The struggle ended abruptly when the Confederate leader was killed in hand-to-hand fighting. His men fell back in confusion and threw up breastworks.

An hour later, General Custer and his Michigan Cavalry showed up. He relieved soldiers in the center of the line and deployed a regiment on both flanks. The Southerners retreated southeast to the crossroads at Old Cold Harbor. Custer pursued.

Sheridan received orders to drive the rebels off and hold the crossroads at all hazards. He met little resistance.

Wright pulled back from Totopotomoy Creek for a night march to Cold Harbor.

The rebels attacked Sheridan at dawn. He gave ground but held the crossroads until VI Corps arrived and drove the enemy back. Wright's orders were to attack immediately, but his men were exhausted from a night and a morning on the move. He needed time to assess the enemy's position and strength.

Wright launched his attack that evening. The fighting went on until darkness forced a halt, but VI Corps made little progress. The generals decided to renew the attack at dawn. Hancock was ordered to join Wright at Cold Harbor. He should have been able to cover the nine miles and give his men some rest before the planned battle, but the guide got lost. II Corps didn't reach the launch point until noon. Hancock informed Grant that his men were too exhausted to attack the Confederates. The operation was postponed until the morning of June 3.

General Baldy Smith arrived at Cold Harbor with the seven-thousand-man XVIII Corps that afternoon and joined Wright and Hancock. The Union line extended north and west five miles. IX Corps was deployed along Totopotomoy Creek, extending away from Cold Harbor. V Corps formed the right flank.

The men of II Corps had the afternoon and evening to study the rebel fortifications. They could see the enemy had been busy preparing their defenses. The men in blue stitched notes with their names and where their families lived into their jackets so their bodies could be identified. They were preparing to die.

Kennedy's conversations with fellow NCOs confirmed an ominous fact. None of the general officers had been seen studying those defenses in preparation for the planned assault. They would be sending regular soldiers up against one of the strongest defenses of the war, with no idea how it should be attacked.

The sergeant penned a letter and made sure it would be delivered:

June 2, 1864

My Dear Roishin:

I write this with great sadness and anxiety. I fear this may be my last chance to say goodbye to you. We attack at dawn.

The enemy has been diligently preparing for this moment. They have thrown up impressive fortifications. Perhaps the best I have ever seen.

Our leaders have been lax in their duties. None have come here to study the rebel works as required to properly plan an assault.

Between their industry and our sloth, we will be charging into a slaughter. I am not sanguine about my chances.

But I promise that if I do survive, I will find a way to come to you and apologize for upsetting you unnecessarily.

Yours always, Seamus

The assault on the morning of June 3 was worse than any of them had imagined. It started at 4:30 and had ground to a halt by 6:30. Veteran soldiers dropped to the ground to avoid the scathing enemy fire.

The heavy artillery troops assigned to Barlow's division of II Corps, fresh from garrison duty, achieved fleeting success. Their spirited charge carried them past the pickets and into the outer trenches of the Confederate line. Those trenches were flooded and undefended. The Union charge got no further. The main Confederate line was impenetrable. Their counterattack sent the converted artillerymen racing back to the Union line under a hail of musketry.

The Federals began entrenching and throwing up parapets. They would hold what little ground they had gained. In the contested space between the Union line of defense and the Confederate line, thousands of wounded, dying men lay trapped alongside thousands of their dead comrades.

Meade ordered a second charge. Whether soldiers refused the command or were unable to carry it out, no one moved. Charging into a hail of gunfire is unnatural. Charging over the bodies of your fallen comrades into a hail of gunfire is unthinkable.

These men had done it before. But this time, they were worn out. Used up. Exhausted. They wouldn't make another suicidal charge.

Officers went up the chain of command, arguing against another attack. Eventually, Grant came out to assess the Confederate works. He returned to his headquarters and called off all further assaults.

The day ended with the main Union line six hundred yards from the Confederate works. Union troops manned a ragged line of hastily dug trenches and improvised parapets running dangerously close to the Confederate line. A killing field littered with the dead and the dying stood between the two armies. The stench of rotting flesh was overwhelming, but there was no escape.

The sharpshooters were relentless. A hat on a rod pushed above the protective barrier drew a score of musket balls. No one dared to lift his head above that barrier.

When the men needed their canteens filled, they drew lots. The loser collected all the canteens he could carry and sprinted to the Union line. If he made it there safely and filled the canteens, he smoked a pipe with some buddies while screwing up his courage for the return trip. Then he gathered his haul and raced back through the sharpshooters' harassing musketry.

Nevertheless, Yanks and Rebs talked across the chasm like old buddies. They traded coffee, tobacco and sugar by tossing packets over the gap.

In the days that followed, this outlandish behavior became normal.

The injured men trapped in that no man's land lay in the open, exposed to the blazing summer sun without food or water, while insects feasted on their bodies. Their screams and cries assailed their comrades continuously.

On June 7, four days after the suicidal assault on the Confederate redoubt, a cease-fire allowed soldiers to retrieve the dead and wounded. Very few of those who had survived being shot survived the days of waiting for rescue. The dead could not be moved. Their bodies were too decayed.

Three days later, orders came to draw four days' rations, a sure sign of another flanking movement. II Corps and VI Corps pulled to the rear. The front line was contracted. Two divisions from V Corps began preparing for the move.

Camp rumors had Sheridan leading the cavalry west around Lee's position toward Richmond.

On the night of June 12, the Army of the Potomac slipped away from Cold Harbor and marched south. II Corps reached Wilcox Landing on the James River late on the afternoon of June 13. A few hundred yards downstream, Army engineers were busy creating a bridge across the river. It was a wonder - 2100 feet long with a gateway for ships in the middle.

Over the next four days, troops were ferried from Wilcox Landing across the river while the bulk of the army crossed on the new pontoon bridge. One hundred thousand soldiers, five thousand wagons, 56,000 horses and mules, and 3500 cattle made it safely across the James River. Grant had finally won a round in the chess match with Lee. The question weighing heavily on the minds of his soldiers was whether he would be able to win the war.

55

June 9, 1864

My Dearest Mother,

I have read your most welcome letters. I am well, having survived weeks of intense fighting and the most strenuous labors required to move our supply wagons.

We endeavored to get around the enemy and into his rear to capture his supply depot. He launched a surprise attack that led to bloody skirmishing and a standoff that went on for ten days. Our casualties were limited because of our well-constructed breastworks.

Food and other supplies have been our biggest concern. We could not rely on the railroad. The rebels tore up the tracks as they retreated. Replenishing supplies by wagon has been uncommonly difficult. Steady rains have turned the ground to mush. Roads have disappeared. The livestock readily handle these conditions. We have beef aplenty but nothing else.

Foraging is being tolerated in spite of General Sherman's orders. That will likely continue as long as it does not get out of hand.

When I caught some men preparing fresh mutton and chicken, I told them stealing from the local farmers was a violation of General Sherman's directives. One man who seemed to be their spokesman assured me they had negotiated with the owners.

He told me about one woman in particular who claimed to be a widow. He said he assured her he was sorry for her plight, but it was self-defense. Her man had fired the first shot. That got a big laugh. We are becoming barbarians.

We captured Allatoona Pass and gained control of the railroad a week ago. Two days later, we discovered that the rebels had abandoned their defenses along the roads that intersect near New Hope Church.

Some thought they had pulled back to Atlanta, which is protected by stout defense works. Our scouts report that they have not crossed the Chattahoochee River, the main barrier between us and Atlanta. No one seems to know where they are hiding.

The railroad crews are making good progress. It only took them three days to replace a bridge the Johnnies destroyed. They repair more sections of track every day. Everyone is bored. There's little to keep us occupied while the railroad is repaired. No marching or fighting. No artillery duels. We can move around during the day without worrying about sharpshooters, and sleep at night instead of improving our defenses. But all that feels unnatural after what we've been through, and the rain makes us all miserable.

We are near Atlanta. But I am told we are going to capture the rebel supply depot at Marietta first. That will put us halfway to Atlanta. From the preparations we are making, I expect we are about to take on another big fight in mountains covered with trees and bushes and other vegetation that will make our progress very difficult.

But every man I have talked to is of the same opinion. The rebels are only delaying the outcome. Grant is going to take Richmond, and we're going to take Atlanta. That will end this war, and we can go home to our families.

I will write again when I have more news to share with you.

Your devoted son,

Tom

56

Kennesaw Mountain

As soon as Sherman gained control of Allatoona Pass, the rebels abandoned their lines along the roads near New Hope Church.

The Confederates' natural line of defense lay along the Chattahoochee River. But the wily Johnston encamped in the uncharted highlands west of Kennesaw Mountain to wait for his adversary's next move. The rocky hills and tangled woodland made a battleground more suited to the feisty, undersized Southern army than Sherman's juggernaut. Hundreds of streams crisscrossed the area. Wild undergrowth, scrub, bushes, vines and shrubs filled the spaces between trees. And the Confederate general's supply depot was only a few miles to his rear.

On the morning of June 10, with a break in the rain, Sherman ordered his forces to advance and make contact with the enemy. The initiative extended the Federal line on a southwest diagonal from Brush Mountain to Lost Mountain.

After days of continuous rain, saturated earth oozed underfoot as Yankee soldiers slogged forward.

Mounted infantry from the Lightning Brigade had driven off a division of Confederate cavalry the previous afternoon.

McPherson advanced along a road connecting Acworth to Marietta by way of Big Shanty. He came up against Confederates massed on Brush Mountain and began to entrench.

Thomas divided the Army of the Cumberland into three columns. Howard, in the middle, led the advance toward Pine Mountain. Palmer, on his left, maintained contact with McPherson. Hooker, on his right, extended south toward the Army of the Ohio.

On the Union right wing, Schofield divided the Army of the Ohio into two columns. Haskell followed Allatoona Creek southeast from Kemp's Mill. Cox, on the army's extreme right, followed Sandtown Road. He found the enemy entrenched over Allatoona Creek about a mile in front of Gilgal Church.

Stoneman, patrolling the right flank with his cavalry, discovered unoccupied trenches on Lost Mountain. A single division of Confederate cavalry was protecting Johnston's left flank.

Rain began falling again that afternoon. At times, it poured down in sheets, drenching clothing and equipment and drowning out cooking fires. Union soldiers, worn out from a hard day of marching, constructed stout defenses before lying down to get what sleep they could.

Winds blowing from the east brought cold air and moisture to feed the monsoon. This was not the Sunny South

Union troops had expected. They dug trenches and put up breastworks to keep busy and stay warm.

The rain let up on Tuesday, the fourteenth. Sherman ordered skirmish lines to attack the rebel works across the entire front. He wanted his infantry to entrench close to the enemy without assaulting its fortifications.

The right wing under Schofield and the left wing under McPherson pushed skirmishers back to the Confederates' main line of defense. Thomas ordered Palmer to attack a weakness on the slopes of Pine Mountain. That thrust nearly broke the Confederate line.

Johnston watched the Federals close in and entrench from a vantage point in the hills. He stood with Hood and Polk in plain view for some time. Union artillery took aim. In an instant, Reverend Lieutenant General Leonidas Polk disappeared. A cannonball struck his midsection and knocked him back into a tree before exploding. Later that night, as the story made the rounds, it ended with, "It's a sign from God. The rebel cause is doomed."

The next morning, Hooker attacked rebels holding earthworks that connected Pine Mountain with the main Confederate force. He won the trenches in a sharp battle. Then he sent his Second Division against the rebels' principal line, but the Yanks couldn't break through those defenses. They were forced to retire after losing several hundred men.

Schofield's Second Division drove advanced pickets from positions along Allatoona Creek back to the main line at Gilgal Church. They captured a hill that made an ideal platform for bombarding the entrenched Johnnies.

The Union army now encircled the Confederate army. The two forces stood toe-to-toe, their muskets bickering incessantly.

The downpour had resumed, soaking everything. Men marched, sat and slept on waterlogged ground. Wood had to be dried before it could be burned. Whiskey often replaced coffee. No fire needed. Clothes never dried. Men began reporting sick to get a few hours of relief inside the hospital tent.

Supply problems added to the misery. Attacks on the trains and tracks by Southern militias and partisans interrupted the flow of supplies. The marshy, rain-soaked ground bogged down wagons bringing supplies to the front. Meat, hardtack and coffee were always available, but tobacco was in short supply. Men who'd been struggling for weeks in rain and mud could not clean themselves or their clothes. There had not been a delivery of soap in weeks.

Even ammunition ran dangerously low.

Tom refused to leave his post. Others looked to him as a role model. When he led a detail to the rear for supplies, he crossed paths with Kat. Their eyes met, but he looked away. Holding that gaze when he couldn't throw his arms around her was too painful.

On Thursday morning, June 16, Schofield maneuvered his two divisions for an assault on Johnston's left flank. He gained high ground, where he set up his artillery to enfilade the rebel works. Those stout defenses, impervious to a frontal assault, could not hold up against an oblique, crosswise attack.

That night, the Confederate left wing pulled back. Schofield and Thomas set out in pursuit early the next morning. Massed Union infantry overran Southern horse soldiers posted to delay them and pushed on.

The Army of the Ohio marched east toward the river along Sandtown Road until it reached the road to Marietta. Schofield ordered his lead division under Cox to take that route, which led to a broad valley carved out by waters running off Kennesaw Mountain. Mud Creek ran through the basin, parallel to the road. A high ridge shot up on the stream's east bank. Cox found the rebels entrenched along that eminence. Their artillery had been deployed to cover a mile of open bottomland.

The target area in front of the rebels offered no cover except for a couple of hills that had survived the ebb and flow of flood waters. Cox's division raced to one of the hills and took up positions just below the crest, making it a natural parapet. Cockerill's Ohio Battery unlimbered and began firing on the rebels. An hour-long artillery duel silenced the Confederate guns.

Hooker, who'd been advancing along the Dallas-Marietta Road, moved forward and extended his line to cover the Confederate left flank. Howard, following the Burnt Hickory Road, moved into position on the Confederate right flank.

Early on the morning of the eighteenth, Howard sent two divisions on the offensive. They crossed rain-swollen creeks and stormed the rebel trenches. The Southerners fell back, but unwilling to give up their stronghold, they counterattacked. The Yanks, refusing to surrender what they had gained at great cost, fought off three desperate assaults. During the night, they improved the trenches and added parapets. By morning, IV Corps was dug in a few hundred paces from the main Confederate line.

With his front collapsing, Johnston pulled his army back to Kennesaw Mountain on the night of the eighteenth. His men had to haul artillery pieces and support wagons through a heavy downpour over rain-soaked mire to reach the safety of their new defensive line.

The next morning, Sherman ordered his army forward. They found the enemy firmly lodged in a line that crossed formidable mountains blocking the way to Marietta. The Confederate line stretched from Big Kennesaw, in the north, across Little Kennesaw and Pigeon Hill. It extended down the southern slope of Pigeon Hill in a broad sweeping arc that crossed the Dallas-Marietta Road, the Powder Spring Road and Ollie Creek, cutting off all routes that led directly to Marietta.

The Federals spent most of Sunday, June 19, maneuvering into position for a renewed assault. Mud sucked at soldiers' boots. Rain poured down on them. The rebels peppered them with musket balls and shelled them from their batteries on Pigeon Hill.

On the Union left flank, McPherson pushed the Confederates off Brush Mountain and extended his line to cover the railroad.

Thomas anchored the center of the Union line. Howard was on the west bank of Noses Creek, where the road from Gilgal Church to Marietta crossed the stream. Palmer, on his left, had his division positioned at the base of the mountain, where it began to rise from the plain. Hooker, on his right, was also on the west bank of the creek. The stream bent sharply to the west, creating a large gap between him and the Confederate line. The three divisions of XX Corps had to cross to the east bank of the rain-swollen creek using a rickety bridge that looked as if it might be carried off at any moment by waters rushing down the mountain. Tom led the Second Division across the bridge. The rest of XX Corps followed.

Schofield had the right flank. XXIII Corps, led by Cox's division, marched three miles down Sandtown Road to a crossing of Noses Creek. Planking had been removed from the bridge to prevent the Federals from using it. The stream had overflowed its banks and created a waist deep lake that blocked the approach to the bridge. The stream could not be forded. Yankee soldiers dug in on the far shore and engaged the Southern cavalry, but made no serious attempt to cross the creek.

Union cavalry under Stoneman reconnoitered the area as far as the village of Powder Springs, four miles south of Schofield's position.

The next day, the Yanks stepped up pressure on the rebels.

Sherman ordered a demonstration along his entire line while XXIII Corps continued its efforts to turn the enemy's left flank.

Schofield ordered Cox to cross Noses Creek and drive the Johnnies back. By the end of the day, he had established a foothold at the intersection of Sandtown Road and Powder Springs Road, which wound east around Kennesaw Mountain into Marietta. That position set Sherman up with two flanking options.

Cox made his headquarters at the Cheney farm, which was near the intersection. His division encamped at the rear of the farm on a knoll overlooking Ollie Creek, another stream flowing southeast from the Marietta plateau.

Sherman immediately shifted his army to take advantage of Schofield's new position. McPherson relieved Palmer, who relieved Howard. He took over Hooker's position, and Hooker moved south to the hills on Kolb's farm.

XX Corps reached its new position in the early hours of June 22. The morning dawned bright and clear. A heat wave was about to follow the monsoon.

The sound of big guns broke the morning stillness. The rebels had moved artillery to a plateau near the top of Little Kennesaw and were blasting away. From Tom's position in the southern hills on Kolb's farm, it was a sight to behold. The shells were landing in the Union rear, threatening supply wagons, field hospitals, command tents, and the people working there. The attack did little more than force a mad scramble to move the wagons and tents out of range.

Hooker set up his headquarters at the farmhouse. To his front, XX Corps commanded a ridge line overlooking a broad, open field. Butterfield was on the left, Geary in the center and Williams on the right. The only weakness was a deep ravine that separated Geary from Williams. The troops immediately began entrenching and setting up artillery because captured rebels had revealed that Johnston was preparing an assault on the Union right flank.

There was still a gap between Williams's division on Hooker's right and Haskell's division on Schofield's left.

A rebel war whoop shortly after five in the afternoon signaled the start of the Confederate attack. Hood sent a division across the field in front of XX Corps. Lethal artillery fire shredded the division before it got halfway. The rebels kept coming. Musket fire took its toll on those who had survived the shelling. A marsh waited for them at the end of the field, and on the other side of the marsh, a grove of trees. The trees provided some respite, but the Federals continued pouring artillery and musket fire on the trapped rebels.

The Johnnies who could still move on their own made their way back to the Confederate line under the cover of darkness. Many brought wounded buddies along as they crossed the field. Ambulances could be heard retrieving the wounded and dead throughout the night. Hood had paid in blood for New Hope Church and Pickets Mill.

57

On to Petersburg

The move from Cold Harbor across the James River to the south bank was a stunning success. Grant had produced the plan in two days, and his army had executed flawlessly. There were no significant breakdowns. The Confederates did not send gunboats to attack the Army of the Potomac while it was crossing the river.

The commanding general's luck didn't hold. Miscues and Southern resistance combined to foil a brilliant plan.

General William Baldy Smith was returning from Cold Harbor to Bermuda Hundred on June 14 when he received orders to lead XVIII Corps against Petersburg. The objective was to capture the railroad hub that collected goods from all over the South and funneled them to Richmond and its defenders, Lee's Army of Northern Virginia.

The city, a port on the Appomattox River, was protected from an infantry attack by the Dimmock Line, a ten-mile bulwark with artillery turrets, rifle pits and trenches behind a six-foot wall along its eastern border. The battlement had been built by Confederate soldiers and impressed colored workers in 1862 and 1863 in response to McClellan's unsuccessful James River initiative. Work was halted in May 1864 when Grant crossed the Rapidan in concert with Sherman's move into Georgia.

Smith was to reach the city on the morning of June 15. Hancock was supposed to join him with II Corps later that day. But XVIII Corps was delayed by a fight with an entrenched rebel skirmish line. The first Union troops did not reach the objective until early afternoon.

After a reconnoiter of the defenses around the city, Smith spread his troops out in a reinforced scrimmage line and charged. He overran the defenders and captured a three-mile section of the Dimmock Line. II Corps arrived after dark, just as the battle was ending.

Hancock had gotten a late start because supplies he needed were not waiting for him when he reached the south bank of the river. The supply wagons had been forced to detour because the planned route was impassable.

II Corps was further delayed when it was sent on a circuitous route to Petersburg.

Flaws in the Union command structure doomed the operation after a brilliant start. Smith's use of skirmish lines instead of columns had taken the Confederates by surprise. They were defeated before they could figure out how to respond. However, his shortcomings as a leader gave them an opportunity to regroup and mount a successful defense of the city.

By the time the generals got together, Smith had decided to rest for the night and resume the attack in the morning. Hancock and his men had been marching for days in extreme heat and choking dust. He was in severe pain from the wound he had received at Gettysburg. His orders were to support Smith, and that's what he did. Hancock deployed his men as requested and ordered them to reconnoiter the enemy's position for strengths and weaknesses.

As the first day of operations against Petersburg drew to a close, exhausted leaders with exhausted forces let the initiative slip away.

Kennedy and Goldman joined others around a fire with their pipes and their thoughts. The big question was why hadn't they done more?

XVIII Corps should have attacked sooner, but Smith was overly cautious. Hancock was another matter. Everyone looked up to him. Why hadn't he come straight to Petersburg and taken charge?

As the discussion proceeded, a burly black man joined them. The stripes on his sleeve made him an NCO. He took a seat and lit his pipe. Someone growled, "And who might you be?"

"Jeremiah."

"Gotta last name, sergeant?"

"Smith. I growed up on der plantation. But ah been Jeremiah all ma life. Call me dat."

Kennedy said, "I see you boys took some of the turrets and captured artillery pieces."

"We hit dem boys hard and dey run like scared rabbits." Jeremiah took a long drag on his pipe and exhaled smoke in one long breath. "What I don' get is why we ain't out der chasin' 'em 'n' baggin' 'em."

Goldman nodded. "We've been thinking the same thing."

Wilcox said, "Anybody with a brain in his head would know that today was the day to take Petersburg." He laid out a map he was carrying. "Here's Petersburg," he said, pointing to a spot on the map. Pointing to another spot a few inches away, he said. "Here's Lee. He'll be in Petersburg tomorrow and we'll be looking at another Cold Harbor."

There was some half-hearted dissent, but every man in that group knew Lee and the Confederates well enough to believe beyond a shadow of a doubt that Wilcox was right.

General George Meade was enjoying a relaxing dinner with his staff as guests of Admiral Samuel Lee, commander of the James River Flotilla, when he received word of Smith's success and plans for renewed battle in the morning. That was the first Meade had heard of plans to attack Petersburg as soon as II Corps reached the south bank. He immediately left his meal to fix a logistical problem. IX Corps was on the north bank of the James, waiting for II Corps' supply wagons and artillery to cross the pontoon bridge. The commander of the Army of the Potomac had to stop the supply wagons so his infantry could get across the bridge and be ready for an attack on Petersburg in the morning.

Smith was awakened at dawn by General Butler's aide, who had been trying to reach him all night with orders to resume the attack immediately.

By the time Meade and his staff reached City Point, Grant was on his way to the battlefield. When Meade caught up with him, the commanding general handed over responsibility for Petersburg. Meade raced ahead and caught up with IX Corps. The men were suffering from the heat, the dust and a night of marching. Meade rode on to consult with Hancock.

At II Corps headquarters, he was told that although operations had gotten off to a late start, the troops had conducted an aggressive probe of the enemy positions and captured an artillery battery.

Smith was called in, and the three generals spent the next few hours making plans for an assault.

The attack began at six. Fighting continued until nightfall. Several outposts were captured, but Union forces failed to break through the rebels' new line along Harris Creek.

The Yanks were exhausted. They lacked the vigor and enthusiasm needed at that moment. And they failed to notice that the Confederate commander had left three miles of the Dimmock line unguarded.

It took Burnside until three in the morning to launch an attack that had been scheduled for midnight. But IX Corps delivered. More than half a mile of the Harris Creek line was captured, and several hundred rebels were taken prisoner.

As the sun rose above the horizon, bad news began arriving. The heat and humidity were already oppressive. Men were sweating. It was going to be a miserable day for fighting. Hancock, the one man they needed at the front, could barely get out of bed. He turned the fighting over to his division commanders.

Lee was reportedly on his way south with troops to defend Petersburg. He retook the old Confederate line across the neck of Bermuda Hundred that evening. Grant ordered Butler to push him back.

Butler did nothing. His division commanders refused to follow him into battle against the legendary Confederate general.

An attack on the Harris Creek line by IX Corps, supported by a division of II Corps, was repulsed with heavy losses. A second attack was initially successful, but the Southerners were able to recapture lost ground with a counterattack.

Kennedy and his friends gathered to discuss the situation and boost their spirits with whisky. The men recounted what they knew of events from the past few days. It was a puzzle to which each man's recollection added a piece. When they were confident that they had the whole picture, they agreed that the battle was over. They had failed to take Petersburg, and they would fare no better in the days ahead.

At two in the morning on June 18, Hancock turned over command of II Corps to his senior division commander, Major General David Birney.

Meade renewed the assault at dawn. It would be another day of fighting under a scorching sun. The Union troops were greeted with light musketry. They found the enemy trenches abandoned. Advancing cautiously, they came upon the new line of defense as the sun was reaching its zenith.

Meade ordered an assault by all units at midafternoon. At the appointed hour, his army staggered forward in a futile, uncoordinated offensive. II Corps advanced piecemeal. V Corps and IX Corps delayed their start while they completed preparations. Musketry and artillery from the defensive line cut the attackers to pieces. The Yanks continued fighting, but weary soldiers who'd spent an entire day toiling under a blazing sun could not muster the force to overrun an entrenched enemy. At six, Meade called off the assault and ordered his troops to dig in.

Kennedy and his friends were gathered around a fire, debating the day's efforts. Jeremiah found them and took a seat. Everyone watched as he settled himself and lit his pipe. He studied the group before fixing his gaze on Wilcox. "You right. I heer'd Gen'r'l Lee hisself is here. Took his time but he come wi' da posse."

When no one replied, Kennedy said, "Birney was in command of II Corps today. Hancock was too sick."

"It's that wound he got at Gettysburg," Goldman observed.

Kennedy nodded. "Probably been bothering him for a while. That'd explain what's been going on for the last few days."

"An article in the newspapers quoted Smith as saying we could 'a captured Petersburg on the fifteenth if Hancock had done his job."

"I hear the division commanders are blaming each other for that."

"Hancock jumped on them after he read that article."

"That's only half the problem," Wilcox interjected. He inhaled and blew out a puff of smoke. "This is not the same army that defeated Lee at Gettysburg. Most of those veterans are gone. Many went home when their enlistment expired. Fighting over the last six weeks has cost us thousands. We still have a hundred thousand men, but many are draftees or even worse, bounty men."

Jeremiah chimed in. "Hirelings who run from da wolf like da Lord said."

Kennedy shook his head. "There are still a lot of men out there fighting. Maybe most of them are green, but they'll get over that. I have to believe that we've got enough left to see this through. We can't lose after three years of fighting and bloodshed."

Josh Goldman had joined the group but kept his peace during what he saw as a lively discussion. "Jim, there's more bad news. Black John Hunter and his cavalry had to withdraw from a confrontation with Early at Lynchburg. The

Confederates have regained control of the Shenandoah Valley."

That night, word spread that there would be no more assaults. The Army of the Potomac was again face-to-face with the Army of Northern Virginia on ground that favored a defensive stand by the Southerners. The commanding general had decided on a siege. He would force Lee to surrender by cutting the railroads he needed for supplies and communication.

58

June 19, 1864

Me dearest Seamus,

'Tis a grand Sunday. I was at Mass this morning, bless me soul. This afternoon, I took a wander round City Point. New hospitals they're building. Each Corps will have its own, mind ye. I'm with the II Corps. But you're not here, so you must be at the front, leading the lads, brave as ye are.

I found meself a room with a local widow, she's got a grand big house. She's taking in boarders, like meself, to pay her bills. We're a lively bunch – Mrs. Kirsch, meself, and three others. We have coffee and flapjacks in the morning, and we sit down for dinner together in the evening. And betwixt the two, we work our fingers to the bone. The wounded and the dying fill our tents as fast as they're put up, God help us.

The town's fair swarming with contrabands. That's what they're calling the Africans, ye see, who've come here escaping a life of slavery on the plantations. I'm nay sure the cure's better than the disease itself, mind ye. They're given all the hard work, like loading and unloading the ships that show up, day in, day out. I've been put in charge of a dozen women doing laundry. They don't really need minding, but the officers prefer having a chat with an Irish immigrant like meself, brogue and all. They're living in great big tents, with several families crammed into each, God love them. Barely a stitch o' clothing on their backs, and divil a thing else to their names.

Ye made a promise now, in yer letter from Cold Harbor. I'll be expecting payment in full, aye, as soon as General Grant can spare ye for a few days.

Me whole heart is with ya,

Roishin

59

June 20, 1864

My Dearest Roishin,

You are as enterprising as you are fetching. I look forward to joining you at City Point. But I doubt that I will get a furlough as much as it is needed. We are moving toward the enemy and digging in. I am certain that we will go on the attack soon.

Signs of fatigue are everywhere. The heat makes every undertaking doubly hard. We are good soldiers and manage to get done what has to be done. But we have our limits, and heat exhaustion has claimed some good men.

We are caught in a difficult situation. Experience has taught us to press forward. The rebels make good use of every minute we rest. That has cost us dearly.

We must strike them now, but we need time to rest and heal if we hope to defeat them.

President Lincoln conducted an informal review. When he stopped for a visit with II Corps, I got to shake his hand. He told me I reminded him of General Meagher. There could be no greater compliment for a poor Irishman like myself.

I am closing for now. I make no promise except that I will come to you at City Point.

Yours truly,

Seamus

60

Over the Mountain and to the River

An air of grim determination settled over the battle-field. The armies were deadlocked. A Union assault on Kennesaw Mountain would be suicidal. On the other hand, Johnston's army would be destroyed if he attacked Sherman. And the Southerners dared not retreat. Atlanta was their only remaining bastion.

According to rumors circulating through the camp, Sherman was dead set on going around Johnston. But Schofield had warned that XXIII Corps was too small to outflank the rebel position along Sandtown Road.

Sherman blasted away at Confederate artillery positions on Thursday, June 23. The next day, Union artillery only fired for an hour. The rebels did not answer. Irritating musketry never stopped. Both sides were gathering themselves for the next battle.

On Saturday night, June 25, Mac found Tom sitting by a small fire and puffing on his pipe. "Smells like tobacco. Where'd you get that?"

"There's plenty back at the wagons," Tom said as he went to his haversack and dug out a plug.

"I tried smoking dried coffee grounds," Mac grumbled. "I'd rather die."

Tom tossed the chestnut-colored bar to his friend. "Not much longer," he declared as he returned to his seat by the fire. "Marietta's just a few miles away. Atlanta's a day's march after that."

"Maybe. But the Johnnies aren't gonna just walk off that mountain. They're digging in."

"Busy work. They're trying to scare us."

"They're doing a good job. Kennesaw Mountain is the most perfect fortress in the history of warfare."

"We're gonna slide around their left and take Marietta."

"It's too quiet. I think something else is going on." Mac pressed his lips into a grim line and nodded. "And I think that's what the Johnnies think."

On June 26, Sherman ordered Schofield to make a lot of noise on the right flank as part of his plan to force Johnston to abandon his Kennesaw line. In turn, General Cox was ordered to move his division south on Sandtown Road and find a way to cross Ollie Creek.

The bridge was blocked by a brigade of dismounted Southern cavalry entrenched on the east bank. Cox began skirmishing with the rebels while he sent a brigade upstream to find another crossing. When the detachment found a suitable spot a mile north, they built a bridge and set up a defensive position in rebel territory.

That evening, Sherman issued orders for a frontal assault on the Confederates entrenched on Kennesaw Mountain and Pigeon Hill. The brigades that were going to carry out the attack had to be maneuvered into position for their launch. Troops marched all night. Some from the flank to the center. Others from the center to the flank. McPherson's pioneers cut a road through dense woodland so his artillery could move into position to support the attack.

Regimental commanders were briefed an hour before the assault. They had fifteen minutes to pass instructions to their troops and get them lined up. Soldiers, most of them fully aware of the danger they were about to face, gulped down a last meal, wrote a note for a loved one, and left their packs with a rear guard. They set out with sixty rounds of ammo and a canteen.

At 7:45, Union artillery began pounding Confederate positions. At eight, a well-planned, well-organized, three-pronged assault moved forward. Within minutes, shallow creeks overgrown with vegetation muddled the rhythm of thousands of marching feet. Rugged rocky ground covered with trees and vines finished turning Sherman's army into a fierce, determined horde.

The Northerners swept up the slopes of Pigeon Hill and little Kennesaw like a blue wave thrown ashore by a great ocean. Heroic men, veterans of many battles, drove forward until they reached a high point. Ran out of energy. And fell back.

A few made it all the way to the rebel works and were killed or captured. Many were wounded within a stone's throw of the target. They lay helpless. Dying. Waiting for someone to carry them back to friendly ground.

Retreat turned into a chaotic scramble for safety. Hapless Yanks raced back to the Union lines while bloodthirsty rebels fired from behind their parapets.

McPherson tasked XV Corps, led by Logan, to capture the rebel works on the saddle that connected Little Kennesaw and Pigeon Hill.

The troops moved out smartly and emerged from a wooded area, surprising Confederate skirmishers. Overwrought Yanks fell upon shocked rebels and drove them from their trenches, capturing over a hundred. Continuing their advance toward the main rebel works, they crossed a ravine only to discover a perpendicular wall in front of the enemy entrenchment. Heavy musketry raining down from the top of that wall brought the Union advance to a halt.

On McPherson's right, Howard faced the center of the Confederate line along the southwest slopes of Pigeon Hill. Major General John Newton, a Virginian by birth, was tasked with breaking through the Southern defenses. Newton had fought well in several battles, including Fredericksburg, Chancellorsville, and Gettysburg. But he was under a cloud for using his connections to pressure Lincoln to dump Burnside after Fredericksburg. He deployed his brigades in three stages.

Haskell went first. His soldiers descended into the valley of a small creek and up the steep slopes on the opposite bank. When they emerged onto level ground, they raced across an open field.

A heavy skirmish line led the way, driving Confederate pickets from their trenches and advancing to an abatis of tree trunks and branches that blocked the final assault on the Confederate redoubt. The skirmishers dropped to the ground at the edge of the barrier.

Soldiers at the front of the Union column foundered when they hit the barricade. They spread out and dropped to the ground alongside the skirmishers. The sudden halt rippled back down the column like a wave. Men at the tail end of the column were still crossing the creek when they were forced to stop because the men in front of them were no longer moving. The men in the middle were trapped in the open, easy targets for rebel sharpshooters.

Haskell rode his white stallion to the edge of the abatis and, brandishing his saber, roared, "Forward men and take these works!"

Soldiers jumped to their feet to follow his lead. But a musket ball hit him in the chest, knocking him to the ground. An instant later, his horse was shot and killed. Quick-thinking soldiers grabbed their commander and carried him back to safety. The charge had been quashed.

Minutes later, retreat was sounded. The withdrawal turned into a melee as men raced to get to the ravine before they were shot in the back.

George Wagner lined his brigade up on the left of Haskell. He stacked his five regiments one after the other, each spread out in a line of battle. His column was short and broad. At the signal, the men moved forward across the creek and up the steep slope to reach the plain where they charged the enemy. When the lead regiment ran up against the abatis, some men threw down their weapons and began tearing apart the obstruction, while others provided covering fire.

But it was a losing effort. Wagner's whole column was forced to stop. Two regiments were stuck in the defile. Two were caught in the no man's land between the ravine and the abatis, easy targets for a thousand rebels firing from behind a wall as fast as they could reload. Yanks fell by the hundreds before they gave up and dropped to the ground.

The order to retreat was not long in coming. It was obeyed immediately.

Nathan Kimball, on Wagner's left, also lined up his brigade in a column of regiments. But he didn't get orders to advance until nine, an hour after everyone else had gone. Wagner's men were still trapped in no man's land when Kimball led his brigade into the valley, across the creek, and back up the steep slope on the far side. If there was some hope that the rebel defense was spent or at least occupied with a brigade now tearing at their abatis, it quickly evaporated. As soon as Kimball's column crossed over the Union skirmish line and started down toward the creek, a barrage of musket balls assailed them.

When the lead regiment reached the abatis, men began working through the dense tangle. Those who reached the rebel fortress were killed or captured. Most of the brigade was trapped in the killing zone for half an hour. The men got down on the ground to take advantage of whatever shelter was available, but the losses were horrendous.

Newton called off the assault at ten.

Palmer was on Howard's right, south of the Dallas Road, where two streams came together to form John Ward Creek. The salient in the Confederate line, known as The Horseshoe, was directly to his front. That was his objective in this assault. He assigned brigades led by John Mitchell and Daniel McCook. Both reached the Confederate redoubt, and both were repulsed.

Colonel Daniel McCook was one of seventeen "Fighting McCook's" serving in the Union army. Two of his brothers were generals. His former law partner, William Tecumseh Sherman, who now commanded the army, had hand-picked him for this mission.

He formed his unit in a column of regiments five deep. Mac was at the rear of the formation. As the moment approached, Colonel McCook ordered his men to fix bayonets. Then he said to them,

"Then out spake brave Horatius, the Captain of the gate:
'To every man upon this earth death cometh, soon or late.
And how can a man die better than facing fearful odds,
For the ashes of his fathers, and the temples of his gods.'"

The men were quiet but fidgety. When the Union artillery opened up, Mac turned to look back at the batteries. He watched shirtless men, sweat glistening on their exposed skin, loading the big guns and firing them with mechanical efficiency.

Bugles sounded the charge.

Soldiers surged forward as a unit, briskly covering the fifty feet to Morgan's line. They passed through the skirmish line and broke into a trot. They crossed the sluggish, marshy stream and ascended the opposite slope. Enemy musketry and artillery began hitting them as soon as they emerged from the ravine. They forged ahead and captured a line of rifle pits. They soldiered on. Batteries on their left and right peppered them with grape and canister. Good men fell never to rise. But they pushed on toward the bastion at the top of the hill. The deluge of steel grew more terrible the closer they got. When they got very close, the Johnnies threw rocks and hand grenades and yelled, "Chickamauga!"

Piles of tree trunks and branches shaped like pikes, covered with steel blades and stacked like hay, covered the ground in front of the rebel fortifications. As soldiers at the head of the charging column reached the obstruction, they grabbed the pikes and carried them off endwise to make a path for the rest.

Colonel McCook led the way, striding through a torrent of bullets unharmed as if protected by a magic charm. When he reached the edge of their stronghold, he turned and yelled, "Come on, boys, we've won the day."

Turning back, he leaped to the top of the parapet. He parried a bayonet thrust with his saber and killed the man with a counterstroke. He bellowed, "Surrender, traitors!"

One of the rebels raised his musket and shot McCook in the chest. He fell back, critically wounded but not dead. Soldiers grabbed him and carried him to the rear. In quick order, three more colonels stood to take command of the brigade, and each was shot dead on the spot.

The men in blue dropped to the ground to escape the never-ending musketry. Some used dead bodies as a shield. They were right under the enemy works, less than twelve feet away, but in no position to load and fire their muskets. The order was given to fall back twenty paces and form a new line. One by one, they worked their way back, leaving the dead and wounded to their fate.

Half the men kept firing while the other half, lying face down, used bayonets and tin cups to create a bulwark that would give them some protection. That effort took hours. It was midafternoon before they felt safe.

The sun beat down relentlessly. Their ammo was low. They had no food. They were out of water. They kept trading lead with the Johnnies.

Fresh supplies reached them at nightfall. They were given entrenching tools and orders to hold their ground.

Sherman had advanced troops across the creek. They held the trenches that had been occupied by Confederate pickets. Only a few hundred yards separated the two armies.

Those successes did not change the overall picture. It had taken little more than an hour to inflict three thousand Union casualties while fending off Sherman's brash offensive. The abatis that had taken the steam out of the Yankee charge were still in place. Southern soldiers were still protected by a solid, six-foot-thick wall. They were still able to concentrate musket and artillery fire anywhere to their front.

Throughout that night and the next day, the two armies pounded each other with artillery. Soldiers along the front line sniped from entrenched positions. Any soldier who stood up could expect to be shot. The men kept their heads down and fired blindly. Random Union musket balls ricocheting off the walls of the Confederate fortress took their toll.

But the strategic situation had changed dramatically. The thinly manned Confederate left flank had been breached. Cox had made his move before sunrise. By the time artillery and bugles launched the attack on the Confederate works, he had driven the dismounted cavalry from their stronghold blocking the bridge across Ollie Creek. By the end of the day, he had pushed the rebel horsemen two more miles toward Marietta and had established his camp on a ridge overlooking the valley.

Hooker's Second Division had been placed in reserve, awaiting orders to follow McCook in the attack on the Bloody Angle. But those orders were never issued.

Tom spent a tense day waiting to jump into action. He watched from the division's staging area as the blue waves swept over Kennesaw Mountain and Pigeon Hill, but he did not hear any news of the battle's progress.

The wounded had begun streaming into field hospitals shortly after the assault began. They continued arriving throughout the day. Some died within hours of reaching the sanctuary. It wasn't until late Tuesday, the day after the assault, that Tom found Kat outside the hospital tent. More than twenty-four hours tending to the casualties had left her completely exhausted.

They searched out an abandoned rifle pit that would provide some protection from the sun and prying eyes. They talked as they walked. Kat said, "It's horrible in there. It's like an oven and there aren't enough beds. Those poor men are in agony."

Tom glanced at her but said nothing. She continued, "It's not as bad as Gettysburg, but it's bad enough. We only have three surgeons and they're kept busy taking care of the most seriously wounded. The others are handed off to me and other women. We dress minor wounds and do our best to make sure the men have water and food. I was looking after at least a hundred of them."

Tom put an arm around her shoulder and squeezed. He kissed her on the forehead. She said, "They're rushing these men off to Big Shanty."

"Why?"

"Shipping them to Chattanooga, I think."

"Why?"

"Something about not having enough supplies."

Tom puzzled over that statement, while they walked and Kat went on about conditions in the medical tent. He said, "That only makes sense if we don't have the train to bring supplies. Sherman is going to march us around Johnston's left flank to capture Marietta. That'll cut the rebels off from Atlanta."

When they found what they were looking for, they crawled into the hole, curled into a heap and fell asleep.

The next day, a truce was called to deal with rotting bodies that were creating an unbearable stench. Tom led one detail to perform a task that he had come to see as a necessary part of every great battle. When he and his team had finished their work, he made his way up to the Union breastwork near the Bloody Angle. He found Mac stretched out, relaxing, but not sleeping.

Tom paused to observe what appeared to be a Sunday social in the no-man's land between the two fortified works. Officers and common soldiers were passing the time in casual conversation with the enemy. Yanks mixed with Johnnies as if they were next-door neighbors. Some were serious. Others joked. In one bit of conversation, a man with a drawl was talking about his family back home. In another, two officers, one in gray, one in blue, who had apparently served together before the war, were catching up on their lives.

Tom asked, "Why aren't you out there socializing?"

"I already got my fill. Besides I talked to them some yesterday and last night. Tossed them a bag of coffee for a plug of tobacco."

"That sounds pretty chummy. I thought you were shooting at each other."

"We been doin' that too. There really isn't much point in making friends with them. They know we're getting ready to attack them just like they're getting ready to jump us."

Tom studied the rebel fortifications. "You're planning to storm that wall?"

"Nah," Mac said. He pointed toward a hole that looked like the entrance to a tunnel. "We're gonna blow them to kingdom come."

"Do they know that?"

Mac nodded and grinned at his friend. "Yeah. A couple of them came down here and looked at the tunnel. They said they knew that's what we were up to."

"How long will it take?"

"A couple more days." Mac chuckled. "We're gonna do it on July Fourth."

"How's life up here?" Tom asked.

"Terrible. We're cramped together and you can't stretch out. You can barely move without gettin' shot. But as long as we're here they ain't whipped us."

Tom laughed. He reached out and shook his friend's hand. "By the way, Schofield got around the left flank. We're going around them just like I said."

He turned and trudged back down the hill to his unit.

The Federal encampment became a beehive of activity. Troops were rotated in and out of the entrenchments captured from the Confederates, and the unexpected position just yards from the salient on Cheatham's Hill. Sherman could renew his assault, or he could undertake a siege, the strategy preferred by Thomas.

Troops began accumulating rations for a ten-day march away from the railroad. Each regiment was allowed one wagon to carry the ammunition it would need.

Field hospitals were emptied. The sick and wounded were shipped to Chattanooga or the new hospital at Rome. Kat was scheduled to go to Rome, but Geary insisted he needed her at his headquarters.

XX Corps stretched its line south to relieve Haskell's division of the Army of the Ohio so it could join up with Cox's division. This put the Army of the Ohio in control of all the roads to Marietta, Ollie Creek, Nickajack Creek, and the hilly ridge separating the two valleys. The main road from Sandtown on the Chattahoochee to Marietta passed through Smyrna Station, five miles south of the Confederate supply depot.

Stoneman's cavalry reached the Chattahoochee River and covered Sherman's right flank.

By July 1, McPherson was ready to move the Army of the Tennessee around the Army of the Cumberland so he could join up with Schofield and the Army of the Ohio. The move was to be made the following night after dark and completed before the rebels knew what was happening.

On the morning of July 2, Sherman staged a demonstration against the rebels. It opened with artillery fire followed by a reconnaissance in force all along the line. That afternoon, the Army of the Tennessee's supply wagons got an early start. Soon after McPherson's wagons began moving, observers spotted Confederate supply wagons making a similar move.

Mac woke with a start and bounced up, ready to fend off an attack. He sensed that something was moving about. It was two or three in the morning according to the position of the moon. A voice called out from the darkness, "Hey, Yanks, don't shoot. I wanna surrender."

The seceches had put out cotton balls soaked in pitch and set on fire to light the space between the two entrenchments. Mac could not locate the speaker despite the flickering flames. In a loud voice, he ordered the man to "Step forward and show yourself."

A tall, gaunt figure stepped into the light. He held a musket over his head. After a moment, he said, "They're all gone. I wanna surrender."

"Put your weapon down and walk over here slowly."

The man lowered his musket to the ground, and eased toward Mac with his arms raised. Mac demanded, "What's your name?"

"Elijah. Elijah Johnson." When he reached the parapet, he said, "They were gone an hour ago. I reckon Uncle Joe figured he'd better git out while the gittin' was good."

Mac ordered a full alert. Everybody got up, ready to shoot anything that moved. Then he sent two scouts over to check the rebel works. "Throw a couple of them balls over the wall and make sure nobody's back there waitin' to ambush us."

After the point men had looked over the wall and declared the trenches empty, Mac detailed soldiers to escort Elijah back to headquarters and report the situation. He set out on a more thorough investigation.

By four, skirmishers from all divisions were working their way up the mountains. Troops crept forward, dreading what might be waiting for them. They celebrated exuberantly every time they found a position empty.

Mac reached the top of Big Kennesaw as dawn was breaking. Others were close behind him.

On the other side of Noyes Creek, Sherman had borrowed a surveyor's glass to get a good look. He experienced a moment of exultation that he would never forget when he confirmed the men on the peak of Big Kennesaw were his.

By six, Thomas was marching the Army of the Cumberland to Marietta. He found the town virtually empty. All the military supplies and most of the population had been moved by train to Atlanta after the battle on June 27. Sherman reached the city at 8:30. He was furious at the half-hearted pursuit of the Confederates. "It is imperative," he said, "that we catch Johnston on the move."

Thomas advanced south along the railroad track and found the Confederates entrenched at Smyrna Station. Sherman ordered an attack with heavily reinforced skirmish lines. Howard hit the rebels' right flank at four. At the same time, Dodge attacked their left flank. The battles were hard fought, bloody and costly. But the Southerners were pushed from their trenches.

That night, Johnston pulled back to his last defensive line west of the Chattahoochee River. Time and energy had been put into making this one formidable. The architect was Johnston's artillery commander. The Georgia militia had built it with the help of impressed slaves. It was six miles long, extending from Paces Ferry to Turners Ferry and blocking all three bridges leading to Atlanta. Detached redoubts guarded ferries along the river.

Sherman paused to establish his line and develop a strategy.

61

July 6, 1864

My Dearest Mother,

By the grace of God, I am alive and well. The battle on Pigeon Hill, which you have no doubt read about, was fierce and bloody. We were not able to drive the Confederates from their mountain stronghold, but in a matter of days, General Sherman's maneuvers forced them to abandon it. They have now fallen back to a fortress on the banks of the Chattahoochee River. It looks invincible. But I'm sure we will force them to surrender it.

Three days ago, we were awakened in the middle of the night with news that they had slipped away from their works on Kennesaw Mountain. We moved forward to investigate, and much to our delight, we found the report to be accurate.

We had done a great deal of damage to their fortifications, and they would've been forced to withdraw eventually. Trees the size of a man's leg had been cut down by musket balls. Likewise, musket balls had cut big chunks of wood from the logs they were using at the top of their breastwork. The walls of their trenches bore thousands of pockmarks where mini balls had hit and bounced off. They had dug caves to hide from our balls bouncing around inside their fortress. They must have suffered many casualties while hiding in those fortifications.

We scooped up many stragglers as we chased the rebels fleeing to Marietta. These men were tired and discouraged. They were happy to become our prisoners because they realized the South could no longer win.

Now Atlanta is plainly visible from our encampment. We are about to capture it and end this war.

But it is not over. Many thousands will continue fighting as long as their leaders refuse to recognize that there is nothing left to fight for.

Your devoted son,

Tom

62

Hostilities Renewed

The Army of the Potomac had made significant gains despite failing to capture Petersburg. Grant intended to rest his troops, but he had to capitalize on what had been accomplished. He began making plans and surveying the territory the day after the disastrous battle of June 18.

Meade's forces had ended up southeast of the city after crossing the James River. The Jerusalem Plank Road, running south from the Appomattox River through the eastern suburbs of Petersburg and into the countryside, provided a natural defensive line for the Federals. Warren was ordered to extend his line as far as the Jerusalem Plank Road. II Corps and VI Corps were pulled out of the trenches facing Petersburg and posted behind V Corps.

Grant rode with Butler along the James River, looking for a crossing and a route to attack Petersburg from the northeast.

Spies reported that Lee attended services at St. Paul's Episcopal Church on Sunday, June 19.

That night, Kennedy and Goldman sat smoking their pipes and discussing the situation over coffee. Goldman said, "He'll use the same strategy he used at Vicksburg."

"Oh yeah. What was that?"

"Surround them and wait for them to run out of food. That won't take long after we cut the railroads."

Kennedy grimaced and shook his head. "Lee won't let that happen. He's had an answer for every strategy Grant's tried."

Wilcox joined them. "Hi, boys. Hope you're enjoying the weather."

Kennedy said, "A sunny day in hell. At least it ain't rainin'."

"Shouldn't you be guarding your howitzer?" Goldman growled.

"I left it in good hands. I was feeling a little down and I thought spending some time with lads who are really suffering would cheer me up."

Kennedy said, "You better have something good. I'm of a mind to shoot somebody."

"We're going to be here a while. I was part of a detail escorting Grant today. He and Butler scouted the river for a good place to cross and launch an attack north of the city."

"Find anything?" Goldman asked.

"A place called Deep Harbor. It's a few miles upstream. We'll have a pontoon bridge in place in a couple of days."

"What about us?" Kennedy asked.

"We're going to attack," Goldman snapped. "We're not going to wait for them to get comfortable."

Wilcox nodded sagely and sipped his coffee.

II Corps started moving to the east shoulder of the Jerusalem Plank Road early on Monday, June 20. Soldiers marched through choking dust as the sun climbed higher in the sky and the temperature soared. By midday, they were positioned along the road to the left of V Corps. They spent the rest of the day fortifying a two-mile stretch parallel to the highway.

That was dangerous work for the exhausted soldiers. It could be fatal in the oppressive, muggy heat. As the afternoon wore on, men had to be carried to the rear after collapsing from heat stroke.

A party on horseback approached them late that afternoon. They were escorting a giant of a man dressed in black like an undertaker. President Lincoln had come to pay a visit to the men fighting the war. He was gracious and even shook hands with several of the men.

VI Corps moved to the left of II Corps. Entrenching along Jerusalem Plank Road continued well into the night.

Word spread around the camp that night that skirmishers had cleared the way for an attack on the Weldon Railroad, which connected Petersburg to Weldon, North Carolina. It snaked through the hills five miles west of the Jerusalem Plank Road, carrying supplies and troops to Petersburg and Richmond from parts of the South untouched by the war.

Union cavalry set out for Reams Station on the Weldon Railroad at three in the morning on June 21. Its mission was to torch the station and tear up track, disrupting the flow of supplies into Petersburg.

Both II Corps and VI Corps started across the highway before dawn. Marshy, vegetation-choked woodland made organized movement practically impossible. Wide gaps opened up between the two corps. Closing those fissures took time and slowed progress.

The overall movement was a line rotating north as it moved west. II Corps was on the inside. Two of its divisions reached their goal early and had fortifications in place by midday. They faced north, ready to fend off attacks from Petersburg. The Third Division, under Barlow, had the additional responsibility of maintaining contact with VI Corps. Kennedy's job was to control the skirmish line that maintained the connection between Barlow's division and VI Corps. But Wright's men were not keeping pace.

Around midday, Wright came up against Confederate opposition. He ordered his men to form a line of battle and entrench. Barlow sent a message to headquarters informing Meade of the situation. The commander ordered Barlow to cut ties with VI Corps and proceed with his mission.

The Barlow moved his men into position on the left of the Second Division, but that exposed his left flank. An attack from the west would be devastating. He curved his line to face a strike from that direction.

At three o'clock, rebel war whoops rang out. Confederate troops emerged from a ravine in the Union rear. They streamed onto the battlefield as if from nowhere, charging at a dead run, shouting and firing their muskets.

The Yanks, who had been digging trenches and setting up bastions, were caught in the open with their weapons stacked. The left side of Barlow's line broke and ran for the safety of the Jerusalem Plank Road. The center quickly collapsed under pressure from the Confederate attack. The right didn't hold out much longer.

II Corps reorganized behind the bastion it had constructed east of Jerusalem Plank Road the day before. They fought the pursuing rebels the rest of the afternoon and into the night.

In the morning, skirmishers pushed west across the highway again. They met no resistance. The Confederate forces had pulled back inside their defenses around Petersburg. Birney, still standing in for the ailing Hancock, put II Corps to work connecting the fortifications constructed on June 21 with those on the east side of the Jerusalem Plank Road.

That was the beginning of a network of forts with interconnecting trenches that would eventually encircle Petersburg and Richmond like a noose, choking the life out of the Confederacy.

With a temporary pause in the fighting, Kennedy asked for and was granted a furlough. He made his way to City Point to spend a few days with his wife. Roishin stayed away from the hospital to coddle him. She led him to her rented room and shut the door. They tore off their clothes and went at each other like starving beasts. When they stopped to rest, she said, "Ah, that beard's gotta be goin'."

She drew a bath for him. Shaved his beard. Trimmed his hair. They joined the other boarders for dinner. And returned to their lovemaking. Kennedy slept till noon. Roishin brought him eggs and toast with coffee for breakfast. Later, they strolled in the afternoon sun.

They could not avoid the war. It was everywhere. All day, every day, supplies were unloaded from ships at the wharves and reloaded for transport to Grant's army. Soldiers in uniform, officers and enlisted men, were out and about on their official duties. Ambulances brought the wounded to the hospitals.

Newspapers reported on developments. One big story concerned the cavalry and the Shenandoah Valley.

Union General David Hunter and the West Virginia cavalry had disappeared. They had not been seen for two weeks after withdrawing from Lynchburg without a fight. Hunter had been successful in early June, defeating the rebels at Piedmont. But when he found the Southerners entrenched and ready to make a stand at the railroad hub in Lynchburg, he had retreated after launching a few feeble attacks.

Newspapers reported the Southerners had conducted an elaborate ruse to make their army appear larger than it was. The Union general had been fooled and given up without a fight rather than risk defeat.

As a result, Confederate General Early was running amok in the Shenandoah.

63

Across the Chattahoochee

The Army of the Cumberland pursued the Confederate Army of Tennessee as it retreated from its trenches around Smyrna Station. Howard, on the left flank, followed the Western and Atlantic Railroad to Paces Ferry on the Chattahoochee. McPherson and the Union Army of the Tennessee advanced to Turners Ferry on the right. The cavalry under Stoneman bivouacked near Sandtown, covering McPherson and searching for an unprotected crossing.

A Confederate fortress blocked the main routes to Atlanta. Abatis obstructed approaches to the rebel stronghold. Artillery and musketry greeted Thomas as soon as he got in range. He deployed a line across the front of the stronghold rather than attempt a suicidal attack.

IV Corps found a pontoon bridge protected by a brigade of dismounted cavalry at Paces Ferry. The Yanks drove the defenders off, but the rebels destroyed the bridge as soon as they had crossed the river. Howard encamped on high ground overlooking the ferry while he waited for pontoons for a new bridge.

Garrard's cavalry explored the road as far as Roswell, eighteen miles upstream from the Confederate bastion. The bridge connecting the town to Atlanta had been destroyed. Garrard burned the town's factories and sent the workers north to prevent them from supporting the war effort.

The Army of the Ohio was kept at Smyrna Station as a mobile force that could support either Howard or McPherson.

Sherman set up his headquarters on high ground overlooking Johnston's fortress. From there, he could see the whole Chattahoochee Valley, including the defensive works surrounding the besieged city and houses within its walls.

A month had passed since Sherman and his army had crossed the Etowah, a hundred miles northwest of Atlanta. They had persevered through extreme weather as they marched, skirmished, and even fought a few major battles. Now, they were preparing to cross the Chattahoochee, less than a dozen miles from the city.

A heavy price in life and limb had been paid. Their most important victory was over themselves. Three separate armies, thrown together in May, had become a single, indomitable fighting force in July.

Sherman tasked Schofield with finding a way to cross the Chattahoochee. The general surveyed the river in person, from the burned-out bridge at Roswell to Turners Ferry. He selected a place midway between the ferry and the rebels' main fortifications where Soap Creek emptied into the Chattahoochee. Steep ridges towered two hundred feet above the river on both banks. The creek ran parallel to the ridge on the north bank for several hundred yards before making a sharp turn to join the larger stream. The commanding general ordered Schofield to make the crossing the following day.

On July 9, Cox led Schofield's little Army of the Ohio from Smyrna Station to the jumping off point. He brought canvas boats for a crossing and pontoons for a bridge. The boats were set up out of sight behind the ridge while a regiment of Ohio infantrymen made its way upstream to a fishing dam submerged below the rain-swollen waters of the river.

The attack launched at 3:30. Union soldiers clambered across the narrow top of the sunken fishing dam. At the same time, boats carrying Union troops burst onto the Chattahoochee and crossed to the south shore.

The rebels had one cannon to block the crossing. They got off one shot before Federal sharpshooters found their range and made it too hot for the Southern artillerymen. The Johnnies abandoned their post and raced away to report the situation.

Cox recognized that the high ridge he had just captured on the south bank was an ideal defensive position and began digging in.

Pioneers went to work on two pontoon bridges. They had one ready by dark.

The next morning, the Southern cavalry attempted to dislodge Cox. They gave up after one charge. Sherman had outflanked Johnston again.

While the Army of the Ohio completed its crossing of the Chattahoochee, Howard forced a crossing at Paces Ferry, and Dodge's division of McPherson's Army of the Tennessee marched upstream to replace the bridge at Roswell.

Sherman watched the Confederate reaction to these forays from his vantage point and planned his next move. The Union army spent a week preparing for a final push to capture its prize, the Gate City, Atlanta.

Railroads were repaired, and supplies began flowing to the troops. Warehouses at Allatoona and Marietta were provisioned. River crossings were improved and strengthened. On the morning of July 18, Sherman's army pushed forward from the banks of the Chattahoochee to force the surrender of Atlanta.

McPherson crossed at Roswell and marched to the railroad midway between Stone Mountain and Decatur, five miles northeast of Atlanta. Schofield crossed at Soap Creek and proceeded to Decatur. Thomas crossed at Paces Ferry and advanced to Peachtree Creek northwest of Atlanta.

The following day, McPherson began tearing up track and working toward Decatur to join up with Schofield, who was extending his line west to connect with Howard and the Army of the Cumberland. Thomas performed a wheel maneuver and formed into a battle line along the west bank of Peachtree Creek.

Sherman's army advanced more rapidly than expected because the Confederates offered little resistance.

Throughout the morning of July 20, the Army of the Potomac crossed Peachtree Creek and began setting up on the east bank. Newton became concerned about his division's exposure because of a ravine separating it from the rest of Howard's Corps. He curved his left flank along the ravine and ordered his men to erect a log parapet to shield their front.

Hooker was on Newton's right.

About three o'clock, thousands of screaming rebels sprang from a line of trenches and the adjacent woods. They tore across the open ground like crazed animals. Yankee artillery firing from the far side of the creek mowed the Johnnies down. But that didn't stop the charge. Hooker's Second Division took the brunt of the attack. A second wave charged at four and a third at five.

This final wave crashed into the Union line, forcing it back. Sergeant Tom Donal kept his men fighting. They slashed with bayonets and clubbed with rifle butts. After a long, bloody hour, the Yanks began to regain ground. After another hour, the Southerners broke off and slipped back to their defenses. Many wounded managed to make it to those trenches, but the ground between the armies was thick with the dead and the dying.

The following day, a truce was arranged to care for the fallen. Wounded Southerners were hauled into the city. Northerners were carried to field hospitals being set up in Decatur. The dead were buried in mass graves. Crude placards marked the final resting place of many valiant men. The sign on one burial mound read, "Captain William Smythe and thirty-four others."

After the pause, Thomas and Schofield advanced their forces and entrenched close to the rebel works west and north of Atlanta. McPherson tightened the noose from the east. He captured a hill midway between the railroad and the city. It became known as Leggett's Hill in honor of the general who led the assault and forced the rebels to abandon it. Union troops immediately set about reworking Confederate trenches for their own purposes.

On the morning of July 22, Union commanders discovered that the rebels had abandoned their forward positions and pulled back into the defenses around Atlanta. Under orders from Sherman to get as close as possible, Thomas and Schofield pushed forward, driving skirmishers back until they had established a position on a line of hills separated from the city by a valley with a creek running through it. They entrenched and positioned their batteries. The siege of Atlanta was on.

Around noon, while Dodge was marching to secure McPherson's left flank, Confederates burst from the woods east of Atlanta in a devastating assault. They overlapped the Union line and began pushing Yanks from their entrenched positions.

Shortly after the surprise attack, McPherson, racing to take charge of the front, ran into a party of rebel pickets. Rather than surrender, he wheeled his horse and took off at a gallop. The Johnnies opened fire. A mini ball hit the general in the back and traveled up his torso and through his heart before lodging in his chest. He was dead when he hit the ground. The Army of the Tennessee had lost its leader at a critical moment.

The fury and savagery of the battle that followed matched any of the legendary confrontations between the two armies. The Confederates, frustrated by two months of retreat and now backed into a corner, charged like a horde of demons from hell. Veteran Union troops, outflanked and outmatched, gave ground grudgingly. For over an hour, the Southerners forced their enemy back toward Leggett's Hill.

Confederate troops came out of the trenches in front of Atlanta and attacked the Union soldiers holding that hill. Union artillery unlimbered and began shelling the rebels. They kept coming.

The Southerners circled north of the entrenched position on the isolated hill and hit the Yanks from the rear. Battle-hardened Union vets jumped the parapets and repelled that thrust while fighting from the wrong side of the bastion. The next attack came from the front. The vets jumped back over their barrier. Again, they staved off the Confederate onslaught. When the rebels did make it to their line, the Federals fought with bayonets and rifle butts, driving the enemy back.

McPherson's senior corps commander, Black Jack Logan, raced to the front on his black stallion to lead a countercharge.

In an instant, the fortunes of war changed. Yankees held their ground and began pushing the men in gray back to the woods where they had started.

Southern Cavalry skirted the battle and attacked Decatur, where the supply wagons and medical units were stationed. A heroic fighting retreat by Sprague allowed the workers and wagons to pull back to the safety of the main line. Rumors spread that General Walker, the leader of the raid, was shot from his horse and died, one of the thousands of casualties in that assault.

As the sun was setting, the rebel army pulled back inside its fortifications. The Southerners had held onto Atlanta, but they had lost thousands of fighters. And Sherman was still camped on their doorstep.

That night, some survivors of the day's battles meandered through the encampment, swapping rumors and stories with men from Thomas's army. Tom sat quietly smoking his pipe while he caught up on recent events with these wandering newsmen. After they left, he made his way to the field hospital and found Kat. They embraced and held each other for several minutes. Tom said, "I heard it was touch and go for a while."

"I think they came close to capturing us, but Sprague's men fought them off."

"I heard there was a woman on the scrimmage line."

Kat shrugged. Tom said, "I heard she shot Walker off his horse."

Another shrug. Tom hooked his finger under her chin and turned her head so they were eye to eye. Kat pressed her lips into a grim line and shook her head. "The men were out there fighting and dying so we could run for cover. You would have done exactly what I did. I saw a man go down and I raced over to help him. His eyes were shut. He was wheezing. Struggling to breathe. Blood spurted from his mouth with every breath. I grabbed his hand. He squeezed back. There was nothing I could do and we both knew it. I said I need your carbine. His eyes opened. I think he tried to smile. Then he was gone." Kat's brows lifted. She shrugged. "I grabbed his rifle and ammo and I took his place on the line."

Tom grimaced and shook his head. She snarled her answer. "It's my fight too. And I'm the best damn shot in this army."

"So did you shoot Walker?"

Kat's lips curled into a bitter smile. "I shot a few of them, but I didn't get their names."

Tom's hand brushed gently across her cheek and came to rest on her neck. He pulled her in for a kiss. Kat took his hand and led him into the shadows beyond the firelight. He took her in his arms, and they swayed gently, savoring the sweet affirmation of body pressed against body. Tom broke it off and kissed her. "I've got to get back."

She stroked his beard. "Take care."

"You too." He turned abruptly and started back to his tent. As he walked, he wondered whether it was better to have her fighting at his side or far away, where he wouldn't know about it until after the dust settled.

64

Undermining Petersburg

Leaving Roishin's bed at City Point was harder than Kennedy had imagined. The situation in the camp around Petersburg was worse.

The troops were not fighting. They were digging trenches. Expanding their line. Forcing the rebels to stretch their front at the expense of their effective strength.

For Northern soldiers laboring in sweltering heat under a torrid sun, the conditions were extreme.

Wilson's cavalry had returned from a nine-day raid on July 1. According to stories making the rounds, the horse soldiers had reached Reams Station and burned it to the ground on June 22. They began moving west along the Southside Railroad, which ran parallel to the Appomattox River. They tore up track until they reached the Staunton River Bridge. A militia group defending that crossing managed to hold off the Union cavalry long enough for the Confederate cavalry to join the battle. Wilson escaped the trap by sending his men racing along circuitous routes back to City Point.

The Irish were in revolt. When Hancock returned to duty, he found II Corps gutted by casualties, illness, and veterans going home at the end of their enlistment. Its strength had been slashed by thirty percent. He made necessary changes, consolidating units to get the required average strength. When he broke up the Irish brigade, he wounded the pride of men who had fought and served with distinction throughout the war. Those men vowed to never fight again.

Kennedy spent days and nights smoothing ruffled feathers and rebuilding the Irish force. "We can't quit now. We've got them whipped. We have to keep going until they surrender."

When that didn't work, he said, "If you don't keep fighting, you will be betraying your friends who lost life and limb fighting beside you."

Gradually, Celtic pride yielded. The immigrant Irish, whose warrior traditions were older than Western Civilization, bought into Kennedy's way of thinking. They brought the others with them.

When Kennedy connected with Sam Goldman and his cousin Josh, the topic was a project undertaken by IX Corps. Burnside's men were digging a tunnel to bury explosives under the Confederate works southeast of Petersburg. Sam was ecstatic. He declared, "They're halfway there."

Kennedy looked skeptical. "How long is this tunnel?"

"About five hundred feet."

"Isn't that pretty risky?"

"That's what they did before the war. They were coal miners."

Josh said, "Colonel Pleasanton, the man behind the idea, was an engineer with a coal mining company." He looked over at Sam before continuing. "General Burnside likes the idea. It's flashy. Brings some swagger to the siege. But Meade isn't sold on it. He's giving Burnside some rope to hang himself."

"What about Grant?"

"He's putting it on Meade."

"But the work is moving forward," Kennedy suggested.

Sam chuckled. "Yep. There have been a few problems. They had to work past an underground stream and the roof collapsed once. But nothing they couldn't handle."

Kennedy shook his head. "How long have they been working on it?"

"A couple of weeks."

"So, we blow up the Confederate defenses," Kennedy said. "Then what?"

Sam grinned. "We march in and take the city."

Josh said, "By *we*, he means the division of colored troops in IX Corps."

Kennedy shrugged. "What difference does that make? They did a good job in the fighting last month."

Josh said, "It's a hot potato. If they capture the city, they'll get a lot of good press. But, if they're slaughtered in the attack, Burnside, Meade and even Grant will be accused of using them as cannon fodder."

Sam said, "And if white troops lead the charge and get slaughtered?"

Over the next ten days, Kennedy heard rumors that Southern deserters were talking about the mining project. The tunnel was common knowledge inside the Confederate fortifications, and it worried the rebels.

Kennedy ran into Jeremiah, who said he and his fellow troops were excited about the prospect. They were convinced they would capture Petersburg.

On July 27, Hancock was ordered to cross at Deep Bottom with the cavalry under Sheridan in support. Entrenched Confederate forces were waiting behind formidable breastworks at Baileys Creek, a few miles from the crossing. Hancock set up facing them and began searching for weaknesses.

Sheridan captured the nearby heights but was driven back by a rebel counterattack.

On July 28, a brigade from XIX Corps was sent to reinforce Hancock. Sheridan made an unsuccessful attempt to recapture the heights. The following day, Grant, satisfied he had forced Lee to deploy troops to block the thrust, called Hancock and Sheridan back to the trenches.

At dawn the next morning, tremors shook the men of II Corps out of a sound sleep. Kennedy leaped to his feet and out of his tent in time to see a fireball shooting hundreds of feet in the air. The deafening roar of an explosion caught up seconds later. The sound of artillery blasting the rebel works in support of an assault followed immediately.

He knew what it meant. Another promising offensive. Another bloody battle. He was glad it wasn't II Corps. The men needed rest. But part of him yearned to join the fight. He expected it would end badly. All the more reason he should be in the middle of it, doing his damnedest to tip the scale.

By midmorning, reports of fierce fighting circulated through the camp. According to the rumors, hundreds of Confederates had been captured. Kennedy's heart sank. It was the Mule Shoe all over again. Another brutal battle. Another great slaughter. And nothing to show for it.

By noon, it was over. Word spreading through the camp confirmed the sergeant's fears. The Union assault had been repulsed. Thousands had been killed. Thousands more, both white and black, had been taken prisoner.

That night, Sam and his cousin stopped by to visit Kennedy. The correspondent was out of sorts. He seemed tense, anxious. Kennedy started a fresh pot of coffee. Sam said, "Josh was at the crater this morning."

"How did you manage that?" Kennedy asked.

"It wasn't hard. I showed up early and marched with them when they took off for the blast site."

"What happened?"

"The blast blew a huge crater but the entrance was narrow. When we arrived, Confederate prisoners were being marched out. It was bedlam. We were pushing to get in and take control while rebel prisoners were being herded out. No one was in charge. No high-ranking officers were around to give orders. Ledlie never showed up."

Kennedy interrupted. "Ledlie? I thought it was supposed to be Ferrero."

"It was," Josh said. "Meade overruled Burnside at the last minute. He insisted on a different division. He was probably afraid the newspapers would have a field day if the colored troops got shot up but failed to capture the city."

Sam interjected, "Meade's gun-shy. The press has been rough on him."

"And Ledlie is the best he could do?" Kennedy demanded.

Josh said, "I don't know how he came up with Ledlie. He's considered the worst of the four division commanders. It was a late decision and probably never got reviewed. No matter. There wasn't a general or even a colonel on hand to lead the strike. Low-level commanders with conflicting orders had to work through the chaos to get the attack going."

Kennedy said, "They never made it past the crater. Did they?"

Josh shook his head. "The hole was too small for a division. The entrance was just a narrow gap. We had to push our way in. That gave the Johnnies time to recover. They jumped over the lip and started pushing our boys out."

He paused to sip his coffee.

"Did the black troops ever get involved?" Kennedy demanded.

"Eight o'clock. They came marching up in two columns but there was no place for them to go. Some companies went to the left of the pit. The rest went to the right. By that time the Johnnies were dug in on both sides." He paused to sip his coffee and study his friends. "At eleven, Meade's chief of staff showed up and ordered everybody to pull back."

A truce was arranged so the dead could be buried. The Confederates placed guards to prevent Union troops from entering the crater. Southern soldiers carried the bodies out of the pit and handed them over to Northern soldiers. All the corpses were black and bloated. The only difference between the whites and the blacks was their hair.

Idlers from both armies began to fraternize while the gruesome business moved forward. A Confederate army band came out and began to play. When a Union army band joined them, the two bands took turns.

Josh Goldman brought a rebel soldier to Kennedy. He said, "This is Seth Brown. He wants to surrender. You should listen to what he has to say before you decide what to do with him."

Kennedy turned to the deserter and nodded. Seth began, "Ah'm tired of all this. It ain't worth it. Ah've seen things no man should see and ah've done things no man should do. But no more." He paused to get the sergeant's reaction. Kennedy stared impassively.

"Yestiday they marched yer boys through the streets. They were mixed together. A column of whites and a column of niggers. The whole town turned out for the show. It was the strangest thing we'd ever seen. People jeered. Razzin' them white boys was great fun. See what happens when you treat niggers like they's yer equal?" Seth turned and spat. "Thet was them thet survived. Right after the battle, when the prisoners were being rounded up and tallied, a lot of niggers were shot and bayonetted." The rebel's face twisted in disgust. "My brother's a nigger. Pa picked out a pretty slave and knocked her up. I couldn't stop seeing Lijah while them Johnnie Rebs murdered unarmed prisoners right in front of me. I told myself I was gettin' out first chance I got." He pressed his lips together and nodded. "Ah surrender. Ah'm yer prisoner."

That night, Kennedy was sitting by his fire, drinking coffee and puffing on his pipe, when Jeremiah appeared from nowhere. The big man looked beaten, but he radiated white-hot anger. Kennedy motioned for him to sit while he poured whisky into a spare cup and dug out a plug of tobacco. "We all heard what happened."

"Meade don' truss colored troops. If he was a nigga, he'da sent us in 'n' we'da capture da city."

Kennedy had no response. The two men sat in silence, nursing their drinks. After a while, Jeremiah got up and walked away.

The Union had lost four thousand more men and frittered away another opportunity to capture Petersburg. Major General John Parke replaced Burnside. His military career was over. Ledlie was sent home and told to wait for further orders. His military career was over.

Hunter's failure to rout Early at Lynchburg was a bigger problem for Grant. The Union general and his cavalry had disappeared after withdrawing from the battle. The Confederate cavalry immediately moved into the Shenandoah Valley and marched north, burning and looting as it went. After crossing the Potomac, Early turned east to threaten Washington. Grant was forced to dispatch VI Corps under Wright to bolster the depleted forces guarding the nation's capital.

The Southerners got close. A non-combat brigade stationed in Baltimore intercepted Early forty miles from Washington and forced a daylong battle. The Confederates moved on to the fortifications outside the capital but paused for a day to regroup.

Wright reached Washington at the same time as Early. He used the Confederates' one-day delay to deploy his corps in a strong defensive position. Two days of heavy skirmishing followed. The Southerners abruptly gave up and headed west to continue their reign of terror. Wright pursued.

Early torched the town of Chambersburg, Pennsylvania, on the same day that Burnside blasted a hole in the defenses around Petersburg.

Grant arranged a meeting with Lincoln in Washington to discuss strategy. On his way to that meeting, he cornered Hunter, who offered his resignation. Grant accepted and assigned the task of hunting down Early and finishing him off to Sheridan.

65

July 25, 1864

My Dearest Mother,

Trains with supplies reached our encampment outside Atlanta today. The bridges over the Chattahoochee River have been fully repaired.

We were attacked twice last week. The battles were bloody but we defeated them soundly. I was not injured in the fighting.

I believe the Confederates have grown tired of General Johnston's delaying tactics. They replaced him with General Hood who has lived up to his reputation as an aggressive leader. But it looks like his approach will be better for us.

Our Army has also had to make some changes in leadership. General McPherson, the commander of the Army of the Tennessee was killed last week. General Sherman chose General Howard to replace him. He has proved to be an effective field commander throughout this campaign. General Hooker has resigned and General Slocum who was our commander at Gettysburg will take his place. It appears that the promotion of General Howard was too much for General Hooker. It's an old grudge. General Hooker still blames General Howard for his loss at Chancellorsville.

I believe we will now be moving aggressively against the city of Atlanta. That means more fighting and killing but capturing the city will be worth it.

Your loving son,

Tom

66

Atlanta Under Siege

A few days of relative peace followed a month of intense action. The Union army had driven the Confederates off Kennesaw, crossed the Chattahoochee, and established itself close to Atlanta's defenses. Two major attacks by the Confederates under their new commander, Lieutenant General John Bell Hood, had taken a heavy toll in life and limb on both sides. Some guessed that the Confederate Army of Tennessee had lost a third of its force in those sorties. No one expected the rebels to attempt another assault.

Men and horses needed time to recover, and engineers would have to rebuild the railroad bridge across the Chattahoochee before the Union army began its next offensive.

The respite allowed Tom and Kat to spend nights alone together for the first time in a month.

General Tom Sweeny, one of the many Irish immigrants in Sherman's army, was the hero of a story making the rounds. He had risen through the ranks to command a brigade in spite of having lost his right arm in the Mexican War. He spoke English with a tolerable brogue except when he reverted to his native Irish lingo. He could cuss with the best of his sergeants. In this account, he had turned on a fellow general and accused him of cowardice during the battle on the twenty-second. The argument got heated and loud. Dodge stepped in to break up the confrontation. Sweeny turned on him and dressed him down for bypassing the chain of command and giving orders directly to the Irishman's subordinates. Infuriated, Dodge slapped Sweeny across the face. Sweeny threw a punch that sent his commanding officer to the ground with a bloody nose. He then tackled his fellow officer and wrestled him to the ground. It took three men to pull the Irishman off his victim and restrain him. Dodge scrambled to his feet and ordered Sweeny arrested.

McPherson's death forced a shake up in the command structure. Hooker, the former commander of the Army of the Potomac, was the obvious choice to take over command of the Army of the Tennessee. He was one of the most senior officers in the Grand Army. But Sherman had lost respect for the man. Thomas found him unruly and obstinate.

Black Jack Logan, interim commander of the Army of the Tennessee, had proven himself in combat. He was popular with the men. But Thomas faulted his education. He hadn't come out of West Point. He was a political general.

Sherman tapped Major General Oliver O. Howard for the position. He had graduated fourth in his class at West Point. And he was manageable. He worked well with his fellow officers.

Hooker took the choice as a slap in the face. Not only was Howard his junior in rank and experience, he was responsible for the loss at Chancellorsville. Fighting Joe submitted his resignation a second time. And again, it was accepted without discussion.

Although Hooker was popular, his departure was accepted with little comment. His replacement, Major General Henry Slocum, had led many of these men at Gettysburg. General Alpheus Williams, commander of the First Division, took over as interim corps commander while Slocum completed the transfer from his post at Vicksburg.

Reaction to the appointment of Howard as McPherson's replacement was a hot topic at the nightly gatherings. General Logan had recruited the men of XV Corps and led them through all their battles. General Blair had the same relationship with the men of XVI Corps. He had organized the militia that drove the Confederates out of St. Louis and kept Missouri in the Union. Howard was a stranger to these men and a cold fish, well known for quoting the Bible.

By July 25, the train bridge over the Chattahoochee had been rebuilt, and supplies were flowing directly to the Army of the Cumberland. Supply wagons, the field hospital and ambulances were relocated from Decatur to Peachtree Creek in Thomas's rear.

The Army of the Cumberland was sprawled out in a tent city that dwarfed nearby Atlanta. One might easily believe that Thomas could bring Hood to his knees if given the order to advance on the Gate City. But that city was perched on a mesa protected by a network of trenches with stout parapets and abatis in the surrounding foothills. It was going to be a tough nut to crack.

Sherman chose to sit outside those defenses and conduct a fitful bombardment of the city while he focused on isolating Atlanta by destroying tracks south of the citadel.

The Macon and Western Railroad brought supplies from Savannah. The Atlanta and West Point brought supplies from Mobile and Montgomery. Both lines terminated at Eastpoint, five miles south of Atlanta. From there, a single track carried supplies into the city.

Howard's first mission as commander of an army was breaking that stretch of track.

The operation began July 26 with a cavalry raid designed to tear up track well south of the city. General Edward Moody McCook led a force of three thousand horse soldiers west to Campbelltown on his way to Lovejoy Station. General George Stoneman, starting from Decatur with another three thousand, circled east, aiming to join up with McCook at Macon before hitting the railroad.

That night, the Army of the Tennessee began sliding one division at a time north and west around the rear of the Army of the Cumberland.

XV Corps under Logan led the way. XVI Corps and XVII Corps followed. They reached Elliott's Mill on Proctor Creek during the early hours of July 27 and started south on a country road that led to Ezra Church. Sherman and Howard rode at the front of the column. They reached the old Methodist meeting house around noon. Rebel activity in the area alerted Howard to a planned attack. He knew Hood well from their time at West Point. Attacking a column in motion was a strategy that appealed to his former schoolmate. Howard ordered Logan to get his men in position on the high ground around the church.

XV Corps began entrenching. Its line followed the road from Elliott's Mill south to Lick Skillet Road, where it turned west, curving horseshoe-like around the church before ending on a small rise that would become known as Battle Hill. The men grabbed pews from the church, rails from nearby fences, and anything else they could use for breastworks. When they ran out of material for the hastily constructed parapets, they pushed dirt into mounds that provided some semblance of cover.

Lick Skillet Road originated at a race course in the Atlanta suburbs and wandered southwest through the countryside, past farms and plantations, to the town of Lick Skillet. Confederate troops had marched along that road to intercept the Union forces heading south toward Eastpoint.

In the middle of the afternoon, the rebels launched their attack with their fearsome yell. Moments later, a long gray line charged out of the woods and across the road toward the Union position. An open field separated the two armies. XV Corps waited at the top of a hill behind the flimsy fortifications they had cobbled together. They were not going to give ground. Black Jack Logan roamed behind his men, roaring, "We hold this hill 'til hell freezes over."

The Southerners made six charges that afternoon. Each was bloodied and repulsed. As the sun was setting, the boys in blue along the crest of the hill could see Confederate officers on horseback, sabers drawn, ordering another charge, and the men in gray on the ground refusing to move.

The battle was over. XV Corps and the Army of the Tennessee controlled the high ground overlooking Lick Skillet Road. They were lodged two miles from the railroad. Howard had won his first major battle and the respect of the men in his new command.

Hood had lost another five thousand men in the gambit, but he had managed to halt Sherman's drive toward the vital railroad hub south of the city.

The rebels did not withdraw. They continued to confront Howard, provoking skirmishes and artillery duels as July slid into August.

The cavalry raid on Lovejoy Station south of Atlanta had flopped. Stoneman never reached the rendezvous point. He ran into a Confederate cavalry brigade and lost the fight. Most of his men escaped, but seven hundred of them were taken prisoner along with the general.

McCook gave up on him and proceeded to Lovejoy Station, where he tore up track and burned rolling stock. When he was satisfied, he started north with four hundred prisoners but ran into a brigade of rebel cavalry. He managed to escape the situation, but he lost the prisoners and suffered six hundred casualties.

Sherman ordered Schofield to march the Army of the Ohio around Thomas and south to Lick Skillet Road on August 1. The next day, Schofield formed a line along Utoy Creek south of the Army of the Tennessee. Howard wheeled his corps and advanced to line up with the new arrivals. On August 3, Palmer was directed south to the right of Schofield. He was ordered to report to Schofield, who would be in charge of overall operations. Palmer objected that he outranked the commander of the Army of the Ohio. He would cooperate with Schofield, but he would not take orders from him.

An assault set for six the following morning was delayed because one of Palmer's division commanders informed Schofield he did not recognize the major general's authority to issue orders.

Sherman rode out to confront Palmer and make him understand that Schofield was the ranking officer and his orders were to be obeyed.

But the following morning, Baird, another of Palmer's division commanders, ignored Schofield's orders for a couple of hours while he waited for the orders to come from his corps commander. He made a good start, but around noon, he halted for the day.

Schofield reported to Sherman that he was unable to make any significant progress without the cooperation of XIV Corps.

Sherman relieved Palmer of command and replaced him with a brigadier general who could follow orders.

By the time the squabble over rank had been resolved, the Southerners had gathered in force to make a stand. They could be heard chopping down trees throughout the night on August 6. In the morning, Union forces had to work past trees and limbs strewn haphazardly over vines and bushes as they moved forward, searching for the rebel stronghold. When they reached a clearing in front of the rebel fortifications, they could see the Johnnies entrenched behind stout breastworks. A day of probing and skirmishing proved that the Yanks would not be able to break through to the railroad.

Sherman had to stop the bombardment of Atlanta on August 12 when his ammunition ran out.

He tried his cavalry again. This time, he sent Brevet Major General Judson Kilpatrick with five thousand horsemen south of Eastpoint to destroy Jonesborough station. Kilpatrick routed a small contingent of rebels protecting the station, torched it, and began tearing up track. He was forced to stop working when a torrential downpour made it impossible for him to burn the ties and destroy the rails.

A counterattack by Confederate cavalry sent him scuttling back north. The escape went well until a brigade of dismounted cavalry blocked his route. With his pursuers closing in, Kilpatrick sent Colonel Minty and a brigade of

Yankee horse soldiers racing through a hail of musketry and artillery to get past the entrenched cavalrymen. After breaking through the ambush, Minty turned his men back and drove the Texans from their trenches, clearing the way for the rest of the Union cavalry.

Kilpatrick gave a glowing report of his accomplishments, but within days, the railroad was back in service, bringing supplies into the besieged city.

67

The Battle for the Weldon Railroad

August 9, 1864 - a day never to be forgotten.

Grant was on his way back to City Point after a meeting with Lincoln in Washington.

Josh Goldman was on his way to lunch with an officer, hoping for a scoop.

A flash of light and flames shooting into the air caught the reporter's attention. Almost immediately, he heard the roar of an explosion, and a shockwave knocked him to the ground. While he lay motionless, trying to make sense of it, something landed on his back, knocking the wind out of him. A limp black arm slid from his shoulder to the ground. It was attached to a headless torso. The remains of some poor dockworker who happened to have been in the wrong place when the cargo of an ammo ship exploded.

The blast knocked down buildings and blew away tents. It killed and injured people a hundred yards from the ship. It disrupted daily life for weeks around the boomtown created by Union army operations.

Investigations failed to determine a cause for the explosion. It was written off as an accident. Skeptics blamed it on Confederate spies who operated freely in the town.

Three days later, II Corps marched to the docks to board ships bound for an undisclosed destination. The troops were upbeat. Many believed they were headed for Washington. But it didn't matter where they were going. They were getting away from Petersburg. Many took time to look up a friend, acquaintance, or relative while waiting for their turn to board a ship.

Kennedy sought out his wife. She was delighted to see him, but when he mentioned Washington, she pulled back and eyed him skeptically. "Has Lee given up?"

"I don't think so."

"We'll be stayin' put in this spot 'til he does."

Kennedy grimaced. She was right.

"I've had a good yarn with many rebel lads in the hospital. Lee's the man. As long as he's leadin' the army, they'll keep up the fight."

Kennedy closed his eyes and nodded. "I know."

Roishin threw her arms around his neck and kissed him on the cheek. "When ye get to Washington, be sure to drop us a line. Begorrah, I'll come even if I have to walk the whole way! In the meantime, I'll be grand, just keepin' on as I am now."

The ships took their human cargo to a small inlet a few miles downstream. After midnight, they sailed back upstream to Deep Harbor. Flaws in the plan tripped up the execution.

Hancock had inspected the docks while his troops were embarking on the transport ships. The rotting wharf was unusable. He organized a work crew to get it ready to handle the landing.

Getting the entire corps from ship to shore took hours longer than expected. The three piers were too narrow for the planned operation. Soldiers on some larger vessels had to use a gangplank to transfer to a smaller ship to disembark.

The ten-thousand-man force led by Barlow was three hours late starting its march into enemy territory. The sun was already high in the sky. Scorching heat and humidity quickly took their toll on men who had been crammed into a dark, sweltering hold for an afternoon and a night. As the march across Curls Neck progressed, men fell out from fatigue. Some went into a seizure. Some died.

Entrenched Confederates blocked the road at Fussels Mill. Barlow deployed his soldiers to drive them off, but his disjointed attacks failed to dislodge the rebels. The general blamed his men's lackluster performance. "They did not show their usual dash."

The general fell short as well. His leadership lacked the acumen and energy that had saved his division at Spotsylvania. He was a shadow of himself, worn down by pain from his wounds and battle fatigue.

X Corps, led by Birney, was no more successful. They marched across the pontoon bridge in the early hours of that Sunday and fought their way north to New Market Heights, where strongly entrenched rebels stopped them.

Hancock ordered Birney to march his men to Fussels Mill for a dawn attack on the enemy's left flank.

The movement proved too much for X Corps. They did not reach the mill until midmorning on the fifteenth. Birney let his men rest while he studied the enemy defenses. That night, he sent a message to Hancock saying he had found a weakness and would attack in the morning.

The Union cavalry, led by Gregg, set out at dawn on Tuesday, August 16. They advanced steadily along Charles City Road despite resistance from rebel skirmishers. They were close to White's Tavern, and Richmond was visible on the horizon when they stopped to rest.

Unexpected difficulties delayed Birney's offensive. He launched his attack at ten. Pushing a skirmish line out of the way, he advanced to a clearing in front of the main rebel works. His first line suffered heavy casualties from the guns of entrenched rebels. His second line crossed the clearing and swarmed over the enemy parapets. A brief hand-to-hand scuffle drove the Johnnies from their position.

The counterattack came quickly. Southerners drove the Yanks back and reclaimed the works they had abandoned.

Confederate resistance along Charles City Road stiffened, stopping Gregg short of White's Tavern and forcing him to retreat to Deep Bottom.

Wednesday was quiet. A truce allowed both sides to remove their dead and wounded from the battlefield. The Confederates seemed content to strengthen their left flank so the Yanks could not get around them and attack Richmond. Hancock studied the situation and made plans.

South of Petersburg, V Corps set out at dawn on Thursday morning. Warren was under orders to set up camp on the Weldon Railroad as near the enemy lines as possible and tear up track. His lead division reached the railroad near the Globe Tavern at nine. Skirmishers were deployed and a perimeter was established while other soldiers were set to work destroying the tracks.

Warren's last division reached the encampment and began working on the tracks around eleven. Stifling heat slowed the men down, forcing them to fall out and rest frequently.

In the afternoon, Confederates attacked Hancock and Gregg east of the besieged city. The fighting went on until after dark, but the Federals held their ground. Lee's forces returned to their works with only dead and wounded to show for their efforts.

In the morning, Warren advanced his troops north, toward Petersburg. Ayres deployed along the tracks. Crawford, on his right, was working through a densely wooded area about a half mile north of Globe Tavern when a Confederate force attacked. The lead Yankee brigade was caught by surprise and driven into a panicked retreat. But the dense woods hobbled the rebel charge. Crawford's division surrounded the Southerners, hitting them head on while simultaneously attacking their flanks. The outnumbered rebels beat a hasty retreat.

By seven o'clock, a steady rain was falling. Warren sent a message to Meade informing him that V Corps would be able to hold its position. His only concern was a large gap between his right flank and IX Corps, entrenched along Jerusalem Plank Road.

At two in the morning, Warren decided he had to act. He ordered General Edward Bragg, who had only recently been promoted, to move his brigade into a position connecting V Corps with IX Corps. The Wisconsin native had his troops entrenching by four.

Meade, wrestling with the same concern, ordered Hancock to dispatch a division to Globe Tavern to reinforce Warren.

As soon as the sun was up, cavalry units set out on patrol, searching for signs of an enemy assault. The men of Ayre's and Crawford's divisions went to work improving their fortifications and laying abatis to slow an enemy charge.

Reinforcements from IX Corps reached Globe Tavern later that morning. The division from II Corps arrived in the early afternoon. The new arrivals were placed in reserve. They had to stand in the rain, ready to respond to any attack by the Southerners.

That afternoon, Bragg reported that the line connecting V Corps with IX Corps was complete despite the pouring rain and challenging landscape. He warned that the coverage was thin because the gap was too big for a brigade.

An hour later, Confederate forces crashed through Bragg's flimsy line and attacked Crawford's exposed flank. One brigade was quickly captured. The other two kept fighting despite being surrounded and outnumbered.

Sounds of the battle brought Union artillery to life. Suddenly, big guns that had been silent all day began pouring shot and shell into the wooded area where the fight was in progress. Crawford's men, under attack front, flank and rear by enemy troops, had to scramble for cover from Union missiles exploding overhead. One brigade made it back to the Globe Tavern. The other disintegrated. Some escaped. Many surrendered.

They had held on long enough for Warren to send his reserves against the Confederate offensive. The fresh troops proved too much for the rebels. They retreated toward Petersburg.

Couriers raced through the rain between Meade's headquarters and Warren's as the two generals assessed the damage and made plans for the next day. Ayres had taken heavy losses. One of his brigade commanders was missing.

Crawford had lost one brigade, and many of his men were missing from the other brigades. Presumably captured. Cox's division was intact but disorganized.

Meade wanted the line connecting V Corps to the entrenchment at Jerusalem Plank Road repaired. Warren responded that the linkage could not be repaired immediately. But V Corps would be able to hold its position on the Weldon Railroad.

In the morning, IX Corps extended its line to connect with V Corps. Ayres continued improving his front west of the railroad in spite of constant harassment by Confederate sharpshooters. In the afternoon, a confident Warren assured Meade he could hold his position against any attack.

Both men expected another attack.

That night, Warren pulled his troops back into a tight perimeter around the Globe Tavern. His men worked through the night preparing new earthworks.

Hancock withdrew back across the James after dark. II Corps crossed the pontoon bridge and Bermuda Hundred in a torrential rainstorm. Thunder rumbled as lightning strikes flashed across the night sky.

Confederate artillery opened up on the Union forces holding the Weldon Railroad at nine in the morning. Yankee guns answered. When the duel died out, the men in gray charged out of a cornfield.

The men in blue, standing behind crude parapets, blasted away, decimating the enemy line and cutting corn stocks to the ground. Warren rode behind them yelling, "Fire low. Fire low."

The rebel charge staggered and pulled back. The battle for the Weldon Railroad had been won.

Kennedy was rousted from his tent at noon. He was still exhausted from the long overnight march back to the entrenchments outside Petersburg. His new orders were to march to the Globe Tavern and extend Warren's left flank.

Barlow had taken sick leave and turned the division over to his senior brigade commander, General Nelson Miles.

Weary soldiers trudged in the rain on mushy roads all afternoon to reach a farm to the left of V Corps. There, they halted and set up camp on waterlogged ground.

On Tuesday morning, August 23, Barlow returned from sick leave and took command of the division. Miles went back to his brigade. The men of the First Division tore up track as they advanced toward Reams Station.

Barlow sent a regiment to drive Confederates from the station and establish Union control.

That night, Hancock informed Barlow he was coming to Reams Station with reinforcements.

General John Gibbon, accompanied by Hancock, led the Second Division from its encampment along Jerusalem Plank Road at 3:00 a.m. They reached Reams Station four hours later. Barlow had turned command of the First Division over to Miles and put himself back on sick leave.

The cavalry again fanned out, searching for evidence of rebel activity. They encountered a roadblock at one intersection and drove the defenders off. It looked like the rebels had given up on Reams Station. But Federal signalmen observed thousands of Southern troops leaving Petersburg and moving toward the exposed Union left flank.

Both Meade and Grant were alerted. Meade passed the intelligence to Warren and Hancock that evening. But he did not issue any orders.

A cavalry sweep in the morning found no evidence of hostile forces. Hancock sent Gibbon to continue destroying the track. He ordered Miles to improve the defensive works around Reams Station.

At noon, pickets warned Hancock that they were being probed by a large rebel force. Miles prepared for an assault. Gibbon stopped work on the railroad and readied his men for combat.

At two, Hancock sent Meade an assessment of the situation with a warning that he might be cut off from Warren.

The fight began as a battle between Gregg's cavalry and a large force of Confederate horse soldiers. An Infantry assault followed. Union pickets tumbled back and scampered out of the way. Rebel troops whooped and charged at the north face of Hancock's bastion. Troops of the First Division opened fire. Behind them, cannons poured grape and canister into the long gray line. The assault ground to a halt. Rebels raced for safety, abandoning their dead and wounded.

Hancock received word from Meade that reinforcements were on the way. But poor road conditions would prevent them from reaching him in time.

The second assault began an hour after the first. Withering musketry and artillery fire forced the rebels to retreat.

At five in the afternoon, the Confederates launched an attack aimed at a weakness in the Union defense. The Weldon Railroad ran through the northwest corner of Hancock's works, creating a gap that could not be closed. The rebel line was again subjected to murderous rifle and artillery fire. But before they gave up and retreated, Union soldiers defending the northwest corner near the gap panicked and raced for the rear.

Triumphant Johnnies surged over the undefended walls. Panic spread in the Union ranks, sending more defenders scuttling for safety. The 61st New York Regiment on the south side of the railroad held, but soon found itself locked in a slugfest with the rebels pouring into their works.

Hancock, sword in one hand, hat in the other, vainly tried to halt the stampede. Miles mustered enough men to mount a counterstrike that blunted the rebel onslaught. Hancock was organizing a full-scale offensive to retake his position when Gregg told him the cavalry could not hold the escape route back to Jerusalem Plank Road. The II Corps commander decided to retreat rather than risk being cut off and surrounded.

The order to withdraw was issued at eight o'clock. By nine, the men of II Corps were marching east in the dark, with rain beating down and thunder and lightning crackling overhead. The Southerners let them go. After a hard day of fighting, they had prisoners, regimental flags and other trophies.

Hancock fumed.

Meade was sympathetic. "II Corps had suffered some bad luck."

He was supportive. "This defeat could not tarnish the hard-won reputation of II Corps in either the public's eye or the army's estimation."

But everyone in II Corps, from the commanding general to the lowest private, knew it was a black mark on the distinguished record of one of the army's storied fighting units. Hancock blamed the humiliating defeat on everything and everyone but himself, although he did concede his soldiers may have been asked to do more than was humanly possible.

Men sitting around a fire at night, discussing the situation, had little interest in what their officers thought. For the first time in more than three years of fighting, they had lost regimental flags and given up artillery pieces. These men had slugged it out with the rebels for twenty-four hours at the

Mule Shoe on Laurel Hill. But this time, they threw down their weapons and ran. It was embarrassing.

Someone pointed out that the veterans of Laurel Hill were gone. Replaced with green troops - many of them draftees. Others countered that even the veterans had been unwilling to fight. It was well known that the backbone of the corps, the Irish, had threatened to quit fighting after Hancock's reorganization.

When Kennedy heard this, he bristled. "I fought and everyone with me fought. We stopped them and sent them running. But the fool rebels came at us one more time and the middle of our line folded."

A private demanded, "Is that why you turned and ran?"

"We didn't run," Kennedy snarled. "After the center collapsed, our flank was exposed. We were forced to retreat. But we made them pay for every inch they gained."

Somebody else threw in, "It was them mishmash regiments put together by Hancock. A green soldier ain't gonna fight like a veteran. It's the same for regiments."

Kennedy nodded. "The Irish Brigade had pride. We earned it by fighting in battle after battle. Hancock took that from us. Now he has a brigade with numbers that look good on paper. But it goes into battle without history or pride or spirit."

Discussions like this were hurtful, but they became common after Reams Station. A debate that never ended. Days spent digging trenches in the brutal summer sun made matters worse.

68

Atlanta Fairly Won

Sherman was forced to accept the grim truth. He would have to move south in force to cut off the railroads supplying Confederates barricaded in the Gate City. On August 23, after consulting with Thomas, Schofield, and Howard, he authorized two days to collect supplies and make other preparations for the move. XX Corps, now under Slocum, would remain in the entrenchments north of Atlanta to protect the railroad bridge across the Chattahoochee and threaten the rebel stronghold.

While these preparations were underway, news of Farragut's victory at Mobile Bay spread across the country. He had captured the last port available to Southern blockade runners.

But that triumph got little notice in the newspapers. Many northern papers followed the lead of Horace Greeley, who had written that Lincoln was already defeated. In Greeley's published opinion, the Republicans had to replace Lincoln as their candidate for president if they hoped to win in November.

Grant and Sherman were also under attack. Several papers reported that Sherman's grand strategy had failed. He had been reduced to making meaningless cavalry raids on railroads.

Southern papers blasted the general's bombardment of Atlanta as a cruel tactic aimed at women and children trapped in the city. They crowed that Hood had crushed Sherman in battle on July 22 and predicted the Union army would soon retreat from its failed effort to capture Atlanta.

Philadelphia Inquirer war correspondent Patrick Burns cornered Tom. "Can you answer a few questions, sergeant?"

Tom nodded. The reporter continued, "Is the army getting ready to pull back from Atlanta?"

Tom grinned and shook his head. "We're winning. This is just about over."

Burns laughed. "Sherman's lost every fight since you crossed the river a month ago."

"I've been out of the action since they jumped us at Peachtree Creek. But we gave them a whooping that day."

"What about the next day?"

"What I heard was they got on top of us but we kept fighting and drove them back into Atlanta."

Burns scoffed, "All Sherman has done since is send his cavalry to tear up railroads."

Tom said, "I've read an army marches on its stomach. After we break up their railroads they'll be marching on empty stomachs."

"What makes you think you'll be able to do that?"

"General Sherman got us from Dalton to Atlanta by being smart. He'll capture Atlanta the same way."

"Time's running out. People up north are tired. They want this war to end, even if that means making peace with the Confederacy. They're ready to vote for McClellan."

Tom nodded. "I reckon General Sherman knows that and he's getting ready to do something about it."

On the morning of August 25, Howard marched south from his position along Lick Skillet Road near Ezra Church.

Thomas pulled out of the trenches northeast of Atlanta and started south to join Howard. Slocum stayed behind to protect the supply line and threaten the rebel stronghold.

Schoefield continued to hold his position at Utoy Creek.

On the night of August 26, the Union army was camped along Sandtown Road as if it might be withdrawing across the Chattahoochee without its supply train.

The following day, the supply train moved to Mount Gilead Church, four miles southeast of Eastpoint. Thomas trailed the wagons to Red Oak Church, a station on the West Point Railway, one of the two lines still bringing supplies to Atlanta. Howard moved to Fairburn, another station on that same line.

On Sunday, August 28, the Army of the Cumberland and the Army of the Tennessee thoroughly tore up and destroyed the tracks between the two stations.

Howard continued his march south on August 30. Logan led the column on his left. Ransom, filling in for the wounded Dodge, the column on his right. Kilpatrick's horsemen rode in front, screening the movement. Resistance from the Confederate cavalry was light.

When the Army of the Tennessee reached the Flint River, they found the bridge guarded but undamaged. Kilpatrick's cavalrymen dismounted and engaged the troops defending the crossing. Logan sent a division to seize the bridge and drive the Johnnies from their barricades.

XV Corps pushed on to the nearest high ground and entrenched a half mile from Jonesboro Station. XVI Corps encamped on the west bank of the river.

In the distance, tracks for the Macon railroad emerged from the woods onto a ridge along the hills before descending into Jonesboro Station. The ground between the tracks and the river was hilly with little natural cover. The Confederates were dug in around the station.

Howard decided to establish his defenses rather than launch an attack. It was late. The men had been marching all day, and Blair would not arrive with XVII Corps for several more hours.

The movement to Jonesboro had isolated Schofield on the left wing of the National Army. He entrenched, preparing for an attack by rebel troops stationed in Atlanta.

In the morning, Schofield set out to capture the Macon and Western Railroad between Atlanta and Jonesboro. Stiff resistance by dismounted cavalry slowed his progress. When he reached the tracks in the afternoon, he found strongly entrenched rebel troops waiting for him. His lead division charged the rebel fortifications and captured them after a bloody fight.

Stanley led IV Corps to the same rail line on a road parallel to Schofield but a few miles farther south. He began working toward Jonesboro, tearing up and destroying the tracks as he advanced.

Howard received reports of Confederate troops arriving throughout the night. In the morning, he observed a large rebel force organizing for action in front of the station. They would have to push him back across the river if they hoped to hold onto Jonesboro. He ordered his corps commanders to entrench and prepare for the onslaught. The Yanks dug in and threw up parapets while they waited for the Johnnies to launch their offensive.

At three in the afternoon, Southern artillery began bombarding Howard's position. Moments later, a line of men in gray launched themselves toward the Army of the Tennessee with a bloodcurdling yell. The rebel line stretched across Howard's front, but most of its strength was aimed at the center, a bulging arc manned by Logan's XV Corps.

The Union skirmish line gave way. The rebels rushed forward. As they neared the fortification, the order to fire was given, and a sheet of flames from behind the parapets hurled mini balls into the charge. Half the rebels fell from the charging line. A second round from the Yanks halted the charge in its tracks.

The Southerners regrouped and charged again with the same result. When a third charge was ordered, rebel troops went to ground, refusing to make another suicidal assault on the entrenched Union infantry.

They pulled back to their lines around the station, leaving hundreds dead on the field in front of the Union trenches.

By Wednesday, August 31, Sherman could see that Atlanta was about to fall. Its supply lines had been cut. It could not survive. Hood was isolated in the city with one of his three corps. His other two were under siege at Jonesboro Station.

Sherman issued orders for Slocum to determine the status in and around Atlanta. XX Corps should enter the city if at all possible.

Davis was ordered to move XIV Corps into position on Howard's left. Stanley was to march IV Corps down the tracks, causing as much damage as possible, before taking up a position to the left of Davis. Schofield was to move south, tearing up track as he advanced.

On September 1, Sherman accompanied Davis as far as the Flint River before joining Howard at his headquarters. He learned from Howard that one of the Confederate corps had left Jonesboro during the night and marched north. Sherman immediately issued orders to concentrate the Army of the Cumberland for an attack on Jonesboro station that would either capture or destroy the isolated corps holding the railway depot.

The Confederates, taking advantage of the Union's slow-developing assault, shifted from a north-south line confronting the Army of the Tennessee to a fishhook with a salient facing north while improving their fortifications.

Davis connected his right with Howard and extended his left past the salient in the Confederate line. He launched his attack at four. His lead brigade quickly brushed aside rebel skirmishers, but just as it was about to fall on the main line, a well-timed volley tore it to shreds. His second wave reached the salient so quickly that the rebels were unable to reload. The men of XIV Corps overwhelmed the Southerners. But even as they were scooping up prisoners, the Johnnies formed a new defensive line to keep Davis from advancing any further. The battle raged until darkness fell, and the Federals pulled back.

Stanley marched IV Corps around the battle to reach the Confederates' rear. He found abatis and troops manning a strong bastion waiting for him. It was late and getting dark. He decided to wait until morning to attack the position.

At midnight, the sound of artillery and musketry reached the Union encampment around Jonesboro. Flashes from the explosions filled the night sky. It sounded like Hood was attacking XX Corps, but the rhythm was strange, unlike any battle these veteran soldiers could remember.

In the morning, Sherman learned the Confederates had abandoned their trenches and slipped out of Jonesboro. He sent Stanley in pursuit and dispatched a courier to get a report from Slocum.

That afternoon, he learned that Slocum had entered Atlanta and taken control of the city. But Hood had escaped, and the Confederate Army of Tennessee was dug in around Lovejoy Station.

Stanley reported that IV Corps had demonstrated against the rebels and found their fortifications too strong.

Sherman reported to Halleck, "Atlanta is ours. And fairly won."

The Army of the Potomac marched to Lovejoy Station to probe Hood's new position. They skirmished and demonstrated for two days before Sherman decided an attack would be too costly. Declaring the capture of Atlanta a successful conclusion of his mission, he returned to the city to rest his men while he planned his next operation.

69

September 7, 1864

My Dearest Mother,

Atlanta is ours. We are on garrison duty, resting and getting ready for a new operation against the seceshes.

The night of September 1 was scary. The rebels pulled out of the city after dark. On their way out they set fire to clothing and equipment and even food that they could not carry with them on the race south to Lovejoy Station. They set fire to wagon loads of ammunition that began to explode around midnight and continued for several hours.

In the morning, General Slocum set out to inspect the trenches. He was met by the mayor of Atlanta. He assured him the Confederates were gone and asked him to enter the city and establish martial law.

We were instructed to be on our best behavior and we have been with a few exceptions.

We must have presented quite a sight marching through the streets. Many of the residents watched from their windows or stood on their porches. Some people showed Union sympathy. I saw a sign that read, "United we stand. Divided we fall."

Some of the young women got as close as they could and flirted with us. They giggled and waved handkerchiefs.

The blacks seemed especially happy to see us. They cheered, made music and danced.

I have heard that the news of our success was met with cheers back home. Folks up north have changed their attitude overnight. It looks like Lincoln will win the upcoming election. I hear General Sherman is being compared to Napoleon and even Julius Caesar.

I don't think this war can go on much longer. I look forward to coming home.

Your loving son,

Tom

70

Richmond Under Siege

Grant had pared the struggle between the Union and the renegade Confederacy to a showdown between his Army of the Potomac and Lee's Army of Northern Virginia. Fighting was still widespread, but the fate of the rebellion hinged on the outcome of the face-off between the Union commanding general and Confederate General Robert E. Lee.

His headquarters at City Point lured newsmen and spies in search of information. Major Northern newspapers placed a team of correspondents in the settlement and set up a field office if they could justify the expense. The *New York Herald*'s headquarters rivaled General Meade's. It was housed in a hospital tent with multiple rooms. It had a stable of horses and two ambulances that could be put at the disposal of important guests. The reporters all had national reputations.

Josh Goldman survived at the bottom of the newsgathering community. He wrote well enough, but his access to information was limited. His pieces were published and he was paid, but his income didn't always cover his expenses. His cousin Sam would help him out with a meal. So would Jim Kennedy. Roishin Kennedy would feed him and put him up for a night in a pinch.

Goldman did his best work in the field. He spent much of August with II Corps at Fussels Mill and Globe Tavern. He had marched with the troops in a thunderstorm when Hancock pulled back across the James. He had walked beside Sam in the pouring rain on the long trek from Reams Station. The reporter doubted that Hancock knew or cared who he was. Brigade and regimental commanders were his key sources.

Other men with a talent for gathering information and a taste for adventure spied. They moved about in pine-forested hills beyond the elaborate entrenchments around Petersburg and Richmond. They took great risks to gather intelligence on one of the armies for leaders of the opposing army.

Judson Knight left his position as a sergeant in the infantry to join Hooker's Bureau of Military Information in 1863. He was spying for Meade by the end of that year. He went on to become an important asset for Grant as the campaign moved from Chancellorsville to Petersburg.

At City Point, he was assigned to maintain communications with Richmond socialite Elizabeth Van Lew. She was an abolitionist who had inherited her father's fortune and his slaves. Starting with a mission to aid Union prisoners at the infamous Libby Prison, Crazy Bet developed a spy network with tentacles reaching into Lee's army and navy. She depended on Knight and men like him to communicate with Union leaders.

George D. Shadburne, Knight's Confederate counterpart, was a sergeant in a partisan militia engaged in guerrilla warfare. Despite his notoriety, he managed to infiltrate Union lines and collect information on the disposition of Union troops, which he passed on to Lee.

News that Sherman had captured Atlanta reached City Point several days after the mayor turned control of the city over to Slocum. Union troops celebrated with musketry and artillery blasts at midnight. They taunted rebels with chants of "Atlanta. Atlanta."

A week later, Confederate cavalry, in a daring raid behind Union lines, made off with 2500 head of cattle. The press and popular opinion blamed Meade. He did not comment in public. In private, he complained that he had done what he could to prevent a sortie like that.

When Josh Goldman got together with his cousin and Kennedy, he told them that officers he had talked to believed the raid was too neat. They all agreed the guard detail had been undermanned, but that was because the herd was in the rear. The rustlers had been able to sneak past the outer defenses and surprise the pickets without raising any alarms. They drove off a large herd of cattle without being challenged. It looked like someone had provided them with detailed information about where Union troops were positioned and the best routes to get around them. Shadburne was the most likely suspect.

Grant did not comment on the raid except to joke that he would never starve the Confederates out of Richmond if his army kept providing them with beef. He planned to use Sheridan to deliver his response.

Reports from the Shenandoah Valley generally favored the Confederates under Early. That changed on September

21. Sheridan defeated the rebels in a series of battles and forced them to retreat up the valley into the mountains. The Union general turned around and marched north, plundering and wreaking havoc on Lee's breadbasket.

On September 28, Butler, under orders from Grant, sent X Corps with a division of colored troops from XVIII Corps north to attack New Market Heights. That night, XVIII Corps, led by General Edward Ord, set out for Fort Harrison on the western edge of the Richmond defensive perimeter.

Early the next day, a brigade of colored troops charged up a hill cluttered with abatis to dislodge rebels entrenched at the top. Blazing musketry from the bastion inflicted heavy losses and drove them back. Birney reinforced the assaulting line and made a second attack. With a division from X Corps, they flanked the Confederates, forcing them to retreat to nearby redoubts.

While X Corps was capturing the line along New Market Heights, XVIII Corps stormed Fort Harrison and captured the stronghold.

Birney turned his troops northwest and attacked two smaller forts that supported Fort Harrison. The battles were hard-fought, but the Union forces were repulsed.

The Federals labored through the night preparing for Confederate retaliation.

Richmond newspapers called the loss of Fort Harrison insignificant. A minor victory for the Northerners. At the same time, Lee collected eight brigades from Petersburg to reclaim the stronghold. The following day, September 30, he led a force of ten thousand in a counterassault. Union troops fought off a series of uncoordinated attacks, inflicting heavy losses and forcing the Southerners to retreat. The

Confederates immediately began constructing a new line of works to prevent further incursions.

South of Petersburg on the same day, Warren, commanding two divisions from V Corps, two divisions from IX Corps, and a division of cavalry, moved against the Confederate supply line on Boydton Plank Road. The advance encountered little resistance from the depleted rebel forces until it reached the partially completed works along Squirrel Level Road. Warren deployed his men in front of Fort Archer, the strong point of that line. A brigade led by General Charles Griffin attacked the redoubt and overwhelmed the defenders. The Johnnies abandoned their works along Squirrel Level Road, retreating to their main defensive line along Boydton Plank Road.

While V Corps consolidated its position around Fort Archer, Parke, who had replaced Burnside as commander of IX Corps, probed the Confederate trenches that protected the supply route. A charge by a brigade from IX Corps was soundly repulsed and driven back. The Johnnies came out of their trenches and pursued the Yankees. Warren dispatched two brigades from V Corps to quash the rebel counterattack.

Union soldiers spent another night entrenching and preparing for more fighting in the morning.

On October 1, the Confederates launched a two-pronged attack south of Petersburg. They renewed their offensive against IX Corps and attacked the cavalry, led by Gregg. The rebel infantry drove pickets back and retook some forward positions but failed to dislodge Union troops from their line, which now extended west toward Boydton Plank Road and the Southside Railroad.

The Southern cavalry initially retook positions along Vaughn Road. A division of Union Cavalry under Davies counterattacked in the afternoon. An hours-long battle ended with Davies forcing the Southerners to retreat.

The Third Division of II Corps came forward overnight to reinforce Warren. The fresh troops attacked at dawn, aiming to establish a position on Boydton Plank Road. They easily captured Fort McRae, another Confederate stronghold, but they soon encountered rebels strongly entrenched and ready to protect their supply route. General Meade called off the operation, choosing to consolidate his gains rather than risk more losses.

The war returned to a slow grind south of Petersburg while a daily back-and-forth continued north of the city. Confederate thrusts attempted to retake Fort Harrison and dislodge the Union line along New Market Heights. Union sorties probed the defenses around Richmond, sometimes reaching the gates of the capital.

Civilians fleeing from Richmond to take refuge behind Union lines told tales of chaos. Males as young as fifteen were pressed into service in the trenches. Businesses had been shut down. People were afraid to leave their houses.

A few weeks after the capture of Forts Harrison, Archer and McRae, Confederate General Early, whose cavalry had been stalking the Federals as they destroyed food supplies in the Shenandoah, mounted a dawn attack. Union troops were caught by surprise. Their flank was rolled up, and they were forced into a hasty retreat.

Sheridan, who had been in a meeting with Grant, raced to the battle and took control. He rallied his men and reestablished their lines. Soon, he had turned the tables on the attacking Southerners. His cavalry and Wright's VI Corps demolished Early's forces, ending the threat of a Confederate offensive in the Shenandoah. Grant brought Sheridan and Wright back to the lines around Petersburg.

A week later, Grant launched another offensive, aimed at seizing Boydton Plank Road and disabling the Southside Railroad. Preparations had been thorough. Maps and intelligence reports had been studied. Days had been devoted to developing plans. Grant and Meade would use the one-two punch strategy that had worked in their previous initiatives. First attack east of the city and then launch the main thrust to the west.

On the morning of October 27, Butler led X Corps and XVIII Corps north of Fair Oaks in an attack on the defenses around Richmond. The Confederate defenders easily repulsed the attack, wreaking havoc on the Army of the James and capturing hundreds of prisoners.

Early on that same morning, with rain pouring down, brigades from across the Union line south of the city pulled out of their trenches and started toward Boydton Plank Road. IX Corps, led by Parke, reached the objective first. But he was behind schedule. Foul weather, muddy roads and dense woods had slowed him. When he did reach the road, he found well entrenched defenders waiting for him.

V Corps, led by Warren, trailed IX Corps. Warren's mission was to support either Parke or Hancock as soon as one or the other made a breakthrough. But a third of his men were green soldiers going into combat for the first time. He doubted the operation could succeed. As he cautiously advanced his corps, a dangerous gap developed between it and the other two corps.

Grant and Meade, escorted by a hundred staffers, reached Parke at nine. Meade assessed the situation and immediately sent a message to Hancock, telling him IX Corps was stymied. That part of the plan had no chance of succeeding.

After ordering Parke to entrench and hold the rebels in place, Grant and his party rode south to meet with Warren. The V Corps commander had established his headquarters at Armstrong's Mill. The Commanding General's party reached the encampment just as Warren returned from a tour of his front. His forward units had encountered rebel outposts north of the mill. A reconnaissance in force west of the mill had come up against a line of breastworks. Meade gave Warren direct orders to dispatch a division to close the gap between him and Hancock. Those orders specified that the division was to use the west bank of Hatcher Run to join up with II Corps. That route turned out to be so difficult that Crawford's division never reached Hancock to provide the desperately needed support.

II Corps made good time as it wound through the countryside to Vaughn Road, where it turned south to the crossing at Hatcher's Run. There, the lead division encountered its first serious opposition. The crossing was held by a company of entrenched Confederates. An initial charge by Union skirmishers was repulsed. The division commander ordered a brigade to drive the rebels off. A regiment of New Yorkers waded across the armpit deep stream with weapons and cartridge boxes held over their head. They charged up the embankment and over the ramparts to send the Johnnies fleeing through the woods.

With the crossing cleared, Hancock's column continued north to Boydton Plank Road near Dabney's Sawmill. The First Division reached the road by 10:30. The corps was in place by noon. Hancock's troops had come under fire from Southern artillery stationed at Burgess Mill as soon as they began establishing a position across Boydton Plank Road.

Hancock sent a brigade forward to clear the road and drive off the Confederate artillery battery.

Still operating under the assumption that IX Corps was driving toward Boydton Plank Road, he ordered his Third Division under General Mott to proceed along White Oak Road to the Southside Railroad.

An hour later, Gregg's cavalry division, which had been screening Hancock's left flank, reached the II Corps encampment. At the same time, Hancock received orders from Meade to halt operations and wait for further orders.

He redeployed his forces to better cover his position.

Grant's party arrived half an hour later. Confederate artillery in front of II Corps and on its left flank was shelling the position. The officers pulled back out of range for a conference. Grant sent his aides to evaluate the rebel position. Then he listened impatiently to conflicting reports before deciding the only way to get a clear picture was to go to the front and see for himself. By the time Grant returned to the conference, he had concluded it would not be possible to push through to the railroad. He decided to withdraw to the Union's fortified line. But he ordered Hancock to maintain his position for another day to see if the Confederates would attack.

As the Commanding General's group rode off, Hancock received a message from Meade's Chief of Staff warning, "Enemy troops are heading down Boydton Plank Road toward your position."

Confederate infantry emerged from an old, overgrown trail to attack II Corps from the rear. They drove a regiment with its battery back toward Boydton Plank Road. That attack signaled a general onslaught. A flank attack came from White Oak Road. Southern horsemen pressed hard against Gregg's cavalry. Hancock was encircled and under siege.

II Corps responded with its old spirit. Lieutenant Colonel Robert McAllister of Mott's Third Division ordered his men to about-face and charge the rebels coming out of the woods. The Southerners broke and ran but regrouped and fought back. They held their ground, fighting like men possessed as the Union line closed around them and crushed them.

Hancock would describe the afternoon as a continuous series of assaults. As soon as he deployed troops to meet one thrust, another hit him from a different direction. But his men kept fighting. Darkness finally ended what would become known as the Battle of Burgess Mill.

That night, Hancock was given the choice of holding his ground or pulling back. He chose to return to the entrenchments around Petersburg.

Grant and Lee settled in to wait out the winter.

General Winfield Scott Hancock resigned from his post as a field commander to lead the newly formed First Veterans Division. He had never fully recovered from the wounds he received during the Battle of Gettysburg. His corps had suffered forty thousand casualties since crossing the Rapidan in May, but the Union army had failed to bring the Army of Northern Virginia to its knees. The loss at Reams Station weighed heavily on him. He never forgave Parke or Warren for failing him at Burgess Mill.

Meade's chief-of-staff, Major General Andrew Humphreys, assumed command of II Corps.

71

Aftermath: Atlanta Condemned

Sherman's Grand Army now took up a defensive position in Atlanta. Tom, the Twenty-Eighth Regiment, Brigades, Divisions, Corps found work to do in and around the city. Guard duty. Reconnaissance sorties. Foraging parties. Colonel Orlando Poe, Sherman's chief engineer, had the vast defensive works around the city reduced to a network of trenches that could be held by a single corps.

But hopes for a period of rest in Atlanta were short-lived.

The Confederate Army of Tennessee remained south of the city in easy striking distance. The Confederate cavalry was busy attacking the single railroad line that connected the Gate City to Nashville, bringing supplies and providing communications. Sherman was under pressure to deal with these threats by destroying Hood's forces. But the Union commander's army was shrinking. Troops were going home as their three-year enlistment came to an end. Thomas and the Army of the Cumberland were sent back to Chattanooga. Schofield and his Army of the Ohio were sent back to Tennessee.

Many of the city's residents were committed to the rebellion and openly hostile to the presence of Federal troops. Sherman's response was to order an evacuation of the entire civilian population of Atlanta days after breaking off his pursuit of Hood at Lovejoy Station.

He wrote to Hood asking him to provide humanitarian aid to the displaced citizens:

Headquarters Military Division of the Mississippi,
In the field, Atlanta, Georgia, September 7, 1864.

General Hood, commanding Confederate Army,

General: I have deemed it in the interest of the United States that the citizens now residing in Atlanta should remove, those who prefer it to go south, and the rest north. For the latter I can provide food and transportation to points of their election in Tennessee, Kentucky, or farther north. For the former I can provide transportation by cars as far as Rough and Ready, and also wagons; but, that the removal may be made with as little discomfort as possible, it will be necessary for you to help the families from Rough and Ready to the care at Lovejoy's. If you consent, I will undertake to remove all the families in Atlanta who prefer to go south to Rough and Ready, with all their movable effects, viz., clothing, trunks, reasonable furniture, bedding, etc., with their servants, white and black, with the proviso that no force shall be used toward the blacks one way or the other. If they want to go with their masters or mistresses they may do so; otherwise they will be sent away unless they be men, when they may be employed by our quartermaster. Atlanta is no place for families or noncombatants, and I have no desire to send them north if you will assist in conveying them south. If this proposition meets your views, I will consent to a truce in the neighborhood of Rough and Ready, stipulating that any wagons, horses, animals, or persons sent there for the purposes herein stated, shall in no manner be harmed or molested; you in your turn agreeing that any cars, wagons, or carriages, persons or animals sent to the same point, shall not be interfered with. Each of us might send a guard of, say, one hundred men, to maintain order, and limit the truce to, say, two days after a certain time appointed.

I have authorized the mayor to choose two citizens to convey to you this letter, with such documents as the mayor may forward in explanation, and shall await your reply. I have the honor to be your obedient servant.

W. T. Sherman, Major General Commanding.

(Transcribed from *The Memoirs of General William T. Sherman*)

72

Aftermath:
Hood September 9, 1864

Headquarters Army of Tennessee,
Office Chief of Staff, September 9, 1864.

Major General W. T. Sherman, commanding United States Forces in Georgia.

General: Your letter of yesterday's date, borne by James M. Ball and James R. Crew, citizens of Atlanta, is received. You say therein, "I deem it to be to the interest of the United States that the citizens now residing in Atlanta should remove," etc. I do not consider that I have any alternative in this matter. I therefore accept your proposition to declare a truce of two days, or such time as may be necessary to accomplish the purpose mentioned, and shall render all assistance in my power to expedite the transportation of citizens in this direction. I suggest that a staff officer be appointed by you to superintend the removal of the city to Rough and Ready, while I appoint a like officer to control the removal farther south; that a guard of one hundred men sent by either party as you propose, to maintain order at that place, and that the removal begin on Monday next.

And now, sir, permit me to say that the unprecedented measure you propose transcends, in studied and ingenious cruelty, all acts ever before brought to my attention in the dark history of war.

In the name of God and humanity, I protest, believing that you will find that you are expelling from their homes and firesides the wives and children of a brave people. I am, general, very respectfully your obedient servant,

J. B. Hood, General.

(Transcribed from *The Memoirs of General William T. Sherman*.)

73

Aftermath:
Sherman September 10, 1864

Headquarters military division of the Mississippi,
In the field, Atlanta, Georgia, September 10, 1864

General J. B: Hood, commanding Army of Tennessee,
Confederate Army.

General: I have the honor to acknowledge receipt of your letter of this date, at the hands of Messrs Ball and Crew, consenting to the arrangements I had proposed to facilitate the removal south of the people of Atlanta, who prefer to go in that direction. I inclose you a copy of my orders, which will, I am satisfied, accomplish my purpose perfectly.

You style the measures proposed "unprecedented," and appeal to the dark history of war for parallel, as an act of "studied and ingenious cruelty." It is not unprecedented; for General Johnston himself very wisely and properly removed the families all the way from Dalton down, and I see no reason why Atlanta should be excepted. Nor is it necessary to appeal to the dark history of war, when recent and modern examples are so handy. You yourself burned dwelling houses along your parapet, and I have seen today fifty houses that you have rendered uninhabitable because they stood in the way of your forts and men. You defended Atlanta on a line so close to town that every cannon shot and many musket shots from our line of investment, that overshot their mark, went into the habitations of women and children. General Hardee did the same at Jonesboro, and General Johnston did the same, last summer, at Jackson, Mississippi. I have not accused you of heartless cruelty, but merely instance these cases of very recent occurrence, and could go on and enumerate hundreds of others, and challenge any fair man to judge which of us has the heart of pity for the families of a "brave people."

I say that it is kindness to these families of Atlanta to remove them now, at once, from scenes that women and children should not be exposed to, and the "brave people" should scorn to commit their wives and children to the rude barbarians who thus, as you say, violate the laws of war, as illustrated in the pages of its dark history.

In the name of common sense, I ask you not to appeal to a just God in such a sacrilegious manner. You who, in the midst of peace and prosperity, have plunged the nation into war — dark and cruel war — who dared and badgered us to battle, insulted our flag, seized our arsenals and forts that were left in the honorable custody of peaceful ordinance-sergeants, seized and made "prisoners of war" the very garrisons sent to protect your people against the negroes and Indians, long before any overt act was committed by the (to you) hated Lincoln Government; tried to force Kentucky and Missouri into rebellion, in spite of themselves; falsified the vote of Louisiana; turned loose your privateers to plunder unarmed ships; expelled Union families by the thousands, burned their houses, and declared, by an act of your Congress, the confiscation of all debts to Northern men for goods had and received! Talk thus to the marines, but not to me, who have seen these things, and who will this day make as much sacrifice for the peace and honor of the South as the best-born Southerner among you! If we must be enemies, let us be men, and fight it out as we propose to do, and not deal in arch hypocritical appeals to God and humanity. God will judge us in due time, and he will pronounce whether it be more humane to fight with a town full of women and the families of a brave people at our back or to remove them in time to places of safety among their own friends and people. I am, very respectfully, your obedient servant,

W. T. Sherman, Major General commanding.

(Transcribed from *The Memoirs of General William T. Sherman*)

74

Aftermath:
Hood September 12, 1864

Headquarters Army of Tennessee, September 12, 1864.

Major General W. T. Sherman, commanding military division of the Mississippi.

General: I have the honor to acknowledge the receipt of your letter of the 9th inst., with its inclosure in reference to the women, children, and others, whom you thought proper to expel from their homes in the city of Atlanta. Had you seen proper to let the matter rest there, I would gladly have allowed your letter to close this correspondence, and, without your expressing it in words, would have been willing to believe that, while "the interests of the United States," in your opinion, compelled you to an act of barbarous cruelty, you regretted the necessity, and we would have dropped the subject; but you have chosen to indulge in statements which I feel compelled to notice, at least so far as to signify my dissent, and not allow silence in regard to them to be construed as acquiescence.

I see nothing in your communication which induces me to modify the language of condemnation with which I characterized your order. It but strengthens me in the opinion that it stands "preeminent in the dark history of war for studied and ingenious cruelty." Your original order was stripped of all pretenses; you announced the edict for the sole reason that it was "to the interests of the United States." This alone you offered to us and the civilized world as an all sufficient reason for disregarding the laws of God and man. You say that "General Johnston himself very wisely and properly removed the families all the way from Dalton down." It is due to that gallant soldier and gentlemen to say that no act of his distinguished career gives the least color to your unfounded aspersions upon his conduct. He depopulated no villages, no towns, no cities either friendly or hostile. He offered and extended friendly aid to his unfortunate fellow citizens who desired to flee from your fraternal embraces. You are equally unfortunate in your attempt to find justification for this act of cruelty, either in the defense of Jonesboro, by General Hardee, or of Atlanta, by myself. General Hardee defended his position in front of Jonesboro at the expense of injury to the houses; an ordinary, proper, and justifiable act of war. I defended Atlanta at the same risk and cost. If there was any fault in either case, it was your own, in not giving notice, especially in the case of Atlanta, of your purpose to shell the town, which is usual in war among civilized nations. No inhabitant was expelled from his home and fireside by the orders of General Hardee or myself, and therefore your recent order can find no support from the conduct of either of us. I feel no other emotion other than pain in reading that portion of your letter which attempts to justify your shelling Atlanta without notice under pretense that I defended Atlanta upon a line so close to town that every canon shot and many musket balls from your line of investment, that overshot their mark, went into the habitations of women and children. I made no complaint of your firing into Atlanta in any way you thought proper. I make none now, but there are a hundred thousand witnesses that you fired into the habitations of women and children for weeks, firing far above and miles beyond my line of defense. I have too good an opinion, founded both upon observation and experience, of the skill of your artillerists, to credit the insinuation that they for several weeks unintentionally fired too high for my modest field works, and slaughtered women and children by accident and want of skill.

The residue of your letter is rather discussion. It opens a wide field for the discussion of questions which I do not feel are committed to me. I am only a general of one of the armies of the Confederate states, charged with military operations in the field, under the direction of my superior officers, and I am not called upon to discuss with you the causes of the present war or the political questions which led to or resulted from it. These grave and important questions have been committed to far abler hands than mine, and I shall only refer to them so far as to repel any unjust conclusions which might be drawn from my silence. You charge my country with "daring and badgering you to battle." The truth is, we sent commissioners to you, respectfully offering a peaceful separation, before the first gun was fired on either side. You say we insulted your flag. The truth is, we fired up on it, and those who fought under it, when you came to our doors upon the mission of subjugation. You say we seized upon your forts and arsenals, and made prisoners of the garrisons sent to protect us against negroes and Indians. The truth is, we, by force of arms, drove out insolent intruders and took possession of our own forts and arsenals, to resist your claims to dominion over masters, slaves, and Indians, all of whom are to this day, with the unanimity unexampled in the history of the world, warring against your attempts to become their masters. You say that we tried to force Missouri and Kentucky into rebellion in spite of themselves. The truth is, my Government, from the beginning of this struggle to this hour, has again and again offered, for the whole world, to leave it to the unbiased will of these States, and all others, to determine for themselves whether they will cast their destiny with your Government or ours; and your Government has resisted this fundamental principle of free institutions with the bayonet, and labors daily, by force and fraud, to fasten its hateful tyranny upon the unfortunate freemen of the States. You say we falsified the vote of Louisiana. The truth is, Louisiana not only separated herself from your Government by nearly a unanimous vote of her people, but has vindicated the act upon every battlefield from Gettysburg to Sabine, and has exhibited an heroic devotion to her decision which challenges the admiration and respect every man capable of feeling sympathy for the oppressed or admiration for heroic valor. You say that we turned loose pirates to plunder your unarmed ships. The truth is, when you robbed us of our part of the navy, we built and bought a few vessels, hoisted the flag of our country, and swept the seas, in defiance of your navy, around the whole circumference of the globe. You say we have expelled Union families by the thousands. The truth is, not a single family has been expelled from the Confederate States, that I am aware of; but, on the contrary, the moderation of our government toward traitors has been a fruitful theme of denunciation by its enemies and well-meaning friends of our cause. You say my Government, by acts of Congress, has confiscated "all debts due to Northern men for goods sold and delivered." The truth is, our Congress gave due and ample time to your merchants and traders to depart from our shores with their ships, goods, and effects, and only sequestrated the property of our enemies in retaliation for their acts— declaring us traitors and confiscating our property wherever their power extended, either in their country or our own. Such are your accusations, and such are the facts known of all men to be true.

You order into exile the whole population of the city; drive men, women and children from their homes at the point of the bayonet, under the plea that it is in the interest of your Government, and on the claim that it is "an act of kindness to these families of Atlanta." Butler only banished from New Orleans the registered enemies of his Government, and acknowledged that he did it as a punishment. You issue a sweeping edict, covering all the inhabitants of the city, and add insult to the injury heaped upon the defenseless by assuming that you have done them a kindness. This you follow by the assertion that you will "make as much sacrifice for the peace and honor of the South as the best born Southerner." And, because I characterize what you call as kindness as being real cruelty, you presume to sit in judgment between me and my God; and you decide that my earnest prayer to the Almighty Father to save our women and children from what you call kindness, is a "sacrilegious hypocritical appeal."

You came into our country with your army, avowedly for the purpose of subjugating free white men, women, and children, and not only intend to rule over them, but you make negroes your allies and desire to place over us an inferior race, which we have raised from barbarism to its present position, which is the highest ever attained by that race, in any country, in all time. I must, therefore, decline to accept your statements in reference to your kindness toward the people of Atlanta, and your willingness to sacrifice everything for the peace and honor of the South, and refuse to be governed by your decision in regard to matters between myself, my country, and my God.

You say, "let us fight it out like men." To this my reply is — for myself, and I believe for all free men, ay, and women and children, in my country — we will fight you to the death! Better die a thousand deaths than submit to live under you or your Government and your negro allies!

Having answered the points forced upon me by your letter of the 9th of September, I close this correspondence with you; and, notwithstanding your comments upon my appeal to God in the cause of humanity, I again humbly and reverently invoke his almighty aid in defense of justice and right. Respectfully your obedient servant,

J. B. Hood, General.

(Transcribed from *The Memoirs of General William T. Sherman*)

75

Sherman September 14, 1864

Headquarters Military Division of the Mississippi,
In the field, Atlanta, Georgia, September 14, 1864.

General J. B. Hood, commanding Army of the Tennessee,
Confederate Army.

General: Yours of September 12th is received, and has been carefully perused. I agree with you that this discussion by two soldiers is out of place, and profitless; but you must admit that you began the controversy by characterizing an official act of mine in unfair and improper terms. I reiterate my former answer, and to the only new matter contained in your rejoinder add: we have no "negro allies" in this army; not a single negro soldier left Chattanooga with this army, or is with it now. There are a few guarding

Chattanooga, which General Steedman sent at one time to drive Wheeler out of Dalton.

I was not bound by the laws of war to give notice to the shelling of Atlanta, a "fortified town, with magazines, arsenals, foundries, and public stores;" you were bound to take notice. See the books.

This is the conclusion of our correspondence, which I did not begin, and terminate with satisfaction. I am with respect, your obedient servant,

W. T. Sherman, Major General commanding.

(Transcribed from *The Memoirs of General William T. Sherman*)

76

September 12, 1864 - Reprieve Refused

S herman received a letter from the mayor of Atlanta dated September 11. The mayor requested that the general reconsider his order for all citizens to evacuate the city. He presented a detailed discussion of the many hardships the citizenry would face not only in packing up and leaving but in getting resettled.

Sherman answered:

*Headquarters Military Division of the Mississippi,
In the field, Atlanta, Georgia, September 12, 1864.*

James M. Calhoun, Mayor, E. E. Rawson and S. C. Wares, representing city Council of Atlanta.

Gentlemen: I have your letter of the 11th, in the nature of a petition to revoke my orders removing the inhabitants from Atlanta. I have read it carefully, and give full credit to your statements of the distress that will be occasioned, and yet shall not revoke my orders, because they were not designed to meet the humanities of the case, but to prepare for the future struggles in which millions of good people outside of Atlanta have a deep interest. We must have peace, not only at Atlanta, but in all America. To secure this, we must stop the war that now desolates our once happy and favored country. To stop the war, we must defeat the rebel armies which are arrayed against the laws and Constitution that all must respect and obey. To defeat those armies, we must prepare the way to reach them in their recesses, provided with the arms and instruments which enable us to accomplish our purpose. Now, I know the vindictive nature of our enemy, that we may have many years of military operations in this quarter; and, therefore, deem it wise and prudent to prepare in time. The use of Atlanta for warlike purposes is inconsistent with its character as a home for families. There will be no manufactures, commerce, or agriculture here, for the maintenance of families, and sooner or later want will compel the inhabitants to go. Why not go now, when all the arrangements are completed for the transfer, — instead of waiting till the plunging shot of contending armies will renew the scenes of the past months. Of course, I do not apprehend any such thing at this moment, but you do not suppose this army will be here until the war is over. I cannot discuss the subject with you fairly, because I cannot impart to you what we propose to do, but

I assert that our military plans make it necessary for the habitants to go away, and I can only renew my offer of services to make their exodus in any direction as easy and comfortable as possible.

You cannot qualify war in harsher terms than I will. War is cruelty, and you cannot refine it; and those who brought war into our country deserve all the curses and maledictions a people can pour out. I know I had no hand in making this war, and I know I will make more sacrifices today than any of you to secure peace. But you cannot have peace and a division of our country. If the United States submits to a division now, it will not stop, but will go on until we reap the fate of Mexico, which is eternal war. The United States does and must assert its authority, wherever it once had power; for, if it relaxes one bit to pressure, it is gone, and I believe that such is the national feeling. This feeling assumes various shapes, but always comes back to that of Union. Once admit the Union, once more acknowledge the authority of the national Government, and, instead of devoting your houses and streets and roads to the dread uses of war, I and this army become at once your protectors and supporters, shielding you from danger, let it come from what quarter it may. I know that a few individuals cannot resist a torrent of error and passion, such as swept the South into rebellion, but you can point out, so that we may know those who desire a government, and those who insist on war and its desolation.

You might as well appeal against the thunderstorm as against these terrible hardships of war. They are inevitable, and the only way the people of Atlanta can hope once more to live in peace and quiet at home, is to stop the war, which can only be done by admitting that it began in error and is perpetuated in pride.

We don't want your negroes, or your horses, or your houses, or your lands, or anything you have, but we do want and will have a just obedience to the laws of the United States. That we will have, and, if it involves the destruction of your improvements, we cannot help it.

You have heretofore read public sentiment in your newspapers, that live by falsehood and excitement; and the quicker you seek for truth in other quarters, the better. I repeat then that, by the original compact of Government, the United States had certain rights in Georgia, which have never been relinquished and never will be; that the South began war by seizing forts, arsenals, mints, custom houses, etc., etc., long before Mr. Lincoln was installed, and before the South had one jot or tittle of provocation. I myself have seen in Missouri, Kentucky, Tennessee, and Mississippi, hundreds and thousands of women and children fleeing from your armies and desperados, hungry and with bleeding feet. In Memphis, Vicksburg, and Mississippi, we fed thousands upon thousands of the families of rebel soldiers left on our hands, and whom we could not see starve. Now that war comes home to you; you feel very different. You deprecate its horrors but did not feel them when you sent carloads of soldiers and ammunition, and molded shells and shot, to carry war into Kentucky and Tennessee, to desolate the homes of hundreds and thousands of good people who only asked to live in peace at their old homes, and under the Government of their inheritance. But these comparisons are idle. I want peace, and I believe it can only be reached through union and war, and I will ever conduct war with a view to perfect and early success.

But, my dear Sirs, when peace does come, you may call on me for any thing. Then will I share with you the last cracker, and watch with you to shield your homes and families against danger from every quarter.

Now you must go, and take with you the old and feeble, feed and nurse them, and build for them, in more quiet places, proper habitations to shield them against the weather until the mad passions of men cool down, and allow the Union and peace once more to settle over your old homes in Atlanta. Yours in haste,

W. T. Sherman, Major General commanding.

(Transcribed from *The Memoirs of General William T. Sherman*.)

77

November 4, 1864

My Dearest Mother,

I have already cast my ballot. General Geary made sure everyone in his division knew about the election and had a chance to vote. Many have gone home on furlough because their state does not have a mail-in ballot clause.

Sentiments here are much like you described in your letter. Support for President Lincoln is strong but so is support for General McClellan. Most of us believe we have won the war but the seceshes are too stubborn to give up.

Many of the men are unhappy about some of the President's policies. Some say he was wrong to free the slaves in the South. Others are angry about the draft. They are against forcing free Americans to serve in the army. They claim this is an omen of things to come if Mr. Lincoln is reelected.

I voted for him because I believe he is the reason we still have a country and I am confident he will do what's best after the war.

General Logan, one of the heroes of our battle for the city, has left camp to stump for the President.

Your devoted son,

Tom

78

Shifting Strategies

The evacuation did not begin until Monday, September 19, but it was completed in good order by the end of the week.

Two weeks later, Hood struck Allatoona Pass, tearing up track and torching facilities at Big Shanty and Acworth. Sherman rushed reinforcements to the fortress at the north end of the pass in time to repulse a rebel attack. But the initiative could not be ignored. Sherman led the Federal Army in pursuit of the Southerners. XX Corps was left holding Atlanta.

Tom and the rest of the garrison guarding Atlanta had no responsibility except to be ready in case something unexpected happened. Work on the trenches went on as usual, and foragers continued to make daily raids on nearby farms.

Little information reached them. The National Army drove the Southerners back toward Dalton. The Confederate general kept his troops just out of reach. Sherman encamped near Kingston at the crossing of the Etowah. Hood moved into Alabama along the south bank of the Coosa River. He tried crossing into Tennessee at Decatur but was repulsed by Union troops entrenched along the north bank. Moving farther west, he made a successful crossing at Florence.

Legendary Confederate cavalry leader General Nate Forrest rode north to join the Army of Tennessee, doubling the size of Hood's mounted force. There would be more fighting and bloodshed in Tennessee.

On November 11, three days after the presidential election, the *Philadelphia Inquirer* correspondent, Patrick Burns, joined Tom and his friends around a campfire. He listened to the back and forth, waiting for a pause, before asking, "What have you boys been up to?"

A private said, "We're layin' up stores. Looks like we're gettin' ready to sit out the winter here in Atlanta."

Burns grinned and shook his head. "You're getting ready for a big move farther into Georgia. Sherman is going to march all the way to the ocean. The plan has been approved by General Grant and President Lincoln."

Tom stared at the reporter while he weighed this revelation. "Are you sure? Where did you hear that?"

"It was in the newspapers yesterday. I did some checking today. No one's denying the report."

"How are we going to do that if the trains are destroyed?"

"I reckon we'll be bumming," Tom said.

Burns nodded. "That's the plan."

Tom objected, "What about Hood?"

The reporter said, "Sherman's got two of his best generals in Tennessee. Enlistments have been up since you captured

Atlanta and all the new recruits are going to the Army of the Cumberland."

As Tom considered the discussion, he realized foraging activities had picked up recently. He had also heard that old and sickly mules and horses were being shipped west. The consensus in talks around the campfires was that the army was getting ready for winter, and there was no telling when the rebels would cut the supply line.

Kat had told him that large numbers of troops were being shipped back to Chattanooga. Some of them had severe injuries requiring long-term care, but many were just too sick to perform regular duties. He had shrugged it off. Sherman worried about supplies and worked to keep his army lean.

Burns had just provided a different explanation. One that felt right.

Sherman had reduced his army to sixty thousand men, fit enough for a long, grueling campaign. Those not selected had been shipped back to Chattanooga. The animals were fat and ready to pull caissons and wagons across the challenging Georgia countryside. The wagons were stocked with ammunition, food, forage and other necessary supplies.

The army was to set out on the morning of November 15.

On Saturday, November 12, Colonel Poe began systematically burning what remained of the Gate City. Mills, factories, and anything else of military value at Kingston and Rome were also destroyed. Sherman gave Thomas command of Federal forces in Tennessee and ordered him to concentrate on Hood and his army. Then he cut communications with the West. The Union army immediately set about destroying the tracks and communication lines between Atlanta and Chattanooga.

XV and XVII Corps reached Atlanta on the thirteenth and set up camp. Sherman arrived the following afternoon.

XIV Corps arrived after dark on the fourteenth. Official duties were suspended to give the men time for themselves. Around the campfires that night, they discussed the final communication from the Major General Commanding: *You have been organized "into an army for a special purpose well known to the War Department and to General Grant. It is sufficient for you to know that it involves a departure from our present base, and a long and difficult march to a new one. All he asks of you is to maintain that discipline, patience and courage which have characterized you in the past; and he hopes, through you, to strike a blow at our enemy that will have a material effect in producing what we all so much desire, his complete overthrow."*

Later that night, Tom sought Kat out and led her to an ambulance to say goodbye. On their way back to their beds, they topped a small rise. Behind them, Atlanta burned like a modern-day Sodom. In front of them, tens of thousands of campfires glittered like stars.

Sherman had divided his army into two wings with two corps in each. General Slocum commanded XX Corps and XIV Corps from the Army of the Cumberland on the left wing. General Howard, commanding the right wing, had XV Corps and XVII Corps from the Army of the Tennessee. A division of cavalry under General Kilpatrick covered his left flank.

Sherman and his escort, the Alabama cavalry, rode along with Slocum, who planned to follow the railroad toward Augusta, tearing up track as he advanced. Communication lines along the track would keep Sherman in touch with Washington and City Point.

Preparations for the exodus began in the pre-dawn darkness. XIV Corps would need the day to draw supplies and ammunition, get new clothes, and ditch excess items. The other fifty thousand men had to be organized into three columns before launching into Georgia's boondocks.

In the XX Corps bivouac, three divisions had to be organized in a line of march along Decatur Road. Behind them came supply trains, artillery caissons and ambulances. The First Division began moving forward at seven. Their path took them over the battlefields of July, still littered with debris from those contests. On their right, flames and black smoke rose from the streets of Atlanta. Colonel Poe and his pioneers were still busy destroying everything of military value in the city.

The division assigned rearguard duty got underway just as the lead division was passing through Decatur, a small village built around a market square. The pace was uneven, with frequent stops to wrestle wagons over rough spots, but XX Corps made fifteen miles that first day. They went into camp in the late afternoon with the hulking mass of Stone Mountain on the horizon. Tom had heard rebel prisoners talking about the giant granite slab that rose abruptly from the plain. For them, it symbolized the Confederacy, its army, and the people of the South in their stand against the tyranny of the North.

Foraging had been poor that day. Parties gathering food to fill the wagons for this march had already picked the area clean.

They started early the next morning. The trail they followed was more a path than a road, even by Georgia standards. Marshy streams stalled wagons, bringing the whole caravan to a halt while soldiers and horses got the schooners back on solid ground. The lurching advance gave men with pent-up energy time for mischief. Tracks were torn up. Cotton fields, cotton gins, and barns with cotton bales were burned. Some isolated, unoccupied buildings went up in flames.

At midday, the Second Division reached the Yellow River, where they found a well-constructed bridge they could use. The trail east of the bridge was in worse condition than the one they had traveled in the morning. But the forage was plentiful. They had left the territory that had been picked clean.

XX Corps was ordered to halt and set up camp for the night near Lithonia. They had covered another fifteen miles.

Blacks began gathering and preparing to overnight a short distance from the Union bivouac. Tom joined a group that accompanied General Geary when he walked over to speak with them. A slender man of medium height stepped forward to meet the general. His easy manner suggested he was used to dealing with white people. He described the living conditions on the farms and said that these people had chosen to walk away from that life. He explained this was a difficult decision because whites were spreading rumors that the Northern soldiers were using escaped slaves as cannon fodder when they went into battle.

Geary acknowledged their right to leave the plantations in search of a better life. President Lincoln had declared them to be free Americans. But he cautioned that he and his men were in hostile territory, headed into battle with the Confederate army. He could not be responsible for the well-being of citizens who chose to attach themselves. He could not feed them. He had barely enough food for his troops. He would not be able to protect them when the fighting started.

The two men talked for some time before Geary and his party returned to their camp.

On Thursday, November 17, XX Corps marched to Social Circle, another small village. As they passed through the settlement, Tom observed women of all ages, some attractive, all hostile. The children clung to their mothers. If there were any men, they stayed out of sight.

The troops were put to work tearing up track, burning ties, and bending the rails into Sherman bows. The railroad station and a nearby cotton mill were destroyed.

Hilly, marshy roads continued to make the trek difficult for the wagons. The rearguard did not reach the camp until midnight.

The following morning, the Second Division diverged from the First and Third and marched along the Georgia Railroad, tearing up track. They encamped at Rutledge. Some of the men were detailed to destroy railroad cars and engines. Others torched public property, including the train station and the local jail.

Pickings had been good for the foraging parties. They returned with plenty of everything. But one party did not make it back.

Saturday morning, November 19, dawned cold and wet. The Second Division continued moving east along the railroad track toward the Oconee River, pulling up rails as they went. The main body of XX Corps marched along a parallel road some miles to the south.

At midmorning, the division reached Madison, a small community of neat cottages and fenced-in yards with flower gardens. There, they paused to visit destruction. Tom oversaw a detail that burned cotton stored near the train station before setting fire to the local jail and the train station itself. He was careful to see that no private homes were damaged.

At the same time, two brigades tore up track, set fire to the cross ties and twisted the rails as ordered by General Sherman himself.

Patrick Burns stopped to chat with Tom. He said he had not expected to see a beautiful town like this in the South and noted that it had many fine women. Tom took a moment to look around at the fires and the smoke rising into the sky. He turned back to Burns and nodded. "If looks could kill, I would be a dead man."

General Slocum held an impromptu review. Troops marched through the town with regimental bands playing "Yankee Doodle Dandy."

After lunch, the division moved on to Buckhead, where they burned cotton mills and presses as well as the train station. They also set fire to several thousand bushels of corn.

The division moved on to Blue Springs, which had one of the best bridges in Georgia. It was two hundred feet long and sixty feet above the waters of the Oconee River at its center. They destroyed that bridge before they set up camp for the night.

The rearguard followed the wagons into camp at midnight. It was raining.

The column set out under overcast skies on a cold, wet Sunday. The Second Division marched south along the West Bank of the Oconee River. Rain had turned the clay surface of the road into a thick, sticky mud that clung to boots and held tight to wagon wheels. Fifteen miles west, the First and Third Divisions took the direct road to Eatonton. The mud was so bad that they had to corduroy the roads for the artillery caissons and the supply wagons.

At Parks Mill, the bridge had been washed out and not replaced. Geary ordered ferryboats collected and destroyed. The Second Division continued along the river until it reached Denham's Tanyard and Leather Factory, which made boots for the Confederate army. Union soldiers helped themselves to new boots and leather before torching the factory. They bivouacked in a nearby field.

Plentiful forage eased the misery of bad roads and bad weather. Every house along the route was visited. Pigs, poultry, potatoes and molasses were collected to feed starving men after a hard day's march.

At Eatonton, XIV Corps soldiers burned the town's large cotton factory and all the cotton in sight. Scouts continued to Milledgeville, the Georgia State Capital, where they stirred panic among the residents and appropriated horses for their trip back to camp.

Driving rain delayed the Second Division's march on Monday morning. When they did get underway, they marched over sodden clay. In places, the mud was knee-deep. Swollen streams with dangerous currents had to be crossed. Men had to help the teams get wagons over every hill.

But foragers continued to visit every house and gather food. They destroyed cotton presses and burned cotton.

By the end of the day, Geary had brought his men to the outskirts of Milledgeville, where they joined the other two divisions. The Third Division had already deployed a regiment to secure the town.

On a cold, blustery November 22, one week after leaving Atlanta, the First Division and Second Division of XX Corps marched through the Georgia State capital, across the Oconee River on an existing wagon bridge, and set up camp along the east bank. The Third Division occupied the city and camped along the west bank of the river.

The following day, XIV Corps joined XX Corps. Sherman set up his headquarters in the Executive Mansion and called for a conference with his top generals.

The men of XX Corps were put to work destroying railroad tracks, but Tom found time to tour the city. He was near the state library when a local woman confronted him. "You are nothing but marauding beasts," she raged.

Tom needed a moment to collect himself. "You sound like you were born and raised in New England," he said, "Maine?"

"New Hampshire," she snapped.

"The 'live free or die' state," Tom chuckled. "I bet you have slaves taking care of your farm right now."

"We don't mistreat them. The darkies live better here than they do in Africa."

"But not as well as they do in Philadelphia, where I come from. They leave your farms and plantations at the first opportunity. They flock to us because they want to live free, too."

"You got no business being down here," the woman shrieked.

"Your men came north in '62 and we fought them at Antietam. They came north in '63 and we fought them at Gettysburg. Now we're down here to fight them in Georgia."

"You're down here robbing and stealing. You take all the food poor folks have for the winter."

"How do you think General Robert E. Lee fed his troops in Maryland and Pennsylvania?" Tom growled.

79

November 23, 1864

My Dearest Mother,

We are in Georgia's state capital, getting ready to move deeper into the state. So far, the marching has been the worst of the war. On a good day, the ground is mushy and progress is difficult for the wagons carrying our supplies. On bad days, progress is next to impossible.

We have marched across mountains and streams in Georgia for the past seven months. We have pushed through woodlands choked with bushes, vines and undergrowth. In the past week, we have seen the state's bounty and beauty. Plantations as big as a city, small farms and villages with cozy little homes.

Farmers in Georgia grow corn, potatoes and cotton. Lots and lots of cotton. They have cows, pigs, horses, mules, chickens and slaves. We are laying waste to all of that. I think we may be worse than the locusts in the Bible. We take their crops and livestock to feed our troops and fill our supply wagons. We burn their cotton, and cotton gins and cotton mills and the barns they use to store the cotton. We take their horses and mules to pull our wagons. We tear up the tracks their trains need and burn the train stations.

It is terrible. Many are left with nothing to see them through the winter, and yet they are defiant. They have an unyielding faith in the righteousness of their cause. I argued with a woman just this afternoon. She accused us of being devils, marauders, robbers and just plain evil. She did not blink when I told her that Robert E Lee had come north and done the same to us. She told me that the slaves here have better lives than they would have had in Africa. She ignored me when I told her the colored folks up north have even better lives and that her slaves wanted nothing so much as to be free.

General Sherman has divided us into 4 columns marching on separate roads because the ground is soft and quickly becomes impassable for the wagons. XX Corps has been using two paths for most of the last week and still men have had to work as hard as the horses and mules to get the wagons over the hills.

I haven't been able to keep up with what is going on in the rest of the army because of the separation. All we do is march and destroy railroads, crops and anything else that could be used by them to carry on this war. No one has the time or energy to share gossip. The only news I get comes from Southern newspapers left behind by fleeing seceshes.

By the time we get to a town, it is practically deserted. Some women choose to stay, but there are never any men around. According to newspapers I have found, the seceshes are most worried about Macon and Augusta, which manufacture weapons and ammunition.

The route our right wing followed took it near Macon making them believe Sherman planned to capture that city. Stories in their papers are all about troops concentrating in and around Macon and how their cavalry keeps driving off General Kilpatrick.

I doubt that there was any intention to try to seize Macon. Sherman has been traveling with us on the left. He would've been on the right if he planned to attack Macon.

We resume our march east across Georgia in the morning.

Your loving son,

Tom.

80

Savannah Under Siege

On November 24, XX Corps rose before daybreak and marched out of Milledgeville to the sound of regimental bands playing "Yankee Doodle Dandy." For the next six days, troops tore up track on the Central of Georgia Railroad as they slogged through the marshy Georgia backcountry. Each day, a brigade was assigned the task of helping the mule and horse teams get the supply wagons and artillery over rough spots.

On Wednesday night, November 30, they encamped near Louisville on the east bank of the Ogeechee River, sixty miles southeast of the state capital. Patrick Burns found Tom sitting alone by a small fire. The NCO picked up a spare cup and filled it with coffee. He held it out to the newspaperman. Burns accepted the offering. "Where are your buddies?"

"They're all bushed, and we'll be crossing more swamp tomorrow."

"But you're still sitting here."

"I figured I'd check on the wagons when they rolled in." Tom puffed on his pipe. "What have you been up to?"

"Riding with Kilpatrick. He was supposed to destroy some bridges, which he did. But he took a couple of regiments north to free Union prisoners from Camp Lawton. The camp was abandoned by the time we got there. All the prisoners had been moved to other locations. Wheeler hit us with a dawn raid on the way back. Kilpatrick didn't have time to dress. He grabbed his saber, jumped on his horse and led us on a wild ride through the enemy lines."

The correspondent paused to sip his coffee. "We rode hard. After two days, everybody was exhausted. Kilpatrick found a spot where we could throw up a line of trenches. Wheeler attacked the next afternoon. We fought him off but we were running low on ammunition." He took another sip of coffee. "Baird sent a regiment to rescue us and bring us back inside XIV Corps lines."

XX Corps continued its migration through the marshy Georgia woodlands as soon as the sun was up. The routes they followed were little more than footpaths that varied in consistency from squishy to ankle-deep mud. In places, the ground would suddenly give way under the weight of an animal, trapping it in a couple of feet of mire. Plank roads had to be laid in to get the wagons across stretches of swamp. Geary led a detachment of XX Corps soldiers to help with the work on one particularly difficult stretch.

There were fewer plantations and farms as the army moved east and south. Forage became less bountiful. Local militia and volunteers harassed Union foragers, killing more than a few. Union horsemen led by Kilpatrick kept the only organized Confederate force, Wheeler's cavalry, engaged in a running fight.

December 7 was an extremely bad day. Frustrated infantrymen, forced to wait while the wagon train was wrestled over one bad spot after another, fell upon the tiny farming community of Springfield like a horde of barbarians. They ransacked houses and raided stores in outbuildings while local citizens cowered.

That night, Burns joined Tom for a cup of coffee while he unburdened himself. Kilpatrick had attacked Wheeler at Waynesboro. He overran the Southerners' breastworks and, with the help of Baird's division, chased the rebels through the town.

Out West, Hood nearly captured Schofield, but the Union general slipped out of the trap and set up a defensive position at Franklin. Hood tried a series of frontal assaults, each ended in a bloody repulse. After nightfall, Schofield led XXIII Corps north to join Thomas and the Army of the Cumberland at Nashville.

On December 9, XX Corps marched east on a road that led directly to Savannah. They came under fire from rebel artillery at noon. Local militia had entrenched across a narrow neck of land between two bogs. Geary sent a regiment into the chest deep ooze on either side of the position to attack it from the rear. The Johnnies quickly abandoned their fortification and fled toward Savannah.

A day later, the corps reached the city's inner defenses. A great lake blocked all access from the west. The Southerners had used their irrigation system to flood the rice fields, merging them with the swamps in the area. Freestanding, disconnected redoubts had been placed in an arc between the moat and the city.

At first glance, a frontal assault was out of the question. Geary sent a regiment into the water to establish a beach-head near the redoubts. The effort was quickly abandoned. The water was too deep and the moat too wide for them to force a crossing.

As the day wore on, more troops arrived. XIV Corps connected on the left of XX Corps. XV Corps and XVII Corps connected on the right. The Union line extended from the Savannah River to the Ogeechee River. Howard and Sherman set up headquarters on the south bank of the Ogeechee, a few miles from Fort McAllister.

That evening, the unofficial newsmen began to circulate, swapping gossip as they moved from campfire to campfire. A pair from XIV Corps was fiercely divided over an incident that morning. Following orders from Major General Jefferson Davis, the soldiers prevented negroes from using their pontoon bridges at the river crossing. A crowd of about a thousand former slaves was stranded and quickly scooped up by Wheeler's cavalry.

Although no one knew for certain, no one doubted the fugitives would pay a heavy price for their attempted escape from the brutal life on the farms and plantations. One of the soldiers, Andy, insisted they should've been allowed to cross the river. His buddy Harry said the negroes should've stayed on the farms until the war was over. He said General Davis had issued the orders because the Africans were interfering with the army's mission to end the rebellion.

"That's crazy," Andy objected. "You've heard the way they are treated. If you were treated that way you would leave the first chance you got."

"Not true," Harry countered. "I'm here. We have marched and fought in heat so bad men died of sunstroke and cold so bad men froze to death. We've charged through musket fire and artillery. We've watched our friends die. When this war started I knew every man in my regiment by his first name. Many of them were boyhood friends. They are no longer with us. But if I decided in the middle of a battle I had had enough and walked away, I'd be shot dead on the spot."

In the silence that followed that pronouncement, a sergeant studied the group sitting around the fire before responding, "We are in Georgia. We are the enemy and those people are runaway slaves."

Andy said, "They aren't slaves. President Lincoln gave them their freedom."

The sergeant said, "Just words until we got here." When no one spoke up, he continued, "We've got Savannah surrounded and we will take it just like Atlanta. When we go in, we will still be the enemy and they will still be runaway slaves."

Everyone sitting around that fire eyed him in silence. He took a pull on his pipe and let the smoke roll from his lips. "We could probably protect them for a while, but Grant's not going to let us sit here. He's going to send ships down to take us north to finish off Lee."

Andy spoke up. "We could bring the colored folks with us."

"This is war. It's about killing and destroying. Taking care of people who have nothing but the clothes on their back is something else."

"That's not fair," Andy muttered.

"I've got a family and a farm," the sergeant rumbled. "I've seen them once in the last four years. Don't talk to me about fair." He looked from his pipe in one hand to the cup of coffee in his other hand, seeming to debate which one he wanted. Then he fixed his gaze on Andy and said, "When my enlistment is up, I'm going back to them. I'm gonna forget this pigsty, this war and all that goes with it. If I never hear the name Sherman, or Grant or Lincoln again, I'll be a happy man. I'm sorry about the Africans and how they're forced to live, but they need to understand that the rest of us aren't living in paradise either."

The conversation quickly turned to what the soldiers would do when the war was over. That was a subject Tom dreaded. He listened in silence until someone asked, "What about you, Sarge?"

He smiled and shrugged. "I reckon I'll go back to Philadelphia and pick up where I left off."

The discussion had about died when a couple of men from the right wing joined them. They were triumphant. "We made it, boys. Sherman's gonna capture Fort McAllister, and the navy's gonna deliver us fresh supplies."

The routines of the siege got them through the next few days. They had the city surrounded, but the Major General Commanding had not revealed his plans for capturing it. There were exchanges of artillery, but the Southern gunners were not regulars and not very effective.

Later in the afternoon on December 13, a cheer started on the far right of the line and moved to the left as messengers on horseback carried news of developments. Fort McAllister had been carried, and Sherman was in contact with the navy. Communications had been restored and supplies were on the way.

Life on the siege line remained unchanged over the next few days. Reveille sounded at dawn. Pickets took their posts while other men worked on trenches. Details were sent out to destroy nearby railroad tracks and to forage. A regiment from Colonel Ezra Corman's brigade crossed the Savannah River and established control of a nearby island.

But no fresh supplies showed up along the siege line.

Mail began arriving on December 17, and the men dropped mundane chores to catch up on news from home. About that time, a rumor circulated that Thomas had crushed Hood in a two-day battle near Nashville. The next day, another rumor had Sherman demanding unconditional surrender from Hardee. According to the rumor, the Confederate general immediately refused.

Normal routines resumed on Sunday, December 18. Foraging parties were sent out to find food. Details went back to fixing the railroads so the Confederates could not use them. Picketing and work on entrenchments kept others busy.

81

December 18, 1864

My Dearest Mother,

I received several letters from you yesterday. We have been out of touch since we left Atlanta.

I am well. We are now in a siege line outside of Savannah. The journey was slow. This is difficult country for an army and its wagons. But there was little fighting. It appears that whatever forces the seceshes have, they are too small to be called an army.

Kat is still with us. I do not see much of her. I am at the head of the column, and we start marching as soon as the sun is up. She is at the very back. Her ambulance does not reach our camp until midnight. The roads here are very poor, if they exist at all. About half the time, we are crossing a swamp. Men and beasts sweat and strain to get fully loaded wagons over ground like that.

Often we have to sit around and wait while the wagons are moved over a stretch of mud or swamp. At one such halt, I went with some others to investigate a Confederate prison, Camp Lawton. Inside the stockade, shelters of various kinds had been built by the prisoners with whatever materials they could get their hands on. Not all the prisoners were able to build shelters to protect themselves from the weather. Many pits had been scraped out around the yard by men seeking at least a little protection from the cold.

Our cavalry went there to rescue the prisoners only to discover that the Confederates had already emptied it. When we reached the place, we found the remains of our fellow soldiers. It looked like they had dropped dead from the hardships, starvation or some disease. Their bodies had been left to rot where they fell. We buried them before we returned to our units, our hearts full of sadness and rage.

Sherman ordered the nearby town burned to the ground. I think he felt as we did that the treatment of our soldiers was unforgivable.

Savannah cannot hold out much longer. I am not sure what comes next, but I have heard rumors that we will be going to Richmond to help defeat Lee.

Your loving son,

Tom

82

Savannah Surrenders

On Monday morning, December 19, Tom received orders to prepare for an assault on Savannah. He was to have his men reconnoiter the Confederate works in front of them and report any weaknesses.

Word that Colonel Corman was moving his entire brigade across the river to establish a beachhead in South Carolina spread through the camp.

That night, rebel deserters began showing up at the picket lines to surrender. Under questioning on Tuesday morning, they said they were sick of the war and the Confederacy. They also warned that a floating bridge had been completed from Savannah to the beaches of South Carolina. The evacuation of Savannah would begin very soon. General Geary passed this information up the chain of command.

On Tuesday afternoon, Confederate artillery began an unusually heavy bombardment of Union positions.

Tom prepared himself for the coming battle.

The rebel barrage eased up around nine that night. Confederate guns stopped firing altogether at two in the morning. Alarmed by the sudden end of the bombardment, Geary ordered a regiment to probe the rebel defenses. When the detail reported that the enemy works had been abandoned, he mustered a brigade and led them at quick time along the main road to the city. As he approached the city limits, Geary was met by a delegation that included the mayor, who was carrying a white flag. That official told the general that the Confederates had pulled out of Savannah, and he was prepared to surrender as long as the safety of the city and its citizens was guaranteed.

After Geary assured the mayor that his community would be spared, as long as the citizens were peaceful and cooperative, he and his men hurried to the wharf. But by the time they reached the water, the rebels had made good their escape and destroyed the bridge so they could not be followed.

Sherman left Geary, his division commander, the former mayor of San Francisco, and the former governor of the Kansas Territory, in charge of maintaining peace and security in Savannah. Preparations for the next move against the Confederacy began almost immediately. The army would have to move north to join up with Grant. Sherman had successfully argued for marching his men through South Carolina and North Carolina.

The existing defensive works had to be modified so a single division could defend the captured city. The troops had to be refitted for a long, grueling march. Supplies had to be accumulated, even though the men would be foraging and living off the land as they had on their journey from Atlanta to Savannah.

The men were kept busy remaking the defensive works and patrolling the city. But they still had time for rest and recuperation in Savannah, a city with a well-earned reputation for hospitality. Its wide, tree-lined streets and many public parks invited a leisurely stroll on sunny afternoons. It offered many dining choices as well as theaters and museums. Sculptures in the various parks honored Revolutionary War heroes. The one that struck Tom was a magnificent sculpture celebrating freedom and liberty in a land that depended on slave labor.

Most of the citizens were tolerant of the boys in blue. Many were friendly or at least acted as if they were. The women were beautiful. Many wore black to mourn the death of the Confederacy. Others were amiable. They seemed to have an eye for the officers but entertained all comers with cards, singing and dancing.

The men were encouraged to participate in church services and socials celebrating Christmas and Hanukkah.

83

December 26, 1864

My Dearest Mother,

I hope you and the rest of the family enjoyed your Christmas. Not being able to join you was a bitter hardship for me. Fortunately the people of Savannah went to great lengths to include us Yanks in their celebration. I attended church services yesterday morning and a social that lasted well into the night.

Many of the people we meet here are courteous and even friendly, but I do not think that is how they feel about us. Most put on a brave face and make us welcome. Even those who are openly hostile avoid clashes. One young woman told me that everyone in the city knew what happened to Atlanta and feared the same would happen to Savannah.

The situation here is bleak. Our foragers have destroyed much of their crop, and we are quickly eating the rest. General Sherman has allowed them to keep their rice so they do not starve. I have heard some rice is being shipped north to be exchanged for meat and vegetables.

Strangers, white folk who've lost their homes, and black folk who have decided they will no longer be slaves, are pouring into the city. They must be cared for. I have heard that some people up North are setting up a colony for former slaves on a nearby island.

General Geary is responsible for maintaining good order in the city. That means I and others in his command must keep people who steal to get what they need from making life miserable for the rest.

We meet many women with husbands, fathers, brothers or sons in the armies fighting to keep this rebellion alive. They often blame us for the war. But many other women are very sociable. Some, both black and white, are willing to satisfy a soldier's needs for a price.

I am certain this war cannot last another year. I sincerely hope that I will be with you for the next Christmas.

Your loving son,

Tom

84

Siege of Petersburg, Winter 1864 - 1865

The arrival of wintry weather curbed active campaigning around Petersburg and Richmond in the late fall of 1864. Grant, determined to finish off the Army of Northern Virginia and end the war, continued to pressure his foe whenever he saw an opportunity. Lee, who was under siege by a larger, better equipped army, had no choice but to parry the thrusts.

The Army of the Potomac had taken control of the Weldon Railroad and destroyed track between Petersburg and Stony Creek Station, twenty miles to the south. That forced Lee to transport critical supplies and war materials by wagon train from Stony Creek. The old general managed to keep supplies flowing despite the challenges.

Southern newspapers reported dire conditions in both Richmond and Petersburg. Food was scarce. Crime was rampant. Robbers raided stores in the cities and ambushed farmers bringing fresh goods to the marketplaces. Food prices were so high that many could only afford enough to keep from starving.

First-hand reports from spies backed up the newspapers.

Both armies had been using the area's woodlands for building materials and firewood. As the readily available supply of wood was depleted, soldiers and civilians were forced to roam greater distances to find what they needed for the upcoming winter.

Nevertheless, the Southerners remained defiant, keeping their spirits up with daily routines and nightly revelry.

The return of VI Corps from fighting in the Shenandoah Valley in early December gave Grant the resources he needed to tighten his noose. He ordered Meade to replace V Corps troops on the siege line with the returning soldiers and detail Warren to destroy the railroad from Stony Creek south to Hicksford on the Meherrin River. V Corps was to be augmented with a division from II Corps and a division of cavalry.

All units reached their designated departure points on the night of December 6. Gregg's cavalry set out at four the next morning. The rest of the army began moving at six on a cold, gloomy Wednesday. Rain fell off and on as the troops marched south along Jerusalem Plank Road into countryside not yet despoiled by war. Advancing a day's march or more from the base of operations around Petersburg was a new tactic for these men. One that left them feeling uneasy.

Warren's enhanced corps reached the Nottoway River at five that afternoon. Crawford's division crossed as soon as a pontoon bridge was in place. The wagons crossed next, followed by Mott's division from II Corps. Two divisions remained on the north side of the river for the night.

Crawford led his men to Sussex Courthouse, five miles south of the river, where they joined Gregg's cavalry.

The horse soldiers set out at 4:30 in the morning, heading due west on the most direct route to the Weldon Railroad. As soon as they reached the railway, they went to work dismantling a nearby railroad bridge across the Nottoway River. Crawford's division reached the tracks at noon and set to work fixing the railroad so it could no longer be used to carry supplies for Lee and his army. They dislodged the track, burned the ties, and melted the rails into useless noodles. They broke up several miles of railroad before they stopped work at midnight.

Infantrymen continued arriving throughout the bright, pleasantly warm afternoon. Many of them lightened their load by discarding overcoats and blankets. They regretted that decision when the sun dropped below the horizon and the temperature fell below freezing. Roaring fires kept them warm in front, but a bitter wind froze their backside.

The troops were up at daybreak to complete their contract with the railroad. The entire corps stretched along the tracks, each division taking a section. As soon as a division finished its section, it moved down the line to a new one. The railroad was being dismantled with remarkable speed and efficiency. Cotton gins and stockpiled cotton were burned at the same time. Many nearby homes went up in flames as well.

While the infantry demolished the rebels' supply line, the cavalry pushed south toward Hicksford. At Three Mile

Creek, the wagon bridge had been destroyed, and the railroad bridge was in flames. One regiment dismounted and crossed the thirty-six-foot wide stream on what remained of the wagon bridge while taking heavy fire from Johnnies entrenched on the far side. They quickly dislodged the defenders, and the march continued.

At the Meherrin River Bridge, they found defenders entrenched on both sides of the river. The lead brigade dismounted and attacked fortifications on the north side, forcing the rebels to flee across the bridge. They set it on fire as they scrambled to safety.

When Warren reached the scene and assessed the situation, he decided against continuing the fight. His men still had to make a three-day march back to Petersburg, and supplies were running low.

That night, sleet and freezing rain fell on the entire area.

On Saturday morning, December 10, troops awoke to a winter wonderland. Frost and ice covered the ground. Icicles hung from tree branches. Frozen, waterlogged tents and blankets had to be abandoned. The infantry took a direct route to the Sussex County Courthouse. By noon, temperatures had risen, turning the roads to mush. Federal soldiers foraged and burned property along their route to the river.

Negroes joined the column as the day wore on. Empty wagons quickly filled with mothers and their small children.

Confederates pressed Warren's rear guard throughout the day in a desperate bid to stop the Yanks from crossing the Nottoway River.

When lead elements of the infantry reached the courthouse, they heard reports of Union stragglers being captured and killed by local irregulars. Detachments were sent out to investigate. They found the mutilated bodies of Union soldiers and retaliated by burning homes in the area.

Warren had his men up and on the road to Freeman's Ford on the Nottoway early. Soldiers from Mott's division came across more bodies of Union stragglers. They had been stripped and their throats cut. Local men were rounded up and hanged if they couldn't provide a good alibi.

Confederate pursuit and harassment only ended when the Union raiding party had crossed to the north bank of the Nottoway.

The men of V Corps were exuberant when they reached the Union line south of Jerusalem Plank Road. Like Sherman, they had lived off the land and destroyed a railroad. The high spirits were soon quashed. The men were sent back to duty on the siege lines, that special kind of hell marking this period of the war. The ground in the trenches was never dry. The food was cold. Vermin feasted on the humans in the trench with them. Danger and death never let up.

During informal truces, soldiers from the opposing armies climbed out of the ditches into no man's land and mingled. They talked, traded, and engaged in contests of strength and courage.

When Kennedy and others gathered around the fire to smoke their pipes, drink coffee and discuss the situation, a man from Mott's division described the five-day mission in detail. He ended his tale with a grin and the observation, "They won't be using that section of track for a while."

"A while," came the response, "but they'll have it back in operation soon enough."

Kennedy guffawed. "Yeah. But I expect there'll be many a cold day in hell before that happens."

The sergeant was granted a furlough to spend Christmas with Roishin. Her present for him was news that she was with child. The baby was due near the end of March.

At the beginning of February, Grant ordered another run at Lee's supply line. He ordered Major General David Gregg to lead a cavalry strike that would destroy the wagon trains used to ferry goods from Dinwiddie Station to Petersburg. V Corps and II Corps would provide infantry support.

The cavalry set out at three in the morning on February 5, a bitterly cold Sunday. They rode past rebel strongholds without opposition until they approached the bridge crossing Rowanty Creek. They easily dislodged Confederate vedettes from their position in front of the bridge. The Johnnies raced across the creek, dismantling the structure as they went. The Yanks repaired the bridge and forced a crossing. From there, they turned west, reaching Dinwiddie Courthouse at one in the afternoon in spite of barely usable roads.

Gregg found a few wagons and some mules instead of the vast supply caravan he had been ordered to destroy. He sent details north and south to search for more. They captured some rebels and found a few more mules.

At three, the cavalry division turned back toward Rowanty Creek, where they planned to spend the night.

The supporting infantry units had set out at seven. V Corps marched south along Stage Road and set up camp a few miles from Dinwiddie Courthouse. II Corps proceeded south along Vaughan Road to Hatcher's Run and then west along the north bank of that stream to Boydton Plank Road, where it set up facing a strongly entrenched Confederate line.

The rebels were quick to respond. They attacked from heavy woods and pushed within a hundred paces of the Union lines. Some of the boys in blue wavered, but the Yankee line held until nightfall ended the battle.

The cavalry got little rest that night. They encamped near Malone Bridge, which they had repaired earlier in the day. They were still eating dinner when Gregg received orders to move to Warren's position. The general allowed his men a few hours' sleep before setting off in the cold and the dark to join V Corps. They got to the new position at dawn and immediately set up across Vaughan Road. Rebels attacked them before they had finished breakfast.

That afternoon, Warren sent an infantry division south on Vaughan Road toward Dabney's Mill and ordered Gregg to push Southern forces back across Gravelly Run. At the same time, Confederate reinforcements were arriving to help the rebels hold their position. As the fighting escalated, the Union cavalry retreated in disarray under pressure from the newly arriving rebel troops.

A counterattack by men from V Corps broke up the rebel offensive. Gregg's cavalry chased the Confederate cavalrymen back to Gravelly Run.

Warren reorganized his battered troops overnight and pushed the rebels back to their line at Dabney's Mill the next day. The Union siege line had been extended five miles from Fort Cummings to Armstrong's Mill.

Troops returned to the warmth and security of their base at Petersburg on February 8.

Major General Gregg's resignation became effective without fanfare on February 9. The longest-serving division commander in the Union army, he was respected by his peers and beloved by his men. But four years of continuous fighting had gotten the best of him. He returned to his home near Reading, Pennsylvania, to take up farming.

A few days later, Josh Goldman sat down with his cousin Sam and Jim Kennedy for a chat by the fire. He said, "I suppose you've heard about the peace conference."

"Read about it in the *Richmond Times* and the *New York Times*," Sam said. He winked at Josh. "And in the *Philadelphia Inquirer*."

Josh grinned and nodded. Kennedy said, "People who have not marched a step or fired a shot made some fiery speeches about fighting for their freedom rather than submitting to northern tyranny."

"Talk about a stiff–necked people," Sam kvetched. "Why can't they just admit they've lost."

"There was a kicker," Josh said. "At the end of January, Congress adopted a resolution outlawing slavery throughout the Union."

85

Carolina

Sherman had hoped for favorable weather at the beginning of the year. Instead, he got the worst rainstorms in living memory. The roads were flooded. Under twelve feet of water in places. Some said a man could row a boat all the way to Savannah, although there is no evidence that anyone tried. The upshot was a two week delay in setting out across the Carolinas and Virginia to join Grant.

The First Division of XX Corps was ordered to advance into South Carolina on December 30. They marched north, skirmishing with rebel pickets for two weeks before going into camp on the Hardee plantation near Hardeesville.

Slocum's wing finished the crossing on January 18. Geary was relieved of his duties in Savannah by General Grover that same day. He set out to join the rest of XX Corps the next morning but did not reach Hardeesville until January 27.

Howard's right wing began crossing the Savannah River on January 3 and bivouacked around Beaufort. It reached the swamp in front of the Salkehatchie River with XVII Corps in the lead on February 2.

The only path across the mile-wide bog was a narrow causeway that was covered by rebel artillery entrenched along the river. Colonel Joseph Anthony Mower ordered his regiment to advance along the ramp and capture the fortifications on the other side of the quagmire. That proved impossible. The enemy artillery easily swept the Yanks off the footpath into the swamp.

The next day, Mower continued his attack but sent two companies to build roadways around the enemy flanks and into the rear of their position. The new roads were completed by the end of the day. That night, the rebels withdrew from their stronghold.

By February 7, Sherman's entire army, except for the Second Division of XX Corps, was encamped along the Charlotte to Augusta Railroad, ready to destroy the track between Midway and Blackville.

Geary was getting his men across the Coosawhatchie Swamp and River. His six-hundred-man pioneer regiment needed the better part of two days to construct corduroy roads and a bridge for the wagons. The planking on the roads had to be held in place with stakes because the roadway was underwater.

He joined the rest of the army at Blackville on February 9. Demolition of that section of the railroad was completed on February 10. The northward advance resumed the next day.

By this time, the army had eaten through most of the supplies stored in its wagons. The prospect of shortages led to changes. Restrictions on the bummers, as foragers were commonly known, were loosened. Independent foraging was tolerated without comment.

By February 15, the left wing was near Lexington, twenty miles west of the state capital, Columbia. Geary was in charge of maintaining order in Slocum's ranks.

The right wing camped along the west bank of the Congaree River directly across from Columbia. The following day, Stone's brigade from XV Corps was ordered to cross the two rivers that unite to form the Congaree and approach the city from the north. The brigade forced a crossing of the Saluda River, but the bridge over the Broad River was destroyed before the Federals reached it. They installed a pontoon bridge and, on the morning of the seventeenth, reached Columbia, where Stone accepted the surrender of the city from the mayor.

Tom heard about these developments on February 19. The next day, he learned that all necessary work had been completed in the city, and the march north would continue in the morning. He also heard rumors of violence and destruction going far beyond Sherman's orders during the three-day occupation. According to the scuttlebutt, several hundred soldiers had been arrested for committing crimes on a night that nearly annihilated the capital city.

Heavy rains caused the Wateree River to rise dangerously and overflow its banks. When Slocum arrived at Rocky Mount on February 23, the bridge was shaky, but XX Corps crossed the river before it collapsed. XIV Corps was stuck on the west bank.

Torrential rains and soupy roads slowed XX Corps to a crawl. They reached Hanging Rock on February 26. The rains let up that same day, but Sherman's army was forced to wait while XIV Corps caught up.

On March 1, Sherman entered Chesterfield with XX Corps. Howard and the right wing were encamped near Cheraw. Confederates holding a fortified position along the banks of the Great Pee Dee River behind the city fought off the Union advance for a day. Slocum arrived on the scene the next day and hit the rebels' right flank, forcing them to abandon their fortifications.

Cheraw was a prize. Its warehouses were well-stocked with goods and military supplies.

That night, Ike Vickers, a sergeant Tom had met during the siege of Atlanta, stopped by for a visit. The two men had quite a bit to talk about. Wilmington had been captured, and Schofield was heading west with the Army of the Ohio to join Sherman. Johnston was now in command of all Confederate forces in Carolina and Georgia. The Confederate Army of Tennessee was in North Carolina, getting ready to block Sherman's path to Richmond.

With the discussion winding down and Ike looking like he was ready to leave, Tom decided to find out exactly what had happened in the state capital. After a thoughtful pull on his pipe, he exhaled the smoke and began, "The more I hear about Columbia, the worse it sounds."

"It was terrible. But it was one dark incident in a terrible war," Ike said. He took some time to consider his next words. "Tom, we're not made for this. You're a shoemaker. I'm a farmer. But our country needs us. Many thousands have been compelled to leave their normal lives and take up arms because of the South's rebellion. We suffer. We fight and we kill. In Columbia, some of us broke."

He pulled on his pipe and let the smoke escape from his lips.

"When I entered the city, Negroes were on the sidewalks handing out liquor they had liberated from the stores. Bales of cotton were in the streets. Some were on fire. We went to work on the tracks and burned the train station. The liquor never stopped flowing."

He took another puff and watched smoke rise as he slowly exhaled.

"A mob formed. Drunken soldiers roamed the streets doing what they had been doing to survive ever since we left Atlanta. They took what they wanted and burned what they didn't. They did some unspeakable things."

He shook his head. Then he looked Tom straight in the eye. "Plenty of us were trying to put out the fires and get the situation under control, but the damage had already been done. Maybe there's no excuse for what happened. But it may also be that something like that was bound to happen sooner or later."

Sherman continued his march on the sixth. The next day, Howard had the right wing tearing up the Charleston and Augusta Railroad. By March 12, he had crossed both branches of the Edisto River and broken the railroad to Columbia at Orangeburg. Confederate resistance was ever present but ineffective. Sherman's wagon trains rolled on unchecked in spite of the never ending rain, marshy roads and swamps.

Slocum got the left wing to Fayetteville on March 11. Sherman entered the city the following morning. A few hours later, a tug steamed up to the port with mail and supplies. It returned to Wilmington loaded with passengers, white and black, who had attached themselves to the army during the march. The next day, more boats loaded with supplies sailed up the Cape Fear River to Fayetteville. They brought meat and sugar, stuff the bummers had collected in abundance. They did not bring boots or other articles of clothing. Sherman's army desperately needed new uniforms and forty thousand pairs of boots.

When they left Fayetteville, Slocum separated XIV Corps and XX Corps to give the foragers a wider range. Two divisions in each corps were to travel light, ready for battle. The remaining division was to stay with the wagons and keep them moving as rapidly as possible. Geary's division was assigned to shepherd the XX Corps wagons.

As they approached Averasboro on March 16, they found the Confederates entrenched on a ridge between the river and the swamp. Slocum ordered two divisions forward in a frontal attack and a brigade around the left to attack the flank. The Johnnies gave way and retreated to a second line of entrenchments. The Yanks renewed their assault and forced the Southerners to retreat again.

The third line of entrenchments was stouter, and the defenders more stubborn. The battle went on until after dark. The Confederates abandoned their position during the night.

Slocum continued his march in the morning, taking the road toward Goldsboro. Over the next few days, the rains got heavier and the roads got worse. On the morning of March 19, XIV Corps was challenged by Confederate cavalry. The Southerners retreated but maintained stiff resistance throughout the morning. At noon, as Davis's corps, led by Carlin's division, neared the town of Bentonville, they found the road blocked by breastworks that curved around a field to their left and into a heavily wooded area on their right. Davis ordered a brigade to skirt the entrenchment and attack the enemy's right flank. At the same time, he sent two brigades directly against the works across the road.

The Union attack was repulsed by heavy musketry from the rebels behind the parapets and shelling from their artillery. Davis deployed a heavy line of skirmishers and ordered his troops to throw up their own breastworks. Slocum arrived and quickly assessed the situation. He sent orders for Williams to bring XX Corps up as quickly as possible. He also sent a message to Sherman notifying him of the situation.

The rebels counterattacked with an assault on Davis's exposed left flank. Union brigades gave way one by one and fell back. But the Yanks were hardened veterans who did not panic. They forced the Confederates to fight for every bit of ground they gained. As the Southerners pushed forward and the Northerners fell back, the line of battle stretched further and further until it was more than a mile long.

Davis collected what troops he could and formed a line along the road. Then he mounted a counterattack against the Confederates' left flank. The rebel assault lost its momentum. Stumbled. And broke to the rear. Yankee soldiers responded by fixing bayonets and racing after the fleeing Johnnies.

Davis halted the pursuit and began forming a new line to meet the rebels' next charge. XX Corps troops began arriving and extending the line to the right. They brought their artillery and set it up on high ground.

The Confederates renewed their attack at five. When it got too dark to continue the battle, the Southerners withdrew to their lines.

Reinforcements from XV Corps began arriving at dawn. Sherman reached the battle site at noon. There was some skirmishing throughout the day, but most of the Union effort went into organizing their lines and erecting parapets.

The Confederates gathered their wounded and pulled out of Bentonville under the cover of darkness.

In the morning, Union forces continued their march to Goldsboro. Schofield and the Army of the Ohio had arrived in the city the day before. Sherman reviewed the troops before releasing them to rest, recuperate and resupply. The men were as ragged as the impoverished Southerners. Their clothing was full of holes. The buttons were gone from their jackets. Their sleeves had been cut up to make patches. Socks had long since been discarded. Many a shoeless soldier kept step with his half shod comrades. But they marched with their heads held high.

The Major General Commanding made arrangements for clothes and other supplies for his men. Then he turned his army over to Schofield and traveled to City Point, where he met with Grant and Lincoln to plan for the end of the war and beyond. The President wanted peace and healing, but he stood firm on his demand that the Confederacy be dismantled and the states return to the Union under the Constitution, including the pending Thirteenth Amendment, which abolished slavery.

86

Collapse

Sergeant Major James Kennedy sat with his friends, smoking his pipe and drinking coffee on the night of March 25. The main topic was a surprise attack by the rebels that morning. It had been well planned, and its initial success sent a shockwave along the Union line. But it had been contained by midmorning, and the Confederates had pulled back to their side of no man's land.

Sergeant Sam Goldman said, "It was a desperate gamble and it failed. They suffered two or three thousand casualties for nothing. They ended up right where they started." He paused to sip his coffee. "Another thing, Lee pulled those troops from other parts of his line. He weakened his position, and believe me, Grant is making plans."

"Not this afternoon," Kennedy said. "He and his wife were riding around with the President and his wife on a tour of the battlefield."

Goldman shrugged. "In a day or two."

The next day, VI Corps hit the Confederate trenches ten miles north of Fort Steadman, driving the rebel defenders back and extending the Union line.

At a staff meeting the next day, Kennedy learned about preparations for another attack on rebel supply lines at Five Forks and the South Side Railroad. Capturing those two objectives would cut off supplies to the Southerners, forcing them to abandon Richmond and Petersburg.

Veterans returning from sick leave and furlough had brought the Army of the Potomac to full strength. Sheridan had just arrived with his cavalry, adding ten thousand men. They needed some rest but were ready to do battle with the Confederates.

XXIV Corps and XXV Corps replaced II Corps in the trenches.

On March 29, Warren led V Corps north on Quaker Road toward its intersection with the Boydton Plank Road. He was blocked at the Lewis farm by entrenched rebels. After a hot battle with attacks and counterattacks, he drove the Southerners back to their main line of defense along White Oak Road and took control of the intersection.

The Union cavalry reached Dinwiddie Station - except for Custer's division, which was escorting the wagon train over sloppy, rain-soaked roads. Grant met with Sheridan the following day. The two generals agreed on a strategy that called for the cavalry to capture Five Forks while V Corps turned Lee's right flank.

The rebels struck first on March 31. They drove Warren back across Gravelly Run. V Corps was able to keep the

Confederates from crossing the stream, but they had lost the initiative.

Unaware of this development, Sheridan set out with two brigades to take Five Forks. He was met by Lee's cavalry and forced back to Dinwiddie Station.

II Corps arrived in the afternoon and helped V Corps drive the rebels back to their line along White Oak Road. The Union infantry reached the rear of the Southern cavalry and attacked, forcing the rebels to retreat to Five Forks.

Miles's division from V Corps repaired a bridge across Gravelly Run and marched through the night on muddy roads to support Sheridan at Dinwiddie Station. They arrived at dawn on April 1. Custer's division had already mounted up and set out in pursuit of the rebel cavalry. He caught the Southern horsemen at White Oak Road, but they repulsed his charge.

Sheridan reorganized and planned a coordinated attack. He would lead his mounted troops against the Confederate center. Custer, on his left, would attack their right flank, while Warren attacked the left flank. Maneuvering Federal forces into position began at noon. The assault was set for four.

At Sheridan's signal, Federal troops rolled over the Confederate defenses like a tidal wave. The rebel forces collapsed and fell back in confusion. They regrouped and set up a new defensive line. Sheridan's troops shattered it. A third defensive line was established and promptly demolished. Union forces had won the battle for Five Forks. They held the road to the South Side Railroad. But it was too late to capture the station.

The rebels dug in. Getting ready to hold out against the attacks that would come as sure as the sun would rise.

News of the victory reached Grant at eight o'clock. He immediately prepared orders for Sheridan to do whatever was necessary to capture the station. He then issued orders for an all-out attack on Petersburg at four in the morning. II Corps was ordered to block Confederate soldiers who deserted Petersburg from joining the fight at South Side Station.

Wright chose Jones's farm as the jumping off point for VI Corps. The men would have a short charge over open ground to reach the Confederate line. They formed a wedge spearheaded by a single brigade, but three divisions wide at the base. The men had to lie face down on the ground for hours, waiting for the moment of truth.

When the signal came at five, thousands of soldiers leaped to their feet as one and charged. They overran the enemy's forward pickets. Surging forward to the main line, they broke the Confederate defenses in a little over two hours. An hour later, General Ord with XXIV Corps joined them. By 10, the combined forces were marching northeast toward the western defenses of Petersburg.

They charged across an open field in spite of heavy fire from two forts a short distance in front of Lee's headquarters. Moats filled with rain and mud prevented them from reaching the strongholds until they found a bridge at the rear. As soon as the Yanks had crossed the ditches, the overwhelmed garrisons surrendered. Lee was seen evacuating his headquarters as prisoners were led away.

Fifteen miles to the southwest of Petersburg, General Andrew Humphreys, in command of II Corps, received orders from Meade to join forces with VI Corps in an assault on Petersburg. Those orders overrode his earlier orders from Grant to block rebels fleeing Petersburg from reaching the South Side Station. He left a division under Miles to carry out Grant's original orders while he led the rest of the corps north to join up with Wright.

Miles decided the best way to carry out his mission was to capture the railroad station. His first three assaults were easily repulsed by the entrenched rebels. While his division rested and prepared for a fourth assault, Kennedy moved among the troops stoking them up for a do or die charge. "This is it, boys. Take this stronghold and the war is over."

Miles divided his troops for the final assault. Three brigades attacked the enemy's left flank. The fourth brigade circled the enemy position and hit the right flank. Bone-tired rebels caught in the pincer maneuver broke and abandoned the station in chaos. Union troops were too exhausted to pursue.

Confederate troops poured out of Petersburg and Richmond throughout the night, leaving the cities in chaos. They followed the Appomattox River west. In the morning, the mayors of both Petersburg and Richmond sought out Union troops to restore order.

Major General Godfrey Wietzel, commanding the colored troops of XXV Corps, formally accepted the surrender of Richmond on the morning of April third. He immediately organized details to bring the fires under control and ordered rations distributed to starving citizens. Later that day, President Lincoln was welcomed as a conquering hero in the former capital of the Confederacy.

At midmorning, Kennedy was informed that he had been granted an emergency furlough to visit his ailing wife. He was to proceed immediately to City Point. The sergeant reached her room at midnight. When he stepped inside, he saw her lying on the bed, holding a bundle to her chest.

She slid to her feet and rushed to greet the grubby soldier. He stammered, "Roishin! What's wrong? Are you okay?"

Tears ran down her cheeks, but she was smiling. She pressed the bundle into his arms. "Our son, Seamus."

He stared down at the infant, then at his wife, before blurting, "They said you were ailing."

She pushed the bundle against his chest and adjusted his arms. "Ah, I might've stretched the truth a wee bit. I'm gettin' meself back, ye know. Sure, bringin' a bairn inta this world is tougher than you could ever dream."

"They said you were ailing. I expected to find you on your deathbed."

She put an arm around his neck and pulled his head down so she could kiss him. "Would ya be standin' here now at all, if I'd told 'em I wanted ya here, to be holdin' yer wee bairn and comfortin' yer missus?" Her face scrunched into a skeptical smile. "Or would ye be off chasin' Robert E. Lee?"

He kissed her on the lips. A long, hungry kiss. "Which is what I should be doing and what I'll get back to in the morning."

Roishin took a step back and assessed her man. Tall, broad-shouldered, but worn to a thin, hard shadow of his former self. Disheveled hair covered his ears and ran down his neck. A sandy beard reaching almost to his chest masked his face. "Ye're too late now," she scoffed. "Ye've lost a day. Ye'll never be catchin' 'em." She grinned. "It's all over. Take the weight off yer feet an' get some rest, why don'tcha? Spend a bit o' time wi' yer wife an' child."

"It's not over. And I'm still a soldier."

"Grant's got thousands o' lads, aye? I've only got the one. And I'm needin' ye more than him."

The Union cavalry caught up with Lee's rearguard on the afternoon of April 3. The fighting continued until after dark.

Grant led his army on a road parallel to Lee's march to get ahead of the Southern army and cut it off as soon as possible. On April 5, a cavalry detachment sent out by Sheridan intercepted a train of Confederate supply wagons. Hundreds of white soldiers and black teamsters were taken prisoner. The wagons were burned. Livestock, horses, mules and artillery pieces were carried off.

A counterattack by Confederate cavalry turned into a running battle. Union troops from V Corps drove off the rebel horsemen.

The next day, Meade sent the Army of the Potomac in a general attack against Lee at Amelia Courthouse. Union troops trounced the enemy in a series of battles, taking a thousand prisoners, including eight generals.

Sheridan led his cavalry around the fighting and took up a position blocking the Southern army's advance. Lee was forced to detour north toward Lynchburg. Fresh supplies were waiting for him at Farmville. If he could push his men hard enough, he could reach them in a day.

Grant got there first. The bedraggled rebels had to march another thirty miles west to Appomattox Station for supplies. A division of cavalry under Custer seized control of the station and burned three wagons loaded with supplies for the Confederates.

Grant sent a message to Lee outlining generous terms of surrender.

On the morning of April 9, rebel infantry attacked Sheridan and drove him from the field. As they pushed forward, they ran up against XXIV Corps and V Corps. A short, bloody battle pushed the Johnnies back to a defensive position where they began entrenching.

The next day, Robert E. Lee, Commanding General of the Confederate armies, surrendered to Ulysses S. Grant, Commanding General of the Union armies, under the terms and conditions proposed by the Union general.

Upon hearing of the surrender, General Johnston contacted General Sherman about negotiating a truce. Johnston needed three days to get approval from Confederate President Jefferson Davis. Sherman agreed to meet him on April 17.

On the night of April 14, John Wilkes Booth snuck into the presidential box at Ford's Theater and shot Lincoln in the back of the head. The president died the following morning. Sherman learned of the assassination while on the train to Durham Station for his meeting with Johnston. After two days of negotiation, Johnston agreed to surrender all Confederate forces in the Carolinas and Georgia.

Sherman's agreement was not accepted in Washington. Grant had to smooth things over to save his friend's career and get Johnston to return to the negotiating table. At a meeting on April 26, Johnston accepted the same terms that Lee had agreed to sixteen days earlier. The rebellion had officially come to an end.

87

April 26, 1866 - Reunion

t ten minutes past noon on Wednesday, April 26, 1866, a woman wearing a long-sleeved black dress, white gloves, and a black hat, her red hair pulled back in a bun, entered a tavern in the Bronx. She stopped the waiter to ask about friends she was supposed to meet. Before she finished her question, a big, blond man in a white shirt, black cravat, and black coat stretched snugly over his broad shoulders stood and waved. A dark-complected man with thick, black hair stood and waved as well.

The woman smiled, waved, and walked over to join them. A woman seated between the two men stood, pushed her chair back, and strode purposefully to greet the new arrival. She was tall, dressed in burgundy, and with child. After the two women embraced, the woman in red gushed, "Kat, you came."

"And so did you, Sylvia." Kat touched the baby bump and asked, "When is it due?"

"A month. Sooner, I hope. I'm tired of waddling around like this."

The two women chatted as they sashayed arm in arm to the table. The swarthy man embraced the newcomer and said, "I'm glad you were able to come."

Kat threw an arm around his neck and pecked his cheek. "It's good to see you, Sam."

The blond man pulled her into a bear hug. "Good to see you, Kat. Where's Tom?"

She hugged the big man and kissed him on the cheek. "He couldn't make it, Jim."

She pushed away and turned to the beautiful, blue-eyed blonde occupying the seat next to Kennedy. The woman had an infant in her left arm and a toddler in the seat on her right. Kat walked over with her arm extended. "Roishin, I am so glad to finally meet you."

Reaching out to take Kat's hand, Roishin said, "Sure, and delighted I am to be meetin' ye."

Kat stroked the little boy's head. "Who is this?"

"James, aye, Seamus wanted him to have an American name." She nodded toward the infant. " This one's Bridget, after his own mather, God bless her." Roishin nodded again. "I'm thinkin' Seamus wants ye ta sit ye'self down, so he can get back ta his feed."

Kat turned. Kennedy was standing behind a chair, patiently waiting to help with her seat. As she walked toward him, she heard Roishin say, "I can see why he'd be thinkin' the world of ya."

The woman in black froze. She glared at Kennedy, then she turned back to his wife. "I can't. I did no more than you and a thousand other women."

"Seamus was tellin' me you're a nurse," Roishin objected.

Kat shot another glare at Kennedy. "I wasn't a nurse. I was too young. Regulations state that a woman has to have achieved her thirty-fifth year."

"But you were taking care of the wounded," Kennedy insisted.

"I had friends like General Geary. Besides, there was so much to be done they needed all the help they could get." Kat grinned at Roishin. "They tolerated me as long as I made myself useful and didn't ruffle any feathers. But I did the same work as you."

When everyone was settled, Sam asked, "Where is Tom?"

"Upstate New York. He took a job with the railroad."

Kennedy said, "You two have been practically married as long as I've known you. I was certain you would've tied the knot by now."

Kat shrugged. "It didn't work out. Tom had trouble adjusting when we got to Philadelphia. He was more comfortable with strangers than with people he had known all his life."

"Philadelphia?" Sam asked. "What happened to your farm?"

"I sold it. We stopped there after the war. I went to the post office. There were three letters from the Department of the Army. One told me of my father's death and one for each of my brothers. Two wanted posters were hanging on the wall. One for Tom and one for me. We got back on the train as soon as we could."

Sam looked shocked. "That was a long time ago. And the war is over."

"It was a hanging offense. We weren't going to take any chances."

Sylvia said, "You sold your farm? I didn't know you had one."

"I was born and raised on a farm in southern Maryland. After the attack on Fort Sumter, my father and brothers signed up as soon as Lincoln called for volunteers. I was stuck running the farm. One day when I was out hunting, a Union patrol took me into custody, thinking I was a secesh. They brought me to General Geary – he was Colonel Geary at the time. After we got the matter sorted out, I volunteered to collect information for him. He insisted that I had to take Thomas as a companion to help and protect me. We learned that Southern sympathizers in the area were forming a militia. We reported it, and the cavalry swooped in to break it up and arrest the plotters. Some of the town folk figured out Tom and I were the informers. We had to slip out of the house and back to the camp to avoid being hanged. The next morning, a friendly cavalry officer took me by my farm. It had been burned to the ground. Geary adopted me and I stayed with him for the rest of the war."

A waiter brought a pint of ale and a plate of beef and potatoes. Kat took a sip of the beer and savored the sensation of the cold liquid on her throat.

She picked up her story. "At the end of November 1863, Twenty Corps was formed with General Hooker in charge and we were sent to Chattanooga to rescue General Rosecrans. The next spring Twenty Corps was attached to the Army of the Cumberland, which became part of Sherman's Grand Army." She turned to Roishin. "Did James arrive before the end of the war?"

"Right before, so it was. They gave Seamus a three-day furlough, after Petersburg settled into a siege. Back he came to his unit, and wouldn't ye know it, I was with child."

Kat smiled and nodded. "You are an amazing woman."

Kennedy pressed, "What happened after you left Maryland?"

"We went on to Philadelphia. Tom's family had sold the shoe shop when John joined his brother Robert in the house-painting business. John, his wife and their baby were living with his mother in the family home. All Tom got out of it was a little money from the sale of the shop. He was lost. He had no idea how to start over."

Kennedy said, "Surely there were opportunities for a man of his talent and ability."

"As an Irish immigrant and a war hero, you were welcome in politics. And now you're a mayor. Sam has a position in his father's bank. I have no doubt he will be a millionaire by the time he's thirty." Kat smiled sadly. "All Tom could come up with was going to California to look for gold or working for the railroads. I talked him out of prospecting. He found a job with the Erie Railroad. I couldn't accept being a railroad man's wife."

She paused to eat, but she could feel the others staring at her, waiting for her to finish the story.

Kat looked at Kennedy and asked, "Does sleeping in your own bed in your own home seem strange after years of roughing it in a tent?" He said nothing. Roishin nodded. Kat continued, "Do you wake up in the middle of the night and reach for your musket?"

This time Kennedy nodded vigorously.

"Tom and I each had our own apartment but we spent many nights together. He didn't sleep much. The war haunted him. He often woke from a nightmare in the middle of the night."

Sam said, "What about his family? He told me how his sisters took care of his brother after he was wounded."

"That was a different time and John's right arm was useless. Tom's wounds were invisible except to people like me."

Roishin said, "I've me own nightmares, and Seamus, he's got his. We get up each marnin', put on a smile, so we can be dealin' wit' the others, gettin' done what needs doin'. A boatload o' sorrow and misery's bein' swept right under the rug." She asked, "How'd ye be meetin' Seamus?"

"Jim and Sam wandered around at night looking for gossip and rumors. They showed up pretty often to sit with Tom and talk about what was going on. I joined them when I could."

Kennedy chuckled, "She looked like all the other privates when she put on a uniform."

Sylvia asked, "What will you do now, Kat?"

"A woman's college in Framingham, Massachusetts has offered me a position, and I have accepted."

"How did you get an offer from a college in Massachusetts?" Kennedy asked.

"Tom's family took me in when we got to Philadelphia. I found an apartment and started looking for work. My search led me to General Geary. He has a farm near the city. When he heard about an opening at the college, he wrote some letters recommending that they hire me."

Sylvia asked, "Is that anywhere near Boston?"

"Twenty miles. Close enough for a shopping trip."

Sam asked, "What will you be doing?"

"Mostly the kinds of things I did for the general during the war. But I'll be teaching history. They're going to get me ready for that before school starts in September."

"History?" Kennedy wondered out loud.

"It's an important subject," Kat snapped. "And I have significant knowledge about one of the most important events in the history of Western Civilization. Our war between the states. Nothing can ever be the same after that."

Kennedy raised his glass and toasted, "To the future."

The others raised their glasses and joined the salute, "To the future."

Afterword

When I was growing up, Mom's family – her father, step-mother and half-sister – lived in Kansas on a farm in a house built by her grandfather, Tom Donal. He moved to Sharps Creek (near present-day Marquette, Kansas) to homestead after his right arm had been severed at the elbow while working for the railroad in upstate New York.

His first marriage ended when his wife died while giving birth to the couple's second child. A year later, he married Adelia Russ, the spinster sister of Cornelius Russ, another veteran of the Civil War. Tom and Adelia built a house and started a farm that stayed in the family for almost 100 years. He died in 1912, five years before my mother was born. Adelia died in 1928.

The four children inherited the farm. My grandfather, the youngest child, bought out his sister and two brothers around 1930 and ran the farm by himself for fifty years.

We didn't get much family history, so I am not sure when I learned that Mom's grandfather had served in the Civil War. As the family historian, I searched the National Archives in Washington, D.C., and Ancestry.com to dig up details. Although I found some interesting information about Tom and his brother John, much of their lives remains a mystery.

This story took root when I discovered the history of the unit my great-grandfather had served in, the 28th Regiment Pennsylvania Volunteers. The twenty-eight-page document is suggestive, but short on details. I did some preliminary work on it in the period after publication of *Demented*, but I wrote a fictionalized memoir, *MacGregor's Final Battle*, first.

I chose Tom Donal's story as my project for a writer's workshop after *MacGregor* was published. The first draft, which would typically take a month or two, required a year. And I still had a lot of work to do.

I knew almost nothing about our Civil War. After a year of following the 28th Regiment's journey, I had barely scratched the surface. While writing the second draft, I learned the importance of places I had never heard of, such as Snickerville Gap. I discovered General George Meade's prominent role in the summer and fall of 1863.

I also came to realize that the end of the war only makes sense when Sherman's conquest of Georgia is told in parallel with Grant's year long struggle to defeat Lee and the Army of Northern Virginia.

Grant's strategy of total war was not entirely successful, but Sherman's occupying the Army of the Tennessee in Georgia while Grant kept the Army of Northern Virginia engaged, was enough to overload the South's resources. Sherman's march north at the beginning of 1865 threatened the Army of Northern Virginia with overwhelming force. Lee's surprise attack on March 25, 1865, was a desperate move to escape Grant's siege before Sherman could join the fight.

The narrative finally came together with the third draft, three years after I first jumped into the project.

While this is a work of fiction, the research behind it was massive and enlightening. The books in the References section contributed significantly to my understanding of major events and the people involved. I have deviated from standard approaches for several reasons. The regimental history, supported by other books, suggests a different interpretation. For example, the Battle of New Hope Church is usually considered a Confederate victory. But that would mean Union forces withdrew from the engagement. The regimental history says the 28th stayed on the ridge in a shooting battle with the rebels for ten days. Cox backs this statement. If the regiment stayed, the division stayed.

The Battle of Kennesaw Mountain generally refers to Sherman's frontal assault on June 27. However, the fight began on June 18 and ended on July 2, when Johnston pulled his forces off the mountain. The attack on the 27th failed to dislodge the Army of Tennessee. But Cox broke through the Confederate left flank, forcing Johnston to abandon Kennesaw Mountain to avoid being trapped up there. I see that as a win for Sherman.

This is a story about a low-level NCO and his fellow soldiers. I have assumed that the men and women at the center of it know little or nothing about what the Southerners are thinking. They don't know that much about what their own officers are planning. My telling of the story leaves those fascinating subjects to others.

I have done my best to report what happened without overwhelming my readers with details.

I wish to thank my editors, Alicia Cregar and Tom Hyman, for their attention to detail, correcting my many errors and making helpful suggestions.

The amazing battle scene on the front cover was created by my friend Sarah Walker (SarahLWalks@gmail.com).

I would also like to thank friends and family who read early versions of this story and generously shared their thoughts and feelings.

References

The following books contributed to my understanding of the war and helped shape this narrative:

The 10 Biggest Civil War Blunders by Edward H. Bonekemper III

28th Regiment Pennsylvania Volunteers "Goldstream Regiment" www.pa-roots.com/pacw/infantry/28th/28thorg.html

Atlanta 1864: Sherman Marches South by James Donnell and Steve Noon

Atlas of the Civil War: A Complete Guide to Terrain and Tactics by Neil Kagan and Stephen Hyslop (*National Geographic*)

The Army of the Potomac: Order of Battle, 1861-1865 by Darrell Collins

The Complete Personal Memories of Ulysses S. Grant

Defeating Lee: A History of the Second Corps, Army of the Potomac by Lawrence A. Kreiser Jr

A Field Guide to Antietam by Carol Reardon and Tom Vossler

Gettysburg: The Story of the Battle with Maps by M. David Detweller and David Reisch

Grant and Sherman: The Friendship That Won the Civil War by Charles Bracelen Flood

The Harp and the Eagle: Irish-American Volunteers and the Union Army, 1861-1865 by Susanna J Ural

The Immortal Irishman: The Irish Revolutionary Who Became an American Hero by Timothy Egan

It's My Country Too: Women's Military Stories from the American Revolution to Afghanistan Edited by Jerri Bell & Tracy Crow Foreword by Kayla Williams

Jewish Soldiers in the Civil War: The Union Army by Adam D Mendelsohn

Kennesaw Mountain June 1864: Bitter Standoff at the Gibraltar of Georgia by Richard A. Baumgartner and Larry M. Strayer

Kennesaw Mountain: Sherman, Johnston, and the Atlanta Campaign by Earl J. Hess

The Last Citadel: Petersburg June 1864–April 1865 by Noah Andre Trudeau

Marching Through Georgia: Pen-Pictures of Everyday Life in General Sherman's Army by Fenwick Yellowley Hedley

The Maps of the Bristow Station and Mine Run Campaigns: an atlas of the battles and movements of the Eastern theater after Gettysburg including Rappahannock Station by Bradley M. Gottefried

Meade and Lee After Gettysburg: The Forgotten Final Stages of the Gettysburg Campaign from Falling Waters to Culpepper Courthouse, July 14-31, 1863 by Jeffrey Wm Hunt

Meade and Lee at Rappahannock Station: the Army of the Potomac's First Post-Gettysburg Offensive, from Kelly's Ford to the Rapidan, October 21 to November 20, 1863 by Jeffrey Wm. Hunt

Meade at Gettysburg: A Study in Command (Civil War America) by Kent Masterson Brown

Memoirs of General William Tecumseh Sherman

My Dear Mother: Civil War letters to Dedham from the Lathrop brothers, transcribed by Stuart R. Christie

No Turning Back: A Guide to the 1864 Overland Campaign, from the Wilderness to Cold Harbor, May 4 – June 13, 1864 by Robert F Dunkerly, Donald C. Pfanz, and David R. Ruth

"Our Crowd": The Great Jewish Families of New York (Modern Jewish History) by Stephen Birmingham

The Overland Campaign: 4 May – 15 June 1864 by The United States Army and Penny Hill Press Inc

The Real Horse Soldiers by Timothy B. Smith

Recollections of a Private Soldier in the Army of the Potomac by Frank Wilkeson

"The Rest of Us": The Rise of America's Eastern European Jews (Modern Jewish History) by Stephen Birmingham

Scouting for Grant and Meade: The Reminiscences of Judson Knight, Chief of Scouts, Army of the Potomac by Peter G. Tsouras

Seven Days in July: A Historical Account of the Battle of Atlanta by Kenneth A. Griffiths

Sherman Makes Georgia Howl by Charles Rivers Editors and J. D. Mitchell

Sherman's Battle for Atlanta by Gen Jacob D. Cox

Sherman's March Through the Carolinas by John G. Barrett

Sherman's March to the Sea: Hood's Tennessee Campaign and the Carolina Campaigns of 1865 by General Jacob D. Cox

Southern Storm: Sherman's March to the Sea by Noah Andre Trudeau

Staff Ride Handbook for the Overland Campaign by Dr. Curtis King, Dr. William Glenn Robertson, LTC Steven E. Clay

The Story of a Common Soldier of Army Life in the Civil War 1861–1865 by Leander Stillwell

The Story the Soldiers Wouldn't Tell: Sex in the Civil War by Thomas P. Lowry, M.D.

A Strange and Blighted Land: Gettysburg – the Aftermath of the Battle by Gregory A. Coco

The War for the Common Soldier: How Men Thought, Fought, and Survived In Civil War Armies by Peter S. Carmichael

War Like the Thunderbolt: The Battle and Burning of Atlanta by Russell S. Bonds